IN
NIGHTFALL

IN
NIGHTFALL

SUZANNE YOUNG

DELACORTE PRESS

Text copyright © 2023 by Suzanne Young
Jacket art copyright © 2023 by Colin Verdi

All rights reserved. Published in the United States by Delacorte Press, an imprint of Random House Children's Books, a division of Penguin Random House LLC, New York.

Delacorte Press is a registered trademark and the colophon is a trademark of Penguin Random House LLC.

Visit us on the Web! GetUnderlined.com

Educators and librarians, for a variety of teaching tools, visit us at RHTeachersLibrarians.com

Library of Congress Cataloging-in-Publication Data
Names: Young, Suzanne, author.
Title: In Nightfall / Suzanne Young.
Description: First edition. | New York : Delacorte Press, [2023] | Audience: Ages 14+. | Audience: Grades 10–12. | Summary: Soon after arriving in the tiny tourist town of Nightfall, Oregon, siblings Theo and Marco break their grandmother's rule not to leave the house after dark and befriend a mysterious group of beguiling girls who are far from what they seem.
Identifiers: LCCN 2022012589 (print) | LCCN 2022012590 (ebook) | ISBN 978-0-593-48758-7 (trade pbk.) | ISBN 978-0-593-48759-4 (library binding) | ISBN 978-0-593-48760-0 (ebook)
Subjects: CYAC: Vampires—Fiction. | Brothers and sisters—Fiction. | Murder—Fiction. | LCGFT: Vampire fiction. | Novels.
Classification: LCC PZ7.Y887 In 2023 (print) | LCC PZ7.Y887 (ebook) | DDC [Fic]—dc23

The text of this book is set in 11-point Bembo MT Pro.
Interior design by Michelle Crowe

Printed in the United States of America
10 9 8 7 6 5 4 3 2 1
First Edition

For my husband, Jesse, who always promises that my books
are "at least 25 percent better" than I think they are.

And in loving memory of my grandmother Josephine Parzych.
If anyone could have wrangled a town of beasts,
it would have been you.

CHAPTER ONE

W/elcome to Nightfall, Oregon—population 876 souls. I watch through the backseat window as we pass the town line, which is marked with a billboard of a glittering ocean bordered by looming pine trees. An oasis in the middle of nowhere. Which I guess is technically true. I haven't seen so much as a gas station in over an hour.

Instead, trees with bright green leaves press in around our car, rows of them suffocating us along the road. There is no open space. No daylight. Only endless pines and the gray, gloomy sky. I already miss the clear Arizona horizon.

To Grandmother's house we go, I sing miserably in my head. Not that my brother or I have ever met our grandmother. She's more like a rumor from my childhood—an apparition a thousand miles away who sends a birthday card with a crisp hundred-dollar bill inside. She's an old-fashioned picture in our family photo album, tucked in the back and never really explained. She's also the woman who will be in charge of our summer, even if our dad is along for the ride.

I look between the front seats at my father, who's driving us to our dreaded summer destination in the rainiest part of

Oregon. My brother groans and thumps his forehead against the passenger-side window.

"Why are we coming here, again?" Marco asks, taking out one of his earbuds. "She probably doesn't even have internet."

"Your grandmother has the internet," our father says. "And you know why we're here. You can't be trusted."

Here we go.

"Dad—" Marco starts, but our father cuts him off.

"I don't want to hear it," he says. "You had your opportunity. And instead, you and your sister"—he hikes his thumb in my direction—"decided to throw a party and destroy my house."

"It's technically our house too, Dad," I say unhelpfully. He ignores me and continues his scolding.

"Forty-six people," our father says. "The police were set to arrest *forty-six* people when they called me." He ticks off the charges like they're baseball strikes. "Underage drinking, disorderly conduct, public disturbance."

Marco turns back to covertly hold up five fingers as he makes a zero with his other hand, mouthing, "It was fifty people," to me. I bite back my laugh.

"While Theodora was doing God-knows-what in her room," my father adds.

"Ew," I say, looking around. "I was watching Netflix with my friends. And why are you using my full name when dipshit over here is the one who printed up flyers?"

"Dipshit?" Marco repeats, offended.

"You're both dipshits," our father says quickly to get back to his point. "You ruined the carpet, broke the handle off the refrigerator, and completely destroyed the pool pump. I mean, how does that even happen?"

Marco chuckles to himself. "Well, Mira Lopez thought it would be funny to put—"

"That was rhetorical!" our father says, exasperated. "Point is, if it weren't for your uncle Gabriel and his law office, you all would have spent the night in jail."

"That's not entirely true," Marco says with a shrug. "Mom said we would have gotten a citation, but it's highly unlikely the Tempe police would have—"

My dad gives him a stern look, and Marco snaps his mouth shut.

Considering our father has been yelling at us for the past two weeks and 936 miles, I can practically recite my brother's half of this conversation by heart. Not to mention that I've already apologized to my father at least ten times. If I had a time machine, I would go back and talk my brother out of throwing an absolute rager of an end-of-the-year party. But it's a little too late now.

"We get it, Dad," Marco says, sounding resigned. "And we get that we had nowhere else to go this summer. Sorry I brought it up." He slips his earbud back in and turns to look out the passenger window again.

His words sting, and I glance in the rearview mirror and see a flash of guilt cross my father's face. It wasn't Marco's intention to hurt his feelings, but . . . well, we're all hurting. Divorce is like that, I guess.

Although my parents have only been officially divorced for a month, they separated two years ago. In an attempt to normalize the dissolution of our family, my parents conducted the entire process as if it were a corporate takeover, devoid of tears or blame. They spoke in legal terms: timetables, asset division, custody.

But in reality, it was more emotional than they admitted.

My mother fell out of love, and no amount of marriage counseling would change that fact. Ultimately, she found some renewed passion with a guy named Dale who sells car insurance and owns polo shirts in about fifteen different shades of blue.

Since the divorce was finalized, my dad has been deeply sad. Honestly, I think he always expected my mother would eventually come home. Now that the possibility is gone, my father has been trying to get his life together. He even joined a cycling team and started therapy. It's also why he wanted to spend time in his hometown. *Find myself again,* he told us in a moment of oversharing. Although how he plans to do that with his seventy-year-old mother and two teenage offspring hanging around is beyond me. We shouldn't even be here.

Marco and I live with our father during the school year—a choice we made because his house is within walking distance of Tempe High. Our summers and holidays are usually spent with our mother at her condo in downtown Phoenix. But due to an *unforeseen complication,* this year's plans changed.

Mom moved in with Dale and his kids. There's nowhere for Marco and me to sleep at his house until they buy a bigger place—together. To say my brother and I are furious about this is a bit of an understatement. I haven't spoken to my mom in over two weeks. Since our father had already requested time off from his marketing job to visit our grandmother in Oregon, he decided to let us stay at our house unsupervised. Marco's going to be a senior and already eighteen and I'll be a junior. It was all set.

And then Marco fucked up. Although in all honesty, I wasn't just watching Netflix either. I was in my room doing shots with the rest of the volleyball team and playing Cards Against Humanity. Which of course I regret.

But it was easily the best party of the year.

Already homesick, I look out the window and twist to stare up at the sky. I assume there's a sky somewhere beyond the trees and thick clouds. I can't stand the dreariness of it all.

"Listen," my father says, drawing my attention again. He glances at me in the mirror, his expression softer, before turning to Marco. "I know things have been difficult. I do. Let's just . . . let's put it behind us and have a good time. You'll like it here."

"I'm sure," Marco says half-heartedly.

Dad looks in the rearview mirror at me and smiles. "Theo?" he asks hopefully.

"I don't know what you mean," I say, deadpan. "I'm already having a great time."

Marco snorts a laugh from the front seat, and the tension in the car dissipates.

Our father nods, a slight smile on his lips. "Excellent," he says. "Because we . . ."

His voice trails off when we notice two people up ahead walking along the side of the road. They're young—our age, I think. A guy and a girl wearing large backpacks, the kind you hike Europe with. I can't see the guy's face, but the girl turns in our direction. She's incredibly pretty, with curly black hair that hangs in tangled waves just past her shoulders and a wide smile. She sticks up her thumb, her expression hopeful.

"Are they *hitchhiking*?" Marco asks, surprised.

"No," I tell him. "She just thinks you're doing a really great job."

He shakes his head. "You suck, Theo."

Our car slows a bit and my heart skips at the thought of my father picking up two strangers in the woods. Isn't that dangerous? My dad watches the couple as we approach, squinting as if to get a better look.

"Dad, are you sure . . . ?" I start to ask if this is safe, when suddenly my father steps on the gas and speeds past them.

My back hits the seat and I turn to see the girl lower her arm, laughing to herself. The guy, however, holds up his middle finger to us in salute.

"Damn," Marco announces, sounding surprised. "That was coldhearted, Dad."

I'm with Marco. It *was* cold, and completely unlike my father. He doesn't meet my eyes in the mirror, staring out the windshield instead.

"Why didn't you pick them up?" I ask. "You slowed down."

"Theo," he replies, "I slowed down to make sure they were okay. They looked fine. Besides, where would we have put them? Those bags were easily the size of you."

I look around our overstuffed car. He has a point there, but still . . . it was pretty rude. Even if they were two possibly homicidal strangers.

"I didn't even know people still hitchhiked," Marco adds. "And I mean . . . where are they going? There's nothing out here."

"They're headed to Nightfall," our father says. "We get a lot of tourists this time of year."

"Tourists?" I repeat. "How do they even know about this place? I'd never heard of it; neither had my friends. Like literally, never heard of it."

"Nightfall is one of those hidden gems," my father says. "A word-of-mouth destination. But that's part of the charm—it's like a secret you've been let in on. Once they're here, some people just . . . stay. They never want to leave."

"Yeah, well," Marco replies, "once our month here is up, I'll be sprinting over the town line to get back home." He looks at our dad. "No offense."

"None taken," he replies flatly.

"How come Grandma has never visited us in Arizona?" I ask my father. "And why have we never been to Nightfall?" It feels weird calling a stranger "Grandma." The word sticks awkwardly in my mouth.

"Yeah, why haven't we been to this secret tourist destination before?" Marco adds with a grin. "And what about Mom? Has she ever been to Nightfall?"

"Your grandmother is a very private person," our father says. "She doesn't like traveling, especially long distances. She's never been on a plane and isn't going to start anytime soon. So, unfortunately, she'll probably never enjoy the Valley of the Sun with us. As for your mother, yes, Rosie did come to Nightfall with me once when we first started dating. But she said it gave her the creeps—small towns can feel that way to some people. Plus, she hated the food," he adds.

Our mother hates the food everywhere, so this isn't a surprise. She owns Rosalinda's, a Mexican restaurant in downtown Phoenix. And truly, no food is as good as hers.

"Wow," I say with smile. "Bad food and a creepy small town. Perfect."

"It's not *creepy*," my dad replies. "It's beautiful. You'll see."

Marco turns to him. "It sounds perfect," he says. "Now please tell us more about our antisocial grandmother. What's she like?"

"She's not *antisocial*," our father says. "Look, in all honesty, she is a bit . . . unusual. Your grandmother has an old-world way of thinking, but it's harmless. Her superstitions make her feel better. When you meet her, just indulge her a little," he adds. "For me."

"Okay," Marco says, nodding. "So when Theo and I wake up with locks of our hair missing and salt circles poured around our beds, we should act like it's all just fine."

"Wait, you think she'll cut my hair?" I ask, playing along. I touch a ringlet that has fallen from my messy bun protectively.

"Your grandmother is not going to cut anyone's hair," our father announces with a sigh. He glances at Marco. "Can you go back to listening to your music and stop talking?" he asks. Marco chuckles and looks out the window again.

I take out my phone to scroll through my list of murder podcasts, deciding which one to listen to next. The fact that I find murder mysteries soothing is probably some major red flag, but we all like what we like. And I like solving crimes, even if only in my head. I've queued up several new series, assuming there won't be much else to do for the next four weeks.

The forest rolls past our windows as we keep driving. I'm about halfway through an episode when my father looks around at us, grinning widely, and both Marco and I take out our earbuds.

"Welcome to Nightfall," our dad says proudly.

In front of us, the oppressive trees suddenly open up to reveal a hilly, quaint town. The ocean glitters in the distance and I gasp at the view. It's still cloudy, but the filtered light touches the roofs of houses and shops, making them almost glow. It's beautiful. I hate admitting it, but it's actually *really* beautiful.

"It's good to be back," my father says. "Almost twenty years and this place is still a revelation. Can't you feel it? Just . . . peaceful."

Marco scrunches up his nose and glances back at me. I think

we'd both rather be home, washing red Jell-O out of the pool pump.

But when I look over at my dad again, he's smiling—the kind of smile that shines in his eyes. There's a ping in my heart, a moment of gratefulness. I've missed seeing him happy. Maybe this *is* exactly what he needs.

Our Forester crests the next hill and the downtown comes into view. The main strip is lined with small, candy-colored shops teeming with groups of people—most of them young. The ocean is at the end of the street, off a promenade, and sand drifts across the road to pile along the curb. Although the sky is covered in clouds, the vibe is entirely beachy: seashells hanging in shop windows, flags for sale that say *I'd rather be surfing* posted outside.

On one of the buildings, there's a large mural of a dark-haired mermaid on a rock jutting out of the sea, a masted ship heading in her direction. I admire it as we drive by, although I notice that the otherwise serene picture is depicting the mermaid luring those sailors to their deaths.

We pass a group of girls wearing sunglasses with matching flannels tied around their waists, and one of them points to Marco. They all turn and wave. Awkwardly, my brother holds up his hand in return before looking at our dad.

"Seems this really is an amazing tourist destination," Marco says. "You've been holding out on us, Dad."

"This time of year there are more tourists than locals," our father responds. "The special weekend is coming up."

"'Special weekend'?" I ask, leaning forward. "What does that mean?"

He points to a massive white-stone building on our right. At first I assume it's a courthouse, but I'm pleased to discover it's the town library. Along the front is a large banner that reads *It's time for the Midnight Dive!*

"Midnight Dive?" I ask, confused.

"It's a week from today," my dad replies. "Next Saturday. A tradition to honor the town's history. Locals throw a giant block party with food, music, costumes—and then at midnight on Saturday, a parade marches all the way to the beach. Everyone walks straight into the ocean, clothes and all."

"Night swimming?" I ask, exchanging an amused look with my brother. "Weird, but that actually sounds fun."

"Oh, it is," our father says. "The whole town looks forward to it every year. Then again, I haven't been to a Midnight Dive since . . ." He pauses to think about it. "Since I was here with your mom. She decided not to join, so I left early," he adds quietly. "God, I barely remember that night."

"Is that why you really wanted to come back here?" Marco asks, seeming impressed with Nightfall now that we know they do at least one fun thing. "To relive your glory days?"

My father doesn't answer right away. The mood in the car seems to change abruptly as he takes a turn off the main street and into the residential area. The rows of trees return, blocking out some of the light. But they're trimmed back to showcase the oversized houses with manicured lawns and large front porches.

"No, Marco," our father replies finally. He turns onto Primrose Lane. "I came home because I didn't know what else to do."

CHAPTER TWO

My father's sadness didn't start with the divorce; that's too simple an explanation. But it's true that since my mom left, his fog of depression has never quite lifted. His admission now is a reminder of that. So although I've been dreading this trip, part of me is glad that my brother and I are here with him. We want to support him in getting his life back together.

About halfway up the block, I hear the rhythmic click of the car blinker. I glance outside as we pull into the driveway of a dark green craftsman bungalow surrounded by shrubs and relatively private.

"Here we are," our father announces, emotion thick in his voice. His eyes shine with tears as he stares at his childhood home. He shifts into park next to a pale blue minivan, which I assume is our grandmother's.

I look around, instantly charmed by the place. The house has a large front porch, rows of flowers that are slightly over-grown, and a gorgeous tree with branches that twist and turn, hanging over the property. It's straight out of a storybook. It's hard to picture my father growing up here, especially since our stucco house is surrounded by pure desert landscaping with muted browns and tans. This is lush and enchanting.

Marco is the first out of the car, stretching and groaning from the nearly two-day, twelve-hour drive. My father leaves his bags behind, heading straight for the house, while I grab my backpack and climb out. The air is *cold*. I wrap my arms around myself.

I hear footsteps in the distance and when I turn toward the street, there's a cute guy jogging by the house. He flashes me a smile.

Mortified, I offer a subdued smile in return. I'm currently wearing a pair of tie-dye shorts, knee socks with slip-on sandals, and a gray ASU hoodie with a ketchup stain on the pocket. My dark hair is in a bun held together with a scrunchie.

Next to me, my brother laughs. "Bet you wish you showered now," Marco says, grabbing his duffel bag from the floor of the front seat.

"I hate you," I mutter, and push him toward the house.

When we left the hotel this morning, there was only time for one of us to shower. Since it was five a.m., I told him to have at it. And he's right. I definitely wish I'd called dibs.

As Marco heads to the front porch, I pause and look around again. It feels so isolated out here, even with all the tourists downtown. I'm reminded of the mermaid on the mural, luring us in. Waiting for us to crash against the rocks and die.

"Theo," Marco calls, annoyed. "Let's go. I don't want to walk in without you."

"I'm not your human shield," I tell him. "Besides, maybe *Grandma* will like you better."

He scrunches up his nose as if he doesn't like the word either. It's too . . . familiar? We've barely talked about this woman, our father's mother. Up until now, she's been the person in the photo wearing a mint-green dress standing rigidly next to an old-fashioned car, our father a toddler in a suit next to her. There isn't a single recent photo of her. She didn't even go to our parents' wedding. I turn to Marco.

"What if she's awful?" I ask him. My worry is spiking and I might be panicking a little. Marco seems to consider the question a moment before shrugging.

"Then I guess it'll be a long four weeks," he replies. "Now let's go, because the anticipation is killing me."

He's right about that. I hike my backpack onto my shoulders and join him on the porch. A windchime made of little bells jingles softly from the side of the house. The noise sounds kind of creepy and haunting as it echoes through the trees.

Our grandmother's door is wide open, but Marco hangs back as I cross the threshold into the house first. I'm caught off guard when I find a small old woman hugging my father in the foyer.

Our grandmother is tiny, barely five feet tall, with gray hair. She's wearing thick-soled black shoes and a blue tracksuit with a fairly large crucifix dangling around her neck. She's significantly older than in any of the photos I've seen, which shouldn't surprise me but does. She's just a little old lady—adorable and pocket-sized. My father looks like a giant in comparison, but she holds him tightly as she comforts him.

As my brother and I wait to be acknowledged, I look around. The inside of our grandmother's house is like a cluttered antiques store. Then again, she's lived here nearly her entire life, so it makes sense she would have collected things. It smells like a combination of old paper and menthol.

Marco bumps my shoulder and points to a photo on the wall. It's of me from eighth grade when I dressed up as a bumblebee and had too-short bangs. Next to it is another gem—a shot of me at a dance recital dressed as Minnie Mouse. I'm both surprised and heartened to find my pictures on the wall, as embarrassing as they are. She must have thought about us over the years. That's kind of nice.

"Do you think she purposely picked your worst photos?" my brother whispers. I elbow him in the gut, making him cough out a laugh.

My grandmother straightens and pats our father's arm. "You're all right now," she tells him. "You're going to be all right, Joey." Dad wipes his eyes and nods. My grandmother is the first person I've ever heard call my father *Joey*. But the tone of her voice is tender and loving—motherly. I smile, feeling tears prick my eyes. My father needed this.

My grandmother turns toward me abruptly, making me jump. She's weirdly fast. We stand in silence for a moment. When I can't take the quiet any longer, I smile.

"Hello, Grandma," I say awkwardly.

She runs her dark eyes over my outfit, appraising me from sandals to scrunchie. She hums out an annoyed sound. "Is this how you dress?" she asks, her tone judgmental. Marco puts his hand over his mouth to cover his laugh.

I scratch at my hair. "Sometimes," I tell her. "The boys seem to like it."

She fights back a smile. "Well then," she replies, "if you're so popular, I guess I should go to you for fashion advice."

Good. She has a sense of humor.

"And call me Nonna," she adds. "It's more respectful."

I exchange a glance with my brother and he shrugs as if telling me to do it.

"Okay, Nonna," I say, deciding immediately that I like it better. It suits her.

She holds her arms open for a hug. "If you want one," she offers, as if she doesn't care either way.

I walk over and bend down to give her a quick hug, feeling how tiny she is in my arms, even though her grip around my shoulders is tight. There is a sudden rush of sadness in my chest. I can't remember the last time someone hugged me. Maybe I needed it too.

When I pull back, Nonna is already looking over at Marco. My brother holds his duffel bag in front of himself like armor. He smiles tentatively.

"Hi, Nonna," he says.

"Well, come on," she says, motioning for a hug.

My brother grins, and as he walks over to her, I look around again. It's like one of those house museums, everything kept exactly as the deceased left it. The thought creeps me out, and I shiver and wrap my arms around myself.

After she separates from Marco, Nonna walks over to take my dad's arm. She glances at us. "Now go get the rest of the bags from the car," she says, shooing us toward the door. "Your father and I need to talk."

She turns away and gently leads my father toward the kitchen, murmuring sweet words of encouragement. Funny how nice she is to him while also being a bit prickly toward us. She reminds me of a fuzzy cactus.

And that's my grandmother—a gray-haired enigma in orthopedic shoes.

★ ★ ★

NONNA WASN'T PREPARED TO have us all in her house at once. She only has three bedrooms. While she and my father get the two rooms on the left, I'm relegated to the small "doll room" on the other side of the second floor. Marco has been shoved somewhere in the attic.

When I walk into the room, I stop short and drop my bags at my feet. I'd hoped Nonna was kidding. But, no. There are a dozen or so porcelain dolls on a shelf near the ceiling staring directly at me. A few are old, really old, with one blinking eye, while others look like they're from the last decade. She sent me a porcelain doll for my birthday once when I was a kid, but I ended up donating it to Goodwill because it scared the shit out of me. I don't know how or if she found out, but she has given me a blank card with money ever since.

"Awesome," I mutter, planning to stuff the dolls into the closet for the duration of my stay. No way I'll sleep with them staring at me all night.

I abandon my bags in the room and head down the hall to the attic. I'm secretly hoping it's a refuge for rejected dolls, because honestly, my brother deserves to be haunted, too.

The door to the attic has a long, old-fashioned key sticking out of the lock. It strikes me as odd that Nonna would lock her attic door, but I make a mental note to lock Marco in there at least once during our stay to mess with him.

Behind the attic door is a steep staircase leading up. As I begin the climb, one of the steps creaks and I hear Marco laugh.

"You're going to love this, Theo," he calls down to me.

I get to the top of the stairs and look around. To be honest, I'd been expecting an inflatable mattress and a doll graveyard, but instead the attic space has been converted into a finished bedroom. There's a large metal-frame bed with a quilted blanket, a nightstand, and a dresser pushed against one wall.

The space is huge, a little cold and a lot dusty. The walls are decorated with gold-framed pictures of landscapes and a mirror with a sheet covering the glass. There is a circular window that lets in some light, which shines directly on the bed. Across the room is an old oversized trunk, big enough to store a body. Although the attic is less cluttered than the downstairs, something about the space feels creepy. A forgotten room in a haunted mansion.

"Who the hell has Nonna been keeping up here?" I ask, looking at my brother.

"Right?" he says. "Maybe this was Dad's bedroom?"

"Yikes," I reply. "In the attic? I hope not. How depressing."

"I like it," Marco says, looking around. He tosses his duffel bag onto the bed. "It's cozy."

"I'm sure the ghosts think so," I tell him.

Marco walks over to sit on the old trunk, a puff of dust rising up around him when he does. "So what do you think of her?" he asks. *"Nonna."* He grimaces, but I can tell that my brother likes her too.

"Not what I expected," I admit. "She's definitely older and smaller than I thought she'd be. And she speaks her mind, which I can appreciate, even if she's a little mean." I pause. "She's really sweet to Dad, though."

"Yeah," Marco agrees. "That was cool to see." We're quiet for a moment. "Our entire summer," he adds. "Can you believe we have to spend the entire summer in this place?"

We stare at each other before the despair starts to feel like too much. We're displaced, alone. And I'll admit that I'm struggling with my mother's abandonment. No, not struggling. Furious. But I quickly swallow the emotion down because I don't want to feel it right now.

Marco sighs loudly and cracks his neck. "Well, I'm already bored," he announces as if changing the subject. "What should we do? Search through all this old shit and uncover some family secrets?"

"Let's do that tomorrow," I tell him. "I need to adjust to Nonna's spooky aesthetic first. I'm not convinced we won't stumble on some cursed object and have to deal with *that* all summer." I smile. "Did I mention there's a bunch of porcelain dolls in my room?"

Marco laughs. "Damn, that sucks."

"Sure does," I agree. I glance out the window, surprised that outside the sky is still bright, even though it feels like evening. "Wait," I say, confused. "What time is it?"

"Just after eight," Marco replies, checking his phone. "My weather app says it doesn't get dark until ten around here. I'm going to check out downtown. Want to go?"

"Uh, I'm not staying here alone," I say. "But who's telling Nonna and Dad that we're leaving?"

Marco smiles. "Not the one who let his friends fill the pool with red Jell-O."

"You're the worst brother," I say, and start for the stairs. To be fair, he does have a point. Our father definitely trusts me more than him, especially now.

I head downstairs to brush my teeth and change into a cleaner hoodie and a pair of jeans. I even rewrap my bun and slick down my baby hairs with water, figuring I should put in a little effort. My cocaptain, Willa, is always trying to give me a makeover, but after an unfortunate incident with an eyelash curler, I stick to the basics. I do slide on some clear lip gloss, though.

Once I'm done, I meet Marco at the bottom of the stairs. I'm startled to find Nonna already standing in the living room entrance as if she's been waiting for us. She eyes us suspiciously as we pause in front of her, my brother courageously standing behind me.

"Hi," I say innocently. "So . . . um. We wanted to go out for a while. That okay?"

She looks past my shoulder at Marco. "You going to cause trouble?" she asks him. "Throw a party and get arrested?"

"I didn't get arrested," Marco says. "And it was a great party. You would have liked it. There were Jell-O shots." He flashes her a smile.

Nonna purses her lips, but I think she's trying not to laugh. Despite her sharp edges, she likes us. I'm sure of it.

My father walks out of the kitchen and crosses the living room, wiping his hands on a red dish towel. "Where are you heading?" he asks. "I was just making us something to eat."

"We wanted to go downtown," I say. "I'm not really hungry, and it's still early—only eight. So we thought we could grab some hot chocolates, check out the beach. Wild stuff, you know?"

My father waits, thinking it over for a moment before shrugging. "Yeah, all right," he says. "Although I don't think you should take the Forester. The air in the front tires is really low." He turns to his mother. "Can the kids borrow your car?" he asks. Nonna breathes heavily out of her nose and gives a curt nod.

"But Nonna drives a minivan," Marco points out.

"So?" our grandmother asks, crossing her arms over her chest. "You need a ride, don't you?"

"Yeah . . . ," Marco admits.

"Then you'll survive," she replies. "The keys are on the front table. But I want you back by the time the sun sets."

Marco laughs. "We're not five, Nonna," he replies, but she doesn't smile.

Our grandmother takes a step toward him and Marco swallows hard. She may be little, but Nonna's eyes are pure fire. "We don't stay out after dark in Nightfall," she says in a low voice. "And in my home, you're going to abide by my rules. You understand?"

Next to her my dad nods as if telling us to humor her.

"Of course," I say, for me and my brother, caught off guard by my grandmother's change in demeanor. Although I have no problem respecting my grandmother's house rules, "home by dark" seems a bit extreme. But I'm hoping she'll ease up the longer we're here.

Nonna steps back, her arms still crossed over her chest. With the matter settled, Marco is first into the hallway, swiping the keys off the entryway table.

"And don't talk to any strangers either," Nonna adds. We hold up our hands in a wave and start for the door. But before we leave, I hear Nonna murmur, "Because they'll sure want to talk to you."

CHAPTER THREE

The world is almost surreal as we drive toward downtown Nightfall. Although it's still light outside, there's a dusky haze cast over everything that feels foreboding. Dreary. The trees glow neon green in the strange light, the houses' front porches tucked in the shadows. On the horizon, orange sunlight begs to peek out from behind the clouds before getting swallowed up by the dark.

"Nonna was a little intense back there, right?" I ask, glancing at my brother as he drives. I'm still thinking about her comment as we were leaving. What could she have meant about the *strangers* who might try to talk to us?

"Dad told us she was superstitious," Marco says, not seeming too concerned. "I'm sure she'll relax after a few days. The real danger," he adds, motioning to the dashboard, "is this monster. I feel like I'm driving a bus."

"It's not that bad," I tell him. "Like Nonna said, you'll survive." Marco huffs out an annoyed sound as he uses both hands to turn the wheel.

It's an older minivan, powder blue with gray interior.

There's a crucifix hanging from the rearview mirror and only three working radio stations. It smells like spearmint.

"You're just saying that because you don't have to drive," Marco says. "You don't understand how annoying this is."

"Luckily you're giving me the play-by-play, so I'll never feel like I'm missing out," I say, smiling brightly at him, and he laughs.

I don't have my driver's license yet. Haven't even studied for the test. Since all of my friends drive, it's never been a pressing issue. Besides, with Marco always taking our father's car, it's not like I'd get to use it much anyway. Last year, my mother told me she'd buy me a car once I passed the test. I wonder if that offer still stands or if she's buying Dale's kids cars instead.

I flinch, hurting myself with the thought. The betrayal of her picking his kids over us. I try to put it out of my head.

Marco takes a left onto Main Street. Once again, I'm reminded of how cute it is here, and that cheers me up a bit. The pink and blue buildings with striped awnings above the entrances. The baskets overflowing with flowers hanging from lampposts and a bike rack on every corner. And of course, there's the mural with the murderous mermaid calling to her prey. I especially love her.

The road is a series of hills, going up and then down. It's impossible to see the end, and both sides of the street are packed with cars parked at angles to the sidewalk. Marco continues to drive, searching for a parking spot. A guy in a golf cart zips past us and Marco groans his frustration. I'm equally annoyed. It'll be dark by the time we find a spot.

"This is impossible," he says. "We should have just walked."

It looks like most of the shops are closed now—definitely the flag store and the one that sells beach gear. But a few restaurants are open, with small crowds hanging out in front of the lit-up spaces. Up on the hill overlooking the water, there's an old mansion that's looks like it's been converted into some sort of public attraction, and we pass a sign announcing that the Liva Museum will open again in the morning.

I notice an open space in front of the library and my heart leaps. "Right there," I call out, pointing to it.

"Finally," Marco says. He pulls up next to a car and backs into the space. He turns the car off and beams at me.

"Pro move," I tell him, making his day.

I climb out of the minivan and take a big gulp of ocean air. It's nice to be on our own after spending two solid days traveling with our father. Even before that, Marco and I were basically on house arrest after the party. I'm grateful to finally have some unsupervised time.

"I don't know about you," Marco says, "but I could go for a scoop." He motions across the street to an absolutely adorable blue-shingled ice cream shop literally called Scoops.

"I could have a scoop," I agree. "Maybe some sprinkles too. You're buying, right?"

"Did you bring money?" he asks.

"No," I say sheepishly. "But you owe me for asking—"

"Yeah, yeah," Marco replies, waving me forward. "Come on, then."

Back in Phoenix, both of us work at our mother's restaurant on the weekends—I'm stuck behind the hostess stand while Marco buses tables. But ever since the party, our mother took us off the schedule—her version of punishment. Marco was angry, but since I'm not speaking to our mother anyway, I wasn't all that hurt. However, my bank account is hemorrhaging. I might have to find a summer job while we're here.

I weave my way through the groups of tourists, my brother already ahead of me. Marco stops in front of the ice cream shop and holds open the glass door for a mother and her child, both of them holding oversized waffle cones. The little boy, who has a ring of chocolate around his lips, bumps into me on his way out.

"So sorry," the mom tells me before grabbing the kid's filthy hand. She avoids my eyes and rushes away.

"No problem," I reply, but she's already too far to hear me. Why is she in such a hurry? Must be past bedtime for her kid.

As my brother and I head inside, tiny bells attached to the handle of the door jingle. The sweet scents of chocolate and marshmallow fill my nose, instantly making me nostalgic for the Cold Stone Creamery by my school. Willa and I go there after practice every Thursday because her girlfriend works there. And also because they'll add gummy worms to your ice cream on request like absolute maniacs. Ugh. I want to go home.

The inside of the ice cream shop is even cuter than its blue-shingled, candy-colored outside. Everything is in pastel colors with gold polka-dot stickers on the walls. There's a human-sized plastic ice cream cone in the corner to take pictures with and a single flower in the small vase at each table. Soft music, dreamy and delicate, plays from a ceiling speaker in one corner. Bowls with fake ice cream, each piled impossibly high with whipped cream and sprinkles, line the counter to show the size options. The cashier behind the register wears a pink hat and a bow tie.

"Can I help you?" the girl asks. She's pretty, with blondish-red hair and freckles, bright green eyes. Marco looks over the choices.

"Am I allowed to taste test each flavor?" he asks. The girl seems to think it over seriously before shrugging.

"I think you'd be a disappointment if you didn't," she says.

My brother laughs. "Wouldn't want that," he replies. "I'm Marco, by the way."

She stares at him a moment before responding. "Erika," she replies. "So where do you want to start?" she asks, motioning to the tubs of ice cream.

"That's an excellent question, Erika," Marco says, glancing over the flavor choices. "I'm thinking pistachio."

"Inspired choice," she affirms as she fills a little spoon for him.

I step up to the glass to check out the flavors. When I look down, though, I see a little chocolate handprint on my jeans from where the kid bumped into me.

"No . . . ," I say dramatically. Marco looks over and I point it out.

"That's why I don't like kids," he says simply, and turns around to take the spoon from the cashier. She laughs.

"I'll be right back," I tell Marco, and head toward the sign for the restrooms.

I go down a long hall and push through the marked door. I grab a paper towel from the dispenser and run it under the tap before vigorously scrubbing at the chocolate handprint on my thigh. It's stubborn, and when the stain does eventually come out, it leaves behind a big wet circle. Great.

My phone buzzes in my back pocket and I tense. It could be my mother again. She's been calling nearly every day to check in, but I've been sending her to voice mail. I'm not ready to talk to her yet. I pull out my phone and am immediately relieved when I see it's Willa FaceTiming me. I lean against the sink and answer.

"Missing you already," I say the moment her image pops

up. Her dark hair is piled on top of her head, with little fly-aways ringing her face. Her septum piercing looks huge from this angle as her broad smile fills the phone screen.

"Maggione," she says in her raspy voice.

"How was practice?" I ask.

"Fine, but everyone's miserable without you," she tells me, her smile fading. "We're playing like shit, so thank your dad for us." She settles into the cushions of her leather couch. In the background, I see her Chihuahua just over her shoulder.

The room is dark—it's nighttime in Phoenix. I suddenly feel a million miles away. I might as well be on the moon, and I miss my friends desperately.

"I still can't believe he forced you to go to Oregon for the summer," Willa continues. "It's like he doesn't care that you're supposed to be training for junior year."

"He cares," I say. "He told me I could go to the Y to stay in shape, and I was like, 'Sure, Dad. I'll just volley to myself. That will really keep me sharp.'"

"It's bullshit." Willa leans closer to the screen and scrunches her nose. "Wait, are you in a public bathroom taking a video call?"

"You know I never miss your calls," I say with a smile. "But yes, I am. Marco and I stopped at an ice cream shop downtown. Oh, and we met our grandmother. She is . . . unusual."

"I bet," Willa says. "Considering she lives in Nowhere, Oregon."

"Nightfall," I correct.

"Same thing," she replies. "So what's she like? Are we talking Miss Havisham unusual or *Flowers in the Attic* unusual?"

"Yikes," I say. "Neither. More like . . . *Golden Girls*. But she also has the potential to have a life-sized gingerbread house with an oven in the backyard, if that makes sense."

"Not at all," Willa replies. "For your sake let's hope she's a Betty White."

Suddenly there's a loud banging on the bathroom door and I nearly jump out of my skin.

"What?" I yell, clutching the phone close to my chest.

"You're taking forever!" Marco yells. "Hurry up."

I sigh, and when I look at Willa on the screen again, she smiles sadly. "Punch your brother hello for me," she says sweetly. "And, Theo," she adds more somberly, "tell your dad it's time for you to come home. We miss you. *I* miss you."

"Miss you, too," I murmur, overwhelmed with homesickness. "Call you later."

I hang up and slide the phone back into my pocket. If I were in Tempe right now, I'd probably be sleeping over at Willa's house or vice versa. We'd be watching true crime documentaries on Netflix and eating nachos. Instead, I'm here on the moon.

When I yank open the bathroom door, I find Marco in the hallway devouring a towering waffle cone of chocolate ice cream. He nods at me. "What did you think of the cashier?" he asks quietly. "She was pretty cute, right?"

"Yep," I agree. "But maybe pace yourself a little. We haven't even unpacked our bags yet."

He rolls his eyes. Marco has a tendency to date . . . everyone. He's not gross about it; I'd kick his ass if he were. But he's a moth to a flame. And then he's on to the next light.

"Okay, Theo," he says as if I'm exhausting. He bites the edge of his waffle cone, crunching down on it. He pulls a wrinkly ten-dollar bill from his pocket. "Here," he says, handing it to me. "I'll meet you outside."

I follow him down the hall, and he waves goodbye to the

cashier before heading out the door. She returns his wave with a bored expression.

With the money my brother gave me in hand, I pause at the counter to examine the flavors of ice cream—my eyes skimming over names like Rocky Road, Bubble Gum Delight, and Chocolate Dream. The cashier appears and waits patiently for me to decide.

After a moment, she points toward the case. "If you're taking suggestions," she offers, "I'm really into the raspberry sorbet right now."

I'm considering it when the little bells on the door jingle. I look over expecting my brother, but then my stomach sinks. The hitchhiking couple walks in wearing their oversized backpacks. I quickly avert my eyes, afraid the girl will recognize me from the car. The car that didn't stop for them.

I feel awful that we didn't pick them up, especially now that we're all in the same room. I watch in the mirror behind the counter as the guy goes to one of the tables, unwinding the backpack from his arms before setting it next to a chair. His sits down and pulls off his hat; his long hair is matted and damp. When he glances over and meets my eyes in the mirror, I quickly look back down at the ice cream.

Okay, I have to say something. As I'm contemplating the best apology, the girl comes to stand next to me at the counter. She smells like rain after a storm, fresh air and carefree. It's wonderful. I look over and smile politely. She stares at me a long moment before returning my smile.

"I'm so sorry—" I start in a rush, too embarrassed to formulate an excuse. The girl holds up her hand to stop me.

"No worries," she says, sounding tired. "Someone else picked us up."

I tilt my head in an apology. "I really am sorry, though," I add, meaning it.

She laughs. "I promise, we're good. You weren't the one driving anyway. I assume that was your . . . father?"

"Yeah," I say. "He's actually from here. From Nightfall."

She smiles as if that's interesting. "I thought he looked familiar," she says with a nod.

She must be local, but it's been twenty years since my dad has been to Nightfall, so I don't know how familiar he actually looked.

When I turn back to the counter, Erika is eyeing the hitchhiker carefully.

"Back so soon, Annemarie?" Erika asks her, setting her elbows on the glass and leaning toward the girl.

"It's been over a month," the hitchhiker says with a smile. "So glad you missed me, Erika. Now can we get two waters?" She motions to the guy at the table. "We're parched."

"I'm sure," Erika replies in a low voice.

"Thank you," Annemarie calls gratefully as Erika heads toward the back.

I examine the hitchhiker for a moment. She's gorgeous up close. Her skin is deeply tanned, with a smattering of freckles over her nose and cheeks. A sheen of sweat clings to her. I wonder how long they've been walking.

"So . . . ," I start hesitantly before she turns to me again. "So, you're from Nightfall?"

"Yep," she replies. "But I've been out exploring." She nods back to the guy. "I met Asa out in Joshua Tree and told him all about the town and the upcoming festival. He thought it sounded fun, so I worked it into our trip. I'm Annemarie, by the way."

"Theo," I reply. I turn to Asa and he watches me with a steady gaze. He doesn't say a word, though. Considering he flipped us off earlier, he might still be mad we didn't pick them up.

"And what about you?" Annemarie asks, drawing my attention back to her. "Pit stop or vacation?"

"Oh, uh . . . ," I stumble. I hadn't considered how to casually answer that question. People expect easy answers, not a rundown of family problems. "Here for the summer," I say simply enough.

Annemarie smiles. "Perfect," she says.

Erika reappears and hands Annemarie two paper cups of water. She takes them to the table and sets one in front of Asa. Erika watches her, seemingly uncomfortable. I can't explain why, but there's a weird tension in the air.

I notice Marco through the large picture window then, his ice cream nearly gone as he waves for me to hurry up. I turn back to Erika.

"I'll take your recommendation," I tell her. "The raspberry sorbet in a cup, please."

Erika has to drag her eyes away from Annemarie and Asa before smiling at me. "Coming right up," she replies. She grabs the scoop out of a bowl of water and turns to the bright pink tub, scraping the scoop along the top.

Her posture has definitely changed since the couple arrived. It's none of my business, but I'm more than a little curious. As Erika sets my cup down, I lean in closer. "Annemarie seems cool," I say quietly. "You friends with her?"

She swallows hard before looking up. "Sure," she says, barely audible. "I'm friends with everyone. Nightfall's a small town." Her gaze drifts past me to Annemarie and Asa. "Too small."

I'm unsure how to address the awkward reply. She doesn't seem to *not* like Annemarie. It's something else and I have no idea what.

Erika looks at me and jabs a spoon into my cup of raspberry sorbet. "Anything else?" she asks. It's abrupt, conversation ending, and I'm a bit embarrassed by her change in tone.

"No, nothing else," I murmur.

Erika hands over my sorbet before tapping a few keys on the register and announcing the total. Awkwardly, I hand over the ten and tell her to keep the change, hoping the tip will soften the moment. She doesn't thank me, so I head for the door.

Clearly there is some drama here and I respect that it's none of my business. When I reach for the door handle, I hear Annemarie.

"Theo," she calls. I turn back to find her smiling from the table where she's sitting with the guy. "It was nice to meet you."

"Nice to meet you too," I reply. "And again, I'm sorry that—"

She laughs. "Seriously, it's okay," she says. "All is forgiven. And we'll see you around. If not in town, then definitely at the parade next week."

"Right," I say, relieved at how friendly she's being. "The Midnight Dive. Yeah, we'll be there. Have a good night."

She lifts her hand in goodbye and glances at the guy next to her. "Asa," she prods. "Tell her goodbye."

He pauses as if about to argue, but then seems to melt under her attention. He glances at me for a distracted second. "Bye," he says vacantly before turning back to Annemarie. She playfully slaps his hand as if scolding him.

I get that we didn't stop to pick them up, but yeah—he's

kind of a dick. He's cute or whatever, but I can already tell that Annemarie is way too good for him.

As I walk out, I glance back at the counter just as Erika grabs a rag from the sink. She says nothing to me. Instead, she begins wiping down the glass case, ignoring me as if I'm already gone.

CHAPTER FOUR

The bells on the door jingle as it closes behind me. I look at my brother, perched on a low wall outside the shop. He's already done with his ice cream and is eating the bottom of his waffle cone, oblivious to the layers of humiliation I just went through. When he sees me staring, he frowns.

"You good?" Marco asks.

"Didn't you see them go in?" I ask, motioning toward the shop.

"See who?" Confused, he glances back into the window. It takes a moment, but then his mouth drops open and he ducks. "Oh, shit," he says. "Are those the hitchhikers?"

"Yeah," I say, waving for him to stand up. "And the girl recognized me. Luckily she was cool about it."

"Awkward," Marco says, widening his eyes. He finishes his ice cream, wipes his mouth with a napkin, and then tosses it into a metal trash can next to the curb.

"She's from here, I guess," I tell him. "Annemarie is her name. The cashier knows her, but she didn't seem all that happy to see her."

Marco looks back at me, intrigued. "Huh," he says.

I shrug. "Small-town shit, I guess." I take a tentative spoonful of my sorbet. It's delicious, tart and bright. Erika definitely hooked me up with a good choice.

Marco looks down the hill toward the promenade. "Should we check out the water?" he asks. "Not sure how much longer we have before it gets dark."

"Well, I already broke the other rule." I hike my thumb back at the ice cream shop. *"Don't talk to strangers,"* I repeat, and we both laugh. Our grandmother is definitely paranoid.

Marco and I head toward the water, people weaving their way around us on the sidewalk, hurrying up the hill. As we pass a small independent bookstore, a large display in the window catches my attention. There is a huge stack of blue-and-white hardcover novels, a smattering of flower petals on a white cloth underneath them, and a banner that reads OLIVIA MILES—*USA TODAY* BESTSELLING AUTHOR OF *RED-BLOODED SUMMER*. I pause to look at the book, recognizing the author's name immediately. I've never read her romance novels, but my mom kept a stack of them on her nightstand when she still lived at home. The memory stings a little.

Next to the display is a picture of Olivia, along with a newspaper clipping. Apparently, she's local. Although I wonder how romantic summers in Nightfall, Oregon, can really get.

When I turn to Marco to point out the famous local author, I find him a few yards ahead. He's staring at the other side of the road, wholly distracted. Enamored, even. Curious, I follow his line of vision.

Across the street and down just a little ways is a Catholic church, or at least it used to be, judging by the stained-glass windows and statue of Mary out front. Now there's a giant billboard that reads *Northwest Estates—Condos for sale!* with a glossy image of a planned condo development. But it's not the building that my brother is staring at. It's the girls.

There are two girls about our age sitting on the low wall under the billboard. Even from here, I can see that they are both beautiful. No, not just beautiful—stunning.

Marco continues walking down the block, watching the girls the entire time. I follow him, intent on telling him to tone it down, but I can't take my eyes off them either. They're mesmerizing—straight out of a movie, almost like a spotlight is shining on them.

As we get closer, one of the girls holds up her hand to wave us over. She's Black with shaved hair, dangling earrings that sparkle in the dim light. She's wearing a sleeveless yellow dress, even though it's fairly cold out. The girl next to her is blond and draped in what looks like a vintage red prom gown. She's grinning, watching us with anticipation.

Marco turns to me and then nods across the street. "Want to go over?" he asks.

I check out the girls again, feeling self-conscious and underdressed. "No, you go ahead," I tell him. "I'm heading to the beach."

"Cool," he says immediately. "I'll text you in a little bit."

"Uh—"

But Marco dashes across the street before I can even voice that I'm a little offended at how quickly he's ditching me. He could have at least pretended to debate leaving me behind.

The girls laugh as he walks up to them, one touching his arm, one messing up his curly dark hair. They really are beautiful, like walking Instagram filters with smoothed-out edges.

The girl with the shaved head looks over at me curiously. I don't want to seem like I'm avoiding them, so I wave and then point to the beach. She smiles and nods like she understands. With that settled, I start toward the water.

For the first time in a long time, I'm alone. It's kind of . . . nice. I got used to people checking in on me since the divorce, but right now, it's just me. Well, me and a bunch of tourists. But the crowd thins out the closer I get to the water.

An icy wind blows in off the ocean. I throw out my mostly empty cup of ice cream and flip up my hood, pulling the strings closed against the chill. Just then, my phone buzzes. I pull it out, guessing it's Marco or Willa, but the caller ID says *Mom*. I have a flash of anger at the idea of her calling from Dale's house, and I click Ignore and put my phone away.

I know I'll have to talk to her eventually, but now is not the time. In fact, I might wait until summer is over. It would serve her right—she's part of the reason we're banished here.

My shoes scrape over the sand as I cross the promenade roundabout, a narrow beach just beyond it. It's a far cry from the Southern California beaches that I'm used to visiting. There isn't much space to lay out, and even if I wanted to, it's too windy and cold.

There *is* a stone bench that looks out over the ocean. It's kind of hidden along a walking path next to the sand, private and decorated with seashells in the concrete. I take a seat, the cold stone chilling me through my jeans. The beach is deserted and it's a combination of peaceful and eerie. I stay, listening to the waves crash against the shore. I'm angry that my mother tried to call me again. And I'm angry that I'm angry. I look up at the overcast sky—dusk at nine at night . . . so strange.

There's a flash of movement as someone sits down next to

me. I turn, expecting my brother, but I jump when I see it's a stranger. The guy immediately holds up his hands in apology.

"Sorry," he says. "I didn't mean to scare you."

I don't respond, staring at him instead as I try to assess his danger level. He's young, my age at least, with reddish-brown hair and big brown eyes. Long lashes. Sharp jaw. When he smiles, a sheen of beauty drapes right over him. It's not lost on me that nearly everyone I've interacted with in Nightfall so far is attractive, but this guy is . . . well, he's hard to miss.

"I'm Parrish," he says. "It's nice to meet you."

"Meet me?" I reply. "When you sit next to a girl who's alone without asking, I'm not sure you can call it *meeting* her."

"You're right," he says apologetically and stands back up. "I'm sorry. I just . . . wanted to see if you were all right. I saw you sitting here and thought you looked kind of pissed off."

Fair point because it's true.

I realize then that the strings of my hoodie are still pulled tight, scrunching my face between the fabric. I quickly yank the strings loose and push the hood down, my ears chilled in the cool wind. But at least I don't look like a total dork anymore.

"Is it okay if I sit here?" Parrish asks, motioning to the bench.

I wait a moment, considering, but he seems harmless. "Sure," I say with a shrug.

He settles back onto the bench and crosses one foot over the other knee. He watches me curiously, a ghost of a smile on his lips. His eyes sparkle playfully in the fading light.

"I'm Parrish," he says again as if we're starting over. "Nice to . . . meet you?" He raises his left eyebrow in anticipation.

I laugh. "You too," I say. "I'm Theo."

"That's an unusual name," he replies.

"Really, *Parrish*?" I point out, and this time he laughs. "It's short for Theodora," I add. "Which is a lot and no one uses it unless I'm in trouble."

"Understood," he says. "To be honest, Parrish is my last name."

"What's your first name?" I ask, curious.

He shakes his head to let me know he's not going to share. "Let's just say I'm no Theodora," he says, settling back against the bench. "And where are you visiting us from?" he asks. "Arizona, I assume?"

His guess catches me off guard, and my heart trips up. "How do you know that?" I ask.

He nods to my sweatshirt, and when I look down, I'm remember that I'm wearing another ASU hoodie. Not exactly rocket science.

"Clearly my observational skills tonight are incredible," I tell him. "Razor sharp."

"You could be a spy," he whispers in agreement.

I can't help but smile, charmed. "I'm from Tempe," I tell him. "Just outside of Phoenix."

"It was an easy guess," he says. "In Nightfall, tourists love to advertise. They come here wearing their UCLAs, their UNLVs, and, of course, their ASUs."

"We're predictable, huh?" I ask.

"In the best way," he replies. "I have yet to see a local walk around with a Nightfall, Oregon, sweatshirt. Then again, our mascot is the wombat, so I'm not sure it would have the desired effect."

"The Nightfall Wombats," I say, and Parrish nods, amused. "Your rivals must be intimidated."

"Oh yes," he says. "The Hellcats and Jackals are terrified of us."

I laugh, promising myself that I'll look up the mascot later tonight. I bet it's hilarious.

Now that my initial startlement is gone, Parrish and I ease into conversation, friendly and relaxed. I'm not sure we're flirting exactly, nothing that obvious. We're just two strangers talking on a bench next to the ocean. He just happens to be gorgeous. But I don't feel self-conscious around him, not even in a hoodie and chocolate-stained jeans.

"You're lucky," Parrish says, turning to look at the ocean. "It's usually raining. Maybe a little cold," he adds. "But I'm sure it's better than that hundred-and-twenty-degree desert heat."

"Debatable," I tell him. "I happen to hate the rain."

He laughs and turns back to me. "What? Nobody *hates* the rain."

"I do," I reply. "In Arizona, we have monsoon season. And everyone goes wild for it—storms, lightning, rain. But after two days of clouds, I feel low and stay in the house, eating grilled cheese and soup. I don't know how I'm going to handle the weather here."

"Enjoy the sun when it comes out," Parrish suggests. "And stock up on soup."

We both turn toward the ocean, watching as waves lap against the sand. I'm cold, but I don't want to stand up. Not yet. For the first time since arriving, I'm not homesick.

"So you grew up here?" I ask, looking sideways at Parrish.

"No," he says. "But I've been here long enough to be a local. How about you, Arizona? How long are you staying in Nightfall?"

"For the summer," I say. "Well, four weeks. Arizona school breaks are short. But trust me, it's long enough to ruin my life."

"I'm sorry to hear that," Parrish says, sounding truly sympathetic.

Now I feel overdramatic and silly—there are real problems in the world. A lot of them. I know realistically that my life isn't *ruined*.

"It's actually our own fault," I admit. "My brother and I . . ." I nearly tell Parrish about the party, but then decide it's not really an important detail. "Never mind," I say. "Marco and I are here for the summer. I'm going to make the best of it."

"That's the spirit," Parrish says, gently elbowing my side. "And I'm sure you've heard about the Midnight Dive—they've plastered flyers about it everywhere."

"I have," I say. "Is it fun?"

He pauses, then nods. "It is," he says. "I think you'll enjoy it. But what's even better is that there's a party tonight. And every night leading up to it."

The beach is deserted. "Really?" I ask, doubtful.

"Not here," he says. "The locals hang out at Sunrise Beach—about twenty minutes away. Breathtaking views. It's very cool. You'll love it. We're heading over there soon if you want to—"

It suddenly occurs to me that the sun has set. I look around, surprised at how quickly the sky has grown dark, stars dotting the blackness. My heart leaps with worry. "Shit," I say. "I have to go. We're supposed to be home by now."

"You sure?" Parrish asks, sounding disappointed.

"Yes," I say quickly. "We're late. I have to get my brother. He's back at the shops."

Parrish and I both stand up. He motions toward the promenade. "I'm actually heading that way to meet my friends," he says. "I can walk with you, if you want?"

"Sure," I say. "That'd be great. And . . . I'm sorry to be so abrupt. My grandmother is just . . . she has this rule and—"

"You don't have to explain," Parrish says, his eyes shining brightly. "Besides, there's always tomorrow night. Or the next night." He smiles at me. "Or the night after that."

CHAPTER FIVE

arrish is next to me as we cross the promenade onto Main Street. I'm surprised to find the restaurants and shops are closed, the tourists gone. The streets are empty. It feels kind of eerie with the sun gone, the crowds gone. Behind us, the waves crash loudly into the sand.

"Where is everybody?" I ask him, a bit anxious.

Parrish slides his hands into the pockets of his jeans. "They don't like the dark," he says. "Which is funny for a town called Nightfall." He smiles. "It's kind of a superstition around here, especially for the adults. Home by dark." He looks sideways at me. "I assume your grandmother told you that?"

I nod. "Yep," I say. "But I didn't realize the whole town was superstitious. I thought it was just her. My dad didn't mention it."

"Your dad?" Parrish asks.

"Yeah, he's with us for the summer," I say. "He's from Nightfall originally."

Parrish's lips part in surprise, and he quickly looks away. "I didn't realize that," he says.

"Good, because I didn't mention it," I point out, and he smiles again.

"Fair point," he replies.

Talking about my father makes me debate calling to let him know Marco and I are on our way, but since he hasn't texted to ask, I don't want to draw attention to the fact that we're not home yet. I should have texted my brother when it first got dark, but I was distracted by a handsome stranger and apparently missed the sunset altogether. Rookie mistake.

I take out my phone to check for a message from Marco, but he hasn't reached out. I'm kind of glad we're being equally irresponsible. I tap the phone icon next to his name before bringing my phone to my ear. It rings four times and then his voice mail answers. "Hi, it's Marco. Why the fuck are you leaving a message? Text me. *Ding.*"

"Answer the phone," I murmur as I hang up. Annoyed, I open my texts.

Are you still at that holy condo building? I write. *We have to get home.*

I wait a moment, but my brother doesn't respond. He better not have ditched me in this unfamiliar downtown. I will strangle him. A little worried now, I pick up the pace. Parrish looks over at my phone before I slide it into my back pocket.

"No answer?" he asks.

"Not yet," I say. "I'm sure he's still at the condos by the ice cream shop. If not, I'll hunt him down and kill him."

"So, you guys are close?" Parrish asks, and then smiles. I laugh.

"We are, actually," I say. "But he's really annoying." I shiver in the cold night air. "What is with this place? I'm freezing. It's supposed to be *summer.*"

Parrish removes his jacket and holds it out to me. "Take it," he says.

"No, stop," I say. "What are you doing? You're in a T-shirt."

"I'm good," he says, shaking the jacket in my direction. "I'm used to this weather, remember? In fact, it's downright hot. You're doing me a favor."

I debate what to do, but ultimately, he seems confident that he's fine and I'm actually cold as hell. I take the jacket and slip my arms though the sleeves. I'm immediately struck by how good it smells. Like a soapy shower, a close shave. It's . . . comforting. I wrap my arms around myself to bring the feeling closer.

Parrish is wearing a black T-shirt, his body lean with muscle, a tattoo twisting around one forearm. Our proximity suddenly feels intimate. I look away, but when I turn back to him again, he smiles shyly.

The sound of a girl's laugh bounces off the buildings. It startles me as I search for the source of it; it seems both close and far away, as if someone is just behind my shoulder and yet far up ahead. *Is it one of the girls Marco was with?*

Parrish shifts his gaze around without turning his head, his expression serious. After a moment, he shrugs as if there's nothing to worry about. "It's just an echo," he assures me.

Despite his calm tone, we walk faster, making our way uphill. The road climbs and then levels out before climbing again, hiding itself from view. I still have no idea if Marco is at the church condos.

There's a small children's park between a coffee shop and a candy store. As we pass, the chains of the swing squeak as it blows gently in the wind. Then I hear a tapping sound and notice a figure near the slide. It's Asa, the hitchhiker from the ice cream shop. He's alone, kicking a hacky sack. I wonder what happened to Annemarie.

"Hey," I call out to him, hopeful he might have seen Marco.

He doesn't acknowledge me at first. Instead, he continues to tap the hacky sack in the air with the inside of his Converse. His oversized backpack lies next to him on the grass. There's a Joshua Tree patch on it, and I think about Parrish saying that tourists advertise.

Finally, Asa lifts his head to look at me, then at Parrish. He nods to us both, but like in the ice cream shop, he's a man of few words. He goes back to his hacky sack and we hear the tapping of his foot all the way up the block.

"I met him earlier," I tell Parrish quietly. "When I was coming into town with my family, we saw him hitchhiking with a girl named Annemarie." I scrunch up my nose. "But we didn't stop. I feel awful about it." I glance back toward the park even though I can no longer see Asa. "But to be fair, he's kind of a jerk."

Parrish also looks back, seeming lost in thought. "Well," he says before turning to me again, "Annemarie has very specific tastes."

"Oh, you know her?" I ask, surprised. Although I'm not sure why I should be—Erika did say it was a small town.

"I do," he says. He takes out his phone to check the time and then smiles at me. The streetlights are dim on this section of the block, which makes his eyes seem endlessly dark, blacker than the night itself.

"It is so dark," I say, glancing around. "These streetlights do nothing."

"It's for the view," Parrish says. "They're set low so that people can see the stars more clearly. Look." He points toward the sky, and sure enough, it's dotted with white pinpoints. So many stars. It's kind of romantic.

Wind rustles the leaves of the nearby trees; the sound is

hollow and haunting. At the next hill, I catch sight of the brightly colored mural again. I examine it as we pass, and this time, I notice something different. The mermaid is still on the rock, beckoning to the sailors with her hair blowing in the breeze. But off to the side and along the shore is a bunch of smaller figures—townspeople.

Men, women, and even little kids are standing and watching the impending doom. And some of them are smiling.

Yikes. That feels kind of morbid.

"Is that him?" Parrish asks, startling me from my thoughts. When I turn back to him, he's pointing up ahead.

I look and am relieved to see my brother still at the church, standing by the low wall in a streetlamp's filtered light. He's alone with the girl with the shaved head and yellow dress, smiling and talking animatedly as she laughs. I wonder where the other girl went.

"That's Marco. At least tonight seems to be going well for him," I say, my heart warming. I haven't seen Marco look this happy in a long time, not even at our end-of-the-year party. In fact, I've gotten so used to his fake smile that I forgot what his real one looked like. I'm glad to see it again.

Parrish doesn't comment, but he slows his steps, falling behind me. I turn back to look at him.

"What is it?" I ask.

He points across the street toward Scoops. The shop light shines in the window, even though the Closed sign is facing out.

"I'm meeting my friend there," he says. "I'm actually late too, so . . ."

"Oh," I say, looking back at the ice cream shop. "Is it Erika?" I ask, sounding as if I know her, when in reality we've only spoken for a few minutes. "I met her earlier."

"You did?" Parrish asks. "Uh . . . no. I mean, I know her, but Erika doesn't typically come out with us after dark. I'm meeting Annemarie, actually." He smiles. "I'm the one who picked up the hitchhikers."

"Of course you were," I say. My embarrassment at our not stopping returns. Parrish laughs.

"It's okay," he says. "I know her, so I wasn't too worried about being ax-murdered. I'm giving her and the jerk guy a ride to the beach. You sure you can't come? It seems like you know a bunch of the locals already. You fit right in."

"I don't know about that," I say with a laugh. "But I'm sorry to miss the party tonight. If I'm not on house arrest, maybe I can make it tomorrow."

Parrish licks his bottom lip before smiling, his gaze locked on mine. There is a flutter in my stomach. We are definitely flirting.

"Well, if you need help sneaking out, let me know," he offers. "And . . . in case you do escape tonight, I'll keep a spot for you near the bonfire."

Which reminds me . . . I start to slip off his jacket, but he shakes his head.

"Keep it," he says. "You can give it back to me tomorrow."

"You sure?" I ask, surprised. My heart beats faster. Keeping it tonight guarantees we'll have to meet up again. Which I guess is the point.

"I'm sure," he says. He glances past me to where Marco is standing. When I turn, both Marco and the girl are watching us. My brother looks puzzled, but the girl seems amused. Parrish holds up his hand to her in a wave. Polite. A bit distant.

"You know her too?" I ask.

Parrish opens his mouth, but before he can answer my question, Marco calls my name.

"Theo!" he yells. "We have to go."

Oh, *now* he's concerned with leaving? He didn't even answer my call. I turn back to Parrish, but he's already started across the road. He spins around, taking a few of the steps backward.

"It was nice to officially meet you, Arizona," he calls to me. "Let's do it all over again tomorrow. Only we'll skip to the good parts."

"Deal," I say, grinning madly. "And I'll keep an eye out for a Wombats sweatshirt, just so you don't feel left out."

He laughs before turning around to hop onto the curb, leaving me gazing after him. I'm warm with attraction and excitement. He's cute. He's sweet. And he smells damn good. Maybe this summer won't be so awful.

"Theo!" Marco yells impatiently. "Come on."

"Seriously?" I say, annoyed. I start in his direction and take out my phone, wagging it at him. "I called *and* texted you."

Marco looks surprised and takes his phone out of his pocket to check it. He scoffs. "No you didn't," he says. "You're the one who didn't answer my texts."

I stop in front of my brother, both of us with our phones out. Sure enough, on his end there are undelivered messages to me. And he didn't get mine.

"Service in Nightfall is spotty," the girl says from the low wall. "Especially after dark."

I turn to her, immediately struck by her dazzling smile and ruby-red lips. There's a hint of vanilla in the air and it makes me nostalgic, although I'm not sure exactly what for. Something from my childhood.

"I'm so sorry," I say, embarrassed that I didn't introduce myself immediately. But even now, I falter a little. She's so shockingly pretty.

Marco puffs himself up. "This is my sister," he tells the girl, motioning toward me. "Theo, this is Minnow—she lives in Nightfall."

For her part, Minnow hops down from the wall to take my hand. Her skin is cool and soft, and her long nails poke into my wrist.

"Hello, Theo," she says. Her voice is low and alluring. Minnow's eyes are light—an amber shade of brown—and I can't help but gaze into them. I feel so welcomed, so . . . special.

After a moment, I blink and take my hand back with a self-conscious laugh. Minnow watches me curiously, sizing me up, but I sense no judgment.

"So," I say to fill the silence. "You're from Nightfall?"

"No," she replies. "But I grew up not too far from here in a small fishing town—that's how I got my name. I relocated because there's more people and better food. I'm currently staying with my friend Beatrice."

There is a sharp giggle behind me. It's the same one I heard bouncing off the buildings when I was at the bottom of the hill. For some reason, the sound pings off my eardrums in an unpleasant way. It's . . . discomfiting.

I turn and see the blond girl in the red prom dress walking toward us. And next to her, I'm surprised to see Annemarie. I look for Parrish, but he's nowhere. The light is still on in the ice cream shop.

The girls are each carrying a bowl of white ice cream with strawberry sauce. Almost immediately, the blond girl smiles at me.

"Annemarie, you're right," she says, even though she's staring at me. "She's positively *adorable*." She pauses. "I'm Beatrice," she says. "And I can already see why the town is buzzing about you."

Her comment catches me off guard, but the flattery works,

and I smile shyly. "Uh, hi," I say, my cheeks warm. "What do you mean *buzzing?*"

"Oh, you know," she says dismissively, and waves her hand around. "Annemarie was gushing about you earlier, and we just bumped into Parrish at the shop. Seems you made quite an impression on him."

The mention of Parrish's name is a shot of electricity, but I try to play it cool, nodding along. Next to Beatrice, Annemarie winks at me and smiles. But Beatrice is sizing me up, running her eyes slowly over Parrish's jacket, its long sleeves hanging over my hands.

"Don't you look cozy," she adds, and then licks the strawberry sauce off her spoon.

Minnow laughs. "Don't mind Bea," she announces. "She's always in everyone's business. An absolute sociopath."

"Psychopath," Beatrice corrects, and smiles.

Minnow strides over to her friend and leans in to swipe her finger through the strawberry sauce on the ice cream. She licks her finger and then smiles at Beatrice. "Delicious," she whispers, and they both laugh.

"I can see the resemblance," Annemarie says, looking from me to Marco. "Some strong family genes."

"Ew," I say under my breath. Marco curls his lip.

Annemarie laughs. Even though I saw her in the shop not too long ago, she looks different—refreshed, her hair fuller and her skin glowing. She must have cleaned up in the bathroom.

"Parrish said he was going to meet you there." I motion toward the shop. "Is he . . . still there?" It's presumptuous of me to ask about him, and it definitely feels weird when the three girls exchange amused smiles.

"For sure," Annemarie says. "He's helping with a few things

before the bonfire. And dropping off my *massive backpack*," she adds, widening her eyes at the other girls. "That shit was heavy."

"I bet," Beatrice responds, although she sounds like she couldn't care less. She's still examining me, judging me for sure. She licks her spoon and then pulls it out of her mouth to point it at me. "I like you," she says as an observation. "You seem interesting."

"Uh, thank you," I say. She's strange, but I don't necessarily mind that. Instead, I'm intrigued and want to get to know them all. To me, they're the ones who seem interesting. I feel kind of cool by association.

As if sensing my thoughts, Minnow comes back over to me and loops her arm through mine as though we're already friends.

"So what do you think of our town so far, Theo?" she asks. "Your brother is *obsessed*."

Beatrice nods, so I imagine they had this conversation with Marco before I arrived. The idea of my brother being "obsessed" with Nightfall is laughable, but I've heard him say weirder shit to impress a girl. For his part, Marco stands by quietly, looking a little impatient to leave, but also curious to learn more about these girls.

"I like the town," I tell the group, mostly meaning it. "It's beautiful, a little quirky," I add, thinking about my grandmother. "We're going to have fun here."

"Maybe you'll want to stay," Annemarie suggests, and Minnow turns to look at her sharply for a moment. Then she smiles at me.

"You're definitely going to have fun," Minnow tells me reassuringly, bumping her shoulder gently into mine before going back to the low wall, the other two girls on either side of her.

"But you might also get sick of it," she adds. "Some people around here get stuck in their ways, resistant to change. Small-town life, I suppose."

"Speaking of resistant to change," I say, turning to my brother. "We were supposed to be home by now. You ready?"

"I hope you're not afraid of the dark," Beatrice says with a pout. "We already have too many of those kinds of people around here."

"Not of the dark," I say. "I'm afraid of Nonna."

Beatrice looks sideways at Minnow, who smiles at me instead. "Nonna?" Beatrice asks her privately.

"Their grandmother," Minnow says sweetly, still staring at me. "That's who they're visiting—Josephine Maggione."

Beatrice falls silent before looking at me again. Annemarie twists a dark strand of hair around one finger, her eyes rounded as she turns to me, fascinated.

Marco furrows his brow at the three of them. "Wait, do you know our grandmother?" he asks.

"Sure," Beatrice says with a shrug. "We know everyone in Nightfall. And your grandmother is just darling." I can't tell if she means it or if she's being polite.

"Uh . . ." Marco turns to me as if asking whether our grandmother could be considered darling. To be fair, we don't know her well enough to judge just yet.

"We should go," I whisper to Marco, and nod toward the car.

Marco makes an affirmative grunt and pulls the keys out of his pocket, clutching them in his fist as he turns back to the girls.

"I'm sorry, but we really have to take off," he says. "I . . ." He looks nervously at Minnow. "I hope I'll see you again?"

"Give me your phone," she says, holding out her hand. My

brother walks over to pass it to her. Minnow quickly taps the keys before handing it back to him. "There," she says. "Now you have my number."

"I'll text you," Marco says, smiling so hard his cheeks might freeze like that permanently. It's embarrassing, but also really endearing.

We start for the car, the night colder now that we're in the open again. Out of curiosity, I turn back to the girls and find Beatrice watching us. She waves her fingers at me. Her long nails catch the dull light, dripping with strawberry sauce before she licks them clean.

CHAPTER SIX

'm still surprised by how dark it really is without streetlights. There aren't any in Nonna's neighborhood and it's as if a curtain has been pulled across the town, submerging it in shadows. The only sources of light are from the front porches of the houses we pass.

"Do you think we're dead meat?" Marco asks from behind the steering wheel before looking at me worriedly. "Is Nonna going to literally carve us up and serve us for dinner?"

"Doubtful," I say. "It's too late for dinner."

"Fuck, we're going to be brunch," he says, sounding disappointed. "I hate brunch."

Once in Nonna's driveway, Marco parks the minivan and kills the engine. Instead of getting out, he checks his phone.

"What are you doing?" I ask. My anxiety is climbing at our impending collision with our grandmother. I was hoping Marco would take the lead on this and bear the brunt of the scolding.

"I wanted to see if Dad texted," he says. "I still don't think there's service, though."

"I didn't hear from him," I say, and look up at the windows of our grandmother's house. No one is watching us, so that's good at least. But the lights are on in the living room.

"We're only like an hour late," I say, looking at Marco. "That's not too bad, right?"

He shrugs. "I guess we're going to find out." He climbs out of the car, closing the door gently, and I do the same. Who knows maybe we can sneak upstairs without anyone noticing.

We head toward the porch and take our time quietly climbing the stairs. When I reach for the door, I smile hopefully at my brother. But just before I touch the handle, the door swings open. I scream in surprise and Marco curses, clutching his chest.

Nonna stands there, her dark eyes narrowed. She holds out her hand for the car keys. Marco fishes them out of his pocket and drops them into her hand.

"You're late," Nonna says, appraising us sharply. "I was just about to come looking for you."

She glances over my shoulder to some bushes near the road. I follow her steady gaze, but there's nothing there. Still, her expression is steely, fierce.

"Now get inside," she says, never shifting her focus from the bushes.

Obeying quickly, Marco and I cross the threshold into her house and Nonna slams the door closed and turns the dead bolt. The three of us stand awkwardly in the foyer.

"I told you to be home by dark," she scolds. "Now, where were you?"

"Nowhere," Marco says. "I mean, just downtown. We got ice cream and walked to the beach."

He's leaving out some key details, of course, but I don't

correct him. Still, Nonna doesn't seem to buy it. Instead, she turns to me sharply.

"And whose jacket is that?" she demands.

"Uh . . ." Okay, now we're busted.

Nonna walks right up to me and takes a big whiff of the jacket's collar. Startled, I fall back a step, bumping into the entryway table and rattling the picture frames on it. Several fall over, loudly banging on the wood.

"Nonna!" I yelp. At the sound of my voice, she straightens and backs away. Her rounded eyes are both scared and angry. "What's wrong?" I ask.

She darts a stern look at Marco but says nothing. Instead, she purses her lips, the lines deepening around her mouth. She's clearly upset. And really, why was she *sniffing* me?

Our father comes strolling out from the living room wearing his reading glasses and carrying a hardcover book. "Hey, hey, what's all the noise?" he asks. "Everyone all right?"

Nonna swallows hard, and then turns, patting her son's arm before heading toward the stairs. "I'm going to bed," she says in a low voice.

"Okay," our father replies. "Well, good night, Mom."

The three of us stand in silence as Nonna makes her way up the stairs, gripping the railing as each step creaks. And then we hear her bedroom door slamming shut.

Our father turns toward us. "What did you do?" he asks, but then smiles, as if acknowledging that our grandmother was the one acting weird. Marco and I both laugh with relief as he breaks the tension.

Marco runs his hand over his dark curls. "So Nonna just sniffed Theo," he says. "Care to explain?"

Our dad turns to me, tugging on his shirt to indicate the oversized jacket I'm wearing. "I'm guessing you talked to strangers?"

I flash an apologetic smile and immediately point to Marco to rat him out. Our father sighs.

"Well, I'm not sure why your grandmother sniffed you, that's a new one, but she did tell you to be home by dark. That's a pretty strict rule in this house. Did you really have to break it the first night?"

"I think it's important we set realistic expectations of failure, Dad," Marco says. Our father swats his arm with the book.

"We weren't trying to be late," I explain. "We just both lost track of time and our phones didn't work. But this home-by-dark thing . . . it's a bit extreme."

"I get it," our father says. "I grew up here, remember? But I'll talk to her. I'm sure we can find a compromise."

I'm still a little worried, though. "You don't think . . . We're not grounded or anything, right?" I ask.

"Yeah, are we?" Marco interjects. "Because I kind of have plans for this week."

"We'll discuss it in the morning," our father says. "But first you both need to apologize to your grandmother for being late. She's just trying to keep you safe."

"Sure," I say. When Marco doesn't say anything, I elbow him in the side.

"Yes, first thing," he says begrudgingly. Sometimes being ordered to apologize automatically makes a person not want to do it. But we both know that we *were* late. That's totally on us.

"So tell me about these locals," our father says, setting the book he's been carrying on the entry table. I snort a laugh when I see it's a copy of *Red-Blooded Summer*.

I opt to maintain my privacy. Before my brother can start to tell him all about the girls, I excuse myself. "Nice chat, but I'm heading up," I announce.

My father eyes me suspiciously. "I see what you're doing," he calls after me. "But you'll have to share details eventually, Theo!"

"See you in the morning," I say, matching his tone and making him laugh. I'd rather stay in the house forever than share details with my father about a boy I met.

As I head upstairs I hear Marco dive into a story about Minnow and her friends.

When I get into my room, I pause to look around at the dolls lining the shelf, their glass eyes studying me. I'll need a ladder to get them down, so it'll have to wait until the morning. Great. I'm sure I'll sleep well.

I slip off Parrish's jacket and hang it on the doorknob of the closet. Then I drag my suitcase onto the bed, unzip it, and pull out a pair of shorts and a T-shirt. I should probably put my clothes in the dresser since I'll be here for a while, but it feels like admitting defeat. I'll do that in the morning, too.

Just as I'm about to yank off my sweatshirt, I realize the bedroom curtains are open. I walk over to close them, but when I look out, I freeze.

The overhead light is on and reflected in the glass. As I stare out over the yard, I swear I see a figure standing at the end of the driveway. My heart leaping into my throat, I dart over to the light switch and turn it off to get a clearer view. But when I return to the window, the moonlight is bright enough to see that it was just the shadow of one of the trees. There's no one there.

I wrap my arms around myself, my pulse calming. Well, that was terrifying.

There's a soft knock on my door and I turn just as it opens. My breathing is still unsteady, and I'm relieved when I see it's my brother.

"Are you decent?" Marco asks, poking his head inside the room with his eyes closed.

"No, but I'm dressed," I tell him.

He opens his eyes and looks around. "Why the hell are you standing here in the dark?" he asks.

"Turn on the light," I tell him, shaking my head. "Sorry, I think Nonna is making me paranoid."

My brother flips on the light and closes the door before going to sit on the chair at the small desk against the opposite wall.

"How is Dad?" I ask.

"Actually, not too bad," Marco says. "He was kind of in a good mood. Did you see he was holding a romance novel?" He chuckles.

"I noticed," I say. "The author is local—I saw a window display when we were downtown. Mom used to read her books."

We're quiet for a moment, and then Marco scrunches his nose. "Hate to bring it up, Theo," he says gently, "but Mom's been calling you."

I lower myself onto the bed, facing my brother. "Yeah, I know," I say. Unlike me, Marco has been taking our mother's phone calls. He's upset with her, too—but he doesn't have the same sense of betrayal. Just hurt.

"I think she's going to marry Dale," I say, my stomach sinking. Marco lowers his eyes.

"Yep," he replies.

It's not that we don't like Dale—he's okay. Nice, even. And we want our mother to be happy. But she moved in with him and his kids, practically abandoning us. It's made me doubt everything. It's this feeling that our family wasn't good enough. I've lain awake at night, thinking back over every Christmas, every birthday, every vacation to Mexico to visit our grandparents, looking for signs that our mom wasn't happy. I'm not sure I'll ever understand.

"It'll be okay," Marco says. "No matter what, she loves us. She just . . . she has to work things out. And so does Dad. It's not all on her."

He's right. I know he's right and yet the pain is still there.

We sit with that thought for a moment, and then Marco leans back in the chair, folding his hands behind his neck.

"So what did you think of Minnow?" he asks, his mouth curving in a smile. "Be honest."

"I liked her," I say. "She seems fun. She's obviously gorgeous, but she also seems super cool. Way out of your league," I add to make him laugh.

"You're not wrong," he says. He takes out his phone. "I hope service is back tomorrow so I can text her. What kind of shitty place doesn't have phone service?"

"Same kind that shuts down after dark," I reply.

Marco checks out his phone another minute before sliding it away and looking over at me. "What was up with that guy you were with?" he asks.

"He's local," I say, immediately embarrassed. I try to play it cool, but I imagine my cheeks are glowing red. "His name is

Parrish. I met him on the beach. He was the one who picked up the hitchhiking couple we left behind."

"Small world," Marco says.

"Small town," I correct. "Anyway, I guess they're all going to Sunrise Beach tonight. And every night until the Midnight Dive."

"That's right," Marco says, nodding. "Yeah, Minnow mentioned that. Well, maybe tomorrow, if Nonna allows it, we can go out there. Sounds fun, right?"

"It does," I agree. "Parrish was nice. Really friendly."

Marco snorts a laugh. "I'm sure he was."

I look at my brother, ready to change the subject. "Did you notice how strange things got after dark?" I ask. "Like, did you see all the people leave?"

"People?" he asks, confused by the question.

"The tourists," I clarify. "When we started walking back from the beach, nearly the whole downtown was empty. Everyone just disappeared. It was eerie."

"To be honest," Marco says, shaking his head, "I didn't really notice anything. Minnow and I were talking and then next thing I knew, it was dark and I started texting you."

It feels strange that we both lost track of time. Then again, we've been driving for two days, living on fast food and broken sleep. It makes sense that we'd fall apart at our first social interactions with other human beings.

It hits me then, how exhausted I am, and I look around the room. The dolls stare back at me expectantly. "I'm sleeping with the lights on," I say, motioning to them.

"Good idea," Marco says, getting to his feet. "I'm heading up, but I'll see you in the morning. Night."

"Night," I reply as he leaves.

Once he's gone, I change into my pajamas and plug in my laptop and phone. I get under the covers, the overhead light still on, curl up on my side, and stare across the room at Parrish's jacket hanging on the closet door. My eyes grow heavier with each blink.

Maybe this trip won't be so bad after all.

CHAPTER SEVEN

wake up in the morning disoriented. I'm in a bed, but not in my room—at least, not my own. It takes a second for me to remember that I'm in my grandmother's guest room. The overhead light is off. Did I shut it off in the middle of the night?

Still out of sorts, I sit up. The sheets are tangled around my legs as if I tossed and turned in my sleep, and my pajamas are damp with sweat. I turn toward the window. The curtains are closed tightly, leaving the room in a hazy glow.

I stretch my arms above my head, rolling my neck, and then climb out of bed. I go to the window and yank back the curtains, expecting a flood of sunshine. Instead, the world is awash in white fog, only outlines of the trees visible. I stare for a moment, completely taken aback. Having spent my life in Phoenix, this is foreign to me.

The mist is eerie but also kind of cool. In fact, I might go outside to check it out once I have something to eat. My stomach is growling.

I turn around and jump, startled by the line of doll faces staring back at me from the shelf. And then I notice a smell.

It's not . . . unpleasant. But it reminds me of an old quarter, an earthy, metallic scent.

It's then that I see my suitcase lying on the floor near the closet, the top unzipped and leaning open. It's strange because I'm sure that I closed it last night. Just like I'm sure I left the light on.

I walk over and crouch down next to it, and I can tell immediately that my things have been sorted through—my balled-up socks are in the wrong spot. I lift the top sweatshirt and gasp. Sitting there, on my clothes, is a tiny doll made of dried green stems—sticks.

"What the hell?" I murmur. The doll is about the size of a Lego person, and its edges appear to have been dipped in metal. Silver maybe? Suddenly, I understand the scent in my room. The sticks are wet and smell like rosemary or some herb that smells like the woods.

I groan. And it's on my *clothes*—they're going to reek. I look around and see a notepad on the desk. I rip off a page and use it to pull the doll off my clothes and drop it into the wastebasket.

"This is deranged," I mutter, staring down at the doll at the bottom of the basket. I glance back wearily at my suitcase. Guess I'm doing laundry today.

I grab the wastebasket and set it out in the hall, then go back into my room and pick up my suitcase. I noticed a stackable washer and dryer in the upstairs bathroom, so I head in there, upend my suitcase into the washer, and then pour in a double dose of Tide. I click the washer on and take a step back.

Clearly the doll had to have been my grandmother's doing. Part of her superstitions, maybe. I can't be out after dark, but it's okay for her to go through my things in the middle of the night and leave me a creepy trinket? I wonder if she did the same to Marco.

I have no idea if anyone is awake yet; it feels early. I quickly wash my hands and head downstairs. I'm halfway there when I realize I left my phone in my room. Before I rush back to get it, I hear hushed voices coming from the kitchen. Well, someone's up.

Still annoyed, I walk into the kitchen, ready to confront my grandmother about snooping through my things. I find her standing near the stove with my father, holding up a wooden spoon as if making a point. My dad's cheeks are flushed with agitation.

"You don't understand," she tells him. "Things have *changed* since you left."

"I have no idea what—"

My grandmother turns abruptly, as if sensing me there. She's wearing a black tracksuit this morning, her gray hair curled and set.

I'm embarrassed to have caught them midargument, and when my father looks at me, he seems equally embarrassed. "Good morning," I say cautiously.

My father smiles and nods hello. He must have just gotten back from a bike ride. He's wearing a pair of cycling spandex and a long-sleeved shirt and has helmet marks pressed into his forehead. Seeing him like that reminds me of home and my anxiety eases.

"Morning," Nonna says in my general direction before stirring a batch of scrambled eggs on the burner, hiding her face.

"How are you, Theo?" my father asks brightly. "You're up early. This place must be a good influence on you."

"A good influence *or* the creepy dolls scared me awake," I say. My father bursts into laughter, turning to Nonna.

"Mom, please tell me you don't still have those porcelain dolls?" he asks. "I thought I hid them all."

"Well, I had twenty years to find them," she replies, a hint of amusement in her voice.

"Not only those dolls," I say. "There was also a stinky stick doll in my suitcase this morning. Any idea how that got there?"

My father appears to pale slightly. Nonna taps her wooden spoon on the edge of the pan before setting it aside. When she looks at me again, her dark eyes scan me.

"It's a good luck charm," she says calmly. "I meant to give it to you earlier."

"It could have waited," I suggest. "You didn't have to sneak in while I was asleep and go through my suitcase."

She tsks. "Don't be dramatic," she says. "I saw your light on this morning and went in to give it to you. But you were asleep, and I didn't want to wake you, so I put it in your bag, where you'd find it."

My reaction does feel a bit blown out of proportion in light of her explanation. My light was on and she came in. That's reasonable enough.

"Besides," she adds, "you were having a bad dream. I thought it would help."

Her comment surprises me. I was having a bad dream? I try to think back, but I slept hard last night. It's plausible that I was having a nightmare, although it's been a long time since I had one that I can remember.

"Well," I say. "Thank you for the doll, but I'm good. No more, okay?"

She stares at me but doesn't answer. Then she purses her lips and turns back to the eggs. "I'm doing my best," she murmurs.

Guilt washes over me and I look at my father, who subtly shakes his head to let me know it's fine. I take his word for it and approach the fridge, parched. When I pull open the door, I'm delighted to see several kinds of juice and opt for apple. My father hands me a glass from a cabinet, and as I pour my drink, he opens the coffee maker to add grounds.

"I'm sorry for being so late last night," I tell Nonna, and take a sip of juice. "We really weren't trying to be difficult. We just got distracted."

"I understand," she says, turning to me. "And thank you for the apology, Theodora."

"It's Theo," I say with a little shrug. "Everyone calls me Theo."

"Of course." She nods. "If I'd had the chance to meet you sooner, I would have known that." She glances once at my dad and then turns back to the stove.

"Mom . . . ," my father says as if starting an apology, but she waves him off.

"Go ahead and sit down," she tells him. "It's almost time for breakfast."

My father watches her for a moment, seeming regretful. Then he pulls out the coffeepot to fill it with water. Were they arguing about me and Marco? I wonder what Nonna thinks has changed? My father seemed to think it was all the same when we pulled into town.

"Should we expect your brother for breakfast, too?" my dad asks me. "Although if Marco Maggione comes strolling in before noon, I might just have a heart attack."

"No way we'll see him this early," I agree. I sit down at the table and look out the sliding glass door. The backyard is covered in a hazy white fog. "Did you ride your bike in this?" I ask.

"I tried," he says. "Although the fog isn't as dense near the woods, it was still unsafe. Should all burn off by midmorning. I might go back out then."

"Makes sense," I say, although I have no idea if it does. But he grew up here, so he'd know more about the weather patterns than I would.

There is a creaking of stairs, and to our collective astonishment, Marco walks into the kitchen.

"Morning," he croaks. His curls are sticking out in every direction and creases from his pillow cross his cheeks. His eyes are a little puffy from sleep.

"This must be the afterlife," our father says, delighted. "Good morning, Marco. Coffee?"

"Yes, definitely," my brother replies.

As our father grabs a mug, Nonna nods a curt hello to my brother. She then uses a large knife to dramatically slice open a package of bacon and adjusts the heat on the pan. Marco takes a seat across from me.

"And how are you?" I ask him, sipping my juice.

"Tired," he replies. "But I couldn't sleep. When I did, I had nightmares."

I immediately look over at our grandmother, who pauses for a long moment, listening to us before she goes back to tending the bacon. Odd that we'd both have nightmares.

"And it was so bright," Marco continues, rubbing his eyes. "There's not even any actual sunshine and the attic was flooded with it from that little window."

"I loved that room as a kid," our dad says. "I'd even sleep up there sometimes, reading horror comics until sunrise. Right, Mom?"

"You did like that space," she agrees.

Marco and I exchange a look. Horror comics? Our dad

never mentioned liking that kind of stuff. I mean, we could have bonded over that.

We're learning a lot of details about our father we've never heard before. It's almost as if . . . he's been hiding his past. At the same time, I feel selfish. I've never really asked about my father's life before us. I should have.

"So how was your first night in Oregon?" our father asks. "It's great here, right?"

"Nightfall is cute," I say. "A little unusual. I have some questions."

My father's expression grows curious as the coffee maker hums to life before sputtering a stream of liquid into the waiting pot. "Let's hear them," my dad says.

I glance at Marco, then rest my elbows on the table, eager to hear more about the town.

"Walking back from the beach last night," I say, "I was surprised that everyone had cleared out. Almost all the tourists were gone as soon as it got dark. Is that normal?"

"Pretty much," our father says. "Once the shops and restaurants close, tourists go home. I'm sure some of the local kids were still hanging out, though." He looks over at Nonna and smiles. "Right, Mom? We always found some trouble to get in to."

Nonna puts more bacon into the pan, the sound of sizzling and spitting grease filling the room. Our father makes a face at us as if we're all in trouble for bringing it up.

"What about the week leading up to the Midnight Dive?" I ask. "Some people were talking about parties at Sunrise Beach."

"Oh, those were the best," my father says with a laugh. "We'd all get together there and have bonfires and listen to music. Bring a few tourists with us. It's a good time. Although I'm sure the sheriff would disagree."

"He was your personal taxi service," Nonna says, flipping over the bacon with a fork, even as it spits angrily at her. "He retired a few years ago," she adds. "His son is sheriff now."

My father curls his lip slightly at the comment. I guess that he and the sheriff's son were definitely not friends. The idea of my father having a childhood nemesis is fascinating. I'm kind of hoping I get to meet this sheriff.

The coffee finishes brewing with a sputter and my dad pulls out the pot to fill two mugs. He brings one over to Marco and sets it in front of him. "Sugar?" he asks.

"Make it a double," Marco says. "I could use the rush."

Our dad chuckles and spoons in a grotesque amount of sugar, which is exactly how my brother likes it. Marco thanks him and takes a sip, aahing gratefully once he does.

Our grandmother starts layering bacon on a paper towel and then gathers four plates. She begins loading them up with food.

"Nonna, do you want any help?" I ask. Marco flashes me an annoyed look. First, because I can't cook, and second, because it makes him look bad that I offered first. I smile at him.

"No, you just eat," Nonna says.

Although the eggs look a bit underdone for my taste, I accept the plate of bacon and eggs appreciatively when she hands it to me. Marco makes a sound of glee, taking a slice of bacon off his plate before Nonna even sets it down.

The four of us eat breakfast, making mild conversation about the weather. At one point, I look across the table to find Marco watching me intently before nodding toward our grandmother. He wants me to ask if we can go to the party tonight. Which sucks, because it's his turn to be the human shield. I relent anyway.

"I was thinking . . . ," I announce cautiously. "I know you

70

said you want us home by dark, but maybe tonight could be an exception? Marco and I would love to check out that party. Just for a little bit."

Our grandmother doesn't look up at first, but our father chews thoughtfully, then takes a sip of his coffee.

"I suppose that'd be okay," he says. He looks at Nonna. "What do you think, Mom? Cut them some slack? They're practically local themselves—by association," he adds with a smile.

Our grandmother is quiet for a really long time, and I swear it's for dramatic effect as my pulse begins to quicken. Finally she gives a curt nod.

"Just be careful," she says quietly. When she looks up and meets my eyes, there's a pressure in my chest, as if someone is walking over my grave. I don't understand her intensity. "You two stay together," she adds. "No running off alone or with strangers. Understand?"

"Yes," I say immediately. It's a small town, so I'm not sure what she thinks is going to happen. But like our dad says, she's superstitious and we should indulge her.

We watch each other for another second before Marco breaks the silence.

"Is there more bacon?" he asks.

Nonna gets up and comes back with a plate, the paper towel underneath the slices of bacon swollen with grease. She sets the plate in front of my brother with a loud clank. Then she takes her own plate and scrapes the rest of her breakfast into the disposal.

She doesn't seem mad. She seems . . . worried. Maybe those stick dolls for good luck were to make *her* feel better more than anything else. She might be lonely. Being here alone, all these years? It must have been terrible not seeing her family.

The buzzer goes off on the washer upstairs. I shovel in a last bite of food and then take my plate to the sink.

"Thank you for breakfast," I tell my grandmother as she grabs the plate from my hands. Standing next to her, I'm reminded of how short she is, a tiny little thing aggressively rinsing the dishes.

"Wait, are you doing laundry at six a.m.?" Marco asks me incredulously.

Across from him, our father sighs as if awaiting a lengthy explanation about the stick dolls. But I just smile.

"Yep," I say. "And by the way—you should check your suitcase when you go upstairs."

I glance at my grandmother, and when she lowers her eyes guiltily, I know that I'm right. My brother has a surprise waiting for him in the attic.

CHAPTER EIGHT

change my clothes over to the dryer and go back to my bedroom. The first thing I see is Parrish's jacket hanging on the closet door. I wonder if I'll be able to track him down today to give it back. Should I go looking? Is that too desperate? I mean . . . I could probably just give it to him at the beach. Better idea. Besides, it's too early for normal people to be out doing things. It'll have to wait.

I sit on my bed and prop myself up on the pillows. The room is a bit cold and I pull the blanket around me, nearly ready to doze off. I'm still exhausted. But then I glance at the porcelain dolls, drawn to a dark-haired one at the end of the row. Her left eye is slightly closed and there's a small crack in one cheek. She reminds of the mermaid mural downtown. Something pretty but also terrifying.

On the nightstand, my computer has been charging, and I grab it and pull it onto my lap. I sign in to Nonna's Wi-Fi, which isn't password-protected. I'll have to mention that to her before she gets her identity stolen or ends up engaged to some rando who drains her bank account.

Out of curiosity, I click the search engine and type in "Mermaid mural Nightfall Oregon."

A few photos and a travel blog pops up. Apparently, the painting is officially called *Only Some Shall Stay,* although it's mostly known as *The Siren of Nightfall.* Not the usual town mural, but then again, my high school has a huge mountain lion painted on the side of the building and those things actually do kill people.

Most of the pictures online are of tourists posing with the impressive artwork, but there is one article about the reclusive artist herself, a woman named Sylvia Ware. She painted it almost fifty years ago. She died a while back, and the local museum commissions artists to restore it every few years.

The article links to an interview with Sylvia in a local paper called *The Nightfall Gazette.* There's a black-and-white photo of her standing in front of the mural with her back to the camera. The caption says that she was twenty-two at the time. Sylvia was tiny, sort of like Nonna. She's wearing a white shirt, a long skirt, and black flats.

Sylvia talks about growing up in Nightfall, the beauty and cleansing nature of the ocean. It's all pretty predictable except for the last question. I read her answer twice.

Q: What was your inspiration for *Only Some Shall Stay*?

A: Nightfall is an enchanting town and many travel here to witness its beauty. But this place is not meant for everyone. The siren symbolizes our fierce nature, our power. We pick and choose. Simple as that.

Pick and choose? What does that mean?

I click out of the interview and pull up a picture of the mural again, confirming what I noticed last night. It's there.

Townspeople watching as the mermaid lures the ship to its destruction. Pretty dark.

My phone buzzes on the nightstand and I nearly jump out of my skin. I settle the laptop off to one side and grab my phone. There's a text from my brother.

Why the hell is there a miniature doll mixed in with my T-shirts?

Good. He found it.

Nonna said it was for luck, I reply. *Feeling lucky?*

Absolutely not. It stinks.

And now you know why I was doing laundry, I write back.

Fuck.

I laugh and set my phone aside. I put my laptop back on the nightstand and glance toward the window. The dense fog still hasn't lifted. I wonder if my father is right and it'll clear up. I hope so. I have plans to go to a party tonight.

I slip in my earbuds and call up the ending of a murder podcast I was on the cusp of solving yesterday. I'm pretty sure the husband did it. It's always the husband, except on the occasions when it's the jilted lover. Either way, the prosecution pretty much has this one in the bag.

While my clothes are drying, I decide to go back downstairs to escape the dolls. But as I descend the stairs, the jury about to announce their verdict, I see the front door is standing wide open, the world white with fog beyond it.

I shiver in the cold breeze and pad over, barefoot, to close it.

"Guilty," the podcaster announces.

I knew it, that sick bastard. I take out my earbuds, and as I do, I hear a scraping sound from just beyond the door. I peek outside, blinking as my eyes adjust, and see my father crouched down in the front yard. What is he doing?

There's a gray jacket hanging on a hook by the door. I grab

it and stuff my feet into my sneakers, bending the backs of them under my heels. I walk outside, closing the door behind me as I pull on the jacket against the morning chill.

"What are you doing?" I call to my father.

He jumps, startled, but smiles as he turns. He's wearing a pair of too-small pink gardening gloves and I see now that there are flowers in little plastic holders just behind him. He holds up a small shovel.

"Your grandmother needed help with her annuals, but I'll be honest," he says, "I'm terrible at this. Pretty sure I killed the first three. Desert landscaping is much easier."

"Well, yeah. That's because our entire front yard is made of rocks," I reply as I cross the lawn to him. "Those are much harder to kill."

"Fair point," he says, standing up. "Any chance you want to help?" He flashes me a pleading smile.

"Why?" I ask. "Are you trying to kill the rest of her flowers?"

He sighs and looks down at the absolute mess he's made of Nonna's garden. Dirt is scattered all over the pathway, and the three flowers he planted lean in significantly different directions, wilted and overworked. "Do you think you can do worse?" he asks.

The misty air is actually kind of nice. And it's not as cold now that I'm outside. "I'll give it a shot," I say. "Which ones do you want to assassinate first?"

"Definitely the purple," my father says, pointing to them with his gardening tool.

He takes off the gloves and hands them to me. But before I put them on, I catch a blur in the distance out of the corner of my eye. It's hard to see the road clearly, but whatever it is, it's heading our way.

"What is—?" I start, and then yelp, my heart shooting to my throat as a large white animal suddenly appears.

My father grabs me by the arm and swings me behind him protectively. It takes a moment before I realize it's a dog. It stops in front of us before sniffing the flowers. Then, as we stand there, it begins to dig them up and thrash them.

"Hey!" my dad calls, taking a step toward the dog before thinking better of it.

The dog is oversized—pure white and honestly stunning. It's some kind of a husky with piercing blue eyes and thick fur. And it's destroying Nonna's garden.

"Cyrus!" a female voice rings out, followed by the sound of footsteps hurrying in our direction.

"If you're looking for a big white dog," I call, "I think we've found him."

The footfalls pause and then quickly resume. A woman appears, a red leash dangling from her hands.

"Oh no!" she shouts when she sees the dog shaking his head, his mouth full of purple annuals, dirt spraying out. "Cyrus, come here!" She snaps her fingers and the dog drops the plants obediently and trots over to her, docile as can be. The woman quickly clips the leash to the dog's collar.

My dad steps forward now that the dog is secured.

"I am so sorry," the woman says. "Cyrus usually stays by my side. He never runs off like this. He ruined them," she adds, clearly distraught as she looks over the flower bed.

To be honest, the entire mess wasn't the dog's fault—my dad had already started the destruction, but I don't offer that tidbit of information.

The woman is petite and adorable, wearing peach-colored sneakers and a white zip-up jacket. Her blond hair is pulled into a tight ponytail and a wool headband covers her ears. She pushes up her tortoiseshell glasses, her blue eyes blazing behind them. She looks . . . familiar.

"He slipped his leash," the woman says. "And he blended in with the fog, and—"

Suddenly the woman looks at my father and her words trail off. A smile slowly pulls at her lips. I shoot a quick glance at my father, the silence between them going on a beat too long.

"Hello, Olivia," my dad says smoothly.

Wait, he knows her?

"Joey?" she asks, her face lighting up. "Joey Maggione?" She quickly rushes over, leash still in hand, and hugs my father warmly. "Oh my goodness," she adds, placing one gloved hand on his cheek. "You look exactly the same."

My father laughs. "I'm not sure I agree with that, but it's nice to see you."

He smiles nervously, but I can hear the joy in his voice. The *flirtation*? Either way it's extremely awkward because I'm standing beside him, unintroduced.

"I'm reading your latest book," he adds to the woman in a low voice. "Pretty spicy."

The woman immediately laughs and closes her eyes, embarrassed. It dawns on me why she looks familiar. She's Olivia Miles—the local romance author.

"You're the writer," I say, pulling them out of their private conversation. My father turns to me, a flash of embarrassment in his eyes, and then he moves to put his arm around my shoulders.

"Theo, this is Olivia Miles," he says, motioning to her. "A friend of mine from town. And also," he adds proudly, "a very famous author."

"I've seen your books everywhere," I say, faltering a little. I've never met a famous author before.

"Theo, is it?" she asks, smiling.

"Yes," my father answers for me. "This is my daughter Theodora. Her brother Marco is inside. He's staying in the old attic."

Olivia's eyes widen. "Oh dear," she says playfully. "I remember that room. Nice, but kind of creepy if you ask me." She looks at me again and smiles.

I'm not sure what else I'm supposed to say, but I know that I instantly like her. She's friendly, and she's gazing at my father like she's truly happy to see him. And they seem to know each other well, like well enough for her to have been in my grandmother's attic. I glance at my father again, reminded that he had this whole other life before me and my brother that he never talks about.

"Would you like to come in for a coffee?" my father asks Olivia, pointing back toward the house. "We can give Cyrus some water to wash down all the flowers he murdered." He smiles at the dog, who now seems perfectly content to be sitting next to his owner.

"I wish I could," Olivia replies, "but I have a call with my publisher in an hour and this one might need a bath." She motions to Cyrus, and his dirt-covered tongue lolls out happily as he pants. "Rain check?"

"Absolutely," my father replies. "And I'm going to hold you to that."

"I hope so," Olivia says, but then her smile fades slightly and she fidgets with the leash. "Will I . . . will I be meeting your wife, as well?" She tries to ask casually, but it's incredibly awkward. Especially for me.

"No," my father says simply. "We're divorced."

It shouldn't hurt as much as it does when he says it. It's a sharp poke in my ribs and I wince. I'm just not used to hearing it out loud, I guess. I dart a look at Olivia to see her reaction.

Olivia's lips part in surprise at my father's revelation, but she quickly recovers and smiles softly. "Well, you know where to find me," she tells him. "Same house. Over on Rosebud Lane."

"I will find you," he replies. She laughs, but I'm internally cringing that I've witnessed this exchange. It's a little too private.

Olivia starts to leave but looks back at me. "And it was great to meet you, Theo," she says. "You're an absolute stunner."

"Oh, uh . . . ," I say, flattered. "Thank you. It was nice to meet you too."

She starts to jog when she gets to the driveway, her peach-colored sneakers smacking the pavement as the dog trots at her side. And then Olivia Miles, the famous author who is apparently friends with my father, disappears into the fog.

CHAPTER NINE

finish helping my father with the flowers just before it starts to drizzle. I'd asked him about Olivia right after she left, but he was pretty tight-lipped.

"Old friend from town," he said. "Pass me the shovel."

To be honest, she appeared to be a bit more than that to me. But since she ran off, my father has seemed distracted, so I decide not to pry. No, not just distracted. A little sad. It occurs to me that the mention of the divorce did it, same as it did to me. So I'm not going to bring up Olivia anymore today.

We go inside and have lunch, my brother checking his phone nonstop the entire meal. I assume he's waiting to hear from Minnow. As our father gathers the dishes and Nonna goes into the living room to watch *Forensic Files,* Marco tells me he'll be in the attic and escapes that way.

The day sort of slides by after that, a haze of clouds and unspoken thoughts. Homesickness. It eventually stops raining, although the sun never does come out. I'm not sure how things grow around here. They certainly do—everything is green. But without sunlight, they're missing an important ingredient.

I shower and it takes hours for my curly hair to dry in the

humidity. I wanted to wear it down tonight, so I suffered with a damp-collared shirt. I'm on my computer playing *The Sims* when there's a sharp knock on my bedroom door.

"Yes?" I ask.

The door opens and Marco pops his head in. "What time you want to leave?" he asks. "Minnow said they'll get there just before dark, probably about nine."

I'm relieved that she texted him back. It's too early in the summer for him to be brokenhearted. I check the time on my phone and see it's almost eight—I'm surprised how late it's already gotten. It's hard to tell the passage of time without the sun.

"Want to leave in a half hour?" I ask.

Marco flashes me a thumbs-up and leaves to go get ready.

Now that the party is impending, I'll admit I'm a little nervous. I glance at Parrish's jacket again, mentally preparing myself for the conversation. I want to sound effortlessly cool when I return it, and yet I can't think of a single phrase to accomplish that. I guess a simple "Thanks for your coat" will work, but I'd hoped for better. Maybe it'll come to me later.

I pick out a long-sleeved T-shirt, a sweatshirt, and jeans for the bonfire. If I had known what the weather was like here, I would have been more prepared for the cold. I didn't think to bring my winter jacket on summer vacation. I put on some makeup, more than lip gloss but not enough that I have to worry about anything smudging at the beach. I hold up my phone, snap a quick selfie, and send it to Willa.

Get it! she writes back, making me laugh.

This would all be so much more fun if Willa were here. I'd told her earlier about the bonfire and she was excited for me. Said a night at the beach sounded amazing. But then I saw on social media that she's out tonight with her girlfriend and a couple of our friends from the team and I'm the one jealous. Feeling left out sucks.

I'll text you when I get back, I reply.

Make good choices, Maggione!

A little bit sad, I try to hype myself up. It *is* going to be an amazing night. "You've got this," I murmur to myself. "Just be cool."

I grab Parrish's jacket and head downstairs. As I slip on my shoes, Nonna comes in from the living room, her arms wrapped tightly around her. She studies me, noticing the jacket I'm holding, but doesn't mention it. She still looks concerned about Marco and me being out at night.

"Are you sure you don't mind if we go to the beach?" I ask. More than seeking permission, I want to know what she's so worried about. My brother and I are a little old for the stranger-danger conversation. "Do you really think it's not safe at night?"

"Your father thinks you'll be all right," she says. "He's been out there. He knows what they get into. So I'll defer to him."

"What do *you* think they 'get into'?" I ask, furrowing my brow.

She holds my gaze for a long moment before shrugging. "Probably nothing," she murmurs, and turns away.

Well, that's not an answer.

Marco comes tramping down the stairs, his hooded sweatshirt covering his face as he yanks it on. When he finally gets it over his head, he gasps for air like he was suffocating. He notices Nonna and me and quickly straightens up and smiles.

"Don't worry, Nonna," he says to her as he comes to stand next to me. "I promise to be on my best behavior."

"I'm sure," she says. She reaches into the pocket of her housecoat and takes out a ten-dollar bill. She grabs my hand

and presses the money into my palm. "In case you need it," she tells me very seriously.

If it's meant as emergency money, I'm not sure how far ten will get us. But it's definitely going to be spent on some late-night Taco Bell on our way back into town. I do note a strong woodsy smell on the money and quickly shove it into my back pocket. Another good luck charm, I guess.

"Thanks, Nonna," I say, and give her a quick hug. She looks me and then Marco over again before adjusting her housecoat and walking toward the stairs to go up to her bedroom.

Our dad looks over at us from the living room couch. "Heading out?" he asks, and groans like an old man as he stands up.

"Yep," Marco says, checking to make sure our grandmother is gone. "And hopefully Nonna has already put the GPS tracker in the car," he adds quietly. "I'd feel safer knowing she was keeping close tabs on us."

Our dad comes into the foyer. "Home by midnight," he says, and then sighs nostalgically. "I had a lot of great times at Sunrise Beach. Brought a lot of dates there, too."

"Please don't elaborate," Marco says. Our father chuckles, holding up his hands innocently.

I consider mentioning Olivia, but I haven't told Marco about her yet. That's an entire conversation and we're just trying to get to the beach.

"All right, you kids be safe," our father says, shooing us toward the door. He hands Marco the keys to the Forester. "Have fun," he adds.

When Marco and I walk outside, I note that the night is a little warmer than I expected, which is definitely a good sign. But as we approach the car, I can't shake the sense of being watched. I turn around and glance up at the house. Nonna is standing at her bedroom window, staring down at us.

I tug on the sleeve of Marco's sweatshirt to get his attention and he follows my gaze to where our grandmother is looming. He smiles and gives her a little salute, but Nonna shakes her head disapprovingly.

"Not weird at all, Nonna," Marco mutters while holding his smile. Then he spins around and clicks open the locks on the car.

SUNRISE BEACH IS STUNNING in its scale. There are large boulders shooting out of the shallow water toward the sky, the ocean shimmering in the moonlight. It looks more like a movie set than an actual place. We don't know exactly where the party is, so Marco parks on the shoulder where we notice a few other cars are parked. Then we start walking along the highway, hoping for a signal of some sort. I grab Parrish's jacket and debate putting it on to shield me from the cold ocean breeze.

The sky is hazy with wisps of gray, the wind blowing even more wildly the closer we get to the shore. The temperature has dropped significantly this close to the water. Just ahead, a couple appears heading toward us, laughing and leaning into each other. The guy is short with black hair; the girl is tall and gorgeous.

"This the way to Sunrise Beach?" Marco asks them. The girl stops to look us over before smiling broadly.

"Yep, just around the next corner," she replies in a smoky voice. Her companion gazes at her, completely enamored. I'm almost embarrassed for him—he looks like a lovesick puppy. "Have a good time," the girl tells us. She takes the guy's arm and pulls him along. As they pass us, she winks at me.

Good for her, I guess. She seems pretty happy to be with him.

As Marco and I get closer to the party, music carries toward us on the wind. There's an orange glow bouncing off the boulders and sand dunes. We make the final turn and the beach opens up to reveal a roaring bonfire sending sparks into the night. There are a few groups of people surrounding it, swaying and talking, and they're lit up by the flames. I can almost feel the fire's warmth from the road.

Marco and I find a break in the guardrail along the side of the pass. My sneakers slip in the sand and Marco nearly eats it, but he catches himself before anyone notices. In fact, no one has even looked in our direction yet. I'm suddenly worried that we won't know anyone here, that this really is just for locals. I clutch Parrish's jacket closer to me and remind myself that we were invited.

Marco and I start toward the fire. Music plays from a speaker on a piece of driftwood, and there are several open coolers with cans of beer floating in the ice. Bottles of wine are wedged in the sand close by. There are a few cars parked on the sand, although I have no idea how they got down here.

The warmth from the fire toasts my cheeks. I glance around and immediately notice the number of college sweatshirts—tourists. We're so easy to spot. Guess it's not *just* locals. But how did we all end up at this party? Who invited everyone?

Someone calls my brother's name and he and I look over to see Minnow resting against a white Jeep parked on the beach. She looks amazing, almost ethereal, in a gauzy, flowing skirt that catches the wind.

"Do you mind if I, uh . . . ?" Marco says to me, and motions in her direction.

"I'll go with you," I say, starting toward Minnow.

Marco winces. "Theo," he pleads. "Really?"

"What?" I say, turning back to him. "I'm just going to tell her hi."

"Sure . . . but, like, you can do that later, right?"

I groan. "Fine," I tell him. "Ditch me again. See if I care."

Marco smiles, gripping my shoulders. "Fantastic," he says. "It's moments like these when I don't wish to be an only child."

"Goodbye, Marco!" I call, even though he's still in my face.

He laughs and then jogs past me toward Minnow. Great. Haven't even been here five minutes and I'm already on my own.

When Marco reaches Minnow she says something to him, and he nods before taking a spot next to her. She reaches into the back of the Jeep, pulls out a beer, and hands it to him. He gazes at her as they talk. They're so comfortable together, like they've known each other for years.

A new song starts, the heavy bass vibrating through my bones. I wander closer to the fire, its warmth easing my nerves as the cool breeze blows my hair around my face. This is kind of nice.

"Hey, you," a girl says.

I turn, delighted to see Annemarie. "Hi," I say, smiling. I glance around for the guy she was with—Asa—but I don't see him.

Annemarie pauses in front of me, the orange firelight bouncing off her glowing, healthy skin. "I was hoping you'd end up here with us," she tells me. "By the way, I love your hair." She reaches over to touch one of my ringlets. "We curly girls have to stick together."

"Uh, right," I reply, a bit taken aback.

Annemarie exhales heavily and lowers her arm to her side.

Her gaze drops to the jacket I'm holding and there's a flash of recognition in her eyes. Does she know it's Parrish's? She must. Oh no. What if this is his thing? His signature move to pick up tourists? Though . . . I don't know. Parrish didn't really seem the type. Then again, I just met him.

"You should grab a beer and stay awhile," Annemarie says brightly, meeting my eyes again. "It's going to be a fun night."

"Sure," I say with a nod. "I can—"

But Annemarie is looking at something beyond my shoulder and she lights up. "Sparrow!" she sings out, and I turn just as a blue-haired girl screams in delight and waves. Annemarie rushes over to her.

"Welcome home, lovey," Sparrow says as the two embrace. "And *good job,*" she adds conspiratorially before the two walk off toward the sand dunes in the distance.

Alone again, I look for my brother. He's still leaning casually against the Jeep with Minnow while she laughs at something he must have said. Right at that moment, Minnow looks over and sees me, and I nod a hello, which she returns.

There really is something about her—I want to talk to her too. But I'm sure I'll catch up with her later.

In the meantime, I'll grab one of the beers Annemarie suggested. I approach the coolers and check out the selection. One cooler has several brands of beer, but they're all craft beers I've never heard of. I move on to the next one, which has even more beer. I reach in, swishing my hand through the ice, turning over cans to find one I recognize.

"You made it."

I look up and see Parrish, his hands in the pockets of his jeans, his head tilted. I have no idea how long he's been standing there. As I straighten, a smile spreads slowly across his face and he looks exactly as he did yesterday, handsome yet approachable.

I'm a bit breathless, my hand dripping with ice water from the cooler. I remember the jacket and thrust it at him, my voice pitched a little too high when I speak. "I thought about bringing this to you earlier," I tell him. "But I didn't know where to look."

Parrish takes his jacket from me, his fingers brushing my wrist. His touch is like a jolt of electricity, a delightful zap through my body.

"You can always find me at the beach, Arizona," he replies easily. "Unless, of course, the sun is too bright."

CHAPTER TEN

stare at Parrish, the firelight playing over his skin and his long eyelashes casting shadows on his cheeks. He slips his arms into his jacket, pulling it over his thin sweater. I wonder if he's cold, and if he was cold last night but played it off to act tough in front of me.

"About yesterday," he says. "I know we're skipping to the good part tonight, but I really felt bad about sitting next to you on the bench like that. It was presumptuous. Kept me up last night. I'm sorry."

"Thanks," I say, appreciating the apology. "And thanks for letting me use your coat."

We nod at each other, the formalities out of the way, but the words between us slightly awkward.

"So . . . Sunrise Beach," I say, motioning around. "You were right. It's gorgeous."

He smiles. "It is. But the beauty is what makes it so dangerous."

"What does that mean?" I ask, intrigued.

Parrish comes to stand right next to me, his shoulder against mine. Another jolt of electricity. He points to the boulders in the distance jutting out of the water.

"See those?" he asks. "They're deadly. And not just them but the ones you can't see. There are more under the surface. They tear right through the hulls of ships that get too close. Split them wide open and the ships hemorrhage their cargo." He looks sideways at me. "Their sailors, too," he adds.

His face is close to mine, and for a moment, I'm struck silent. A thread of attraction stretches between us. Then I blink quickly and turn back toward the rocks.

"I guess those are the real Sirens of Nightfall, then," I say. "I read up on your town's charming mural."

Parrish moves away and reaches into the cooler to pull out a beer, a brand that I've been looking for since I got here, and holds it out to me. I accept it gratefully. He grabs a water for himself and takes a sip.

"What did you learn about the siren?" he asks, curious.

"Just some basics," I tell him, opening the beer and taking a sip. It's icy but a little stale. I swallow. "It was really more about the artist, Sylvia Ware," I add. "She seemed a bit strange."

"Huh," Parrish says, thinking it over. "I can't say I've heard anything about the artist. Most people just want to take selfies with a pretty mermaid and get a few likes on Instagram."

"Oh no," I say suddenly, his words sparking a memory. "I forgot."

"What?" he asks, alarmed.

"The wombats," I reply, and he laughs. "I meant to look up your mascot."

Parrish scrunches his nose adorably. "Yeah well, we just ended the season zero-ten, so you wouldn't have found anything good if you'd looked." He takes another sip of water. "What about you? You play any sports?"

"Volleyball," I say. "Varsity."

"Nice," he says with a nod. "I'm not really a sports guy. I'm one of those car guys. Fixing shit all the time. I know . . ." He shakes his head. "It doesn't fit. I hear it a lot."

I agree—he doesn't seem like a car guy, but I like that he's surprising me.

The beer is cold in my hand and I shiver. Parrish notices and motions for us to move closer to the fire. When we do, a few people look over at us, but I don't recognize any of them.

"So what made you move to Nightfall?" I ask Parrish. "Random place, right?"

"It's a really long story," he says. "But basically I came through here one summer to camp with my family. And we just . . . we never left."

He glances at the sky then, almost wistfully. There is something suddenly vulnerable about him. Raw. Even though we've only just met, I feel like I know him—but even more strangely, I feel like he knows me.

"And what about you, Arizona?" Parrish asks, his dark eyes sparkling in the firelight. "You really plan to stay the entire summer?"

"Trust me," I say, "I don't have a choice." I feel the familiar sting of being dragged from my home combined with my mother's abandonment. I take another sip of beer to wash it away.

"That's too bad," Parrish replies, then adds, "That's a long time to be here."

His words make my chest ache a little. I'd thought he was going to say it was a disappointment that I was leaving at all, but before I have the chance to dwell on it, the bonfire sends a plume of smoke in our direction. Parrish steps in front of me to try to block it. Gray smoke billows around him as he protects me from the worst of it.

"Can I ask you something?" Parrish says, his eyes half-closed against the smoke.

"Of course," I say, trying to get my bearings. Is he flirting with me? I'm so confused.

"Were you gardening today?" Parrish asks. "You smell like . . . you smell like dirt," he adds, his nostrils flaring.

"What? Do I smell bad?" I ask, mortified. I quickly sniff my sweatshirt sleeve, but I can't smell anything over the smoke. I showered and washed my hair, but there must be a smell clinging to me. Why else would he ask about a garden?

Parrish laughs, shaking his head. "No, that's not what I meant," he says. The bonfire smoke trails in another direction, and he moves back to my side. "It's just an interesting scent is all. Maybe it's on your shoes, I don't know."

I suddenly remember the ten-dollar bill that Nonna gave me, the one in my back pocket. It did have a smell, but it wasn't a bad one. Just earthy. Either way, it doesn't feel good that Parrish noticed.

"I'm sorry," he says, wincing. "I shouldn't have mentioned it. You just—"

He's interrupted as someone slips a hand into the crook of his elbow from behind. Beatrice appears; she's close enough for her blond hair to blow over his shoulder. Parrish's complexion pales. A cold splash of realization washes over me as he places his hand over hers where it rests on his arm. They appear to be . . . together.

"Theodora, was it?" Beatrice asks me with a wide smile. "How nice to see you."

"It's Theo," I say apologetically, even though I've done nothing wrong.

Beatrice is a vision in a '50s-style cupcake dress, its bright pink electric against her skin. Unique vintage seems to be her style, and it suits her. Some of her blond hair is pinned up in rolls, the rest blows in the wind, and her feet are bare.

"It's nice to see you too," I add, trying to keep the awkwardness out of my voice. It's unclear if this is a territorial thing, if she and Parrish are together or just good friends. I don't even know if she's actually being nice to me. It's disorienting and I can't quite figure out how to react.

"Listen," Beatrice says with a little pout, "I'm sorry to interrupt, but can I steal Parrish for a bit? A friend of ours is looking for him."

"Go for it," I say. "Although to be fair it's up to Parrish."

She laughs and looks sideways at him, almost amused. But Parrish doesn't say anything, his eyes trained on the fire. In fact, he hasn't said a word since Beatrice arrived.

Beatrice glances at me curiously. "Would you like to come along?" she asks.

Parrish swallows hard. Based on his posture, I don't think I'm really invited—he's completely unapproachable now. Closed down. Pissed off.

Once again, my feelings are a little hurt even though I have no intention of joining them. To be honest, if the two of them are a thing or even a past thing, I feel foolish. I don't want to be in the middle of whatever this is.

"I'm good," I tell Beatrice. "Thank you, though."

"Another time, Theo," she replies, saying my name carefully. She offers a little wave and then pulls Parrish away. He murmurs goodbye to me as he goes, and I watch as they walk to the other side of the hill and disappear behind the sand.

I'm left feeling unsettled and kind of annoyed. Now that I think about it, I'm actually kind of mad. Parrish was the one to approach me—twice. I take out my phone, about to call Willa, but then remember she's out tonight with her girlfriend.

I put my phone away and glance around for Marco, but he's gone. The white Jeep is still there, but he and Minnow have vanished, probably to be alone somewhere. *Gross.*

With no one else to talk to, I circulate around the party, saying hello to a few people as I nurse my beer. I find a cozy spot not too far from the fire and scroll aimlessly through my phone, watching videos with no sound.

"Did you see his face when I told him we were from California?" a voice says, and I look up to see a guy talking to a small group and shaking his head. "And I was like, chill, friend—we're from *Palm Springs.* It's practically its own planet."

The group laughs. The guy talking is Black with curly dark hair and wide-rimmed glasses. He's wearing a white jacket with the sleeves rolled up, fitted khaki pants, and sneakers with no socks—effortlessly cool but possibly too fashionable for a bonfire.

"It's true," the smaller guy next to him says. "We have over three hundred days of sunshine there. Might as well live on Mercury. Or Venus," he adds. "Venus is probably prettier."

I smile, not just because I can relate to the sunshine ratio but because I . . . I think I recognize both of their voices.

"Elijah," the smaller guy continues, "what's the name of that place where you get the date shakes? I was telling them they *have* to try one."

I *definitely* recognize their voices. They've mentioned those shakes on their show. They're the duo behind *Scare Me Silly,* a horror podcast and travel blog. They're celebrities, over ten million subscribers last I noticed. I haven't listened in a few months, but they're *awesome*. And their show has scared the shit out of me on numerous occasions.

Elijah tilts his head as if trying to remember the answer to the question, and I recognize the guy who asked it as his cohost, Felix. I study him, trying to decide whether to go over and introduce myself.

"Oh, you mean Hadley's," Elijah says, snapping his fingers, and Felix nods emphatically.

I linger for another few minutes until they wrap up their conversation and the group dissipates, leaving Elijah and Felix chatting privately. I decide to take the chance and make my way over to them, a little nervous.

I pause next to Elijah, waiting for a moment to introduce myself. Before I can, Elijah stops midsentence and looks at me. My stomach drops; I'm worried he's going to tell me I've interrupted. Instead, he smiles brightly.

"Hello, new friend," he says.

"Me?" I ask, caught off guard. "Hi. I . . . uh, I came over because . . ." I look at Felix, who's waiting for me to finish my sentence. "Because I'm a big fan, actually," I say to them both. "I love your podcast."

Elijah nods graciously. "Thank you," he says. "That's nice of you to say. Well, I'm Elijah, and this is my boyfriend, Felix."

I smile at Felix and he returns it warmly. He's thin and cute with light brown skin and bleached blond hair. He moves to stand next to Elijah and wraps his arm around his waist.

"I like your hair," Felix tells me, motioning to his own for reference. "Bet it took forever to dry in this humidity."

"Hours," I reply and Felix nods knowingly. "I'm Theo, by the way," I tell them.

Elijah carries a large HydroFlask, while Felix sips directly from a bottle of wine dangling from his fingertips. His lips are stained bluish red.

"You're not local," Elijah says, studying me.

"Nope," I say. "I'm from Arizona. How about you?"

Like he'd told the small crowd earlier, Elijah explains that he and Felix are from Palm Springs. I learn that they both graduated from college this year and that Elijah is planning to attend USC in the fall for his master's degree with a full scholarship thanks to their podcast. They're currently living in Elijah's parents' guesthouse. It's all terribly exciting—my varsity volleyball team pales in comparison, but they feign interest long enough for me to exhaust the topic. When I'm done, I take a nervous sip from my drink.

"So," I say, still a bit starstruck, "what are you guys doing in Nightfall?"

"Are you kidding?" Elijah asks. "It's for our show. We've been staying at an Airbnb near downtown. A gorgeous purple Victorian."

"I've seen that one," I say, remembering it. "Very dramatic, totally haunted-looking." They laugh and nod. "But . . . ," I continue. "Why Nightfall exactly?"

Elijah looks surprised. "Have you not heard the stories?" he asks.

"*Scary* stories?" I ask, glancing between him and Felix. They nod. "No," I reply. "But to be honest, I'd barely even heard of this place and my dad grew up here."

Elijah and Felix exchange a knowing look before Elijah moves closer to me, lowering his voice. "Did you listen to our last podcast?" he asks.

"No . . . ," I say guiltily. "I've missed the last few."

Elijah sighs as if that explains everything. "Well, part one on Nightfall is out now. You'll want to have a listen. I thought maybe that was why you came to the beach."

"What do you mean?" I ask. "We came for a party, right?"

There is a long pause before Felix takes Elijah's arm. He smiles brightly. "Hey, Theo," he says, "what are you doing tomorrow? Want to come by our place for lunch? I can pick up sandwiches and we can sit outside and talk, enjoy the sun."

"You've seen the sun?" I ask. "I must be staying in the wrong part of town."

They both smile graciously at my joke, but they seem to be holding back. Almost like they're trying to distract me. Change the subject.

"Come over for lunch," Elijah says, agreeing with Felix. "We'll have a chat. And I can show you around the house. My mother is loving every picture I send her. The place is incredible—you'll see."

"Even if we can't figure out how to turn on the heat," Felix adds. "Although why we need heat in June is beyond bizarre. But who am I to complain when we're used to living on the surface of the sun." He laughs and points at me. "You too."

"Us desert dwellers are a different breed," I say.

Felix smiles, but his attention snags on something beyond my shoulder and he freezes. I turn to see what he's looking at. My gaze drifts over the party until I see Beatrice near the water. She's gliding along the sand toward the fire, a vision of beauty as her dress flutters around her. There is a dazed-looking boy in a Texas A&M baseball cap holding her arm. He's wearing a baseball jersey and a shiny silver watch that glints in the moonlight.

I wonder what happened to Parrish.

"Hi, Theo," Beatrice says as she passes us. She nudges the guy next to her. "Say hi, Greg."

The guy looks over lazily, but his gaze seems to skip past me before he turns forward again. He must be wasted.

"Bye, Theo," Beatrice adds in the same tone as before, and heads toward the fire.

"You know her?" Felix asks, pulling me back. When I look at him, he's intensely curious.

"Met her yesterday," I say. "With my brother. Her and a few other locals."

"Fascinating," he murmurs, watching Beatrice as she pulls Greg's hat off playfully before putting it on her own head. She cups his chin, her nails black against his skin. The guy is smiling, blissed out by her attention.

There is a scream from the water and I spin around, my heart in my throat. But then I hear a laugh, and two girls, Annemarie and her friend Sparrow, go splashing by in their T-shirts. There's a guy with them. I think it's Asa—although he seems different. He wades out toward them, fully clothed and stiff-legged. The girls beckon him forward, laughing as he walks out deeper.

"What are they doing?" I murmur. "It's freezing."

"People have gone in the water the past three nights," Elijah says. "Practice for the Midnight Dive, maybe. Either way, it's dangerous. For several reasons," he adds quietly.

Others at the party watch, a few tourists laughing and nudging each other as if daring one another to go into the ocean. As I scan the bonfire, I realize that Beatrice is already gone, along with her companion.

Suddenly I think of my bother. He's been gone awhile and it's starting to make me a little nervous. Whether it's the fuzziness from the beer I drank or the way those girls laughed in the water, the mood just . . . it feels different. And I realize how very dark it is.

I take out my phone and text Marco. *Hey, you okay?*

It goes undelivered. No service.

Just then, Parrish walks out from behind a sand dune, looking around wildly. He catches my eyes and his are wide, fearful. It sends a wave of panic over me and I instinctively walk toward him.

"Hey, where are you going?" Elijah calls after me.

I keep walking, sure that something's wrong. Not just because of Parrish's worried expression but also because of a sense in my gut. He moves toward me, and as we get closer, we both reach out our hands and he grips my wrists.

"I need to talk to you," he says, his voice urgent.

"What's wrong?" I ask, panicked. "What's going on?"

"It's your brother—"

Fear explodes through my chest. "Is he okay?"

"He'll be fine," Parrish says slowly, as if trying to calm me. "He just . . . he's not feeling well. I don't think he should drive home, but he should probably leave now. You both should."

"What does that mean?" I ask, confused. "Is he drunk? Where is he?"

"Come on," Parrish says. "He's back here."

He tugs me toward the sand dunes, away from the party. It gets colder and darker the farther we get from the bonfire. I look back once and see Elijah watching me, his arms folded over his chest and his brows pulled together in concern. Next to him, Felix looks positively terrified. I hold up a finger to let them know I'll be back in a minute.

My worry grows with each step. I hope Marco is okay— I should have checked in with him sooner.

As we round the sand dune, I spot Minnow crouched down and rush toward her. When she looks up at me, I realize she's crouched next to Marco, who is sitting in the sand, smiling.

I stop, catching my breath, relieved that he's conscious. My heart is pounding as I take stock of Marco's condition. He grins up at me, his head bobbing slightly.

My fear slips toward anger. "Marco, what the hell?" I say. "Are you drunk?" I have no idea how he could have gotten in such bad shape in such a short time. We haven't even been here for an hour.

"Theo," my brother says, his words slightly slurred. "I was looking for you."

Parrish reaches past me to grab Marco under the arms and drags him to his feet, helping steady him. After he does, Parrish casts a steely look in Minnow's direction, but she's gazing at Marco worriedly.

"What happened?" I ask her.

"I don't know," she says. She runs her palm over her shaved head, seeming to think it over. "I guess he drank too much too fast. He started to get kind of sloppy and I worry about your grandmother, you know? She's so strict. . . ." She shrugs. "I asked Parrish to go find you. Figured you'd know what to do."

I stare back at her. *Do* I know what to do? This is a new situation for me. Marco isn't a lightweight; he's usually the one *throwing* the party. Maybe he was trying to impress Minnow and overdid it, or he drank something super strong. Either way, I'm going to kill him tomorrow for humiliating us both.

I look at my brother. "Do you think you have alcohol poisoning?" I ask. "Should I take you to the hospital?"

Marco groans. "No, Theo," he says. "I'm fine. I didn't even drink that much."

"Uh, your lack of balance tells me otherwise," I reply. Great. He doesn't even remember how much he drank. "Okay . . . ," I say, trying to think. Because I have a big problem. How exactly am I going to get Marco home?

With that thought, I glance at Parrish. "I'm sorry to ask this . . . but, um, I actually can't drive us home," I say. "I don't have my license."

Parrish's mouth widens into a smile. "Really?" he asks as if that's interesting.

I can't believe I just had to tell him that. "Can you?" I ask, and he nods quickly.

"Yes," he says. "Of course I can drive you. Mind if we use your car, though? I got a ride here."

"Sure," I say, and then push Marco's shoulder a little more aggressively than necessary. "Give him the keys, dipshit," I tell my brother.

"I'm not . . . ," Marco starts to say but loses track of the argument. He fishes out the keys and jangles them. Parrish takes them, swinging the ring around his thumb before catching the keys in his palm.

"Do you mind if I come with?" Minnow asks, surprising me. "I live near there and I can walk after we make sure Marco gets home safe."

It's sweet that she wants to look after him. Marco must

note the same thing because he moves toward her and puts one arm over her shoulders, a bit unsteady. Minnow dips under his weight and Parrish quickly gets on Marco's other side to help hold him up.

"Come on, buddy," Parrish tells him. "Let's get you home before you puke on us."

"I haven't puked since middle school," Marco announces proudly.

"Seriously going to kill you," I mumble, and lead the way back toward the car.

Unfortunately, we have to walk through the party to get there. Great. We're the tourists who got sloppy at their first bonfire. We'll be lucky if anyone invites us again.

As we make our way through the crowd, I notice there are more people splashing in the water, including Beatrice and Greg. They're with Annemarie, dancing, Greg swaying unsteadily. Well, I guess we're not the only ones embarrassing ourselves tonight.

As I pass the fire, Elijah jogs over. He nods a quick hello to Parrish and Minnow before checking on my brother. He turns to me and I pause.

"Here," Elijah says quietly, holding out a card. I take it and see it's a business card with his name and number along with the podcast information. "We really want you to come by the house tomorrow," he says. "Come for lunch. Just . . . text me when you get home, okay? We'll make some plans."

"Uh . . . okay," I say, flattered by his insistence. And, to be honest, I'd love to hear more about their podcast. "And thank you," I add, holding up the card.

"Take care of him," Elijah says, motioning to my brother.

Elijah falls back then and Felix comes to stand at his side, both of them with grave expressions. It's nice of them to worry about Marco.

"It's okay," I say, calling back to them. "He'll be fine tomorrow. Just hungover. I'll text you about lunch."

They nod and wave goodbye before turning to each other again.

CHAPTER ELEVEN

Marco is propped up in the backseat of the Forester with Minnow next to him. His skin is waxy and pale. He rests his head against the seat and closes his eyes, which I imagine he'll regret, as we drive the winding streets toward Nightfall.

"You should focus on a fixed object outside," I tell him from the passenger seat. He opens his eyes, blinking quickly to focus.

"I told you I'm fine," he says. "Just . . . a little tired, I guess. Now turn up the music," he adds. "I love this song."

Parrish and I both look at the radio, which isn't even on.

"I'm going to bludgeon you in your sleep tonight," I mutter, frustrated. He really should have known better.

I turn the radio on and search for a station, glad for the distraction. When I look sideways at Parrish, he smiles at me and offers a little shrug.

"It could be worse," he says quietly. "Trust me."

"I'll take your word for it," I reply. "Because I think he's really embarrassing right now."

The drive home feels shorter than to the beach, and thankfully, when we pull up at Nonna's, the windows are all dark.

Dad or Nonna seeing Marco in this condition would not be ideal. But hey, at least we're home before midnight.

Parrish and I quickly climb out of the car and open Marco's door. Minnow gets out on the other side and takes a moment to look up at Nonna's house. I can't tell if she's admiring it or studying it, but she definitely seems lost in thought.

I help Marco from the backseat, but he swats me away.

"Theo, relax," he tells me. "Stop making a big deal out of this. You're not Mom."

The words hit me in the chest and I flinch. My brother doesn't seem to notice and he rounds the car, still slightly off-balance, toward Minnow. Hurt, I cross my arms over my chest.

Parrish comes to stand next to me, looking at me carefully. "I'll bring him to the front door?" he asks.

"Sure," I say, still watching my brother as he laughs with Minnow, oblivious to the fact that he hurt my feelings.

Minnow leans in and gives Marco a quick kiss. She smiles at him as she leans back, my brother grinning in total adoration. I might be the one to barf tonight.

Parrish slings his arm around Marco's shoulders. "Let's get you inside," Parrish tells him, exchanging a glance with Minnow before turning Marco toward the house. I watch them walk away, but hang back to talk with Minnow. I want to apologize for my brother's behavior tonight.

But when I turn to her, Minnow is the one to start speaking.

"I'm really sorry about this, Theo," she tells me. She motions toward the house and we both walk that way. "I should have paid better attention to what your brother was doing," she adds. "You probably think I'm a terrible influence."

"No, *I'm* sorry," I say. "On his behalf. I swear he's not normally like this. I have no idea what got into him tonight."

She laughs, and bites down on the corner of one lip. "Can I be honest?" she says. "I think he was trying to impress me a little. But it's okay. I still think he's sweet."

"He's something," I reply as we pause at the porch steps. Honestly, Marco is lucky that Minnow isn't running the other way at this point.

I'm glad she isn't, though. I like her. Minnow seems so grounded and genuine, and when she's next to me, I just feel . . . better. Better about the whole town. Our whole situation.

Parrish gets the front door open and Marco stumbles inside, tripping over the threshold and banging into the entryway table as he tries to steady himself. Parrish turns back to me with a worried expression.

"I should probably make sure Marco doesn't wake everyone up," I tell Minnow. "Did you want to come in for a little bit?"

"That's nice of you," she says. "But I should probably get home. I really appreciate the invitation, though."

"Of course," I say, a little disappointed.

"And you know," she adds, "if you're not too busy this week, it could be fun to have a girls' night. Beatrice and Annemarie have been dying to get to know you better."

"Really?" I ask, surprised by the comment. "I wasn't sure if Beatrice—"

"Oh, that's just Bea's face," Minnow says before I can finish. "Trust me," she adds. "If she didn't like you, you would know. It's just the opposite, really. We're all fascinated by you. Plus, your brother is always bragging about you."

Wow. That's nice of Marco. Now I feel bad for threatening to beat him to death earlier.

"I'd love to hang out," I say, meaning it.

Minnow grins widely. "I'll text you," she says in a bright tone.

Parrish walks over, the door to the house eased shut. He holds out the keys to me before turning to Minnow.

"I'll walk you to Bea's," he tells her. I have an awkward flinch in my stomach, a reminder that there's more between him and Beatrice than I know. If we all hang out again, I might have to ask about it.

When Parrish looks at me again and smiles, that thought slides away.

"It was good to see you tonight, Arizona," he says. "Like I said last night, you really fit in here."

"If you say so . . . ," I tell him with a little laugh. I'm not sure it's true, but I think it's going to work out, at least for the summer.

I wave goodbye and watch as Parrish and Minnow start to walk away. At the end of the driveway, Minnow spins around.

"And, Theo," she says, "welcome to Nightfall."

She looks up at the house again. This time, she smiles and nudges Parrish's arm, prompting him to glance at it also. His expression grows serious.

"Be sure to tell Nonna we said hello," Minnow adds, and then points one of her long nails toward the upstairs window.

Surprised, I turn to find Nonna standing in her window, although the light is off and it's hard to see her. She's mostly a shadow, staring down at us.

"Terrifying," I murmur. "Sorry, Nonna can be—"

But when I turn back, Minnow and Parrish are gone.

Great. They probably think my grandmother is some kind of a creep, standing there and watching us in the dark. When I look again, Nonna's curtains are closed. I pause a moment, overwhelmed by the weirdness pressing in from all angles. But maybe this is normal when you're far away from home. Or at least, maybe this is normal in Nightfall.

I jog up the porch steps. When I get inside the house, I lock the door, leaving the keys on the table, and then make a quick stop in the kitchen to get a glass of water for Marco. As I do, I glance around. Nonna must have been cooking all night because it smells really strongly of garlic in here.

I grab a couple of aspirin from the cabinet for Marco before heading upstairs with the water glass. When I get to the attic door, I ease it open, wincing as the hinges squeak. I know my grandmother is already roaming these halls like a specter, and I don't want to antagonize her.

"Water is a good idea," Marco says when I reach the top of the attic stairs. He's spread out on the bed, one hand pressed to his forehead. "My mouth tastes weird."

"I have aspirin," I say, holding out the two pills.

Marco pulls himself into a sitting position and takes the pills and the glass of water, downing the meds with a gulp. He's paler now, like he's withered since leaving the car. But he's also more lucid. He lies back again and closes his eyes.

"Minnow is never going to talk me again, is she?" he says. "I'm an idiot."

I feel a twinge of sympathy in my chest. "She likes you," I tell him. "She'll talk to you again. But speaking of being an idiot, what did you drink? I know you know better."

"I do," he says, opening his eyes again. "And I'm not kidding when I say I only had a few sips from a flask. Maybe half a beer, not even that much. But then Minnow and I were kissing and . . ." His face flushes, and I gesture to let him know he can spare me the details. "Then I sort of . . . blacked out," he adds quickly. "I barely even remember the drive home. But I'm fine now. I mean, I was fine before too, but I'm really fine now. I just feel drained and have a killer headache."

"What was in the flask?" I ask. Maybe he wasn't drunk after all. He doesn't seem it now.

"I don't know," he says. "A bunch of us were passing it around. The girls and some other guys."

I think about Asa walking strangely into the water. "What about the hitchhiker guy and Annemarie?" I ask. "Were they with you?"

Marco seems to think about it, rubbing at his temples like his head is throbbing. "I think they were actually. Anyway," he says apologetically, "can we talk about this tomorrow? I'm sorry, my head is just . . . it feels like it's going to explode."

"Don't explode," I tell him. "No idea how I'd explain that to Nonna."

He laughs for my benefit and curls up on his side. I sigh, looking down at him. It occurs to me that although he seems mostly fine now, maybe they put something in his drink. That idea is terrifying.

"Do you think they could have drugged you?" I ask, feeling dramatic when I say it.

Marco scoffs. "No way," he says. "Minnow and everyone else were drinking the same stuff and they were fine. And to be honest, they drank even more than me. I don't think it was the alcohol. I probably just . . . who knows. It was probably the mix of drinking and a new climate, new everything. I'll be fine, Theo. Everything's fine. Now go to bed."

I shrug. Honestly, I think my brother probably had more to drink than he remembers. Minnow said he was trying to impress her.

"Night," I tell Marco, and head out of the attic.

As I go into my room, I wonder if our grandmother is still up. I listen closely for any movement, but I don't hear anything.

I do, however, smell something. I wander around, sniffing, until I find the source by my nightstand. I pull open the drawer, and sure enough, there is another little stick doll, still damp. I grab a sheet of paper from the desk and use it to pick up the doll, then discard both in the bathroom trash can across the hall.

I go back into my room, close the door, and lock it. These little dolls are creepy—I wonder if I'll find one every night. I hope not.

I go over to my bed and sit cross-legged on it, then scroll through my phone. Willa was going to email me her schedule for next year so I can try to match her classes. I wonder if she's done it yet.

Just then, I remember Elijah telling me that *Scare Me Silly* had put out an episode on Nightfall. Considering it's a horror podcast, I'm pretty curious. Maybe the mural's mermaid comes to life at night and kills people.

Eager for a distraction, I pull up the podcast and slip in my earbuds. I scroll through until I find the latest episode: "Nightfall, Oregon—Part 1: Where the Night Has Teeth."

A quick check of the date tells me it aired two days ago. I click play.

Elijah's voice is soft, clear, and haunting. "Tucked away in a picturesque corner of the Pacific Northwest," he starts, "there is an idyllic beach town known for its spectacular ocean views, impeccable surfing locations, and quaint downtown complete with a mermaid mural to greet travelers. But the town is not what it appears. It's a place of dark secrets, hidden graveyards, and tales of monsters. Join us and take a tour through the missing persons capital of the world: Nightfall, Oregon."

"I'm sorry, what?" I say out loud to the empty room. Missing persons capital of the world? That's not possible. But . . . would they say it if it weren't true? While the intro song plays, I do a quick search for places with the most missing persons. Nightfall doesn't come up. A bit skeptical now, I set my phone aside and continue listening.

"Nightfall was founded in 1810," Elijah begins. "Its proximity to the water made it an important port of entry to North America. It was in 1814, though, when the curse was said to arrive. A ship crashed near Sunrise Beach, the sailors having driven themselves straight into the rocks instead of the safer waters of the town. There was only one survivor, Alfonse Cardelli, a stowaway on the ship. Cardelli was cared for by the townspeople upon his rescue. They cast him as their beacon of hope against the deadly sea. Eventually, he was even elected mayor. But the bad luck was just beginning for Nightfall.

"Over the next decade, twenty-seven girls went missing. Only six returned, and their families claimed they came back *different*. They would disappear at night, shy away from sunlight, and feast on raw animals in the fields. These girls, by order of Cardelli, were taken into the ocean, drowned, and then beheaded."

I cringe and look around my room. The doll faces stare back at me. I'm scared.

"In addition," Elijah continues, "Cardelli began to reject ships as they headed into port, thereby isolating Nightfall from the outside world. The townspeople grew more fearful and locked their daughters away to protect them from being executed. And yet, eight more girls disappeared. Three of them were drowned and beheaded on their return.

"The population of Nightfall began to dwindle. It had nearly disappeared altogether when Cardelli was unexpectedly lost at sea—incidentally, from the same beach where he had washed ashore. Soon after, the girls stopped disappearing. The next few decades were prosperous ones for Nightfall as the town re-opened and rebuilt after years of solitude. Families settled here. Tourists visited.

"But then, in the 1950s," Elijah continues, his voice filled with righteous anger, "girls started disappearing again—sixteen of them in less than a year, along with sightings of creatures roaming in the dark, bloodstained sidewalks, and freshly dug graves. The locals grew wary of the night; they wanted to close their borders, protect their girls.

"And then, all at once," Elijah whispers, "the disappearances stopped. There were no more strange sightings; there was just . . . quiet. A hush seemed to fall over the town. A secret no one spoke of. A mural went up in the center of downtown called *Only Some Shall Stay,* painted by a twenty-two-year-old local artist. The mural depicts a young mermaid waiting for a ship full of sailors, calling them to certain death along the rocks. On the beach, the townspeople watch. It's believed the mural depicts the ending of the curse.

"But it's our contention that the mural actually depicts the day it began again. . . ."

The podcast's closing music plays.

What does that mean? I'm confused as the episode ends, leaving me hanging for an explanation. What kind of curse? I guess I'll have to wait for part two.

I take out my earbuds and click them back into their case. I have no idea if any of the story is true, aside from the mural. Did Alfonse Cardelli even exist? Did girls ever go missing in Nightfall? Based on my quick internet search, I call bullshit on the entire story. Although, I'll admit, it did make for a pretty great show.

Which reminds me . . .

I reach into my pocket and draw out the business card that Elijah gave me earlier. I put his number in my phone, which I'll admit feels cool because he's famous, and then text him.

Marco and I are home and still alive. Lunch tomorrow?

I'm surprised when he writes back immediately. *Good,* he texts. *Lock the doors and we'll see you tomorrow. I heard it's going to be sunny.*

I don't believe you, but that's okay, I tell him. *See you then.*

Above me, the attic door creaks, followed by the thump of footsteps. They stop abruptly. Marco must be up and moving around. I wait another moment, but when I don't hear anything else, I get ready for bed.

Alone in my room, the podcast has left me on edge. I can't stop thinking about it—thinking about girls drowned in the ocean. About missing tourists. It isn't true, of course—my father would have mentioned that Nightfall was the missing persons capital of the world.

It's just for the show. It has to be.

Right?

CHAPTER TWELVE

When I wake up in the morning, soft light is filtering through the bedroom curtains. Although we've only been in Oregon for a few days, I'm starting to get used to waking up in a place that isn't home. The dolls watch me as I stretch and walk over to the window. I pull back the curtains and gasp when I see a blue sky high above. Holy shit. It really is going to be sunny!

I head downstairs, the house silent as I enter the kitchen. I begin humming as I survey the contents of the fridge, considering what to make for breakfast. Nothing inspires me, so I just grab the orange juice.

But as I turn, I nearly jump out of my skin when I see Nonna already sitting at the table with an open can of Coca-Cola in front of her. I didn't even notice her when I walked in.

"Nonna," I say, clutching my chest. "Make some noise next time so I know you're in here."

"In my own house?" she asks. "Sure, I'll instruct the band to start playing."

I laugh and grab a glass from the cupboard. I bring it to the table and pull out the chair across from my grandmother.

"That's fair," I say. I motion to her soda. "A little early, don't you think?"

"Caffeine is caffeine," she tells me, taking a loud sip. "I've made it this far, so I think I'm doing pretty good."

Once again, Nonna is on point for this early in the morning.

"Can I ask you something?" I begin, leaning into the table. She looks me over for a long moment before nodding.

"Is Nightfall the missing persons capital of the world?" I ask. Her lack of reaction throws me. Could it actually be true?

"Where did you hear something so stupid?" she asks. I let out a breath, relieved.

"A podcast," I tell her. When she stares back at me blankly, I explain *Scare Me Silly*. She listens, but she also looks kind of angry. And to prove it, she takes another drink of soda and sets the can down hard, splashing Coke on the table.

"Those boys need to mind their own business," she says. "Doing a show about Nightfall? And what? Asking more people to come here? Making a spectacle of us?"

"Well, is any of it true?" I ask.

"Does it matter?" she replies. "It was decades ago. And every year, people want to dwell on it." Nonna shakes her head, using the sleeve of her sweatshirt to mop up the droplets of soda. "They're all just asking for trouble," she mutters. "They never learn. I told your father not to bring you kids here. But he didn't listen either."

Her words sting. Marco and I were the ones who were uprooted and dragged here against our will. And now my grandmother is telling us we weren't welcome in the first place?

"You didn't want us here?" I ask, hurt in my voice. "Why not?"

She sighs as if I'm not understanding. But I think she's being pretty clear.

"Nonna," I say louder, "you told Dad you didn't want us to come to Nightfall? You . . . you didn't even want to meet us?"

"He doesn't understand the town anymore," she says in a quiet voice, leaning toward me. "That's all I'm saying, Theodora. You should have stayed with your mother."

I glare at her. That was exactly the wrong thing to say.

"It's Theo," I say. "And in case you missed the memo, my mother doesn't have room for us in her life anymore. Sorry we're such a burden."

"Oh, stop," Nonna says, holding out her hand to me. But I'm furious.

"You know," I say, my voice shaking, "this trip wasn't our idea, either. But you could at least act like you give a shit about us. All these years . . . would it have been so hard to pretend?"

I start to get up, but she takes my wrist, her eyes pleading. "I'm sorry," she says. "Sit down. Please. Of course I'm happy to finally meet you."

Her brown eyes are open wide, her brow furrowed. I ease back down in the chair, willing to hear her out even though I'd rather run away. All the way back to Arizona if I could.

Nonna puts her hands in front of her on the table. "I'm glad you and your brother are here," she says. "I'm happy your father's here—he needs us. But you don't understand this town like I do. You can be content here, but you can't cause trouble. You can't get noticed. You need to start staying closer to home."

"Noticed by who?" I ask, confused. "What am I supposed to be afraid of?"

She hesitates, and I'm reminded of her stick dolls. Nonna believes in the creepy stuff. She believes it wholeheartedly. Which puts this bizarre conversation in perspective. I relax slightly.

My father appears in the doorway. "Good morning," he says, his voice raspy with sleep. "I'm hoping there's coffee."

"By the sink," Nonna replies, but keeps her gaze steady on me. She looks truly apologetic. I feel bad that we just had our first fight. But I've gone my whole life without knowing my paternal grandmother. I think I'd hoped for more.

"I'll make you both some eggs," Nonna says abruptly, and stands. She walks over and pulls out a pan and then grabs a loaf of bread from the bread box.

My father pours himself a cup of coffee and takes a tentative sip. When he sees Nonna put some slices of bread in the toaster, he grabs the jelly.

"You're up early again, Theo," my father says. He comes to sit with me at the table.

"I seem to get up earlier here," I say, studying him. "Hopefully that habit doesn't stick."

"Yes, hopefully," he replies, smiling.

As soon as I'm alone with my father, I'm going to confront him about what Nonna said this morning. I still can't believe she told me she didn't want us here. No matter how she meant it, I feel terrible.

Nonna comes over with a plate of toast cut into triangles. She leaves the plate and goes back to retrieve the eggs, then joins us at the table to eat.

While we chew, Nonna glares at me as if waiting for me to bring up our conversation, and my father texts someone on his phone. I wonder if it's Olivia Miles.

"Who are you talking to?" I ask, trying to see his screen.

He bites back a smile. "I'm sure you don't want to hear about it."

"Uh . . . I might not," I agree, dreading where this might be going. "But maybe give me a version I can handle."

He laughs. "I . . . I went out for dinner with Olivia last night. We had a great time. Really great."

"Well," I say, impressed. "That's very interesting."

"I'm glad you think so," he says, setting his phone aside. "Because I was hoping to have her come by so you and your brother could get to know her better. Would you . . . would that be okay with you?"

The realization hits me. My father's been alone for so long, for years now. And he's finally met someone, or in this case, reconnected, I guess. Wow . . . my father has someone again. That hits me right in the chest.

My father waits for my response. He seems worried, but he doesn't need to be.

"Yeah, Dad," I say with a shrug. "I'd love that. I'm sure Marco would too."

"Great," he says, beaming. "I'll invite Olivia over this week. I promise you're going to like her. I've told her all about you."

"Sounds good," I say, my heart filled with happiness for my father.

Sitting here, I realize my father looks like a different person from even a few days ago. He has more color in his cheeks, and he's happier.

"Are you done?" my father asks, motioning to my plate.

"I am," I say, handing it to him.

As he washes the dishes, Nonna takes her plate to the sink. She hands it to my father before heading upstairs. Without another word to me.

★ ★ ★

I HAVE NO IDEA what to wear to lunch with podcast celebrities. It's nearly noon and I've put away all of my freshly laundered clothes. I stand in the doll room wearing jeans and a sports bra, directionless. My choices aren't exactly inspired. I was too annoyed when I packed to come here. All I have are T-shirts and sweatshirts. Not a single sundress.

"So wait," Willa says on speakerphone, "Joseph has a girlfriend?" I look toward my phone, which I left on the bed.

"It just sounds so wrong to use the word *girlfriend*," I tell her. "How about *womanfriend*? No, that's worse."

"*Ladyfriend?*" Willa offers, and we both start laughing.

"Fine, *girlfriend*," I say. I grab a yellow T-shirt with a flattering cut and pull it over my head, then fall onto the bed and stare up at the ceiling. "Either way," I tell her, "he wants me and Marco to get to know her. I can't believe she's famous."

"What a score," Willa says. "I wonder if she's rich."

"Do authors get rich?" I ask, furrowing my brow.

"Some of them, I think," Willa says. "I know Stephen King is rich."

"Yeah, but he has a billion books. Half a billion TV shows and movies."

"True," Willa says. There's a clicking noise and I know that she's clipping her fingernails while we talk. She hates when they grow out even a little, and I hate it too—one time during practice she scratched my arm like Wolverine.

"Can I ask you something?" Willa says cautiously.

"Of course," I say. I sit up, worried about the change in her tone.

"How do you really feel about this?" she asks. "You weren't

120

too stoked on your mom dating. And I know it's been . . . difficult with her and Dale."

"This is different," I say. "My dad's not moving in with Olivia Miles and forgetting all about us."

"Sure," Willa allows. "But then again, your mom didn't do that right away either. And you were still pissed." We fall quiet. "Hate to ask," she says, "but have you talked to Rosie yet? Because I almost went into the restaurant yesterday but I was afraid of running into her. I knew she'd ask about you, how you were. And she just . . . she misses you, Theo."

My throat feels tight with the beginning of tears. I can imagine my mother rushing over to Willa's table. Friendly. Worried. She'd look beautiful in the red dress she wears to the restaurant, her black hair pinned up with an oversized flower. But her eyes would be sad.

"She loves you," Willa says softly. "You should fix this, okay?"

"I will," I tell her, and then sniffle as a tear runs down my cheek. I quickly wipe it away.

"Then do it fast," Willa adds, lightening her voice. "Because your mother has the best nachos in the entire valley and I am missing them hard."

I smile. "I said I will," I sing out, and hear her laugh.

"Well, good," she says. "And now that we've completed therapy, don't forget to update me on the progress with the new love interest who may or may not have a scary townie girlfriend."

"You will literally be the first person I tell," I promise.

"And you're having lunch with *Scare Me Silly*?" she adds. "I told everyone and they're begging you to post a picture with them. Also, my girlfriend wants you to ask them about La Llorona. She wants the full breakdown, got it?"

"Sure," I say, distracted as I check the time on my phone. "But hey, I have to go. I don't want to get there too late."

"Call me when you get back. And don't forget to tell me everything," Willa replies.

"Every word," I agree. "Call you later."

We say goodbye and I hang up. As I walk out of my bedroom, I glance toward the attic door, wondering if I should check on Marco. It's just after eleven, so he's probably still sleeping. I'll text him later.

I go downstairs and just as I step off the bottom stair, Nonna walks in from the living room.

"Where is Marco?" she asks. "Did you speak to him?"

"Not yet," I say. "He likes to sleep in."

"Sleep all day?" she asks.

"Party all night," I say, joking. But Nonna ignores me and just looks up the stairs, a flash of concern crossing her face. "He's fine, Nonna," I add.

She keeps her gaze trained upstairs.

"Okay," I say when she doesn't ask anything else. "I'm going out now. Not too far from home either. You should be happy."

"I'm not happy about any of this," she murmurs.

I have a spike of anger, a reminder that she really doesn't want us here. Well, joke's on her because I don't want to be here either. I turn and head for the door, yanking it open.

A splash of sunlight spills into the room. It hits my face, and I blink against it, smiling.

I've missed the sunshine.

CHAPTER THIRTEEN

The sun is fully out, any hint of clouds having faded away. And along with them, my anger has faded. I feel like a flower stretching toward the light. This town looks different in the sunlight. I've lived in the desert my entire life, surrounded by earth tones. The colors in Nightfall are unbelievably beautiful when it's not aggressively overcast.

I walk through the neighborhood toward the purple Victorian a few blocks away. The trees are vibrantly green, cherry blossoms and roses everywhere.

At the corner, I check the map on my phone to ensure I'm heading in the right direction. As I do, I regret not checking with Marco. I probably should have invited him along. I'd kill him if he forgot to mention something this cool. I send him a quick text.

How are you feeling? Let me know when you're awake.

When I get back, I'll make it up to him. Bring him toast and water. Maybe a couple more aspirin if he's not feeling well. Hopefully he'll be up before then.

I arrive at the tall Victorian house, stunned by its purple

shingles and pink window casings, the huge porch that wraps around the front, and the castle-tower on the second floor. It's gorgeous, but eerie in how out-of-place it seems in the neighborhood.

I walk up the steps and knock on the front door. When it swings open, Elijah is standing there in a crisp button-down shirt with a smiling Felix just behind him.

"You made it!" Elijah says. "I was worried you'd change your mind." The corners of his mouth pull slightly downward. "By the way, how's your brother?" he asks.

"Hungover, I'm guessing," I tell him.

He pauses for a long moment before nodding, almost like he doesn't believe me. I'm a little confused, but then Felix pushes past him. He's wearing a red puffer vest over a flannel, and I can't help but think of the main character in *Back to the Future*. And yet, on Felix, it works.

"You okay if we eat on the porch?" Felix asks me. "Turns out you're good luck and the sun actually did come out. I want to stay outside and take advantage."

"That would be great," I say.

Felix leads me to a cozy sitting area off to the side, half-covered in potted plants. I take a seat on the couch and Elijah sits across from me in a rocking chair. Felix dashes back inside and reappears with a tray of assorted crackers and cheeses. He sets it down on the coffee table, beaming at me.

"A starter," he says. "I hit up the farmers market this morning."

Elijah immediately reaches in and starts picking, making a cracker-cheese sandwich.

The Victorian isn't far from downtown and several tourists pass, some walking, others on those annoying rental scooters that litter the sidewalks. A few wave to us, which Felix happily returns. The house is a showpiece, and I think Felix appreciates the spotlight.

"So, Palm Springs?" I say, taking a bit of cheese. "I went there a few times as a kid. Do you like living there?"

"Love it," Elijah replies. "Felix . . . not so much." He smiles at him.

"First of all," Felix says. "Your guesthouse is fantastic—I do love that. And Palm Springs is okay, but I grew up surfing in San Diego. I miss it." He shrugs. "Now I spend my weekends antiquing with Elijah's mom, though, so it's not a total loss."

"Stop," Elijah says, slapping his leg. "You're making us sound like an old married couple. I swear we still do fun stuff," he assures me.

"I love antiquing," I say even though I've never done it.

Felix nods at me like I've made a great point. "Who doesn't?" he asks.

I smile. Although technically I've never been *antiquing,* I do love thrifting. Willa and I know all the secondhand shops in Phoenix to find the best outfits. Seems close enough.

Elijah rests back in the rocking chair, crossing one ankle over the other knee. Felix sits next to him on the chair's arm. The air is peaceful around us, warm.

I take another moment to enjoy the sunshine. It's bright enough for me to forget the last few days have been completely overcast. Weather-induced amnesia. The same thing happens in Phoenix after the long summers. The minute the temperature drops below 115, we forget that a few weeks earlier you could fry an egg on the sidewalk.

"So tell us again what brought you to Nightfall this summer," Elijah says, grabbing another piece of cheese. "Your whole family's with you?"

"No, my parents just got divorced and . . ." I pause, not wanting to go into it. "My brother and I are here with our dad," I start again. "Visiting our grandmother. We'd planned to stay in Arizona until my brother decided to throw an epic end-of-the-year party. House got trashed, the police came—it made the local news. After that, he and I lost staying-home privileges and were dragged along to Nightfall."

"Tragic," Felix says, absorbed in my story.

"On top of that, our grandmother is pretty eccentric," I add. "Think *Great Expectations,* but weirder."

I pick up a cracker and crunch down. After a moment, I can't wait to ask them the burning question. I have to know if what they said about Nightfall was true.

"I listened to your podcast last night," I start, keeping my voice neutral. "The first episode on Nightfall."

They glance at each other before Elijah turns back to me. "And what did you think?" he asks.

"It was a great story," I tell him. "Scary, too. But be honest." I lean forward in the chair, a smile at my lips. "Was any of it true?"

Felix winces and Elijah straightens, leaning away from me. My stomach drops as I realize I've offended them. I quickly try to backpedal.

"I'm sorry," I say. "It's just that I—"

"All of it is true," Elijah says, holding up one hand to stop me. "We don't post things we haven't investigated. Of course, there is always room for interpretation, but the story is always based on facts."

"But I looked up the missing persons claim," I tell him. "And Nightfall wasn't mentioned."

"Per capita," Felix clarifies. "Compared to the amount of

people who live here, the ratio of missing people is high. It's about percentages."

I nod. His point makes sense.

"Besides," Felix adds, "I'm pretty sure Nightfall doesn't report every missing person. It's not exactly a big tourist draw."

"Yeah, probably not," I say. "And the story about the shipwreck and Alfonse Cardelli? The missing girls?"

"All can be found in the town library," Elijah replies. "Like I said, we do our research. But that episode is just part one. Trust me, there are more secrets about to be revealed."

"Like what?" I ask, inadvertently lowering my voice. Although I should be thrilled about getting advance details on the next episode, I'm acutely aware that I'm currently *living* in the scary town they're investigating.

Elijah looks at Felix before turning back to me. "Six years ago a couple of kids found a mutilated body half-buried in the sand of Sunrise Beach," he says.

I swallow hard at the abrupt dark turn.

"Apparently it was gory," he continues. "And then someone found another body, two years ago. And it happened again last year. Rumor has it there have been bodies *every* year—for decades—but the town covers it up. Bodies washing up on the beach but never mentioned in the news. We were only able to confirm three through 911 call records."

"Who were the victims?" I ask, wrapping my arms around my stomach. Nerves are making it flutter unsteadily.

"We don't know for sure," Elijah says. "No one has ever been identified because the bodies disappear. We found a few intake forms from the morgue, but the bodies were never taken into custody. They just . . . vanished." He makes a *poof* gesture with his hands.

Considering my grandmother's warnings about the beach, I wonder if there really have been some deaths. Or maybe one that was spun into an urban legend—Elijah did say some of it was rumor. There can't be bodies washing up every year. That would be absolutely insane.

Elijah sighs, senses my hesitance to believe him. Felix puts one hand on his shoulder and continues the story.

"We travel all over the country," Felix tells me, "searching for the unexplained. You wouldn't believe some of the things we've seen. Impossible things. We first heard about Nightfall last year," he continues, his tone growing more solemn. "A friend of mine was out here for the summer to surf, but when he came home, it was weird. He couldn't remember it."

"What do you mean?" I ask. "He partied too hard?"

"No," Felix says. "Brecken didn't drink. But during the month he was here, he stopped contacting his family and friends after the first few days. We were all worried, but figured he was having fun. But then . . . then he showed up in Loma Vista on a bus and borrowed someone's phone to call me for a ride. His surfboard and belongings gone. When I saw him, he started crying. Said he didn't know what had happened or how he got out of Nightfall."

Felix shakes his head and reaches to take a sip of lemonade. Elijah watches on in sympathy and rubs his back.

"He never told us what he was doing in Nightfall all that time," Felix continues after a moment. "But when I first saw him that day off the bus, he had scratches all over him. Marks on his arms."

"What kind of marks?" I murmur, horrified. My body is keyed up with a strange anticipation, the kind you get when you walk into a haunted house, knowing something will jump out at any second. I'm scared of what Felix is going to say next.

"Bite marks," Felix whispers. "Human-sized bite marks."

I don't move for a moment. The image of this kid coming back with scratches and bite marks is terrifying. I turn to look beyond the porch at the street, the tourists walking past, the sun shining. My worry eases slightly with this reality so different from the one Felix just described.

"After Felix's friend came home," Elijah says, drawing my attention back to them, "I started doing some research on Nightfall. I dug into the history of this town. And turns out, this place is creepy as hell."

"Only Some Shall Stay," I say to myself, thinking back on the interview I read about the mural.

"The Siren of Nightfall," Elijah says, nodding. "Yes, she's part of it."

"Part of what?" I ask, hoping he has more information. The mermaid waiting on a rock? Only she isn't just waiting. She's luring sailors to their deaths while the townspeople watch. "What other kind of history did you find?"

"The Midnight Dive," Elijah continues. "They say it's to commemorate the history of the town, the sailors lost all those years ago. But those sailors purposely steered their ship into the rocks to save the town from something. No one says what."

"Disease?" I suggest. "Maybe they were sick. A plague or something—that could've been what was driving the girls mad, making them act strangely at night."

"Perhaps," Elijah says, nodding. "But Alfonse Cardelli survived. And as mayor, *he* created the tradition—the ritual of the Midnight Dive. Only it wasn't called that and it certainly wasn't to commemorate dead sailors. That all came later, when Nightfall started to rebrand itself as a tourist destination. No, Cardelli would order the townspeople . . ." He pauses, but I already know the answer.

"He ordered them to drown the girls," I finish, chills running over my arms.

"Exactly," Elijah says. "Certain girls were rounded up and drowned on his orders. Then they were beheaded and buried just outside of town."

"But . . . why?" I ask. "For real why, not the supernatural stuff. Why kill the girls? Why cut off their heads?" I add with disgust.

"It's said they didn't fully die when drowned," Elijah says. "That they . . . they came back. But in reality? I'm sure it was about control. When it comes to men with a god complex, isn't it always about control?"

I'm caught somewhere between disbelief and revulsion. The history of the town is horrific, unforgivable. Those poor girls. Their poor families . . .

Elijah tilts his head from side to side. "Now," he says in a clear voice, "the townspeople eventually revolted, and Cardelli ran and was lost at sea. And then the Midnight Dive was rebranded as a way to honor the sailors. Girls are no longer being drowned," he adds with a humorless laugh. "But that was the original intent of the Dive. Pretty dark, right?"

"Yeah," I murmur. "My . . . um, my father and grandmother forgot to mention they were part of a cult town."

"Right?" Felix says, widening his eyes. "I'd be pissed if my grandmother lived here."

Despite the morbid topic, they don't seem scared by the story, probably desensitized to horror. My thoughts are racing.

In a way, I'm reminded of everyone in the ocean last night, Asa and the other guy. How the girls had been urging them in. The entire thing seemed . . . strange.

My phone buzzes suddenly in my pocket, making me jump. Elijah makes a small pout. "I'm sorry, Theo," he says. "We don't mean to scare you. And honestly, we're still researching. Just . . . we just want you to be careful." He exchanges a look with Felix.

"That's right," Felix adds quickly. "I'm sure everything is fine. In fact, I'll grab lunch."

As Felix disappears into the house, I check my phone, assuming it's Marco. But I don't recognize the number. I hit ignore and set my phone on the table.

Felix comes out of the house with a tray of gourmet sandwiches and chips. He points out the different types that he picked up from a shop downtown, but I've lost my appetite.

"Thanks," I say with a polite smile, grabbing a chip and biting a corner.

Elijah studies me, his mouth downturned. "Are you okay?" he asks.

"I am," I tell him. "It's just . . . my grandmother said something this morning about warning my father not to bring us here. And last night, my brother got pretty sick. He wasn't the only one, either—there were some guys in the water who were pretty out of it. You don't think . . ." I pause, considering. "You don't think . . . they're drugging and killing people or anything, do you?"

"Of course not," Elijah says. "The answer is never that simple."

My phone buzzes again, startling me. I silence the call and stand up. "I should go," I say. "I want to check on my brother.

Ask my grandmother about the death cult here, typical vacation stuff, you know?"

"You sure you have to leave?" Elijah asks, getting to his feet. "You haven't even eaten. We can change the subject, or if you'd like, we can head down to the library and do some research."

"Together," Felix adds as he moves to stand next to Elijah. "You know, watch each other's backs."

Elijah covertly nudges him. I'm embarrassed that I'm so frightened by their stories. I try to remind myself that they host a horror podcast. This stuff is normal for them.

"Yeah," I say. "Going to go. But thank you for the invite and thank you for lunch—sorry, I . . ." I motion to the tray of untouched food. "And your place is great," I add, indicating the Victorian house.

"Next time we'll actually give you a tour," Felix says. He looks upset, nervous.

Elijah follows me to the porch steps. "We're thinking of having a party this week," he says as I start down the stairs. "I hope you'll come back."

"Sounds fun," I say. Although I'm not sure I want to come back. I want time to digest everything they just fed me.

"Be careful out there, all right?" Felix calls. "Keep your eye out for anything strange."

"I will," I say, giving him a thumbs-up. Felix matches it, although he looks doubtful.

"Good," Elijah announces as we reach the sidewalk. "Because we hope to see you again, Theo."

A chill runs down my spine and I quickly start up the block, away from the house. My heart is racing. It wasn't Elijah's final comment that bothered me, but the way he said it.

As if questioning whether he'd ever see me again.

CHAPTER FOURTEEN

can feel Elijah and Felix watching me all the way to the end of the block, but I don't turn around.

A shadow passes overhead, and when I look up, there are clouds rolling in. Judging by how quickly they're moving, it's going to rain soon. Maybe even storm. Figures. A full sunny day in Nightfall was just too good to be true.

The longer I walk, the less afraid I become, though. The truth is, it's not that outrageous that this could be a creepy cult town— it's pretty remote. But a sketchy past doesn't mean the towns- people are still chopping off people's heads. It's not like Salem is still burning witches.

My phone starts buzzing again. Annoyed, I stop and answer. "Hello?" I say. There's a long silence, and my irritation spikes. "Who is this?" I demand. "I'm really not in the mood for—"

"Hi, Theo," a voice says brightly. "Sorry, my service sucks. This is Minnow. How are you?"

Surprised, I fumble for an answer. "Oh, uh . . . hi," I reply. "I'm good. Sorry, I . . . Wait." I pause. "How did you get my number?"

"Marco gave it to me," she explains. When she mentions

my brother's name, I'm relieved—she must have talked to him, so he's feeling better. I start walking again, honored that Minnow would call me. Completely clueless as to why, though.

"How are you?" I ask. "The sun was nice today, right?" I close my eyes, embarrassed by my horrible social skills.

"Sure," Minnow says. "Look, I'm sorry to bother you, but I was wondering if you were busy tonight. The girls and I were hoping you'd want to hang out with us. Do girl shit, you know?"

I'm stunned for a moment. Although she mentioned a girls' night at her house, I didn't think it would be this soon. Or at all. Minnow laughs softly to fill the silence.

"No pressure, Theo," she adds. "Just think about it. You can text me anytime. You have my number now."

This is awkward even for me. I have no idea why I can't just be cool. "I'd love to go out tonight," I tell her. "I . . . I'll ask my dad when I get back. I'm not home right now." Great. *Ask my dad?* I sound like I'm five.

"Where are you?" Minnow asks, curious.

"Oh, I'm just walking back from lunch with a couple of friends." I wince. "Okay, not really friends, I just met them last night. But they're fun. Kind of death-focused, but you know, we all have our quirks." I laugh, expecting her to laugh in return. When she doesn't, I sink into deeper embarrassment.

"And who are they exactly?" Minnow asks as if nothing I just said fazed her.

"Podcasters," I say. "They host a podcast called *Scare Me Silly.* It's a horror—"

"I love that show," she interrupts. "How fun. We have a couple of celebrities in town for the Dive. The girls will be thrilled. Actually," she adds, and I hear some noise in the background, "I have to run. See if your dad will let you come out tonight and let me know. We would love to have you join us."

"Okay, I'll text you to let you know," I say, trying to sound excited, yet cool.

She laughs. "See you soon, Theo," she sings out before hanging up.

AS SOON AS I walk in the door, I call out to let my father and Nonna know I'm back. But no one answers. Instead, I'm met with eerie silence; there is no distant shuffling, clock ticking, refrigerator humming. It's so quiet it almost feels like I'm submerged underwater. I can't shake the sensation of dread that's crawling over my skin.

"Marco?" I call up the stairs. No answer.

The wood creaks under my feet as I start up the steps, and I hurry the rest of the way. I open the attic door and make the short climb, then open the second door. It's dark in the room, a sheet thrown over the circular window.

"Marco?" I whisper, my heart beating quickly. There's a pile of blankets and a large lump on the mattress that I assume is my brother. "Marco," I say a little louder, but there's no movement.

I go to the window and pull off the sheet, letting a bit of hazy daylight into the room. Dust particles float around me in the air. When I turn back, my brother is curled up on the bed. He's in the fetal position, sunlight from the window cast on the mattress next to him while he's bent away from it. His eyes closed, his mouth agape. His skin is waxy and pale, pinkish-blue circles under his eyes.

He's so still—impossibly still.

I have a sudden and crushing sense of panic. An absolute shudder of horror. I rush over to my brother and when I touch his arm, his skin is cold.

I don't think he's breathing.

With a fresh surge of fear, I violently shake him. "Marco!" I yell, my eyes tearing up.

My brother gasps awake, swinging out his arms. "What? What?" he yells, sounding terrified. His eyes finally focus on mine. "What's wrong, Theo?"

I can't answer right away. I'm trembling as I wipe away the tears blinding me. I honestly . . . I thought he was dead. Holy shit, I thought my brother was dead.

"I . . . I couldn't wake you up," I say weakly.

"So you attack me?" Marco asks, brushing his hair back from his forehead. "What the hell, Theo? I already feel like shit."

My knees are unsteady and I drop onto the bed next to him. The moment I do, I'm nearly struck down by the smell of dirt and rotting flowers. I stand up again and then rip back the top sheet. Marco recoils and covers his nose.

There are no fewer than ten stick dolls arranged in such a way that they were probably surrounding my brother while he slept.

"What in the world is going on?" I say, letting the sheet fall from my hand.

"It was Nonna," Marco says. "While I was half-asleep, she came in with those things, put them around me, and said some shit I didn't understand. The smell makes me sick, but I honestly felt too awful to move. She did promise to make me a grilled cheese, though, so I was trying to wait it out."

"Get up," I tell my brother. "No one's downstairs. I'll make you something to eat and we can wash these sheets. When I asked Nonna not to put these creepy dolls in our clothes, I figured she would understand that applied to all fabric touching our bodies. Come on."

Marco groans as I help him up. He holds up his hands to block the sunlight. "Give me a sec," he says. "I'm a little dizzy."

I step back, and as I take him in, I'm worried. His skin is gray, his eyes rimmed in red.

"Well," I tell him. "Whatever you drank last night, I suggest you never try it again."

"To be honest," he says, "I can barely remember last night. Even before I started drinking. I remember getting to the beach with you. Literally arriving at the beach. All the rest? Fuzzy as fuck."

"That's concerning," I say.

The story that Elijah and Felix told me is stuck in my brain. They said there are others who don't remember their time in Nightfall. Could that be true? Once again, I'm worried that maybe there was something in the alcohol, but I remind myself that they were all drinking it. So what happened? Could the others at the party have built up a tolerance? If they do this every night, it makes sense that they might. Still. . . . Marco trying to impress someone sounds way more likely.

"I was thinking about it while I was dying this morning," Marco continues. "Trying to piece together the night. But all I have are these flashes. Wait, who drove us home?"

"Parrish," I tell him.

"That the guy with the sad eyes?"

I sniff a laugh because it's a weirdly accurate description of him. "Yeah, that's him."

Marco blows out a steadying breath. "Good," he says. "I

was worried you got behind the wheel and that this is the Bad Place." He tries to smile at me, but winces. "Ouch," he says, hand over his forehead. "Being hilarious hurts my brain."

"Hurts mine too," I say, rolling my eyes. "And you know," I add, pushing his shoulder gently, "Minnow was worried about you last night. She came back with us to make sure you got home okay."

"That was nice of her," he replies. He lowers his arm, his expression a mix of confusion and admiration. "Wait, I think I talked with her today. I was half-asleep. Her voice—was she in the window?" he asks, his brows pulled together.

I snort a laugh. "The third-floor attic window?" I reply. "Probably not. But she did call you, and you gave her my number. She invited me out tonight."

"That's right," Marco replies. "It was on the phone. She's really cool," he says, glancing at me. "I like her." He breaks into a smile and I can't help but match it.

"Yeah, I like her too," I tell him. There's a weight lifted by the happiness shining in my brother's eyes. And it feels good. It feels like our lives are moving on. "So don't mess this up," I add, making him laugh.

"Deal," Marco says as if he's hyping himself up. "Now I'm ready to go downstairs."

"Wonderful," I tell him. I wait for him to go first and he leads the way, a little slow, but seemingly all right.

We go into the kitchen, where I immediately check the fridge for options. There's some shredded pork to make chilaquiles, Marco's preferred hangover food from Mom's restaurant, but Nonna doesn't have any tortillas or chips. Grilled cheese it is. Marco still looks pretty horrible, so eating is going to be dicey either way.

I make us both sandwiches and grab a couple of sodas. While Marco takes a few tentative bites of the grilled cheese, I tell him about my afternoon with the podcast boys.

"Drowning people?" he says after hearing the story. "Seriously, Theo? You believed them? They run a horror podcast." He laughs. "I bet they had you going for a while."

"Don't judge me," I say, embarrassed. It does sound completely ridiculous when I repeat the stories. "Besides," I tell Marco, "you're the one who first told me about their podcast last year, remember? And some of their story is true."

"I promise you," Marco says, hand over his heart, "the locals are not sacrificing girls to appease the sea gods or whatever reason you think they're doing it for. In the age of the internet, do you really think we wouldn't have heard about it?"

"Fair point," I say, giving in.

"It's just a story for their show," he says. "And one to scare the tourists. Which, of course, will make more come here. Increase their ratings. What's the alternative pitch? Nightfall, Oregon—the rainiest town in the Pacific Northwest. Sounds like a blast to visit."

I think it over. "I'm not saying I believe them," I tell Marco. "But you have to admit, you forgot some of last night. The memory thing? They said it's happened to several people."

"Sure," Marco says. "But it's summer. We all overindulge, right? Truth is . . . I probably did drink too much, even though I hate to admit it. But you're smarter than me, so you won't make the same mistake." He grins at me and I nod emphatically.

"I really am smarter," I tell him.

He sits back in the chair, folding his hands on top of his head. "So you're going out with Minnow and her friends?" he asks.

"I planned on it," I say. "You think I should, right?"

"Why not?" he asks. "What else are you going to do? Watch *CSI* with Nonna?"

I pause, about to tell him what Nonna said this morning about not wanting us to come to Nightfall, but I hold back. Truth is, Marco is more sensitive than I am in a lot of ways. I don't want to hurt his feelings. I don't really think Nonna meant it the way it came out, either—even if I'm still mad she said it.

"I'm going tonight," I say decisively. "And while I'm out having my exciting, summer-defining experience with the coolest girls in town, maybe you and Dad can go mini-golfing or something."

"Fuck off," Marco says with a laugh.

"Bring Nonna," I add. "I bet she gets a hole in one. She seems the type who could sink the shot."

"Wait," Marco says, looking around. "Where *is* Dad? I swear, I feel like I haven't seen that man since we got here."

"That's right," I say, snapping my fingers, and I lean in. "Marco . . . Dad has a girlfriend."

MARCO'S HAPPY FOR OUR FATHER and the famous author, but the boost of energy he got from the news and the grilled cheese doesn't last long and his hangover starts to settle back in. He deals with it, though, choking down aspirin and some gummy vitamins for old people I found in a cabinet.

An hour later, my grandmother gets home with a van full of groceries. Marco and I go out to help her carry in the bags, the rain clouds still threatening the day. Marco grabs an armful and heads in first, while I hang back with my grandmother.

I loop my arms around several grocery bags, while Nonna

reaches past me to grab an oversized package of paper towels. She's so tiny, the paper towel package looks comically huge in her arms. She backs away enough to close the trunk and we head toward the house.

As we walk, I look sideways at her. "Where's my dad?" I ask. "He wasn't here when I got back from lunch."

"Your father's out," she says.

"Is he with Olivia?" I ask, and then lean in like a conspirator. "Have you met her? Do you like her?"

"You'll have to ask him about Olivia Miles," she says curtly. "I'm not a gossip."

"Seriously?" I ask, coming to a stop while she continues up the porch steps. Well, that was disappointing.

Marco comes out of the house and Nonna immediately passes him the roll of paper towels. Then she walks pasts him, slapping her hands together as if her work is done. Marco glances at me and we both smile. Slick move, Nonna. She didn't have to carry a thing.

In the kitchen I help my grandmother unpack the groceries as Marco drops into a chair and rests his head on his folded arms. He's sweating, his hair damp. He should probably drink some water.

"By the way, Nonna," I say, taking out a box of crackers and putting them in a cabinet, "if Dad tells me it's all right, I'm going out tonight with some girls from town. I wanted to let you know because I know it's breaking your rules. I don't want you to worry, though. I'll be careful."

"I'm not worried about you so much," she says, removing cans of crushed tomatoes and lining them up. "Your brain seems to work. But with the state of things, perhaps Marco should stay home."

"My brain works," Marco says, sounding offended as he lifts his head.

Nonna turns back to him, assessing him as if trying to decide whether that's true. He straightens up with effort. "Then act like it," Nonna mutters, and begins to empty another bag.

"Actually, Nonna," I say, curious, "do you know a girl named Minnow? She wanted me to tell you hello last night."

Nonna goes very still, and then she rolls up the empty bags and stuffs them into a drawer. "No," she says simply. "No, I don't know any person named that."

Why do I get the sense she's lying? "You sure?" I ask. "I thought maybe she knew you."

"Of course I'm sure," she says, turning to me, her dark eyes narrowed. "Now stop asking questions that I've already answered."

I hold up my hands in surrender. When I look at Marco, he widens his eyes to confirm that she overreacted. I finish putting away the groceries and then drag Marco with me to the living room, where we both drop onto the couch.

I find Minnow's number in my phone. I'm sure my father will be fine with me going out with her tonight. In fact, he'll probably be happy I made a friend.

I'd love to go out tonight, I write.

After a moment, she responds. *Perfect. Pick you up after sunset.*

With my plans made, I put my phone aside and glance over at my brother. He's rubbing his temples, his coloring off, skin waxy and pale.

"Still not feeling better?" I ask.

He slowly turns to me, his eyes kind of glazed, his lips really pale. "I'll be fine," he says. "Don't worry about me. I probably just need some protein." He forces a smile and turns back to the television. But I watch him a moment longer.

Then, without saying much else, we binge-watch some re-runs of *The Office* on Nonna's streaming channel. And I wait for the sun to go down.

CHAPTER FIFTEEN

have no idea what to wear and my options are severely limited. I'm also having a tragically bad hair day. I consider calling Willa, but she's out with her girlfriend. I could call one of the other girls on the team, but really, I don't trust their opinions in the same way. Hannah or Jackie will just tell me to contour.

I end up in black T-shirt, one that I tie in the back to make it fit a little better, and faded jeans. To tame my frizz, I slick down my curls, leaving the ends a bit crunchy with gel. All in all, it's not too bad.

It's nearly ten when I head downstairs. I grab my zip-up hoodie and glance out the entryway window. The sun has just set, casting the horizon in a beautiful orange glow.

I look into the living room and my dad is on the sofa with Nonna, while Marco is in the recliner, his head heavy against its back. They are watching *CSI*.

"You look nice, Theo," my father says with a smile. I appreciate that he noticed.

My dad didn't get back home today until close to dinnertime. No explanation. He was quiet, introspective, so neither Marco nor I asked any questions. However, he did tell Marco about Olivia Miles on his own and my brother pretended like it was the first time he'd heard of her.

Marco picks up his head to peek over at me from the recliner. He nods that I look fine and then lies back down. He's been lying around all day. It's like his hangover has gotten worse instead of better. But he's said, repeatedly, that he's fine.

"Shouldn't be out too late," I tell my dad. "And thanks for letting me go."

"I want you to like it here," he says earnestly. "There's a lot to love about Nightfall. You'll see."

Nonna huffs and then picks up the remote and turns up the volume on her show. I stare at the back of her head, frustrated. She's so mean sometimes. I'm trying to understand her perspective, but it's not like she's trying to explain.

I walk out into the entryway. Just as I pull on my sneakers, a horn beeps outside. There's a little jolt of anticipation in my stomach.

"I'll text you when I find out where we're going," I call to my dad. "Bye."

I open the front door, a cool wind blowing around me when I do. Although the rain has been holding off all day, I'm slightly worried that it might finally start while we're out.

In the driveway, the girls are waiting in a flashy black convertible with the top down. Beatrice is driving, her blond hair styled in an impossibly high bun, and Annemarie is in the passenger seat, her gorgeous curls wild around her face. Minnow sits on top of the backseat, half out of the car, and waves for me to hurry up.

"Come on," she calls, smiling. "We're going to be late."

I dash toward the car and wait to be let in, but Beatrice doesn't move, an amused grin on her face.

"Jump in," Minnow says, tapping the side of the car. "You've got this."

I awkwardly climb into the back, trying not to let my shoes touch the seat. I nearly eat shit but make it without too much drama. Starting off cool.

I look up at Minnow, who's still perched on top of the seat.

"Late for what?" I ask her, settling myself in the backseat. "I still don't know where we're going."

Minnow flashes me a smile. "We're going to meet the others. They're waiting on us."

"What others?" I ask.

"Everyone," she replies, wiggling her fingers. "It's the week of the Dive. We have so much to plan."

Then Minnow drops down next to me and she smells wonderful. She's wearing bright yellow eye shadow, expertly applied, hoop earrings, and a choker. Her off-the-shoulder top matches her eye shadow. I really need her to take me shopping.

"Hold on," Beatrice says, and steps on the gas, shooting us back out of the driveway and into the street at full speed without checking traffic. A car skids to a stop before nearly T-boning us and blares its horn. I scream, ducking down.

Beatrice laughs, shifts into gear, and takes off down the road.

My heart is in my throat, but when I look at Minnow, she's still smiling. "Bea is an absolute psycho," she tells me, "but you're going to have a blast."

"Yeah, if I survive," I murmur, icy wind whipping my hair against my face.

Beatrice's driving doesn't improve, and I find myself huddled in the back while she speeds through the residential streets, music blasting.

Minnow holds out a flask. "Take a sip," she says. "It'll help."

I hesitate. "What is it?" I ask, worried. I definitely don't want to end up like my brother.

"What do you mean?" Minnow asks, looking at the flask. "It's sambuca—can't you smell it?"

I'm surprised that they're drinking my father's favorite liqueur. It smells like black licorice, and the scent stings my eyes when I take the flask.

I'm not my brother—I know my limits. I decide to start off with a little sip to help calm my nerves. I take a drink and the liquid slides down my throat, coating it in sweet warmth. Annemarie reaches back to pluck the flask from my hand and takes a drink.

As I smack my lips, I'm immediately calmed. But it doesn't last long. Beatrice takes a sharp turn onto Main Street, knocking me into Minnow, who laughs like this is just the best time ever. I feel a lot more like an unwitting accomplice in a high-speed car chase, and I grip the back of the front seat and hold on.

Downtown is relatively quiet—it *is* after dark. Beatrice races up the hill, sending us airborne with each rise and dip of the street. I'm about to ask her to slow down when she swings the car into an alleyway, the tires crunching on gravel. We slip between two candy-colored buildings into a parking lot you can't see from the street.

Beatrice slams on the brakes, launching me forward before Minnow reaches effortlessly to grab my shirt and pull me back.

"First stop—ice cream sundaes," Beatrice announces. She and Annemarie grin at each other before they climb out of the car. "Then, the beach," she adds.

"Are we going to Sunrise Beach again?" I ask.

Minnow laughs. "Of course. Every night until the Dive.

It's tradition. But it's going to be a chill night. Just locals. Well, locals and you." She grins.

Although I know what Elijah and Felix told me are just stories, the intrusive thoughts slide in. Tradition? Like drowning people? I almost bring it up, but then Minnow hops out from the backseat, chatting with the other girls and waving for me to hurry.

I'm not going to let a podcast ruin my night, so I follow them, glad when Minnow throws her arm over my shoulders and pulls me into the group. It feels incredible to be one of them. And to prove it, the back door of the ice cream shop swings open as we walk up, followed by a gleeful shout.

"The girls are here," Sparrow calls. "What took you so long?" she asks Annemarie.

"Sorry," Annemarie says, giving Sparrow a quick kiss on the cheek as she passes her in the doorway. "We were picking up a new recruit."

Annemarie surprises me by grabbing my hand to tug me forward and Sparrow closes the door behind us.

"I'm so happy you're with us tonight," Annemarie tells me. "We're making plans for the parade this weekend. It's going to be the best one yet."

She keeps hold of my hand and I follow her down the long hallway, heading into the main lobby of the ice cream shop. Melodic piano music is playing, and the sweet smell of vanilla and caramel hangs in the air. I'm suddenly very much craving a sundae.

Erika the cashier is in the lobby. She holds up her hand in hello when she notices me. But like the first time I was here, she's a bit distracted. I'm going to ask Minnow about her later.

"What can we get you?" Annemarie asks, walking behind the counter as Erika watches. "Chocolate?" she asks. "Something more daring?"

"Uh . . ." I feel self-conscious as all the girls watch to see what I choose. "Surprise me," I say.

Annemarie grins. "Great answer," she replies. She grabs the ice cream scoop and starts making a sundae. Tentatively, I look at Erika and find her watching me.

"Sit down," Minnow tells me, appearing at my side. "Annemarie will get us all set up."

Minnow pulls out a chair at one of the tables and I join her, quickly followed by Beatrice. Sparrow joins Annemarie behind the counter, twisting a strand of her blue hair around her fingers as they talk quietly.

I take a moment to look around. Inside this pastel-colored shop, all the girls appear too . . . bold. It's like seeing a supermodel in the grocery store instead of in a magazine. Or like a mirage in the desert. I have no idea why they would find me so interesting.

Beatrice looks mockingly at Erika. "What is your problem?" she asks impatiently. "You've been miserable all week."

Erika's lips part like she's about to argue, when Annemarie appears at our table with a tray of sundaes, blocking Erika from view.

"She's just been working too hard," Annemarie answers for her. "She forgets to have a life outside of Scoops." She passes out the sundaes. "But don't worry," she adds, dropping the empty tray to her side. "She's going to help with the parade. She always does."

"I said I would and I'm here," Erika points out. "Don't act like I'm the one being difficult."

Minnow glances over at her and the room falls quiet. There is a sudden tension in the air.

"Anyway," Annemarie says, waving away the silence. "Let's figure out who's doing what. The sheriff told me he expects more tourists than ever this week. Pretty sweet."

"Yummy," Beatrice replies, swirling her spoon through her strawberry sundae.

As the rest of them start discussing the logistics of the parade, I devour the chocolate and rainbow sherbet mash-up Annemarie created for me. It's inexplicably delicious. The entire weekend honestly sounds like a blast. There will be the parade, live music, and food trucks. And then, of course, the Midnight Dive. Again, I'm tempted to bring up Nightfall's history, but they're all taking it so seriously. I don't want to offend them.

"I nominate Theo to join us as the leads in the parade," Minnow announces. She turns to me. "We're the ones who bring the crowd to the water, sort of like . . . like the queens of the Dive. You'd be perfect. We dress up like mermaids. Everyone loves us." She laughs.

"Yes, Theo!" Annemarie says. "I think that's a great idea."

"Oh . . ." I look around at them. "Um, sure. If that's okay. I know I don't live here or anything."

"No problem," Annemarie says. "We usually have a few tourists mixed in. But only our favorites." She grins at the other girls.

Okay, I'm pretty flattered to be a favorite.

"What about Asa?" Erika asks, earning a sharp look from Annemarie. "Will he be joining us in the parade?"

"No," Annemarie replies after a moment. "No, actually he headed back to Joshua Tree this morning. He didn't really fit in here."

"He was kind of mopey," Sparrow says, sounding bored.

"I liked him," Beatrice says, licking her spoon. "He was super cute. It could have worked. You were just impatient."

Annemarie smiles kind of wistfully. "Probably right," she says. "I do like pretty things." The others laugh. "But like I said, he wasn't the right fit. Oh well." She turns to me with a shrug. "Now back to Theo," she continues. "I think you'll be awesome in the parade."

"Perfect," Minnow agrees. She stands up. "Well, now that it's settled, let's get to partying." She looks around at the other girls. "Sparrow, why don't you help Erika close up here and meet us at the beach?" She turns to Erika, her expression cooling slightly. "Will you be joining us tonight, Erika?" she asks.

The cashier holds her gaze. "No," she says simply. Minnow swallows hard, her eyes narrowed.

"Suit yourself," Beatrice says brightly, getting up from her chair. "You're always such a buzzkill anyway, Erika. You'd think by now you'd learn to live a little."

Erika smiles sweetly and flips her off. Everyone laughs, breaking the tension. The girls toss away their empty ice cream cups, still talking about the parade.

Despite Erika, everyone seems to be on the same page. To be honest, I feel better about how cold she's been to me. She's kind of that way with her friends, too.

And I'm actually excited. Being a queen of the Dive sounds like a blast. It definitely feels nice to be so accepted, so included. I'm grinning madly as I follow Minnow and the others out of the ice cream shop. On the way, Minnow hands me the flask again, and I take an eager sip.

CHAPTER SIXTEEN

Beatrice is back behind the wheel and as terrifying as ever. But when we get onto the Pacific Coast Highway, the world seems to open up. We can see the ocean below us, and the cars whipping past us lessen, until we seem to be all alone on the highway. Minnow and I pass the flask again.

With each turn, the convertible swerves a little, the tires slipping on the pavement. The road is winding, and I'm honestly afraid we're going to go over the side. Crash into the oncoming waves.

I lean forward to hold on to the front seat, balancing myself as my hair lashes against my cheeks. Beatrice turns to look at me. Our faces close.

"You look scared, Theo," she whispers playfully. "Where's your sense of excitement?" She turns back to the road. "Don't you know that danger gets the blood pumping?"

"And it'll keep you young!" Annemarie adds, grinning at me.

I want to agree, but in all honesty, my gut is knotted up with fear. I wish I could be as carefree as they are. Some days, it feels like the weight of the world is on me, but what if I could . . . if I could just let go?

Just then, Annemarie grabs the edge of the windshield to pull herself up, standing in the wind as it blows her dark hair violently. She closes her eyes, lifts her arms in the air, and screams. The other girls cheer.

Startled, I put my hand protectively on Annemarie's hip, hoping I'll be able to hold her down if we take a sharp turn so she doesn't go flying out of the car.

"Aw, come on," Minnow says, pulling my hand away. "Try it!"

"Are you—?" I start to ask if she's serious, but without missing a beat, Minnow stands up in the oncoming wind. She drags me to my feet next to her.

The wind knocks me back at first and the girls laugh. I can barely catch my breath, my lungs filling up with salty sea air. We have to be driving at least eighty miles per hour. Minnow grabs me again, this time holding me up as I keep a death grip on the back of Beatrice's headrest.

"Be free, Theo," Minnow calls, her hand on my back. She looks at me, looks *into* me. I get lost in her eyes and forget about the danger. "It's okay to let go," she says, echoing my earlier thoughts. "I've got you!"

I don't want to, but my throat is still warm from the alcohol, her pressure on my back strong enough to reassure me. So I let go and lift my arms in the air, closing my eyes.

And for a moment, I'm weightless, like I'm a bird gliding on a breeze. The world dissolves around me, my troubles far away. Annemarie screams again, and when I open my eyes, I scream with her.

After I fall back into the seat, laughing and exhilarated, Minnow passes me the flask. I take another sip, this one going down easier, before passing it forward to Annemarie. My pulse is racing, and I don't even mind the cold air anymore. I feel alive—truly alive. I'm so outside my comfort zone that I can't even find it anymore.

I look to my right at the ocean and recognize the massive boulders of Sunrise Beach jutting out of the water.

Beatrice takes a sharp turn off the highway and we begin bumping down a sandy road. She drives straight onto the beach, and I'm surprised when there's no bonfire already roaring, no crowds of tourists. I wonder where everyone is. Maybe we're early.

After she parks, Beatrice opens the door and folds up the seat so I don't have to jump over the side. The gesture catches me off guard, but I'm definitely grateful. The alcohol has left me a bit buzzy and I don't want them to think all Maggiones are lightweights.

The sand is soft under my feet and I have the urge to take off my sneakers and walk barefoot. The air is misty this close to the water, almost otherworldly. Or maybe my head is just swimming away. When Minnow offers the flask, I take another sip.

We start toward the driftwood where the bonfire was the night before. Beatrice and Annemarie are on either side of me, Minnow just ahead.

"Do you love it here?" Beatrice asks me, her frilly pink dress blowing wildly around her legs. "Nightfall is just perfect, isn't it?"

Minnow looks back over her shoulder, anticipating my answer.

"It's really nice," I agree. "Beautiful. But I like the sun way too much to live here," I add. "I love Phoenix."

"Yeah, but your dad's from here," Annemarie says. "Born and bred." She grins at the others.

Minnow spins around to walk backward, facing us. "I bet

your dad misses it," she says. "And Marco told me that he'd live here in a second if he could. So maybe you should consider moving."

"Who's thinking of moving to Nightfall?" a voice says from behind us. I turn and am startled to see Parrish. I hadn't heard him come up, although I guess the sand muted his footsteps. How did he even get here? There's no other car on the beach.

"Parrish!" Beatrice calls out happily, beaming at him. "You're late."

He glances nervously at me before answering Beatrice. "Just got dropped off," he tells her, not matching her enthusiasm. "The others have the supplies."

I'm slightly disoriented, a bit confused that Beatrice was expecting him. I turn to Minnow. "I thought this was a girls' night?" I ask quietly.

"It is," she says. "Parrish just shows up sometimes." She darts a pointed look at him, and then turns to walk forward again. "Even when he's not invited."

"Theo's father is from Nightfall," Beatrice explains, taking Parrish's arm to drag him into step next to us. "And we think he should stay permanently. And that Theo and her brother should join him. What do you think?"

"You're actually thinking of moving here?" he asks, sounding alarmed. Beatrice yanks him slightly closer to her.

"Yes! She's going to lead the Dive with us," she announces. "She's going to be one of us."

"No," I say with a laugh. "I'm not planning on moving here," I tell Parrish. "My life is in Arizona."

"Maybe you'll change your mind," Minnow says. "This place can be pretty convincing."

Before I can argue, Beatrice drops Parrish's arm and goes

running ahead in a fit of mad laughter. She does a cartwheel, the fabric of her dress floating in the air around her.

The other girls clap. I smile as she does a roundoff and then bows to us formally, one arm tucked against her waist. She beckons the other girls.

"Come on, Minnow!" she calls. "Annemarie!"

And then the three girls are racing ahead, taking turns flipping in the sand. Parrish stays next to me.

"I'm surprised to see you hanging out with them," he says, motioning to the others. "How exactly did that happen?"

"Minnow called me," I say. "And honestly, she seems really cool, so I said yes."

I turn and smile at him, but he's watching the girls. There's a mix of admiration and contempt in his expression. I can't really tell if he likes them.

"I have to ask," I start, a bit nervous. "Are you dating Beatrice? Because—"

Parrish laughs. "Dating? God, no." He shakes his head. "Nothing like that. And as for the others, I met them two summers ago. Sort of got pulled into their crowd. If you end up staying, you'll be hanging around with them all the time, too. No other choice."

"What do you mean by that?" I ask. Yeah, there is definitely some disapproval there.

"Let's just say they run the social calendar around here," Parrish replies. "Nothing happens without them planning or knowing about it." He pauses a long moment before seeming to realize that I'm watching him. He smiles shyly. "Small-town life, I guess," he adds.

"But you're friends with them?" I ask, still wondering.

"Absolutely," he says definitively. "Didn't mean to make it seem . . ." He waves off the thought.

I let the topic drop, but I'm relieved to hear that he's not with Beatrice. There's real potential here. I can't wait to tell Willa.

"Hope no one's waiting up for you tonight," Parrish says, bumping his shoulder into mine gently. "Not sure if the girls mentioned, but we stay out kind of late."

I smile at him. "I think I can hang," I say.

"I'm sure you can, Arizona," he says, sliding his hands into his pockets. "I'm just not sure you'll want to."

"There they are!" Beatrice calls from up ahead, pointing to a group of people coming down a sand dune.

I recognize Sparrow's blue hair immediately. She's holding a beach bag and is with two guys who have a cooler. A guy carrying a huge pile of driftwood crests the hill, and I laugh when I see he's wearing a Wombats T-shirt.

I gasp dramatically and look sideways at Parrish, motioning toward the guy. "I want that shirt," I say. "It is, like, number one priority."

Parrish laughs. "I'll get you one," he says. "But avoid Jerry," he adds lightly. "He's a real dickhead."

"Noted," I say. "Well, time for a bonfire?"

"Yep," Parrish says, sighing as if he'd rather be anywhere else. "Looks like the party's all here."

He cuts away from me and heads toward the group setting up behind the driftwood. I come to a stop in the sand, watching him go. I don't get it. He's hot and cold, hard to read. I'm reminded of my brother's description of him: the one with the sad eyes.

But then the buzz of alcohol continues to work though my veins, relaxing my muscles and dulling the social anxiety that would normally be there. I'm in a new place with new people, and yet, I feel like I could be . . . one of them.

"Theo," Minnow sings out from up ahead. "Join us!"

And I jog to catch up with them.

CHAPTER SEVENTEEN

When I reach Minnow, she grabs my hands and then we're spinning in the sand. The wind catches my hair, blowing it around my face, the scene blurred out behind dark curls. I'm laughing, feeling free and wild. I can't remember the last time I've felt this untroubled and carefree, all my sadness and worry somewhere else.

We stop, and Minnow drops to the sand on her back. I do the same, trying to catch my breath. I gasp a few more times before I'm able to slow my breathing.

Minnow sits up. "Oh, good," she says. "The fire's almost ready. Let's go get a spot."

She pulls me to my feet and then we cross toward the driftwood. Beatrice and Annemarie are already there. Everyone is talking; they clearly know each other well. I'm glad Minnow is at my side as we approach, slipping me easily into their world.

When we get on the other side of the driftwood, the sand slopes downward and the air is less blustery. Parrish is adjusting some of the wood while the big guy in the Wombats shirt holds a bottle of lighter fluid and a pack of matches.

I settle in the sand in front of the bonfire and Minnow sits next to me. Beatrice and Annemarie quickly move to her other side. I kind of like that she chose to sit next to me; it makes me feel . . . special. Minnow passes me the flask and I take a sip.

"Sorry we put you on the spot there," she says. "About moving here. It's just that I like Marco. And I like you. I get tired of the others sometimes," she admits quietly. "It would be fun if you stuck around for a while."

Minnow meets my eyes and a splash of warmth flows over me. A vanilla-scented blanket wrapped around me, cozy and soft.

"If you just gave us a chance," she says, her voice humming in my ear, a drum beating along with my heart. "You could forget about home," she adds. "About your mother. About your loneliness. All you have to do is give us the opportunity to show you what it could be like to rule this place."

"What?" I ask, my voice sounding far away. I can feel the flask in my hand, but it's too heavy for me to lift. My body is weighted down, rooted and still. Minnow takes the flask from me and sips, her eyes smiling. "How did you know about my mother?" I ask, and then start laughing. It sounds so silly. She laughs, too.

A big gust of wind whips my hair around my face. I close my eyes against the blowing sand, raising my hands for protection. When the wind settles, I turn back to Minnow, but she's gone. She's on the other side of the bonfire pit now, talking to Parrish. The guy in the Wombats shirt is repeatedly striking a match, the scraping sound loud in my ears. The fire won't catch; the wind keeps blowing it out.

I'm disoriented and my head is fuzzy. When did Minnow walk away? I can't remember what we were talking about, but whatever it was it left me with a mixture of laughter and an overwhelming sense of loss. Did I lose something?

Suddenly, I want my phone. But when I check, it's gone. Did I bring it? I can't remember. It hits me that I never texted my father. No one knows where I am right now.

I stand up, swaying, but I catch myself before I fall. I've only had a few sips of alcohol; how could I be so unsteady already? Was it only a few sips?

The fire bursts to life in a wild explosion of orange heat. The small group cheers and I smile as the warmth radiates forward, drawing me close.

Beatrice appears next to me and wraps her arm around my shoulders as the rest of the girls close in around me. She smells like black licorice, I decide—like sambuca. Something sweet and slightly unappealing in an inexplicable way.

"You look beautiful tonight," Annemarie calls to me. "I'm glad you're here." Next to her, Minnow nods her agreement.

I smile. "Thank you," I say. "I'm having fun."

They laugh and glance at each other. The guy in the Wombats shirt waves hello to me, while the others at the party stay on the edges of the fire, drinking and chatting. One of the guys has a guitar and strums a few chords.

We sit around the flames as the world dances and I lose track of what I was thinking. It's a blur of smiling faces, strangers laughing and drinking.

Parrish comes by and whispers in my ear.

"Are you okay?" he murmurs, his breath cool on my skin. Tingles race down my neck, almost as if he's tracing a line there.

"I'm definitely okay," I say, closing my eyes as I lean into him. But then he's gone again.

I'm enjoying the night. Enjoying being part of the group.

And then Minnow is there, staring right into my eyes. "See how much fun you have with us?" she asks, her smile stretching wide. A little wider. "We could do this all the time," she says. I nod.

There is a loud crack as a log of wood splits, sending up sparks. All of us jump, startled. I blink quickly, a bit disoriented. Instinctively I reach into my pocket again for my phone, and instead touch a still-damp ten-dollar bill—the one my grandmother gave me last night. I forgot about it.

I'm about to joke about her eccentric gift, but when I glance around again, the people look slightly different. Annemarie's beautiful hair is patchy, singed off and missing chunks in places. Sparrow has deep cuts in her face, slashing through her cheeks and exposing her teeth. Jerry is staring at the fire, his brown eyes completely white.

I have a flash of terror. Quickly, I dart a look at Parrish and find him watching me, his skin sallow and slightly grayed. His hair is wet. He tilts his head, as if studying me. He swallows hard.

"Theo," Minnow says, taking my shoulders and turning me toward her.

Disoriented, I reach up to put my hand on my forehead, my vision blurred, my head swimming. And then I look up to find Minnow smiling at me, asking if I'm okay. When I turn to the party again, everyone is back to normal. Parrish is drinking a beer, his complexion rosy in the firelight.

I definitely drank too much.

"Actually," I say, turning back to Minnow. She meets my eyes, seeming eager to help. "Do you . . . do you know where

I can use the bathroom?" I have to go, but I also want a little break. I'm feeling overwhelmed and some air might help.

"Oh," she says, and points in the direction of the sand dunes. "There are restroom stalls up there. Want me to go with you?"

"I'm good," I say. But when I stand up, I'm unsteady. Minnow grabs my arm. "I'm so sorry," I say, flushing with embarrassment. "I should stop drinking."

"I think so," she agrees, brushing my hair back over my shoulders. "We wouldn't want another incident like what happened to your brother out here. But you're already faring much better," she confides.

"I'm glad," I say with a note of triumph in my voice. "Okay, I'll be right back."

Minnow's hand lingers on my shoulder a second longer as if she doesn't want me to leave. But then I break free and head toward the dunes. Just as I start to walk between the hills, I look back at the party and find Minnow, Beatrice, and Annemarie all watching me. I'm in a fog, a haze. Beatrice begins inching in my direction, but Parrish steps in front of her. She pokes her finger into his chest, her mouth a sneer as Parrish shakes his head, responding to her in a hushed whisper.

I'm curious about what they're arguing about, but I don't want to stare. I start toward the restrooms again. Just on the other side of the first dune, I see a green building nestled in the corner of a small parking lot along the highway. I stumble once in the sand, but catch myself, glad that no one saw.

And then my gait becomes steadier. Although I'm still buzzed, the farther I get from the party, the more the fog in my head begins to dissipate. I also realize how strangely I was acting back there, the embarrassing way I was just floating, not a care in the world. The way I leaned closer every time Parrish came near.

I am definitely done drinking whatever is in that flask.

Just as I pass the last sand dune heading up to the parking lot, a glint of light catches my eye. I stop and stare. It's high up in the dune, and I can't make out what it is. Curious, I head toward it, realizing for the first time how bright the full moon is.

As I get closer to the object, it continues to flash in the moonlight like a piece of metal. I climb the sand dune to get a better look, crawling on my hands and knees to keep from sliding back down.

What is it?

I get close and stare directly at the object. It takes me a moment to realize what I'm looking at. It's circular, metal—it's a watch. But . . . wait. My eyes widen and a scream starts in my throat.

Because the watch is still attached to an arm.

There is a white arm poking out of the sand, hairy and slightly bloated. Definitely dead. And there are several punctures—bite marks?—dotting the skin.

My scream tears free as I recoil, losing my balance. I tumble backward down the dune and I slam down hard on my back on the sand, the wind knocked out of my lungs. I gasp, and then I scramble to my feet and run back toward the party.

Annemarie appears first, materializing out of the darkness. I can't see the others. She holds up one hand calmly.

"Whoa, are you okay?" she asks, worried. "You're screaming bloody murder out here."

"I need your phone," I say. My voice is shaking so much it's difficult to get the words out. "Can I please use your phone?"

"Of course," she says, taking it out of her bra. "Whatever you need."

I grab the phone from her and dial 911. An operator picks up, but immediately puts me on hold. I can't believe this is happening. I can't believe this is real.

Parrish comes jogging over, Beatrice close at his side.

"We heard you screaming," he says. "Did something happen?" He looks accusingly at Annemarie, but she only shrugs.

The phone is picked up. "This is the sheriff's office," a male voice says.

"Yes, hi," I say, ignoring the others. "I'm out at Sunrise Beach and . . . and there's a dead body in the sand. A guy, I think."

The line is quiet for a moment.

"What's your name?" the man asks. He doesn't sound worried. There is no urgency.

"Oh . . . it's Theo Maggione," I say. "And I'm serious. I just found a body. Can you come . . . get him?" I ask, not sure what else to say.

When I look up, several more people from the party have arrived, all of them watching me. Annemarie's mouth is set in a concerned frown; Beatrice stares at me questioningly. I'm still buzzed, but I don't understand why no one else is freaking out. *I just found a body.*

"Thank you for your call, Miss Maggione," the man on the phone says. "The sheriff will be out there shortly."

The line goes dead.

I lower the phone from my ear, dazed. Was that it? No follow-up questions or advice? He didn't even offer to stay on the phone until the sheriff arrived.

"Mind if I get my phone back?" Annemarie asks, holding out her hand.

Still shaking, I pass it to her, unsure what to do next. And why does no one else seem bothered by this?

"I'm sorry to ask, Theo," Annemarie says, watching me closely. "But are you sure you really saw a dead body?" Behind her, Sparrow smiles.

"Yes," I say, horrified. I can see still the bloated wrist, skin swollen under the watch.

"Where was he?" Beatrice asks, coming closer. "You might be confused. You've had a lot to drink."

"I'm not confused about this," I say, trying to be clear. "He was right over there." I point behind me. "In the sand dune by the restrooms."

"Yeah?" she asks. "Then who was it?"

"How would I know?" I say, incredulous. "I don't live here. And I didn't see a face. Just . . . just an arm. It was sticking out of the sand."

"Oooh . . . ," Wombats guy says like it's a joke, and looks over at Parrish.

"Mind if I go check?" Beatrice asks me. Another step closer.

She smiles then, and I'm sure that she doesn't believe me. I'm growing frustrated and a little sick. The alcohol in my stomach has made me uneasy. Unsteady.

"Knock yourself out," I say, waving her off. "But maybe don't touch the body."

She laughs. "Thanks for the forensic advice. I'll try not to."

I rub at a dull throb that has started in my temples. This is insane. When I lift my head again, the others are still just standing around. Shouldn't they be calling someone too? Looking around for clues? I don't know what you're supposed to do when you find a dead body. It feels strange to just . . . wait here.

Both Beatrice and Annemarie start for the sand dune to investigate, glancing at me as they pass. The others chat among themselves; Sparrow looks over at me with an amused grin.

Do they think this is a prank? Do they not care? What is wrong with these people?

Parrish comes up to me and puts his palm on my forearm. Instinctively, I place my hand over his. "I'm so sorry that happened," he says. "You must be terrified."

"Theo?" Minnow calls, jogging in my direction. She tucks her flask under her arm, her face a portrait of concern. "I heard you screaming while I was by the water," she says worriedly. "Are you okay?" She looks from me to Parrish, pausing a moment at my hand over his.

"We're fine, Minnow," Parrish replies before I can answer. "Except that Theo just called the sheriff because she found a dead body."

"What?" Minnow says, turning to me, eyes wide. "Do we know who it is?"

I'm about to say again that I don't know when Beatrice announces, "It's Greg." I turn around to see her standing there with the watch dangling from her fingertips.

"I told you not to touch the body!" I say, stepping away from Parrish.

"I didn't," Beatrice says, sounding annoyed. "There was no body, Theo. Just this watch. And it belongs to Greg."

"What do you mean there was no body?" I say, baffled. "There was an arm."

She snorts a laugh. "No, it was just the watch. No arm to speak of."

"I don't understand," I murmur. "That's not true, I saw it."

Jerry busts up laughing, and Sparrow throws her hands in the air as if I'd made a big scene for nothing. The others at the party whisper, most likely about me.

And I stand there, stunned.

"I saw it," I repeat, and look at Parrish. He winces, almost like he feels sorry for me. "I have to check," I say, rushing in the direction of the sand dune.

"Theo, wait," Minnow calls after me, sounding exhausted.

But I don't stop. I need to know for myself. There's no way I imagined this.

When I get to the spot, Annemarie is standing there with her hands on her hips. We glance at each other, and she shrugs apologetically. I move past her, climbing up the dune again to where I saw the arm. I start digging, searching. But there's nothing. I find nothing.

I turn back and the others from the party have come to see what's going on.

"It was there," I say to them. "I swear, there was . . ." But I trail off because now that I have an audience, it sounds ridiculous to say there was a body that disappeared. I'm embarrassed, confused.

In the distance, an approaching police siren rings out. Sparrow curses and tells the others to grab the beers and get out of here. I slide down the sand dune, completely beside myself.

"Party's over, I guess," Annemarie tells the others, shooing them with her hands. As they obey, she turns to look back at me.

"I swear," I tell her. "There was . . . it was there."

"It's okay," she whispers, leaning to put her forehead against mine. "We all have our moments. I mean, *who hasn't* found a dead body in the sand after a night of drinking?" She quickly kisses my cheek with a playful laugh before turning to walk through the sand in the direction of the others.

While everyone's leaving, Minnow comes to stop in front of me, a sympathetic expression on her face.

"We should probably go before the cops get here," she says. "I'm not sure you can explain what just happened without telling the sheriff you had a little too much of this." She waggles the flask.

"I wasn't drunk," I say, adamant. "I know what I saw, I just . . ." I look back at the dune, the nothingness there. And even I'm starting to doubt myself. What if it was just the moon reflecting strangely on the sand? A hallucination—just like at the fire when everyone looked different.

"Right," Minnow says, as if her point is made. "Let's go." She turns to Parrish. "You need a ride, too?"

"Yeah," he says.

Minnow looks him over from head to toe and then smirks. "Sure you do," she says.

We follow Minnow, and I occasionally glance back at the sand dune, as if the hand will just slowly start emerging from it again. But nothing like that happens. It was never really there.

We get in the convertible and I'm wedged between Minnow and Parrish in the backseat. Almost like they're monitoring me to prevent any more outbursts. I definitely messed up tonight. I messed up worse than Marco.

Beatrice drives up to the highway, and as we take a left, flashing police lights come into view on the other side of the hill. She heads toward the police car, the top of the convertible still down. As the sheriff's car gets closer, I start to worry that he'll pull us over.

But instead Beatrice and Annemarie stare directly at him as he passes. He's an older man, about my father's age, with ruddy cheeks and thick graying hair. The girls meet his eyes, but then the sheriff looks away and continues toward the beach.

The flashing lights disappear behind us. Minnow laughs to herself and relaxes into the seat next to me. Parrish lets out a held breath. Sitting between them, I'm not struck with the feeling of freedom I had when we first arrived at the beach. Now I'm unsettled, maybe still a little buzzed, but in a way that makes you sick.

Yet the girls seem unaffected by what just happened. In fact, Beatrice is once again speeding down the highway. She even takes a turn standing while Annemarie holds the wheel, her boot pressed on the accelerator.

And then, into the wind, Beatrice screams that the night belongs to us.

CHAPTER EIGHTEEN

When we pull up to Nonna's house, the lights are all off except for the one in the attic. I have no idea what time it is, and I'm not going to ask. I'm not sure if they're angry with me for calling the police earlier, but I definitely feel like I've ruined the night.

Minnow was texting Marco along the way, and apparently he's feeling better and wants to go out. So he'll be taking my spot with them. I want to tell my brother what happened on the beach, but I know he'll laugh it off.

A dull headache thuds between my ears and all I want to do is go to bed and forget the whole night. I'm confused by all of it, still horrified, and also embarrassed for causing such a scene.

I climb out of the backseat, relegated to jumping over the door again. Parrish does the same on the other side.

"Oh, Theo," Minnow calls, getting up on her knees in the backseat. "Your phone." She holds it out to me. "You must have dropped it."

I stare at it for a moment before taking it from her. "Thank you," I say, puzzled. So I did bring it tonight. It was in the car the entire time.

"It was nice to see you again," Minnow adds, smiling gently.

"Thanks for the invite," I tell her, although my cheeks burn with embarrassment. I start for the house again. "I . . . I'm sorry." She nods, as if telling me that she knows.

"Have a good night, Theo," Annemarie calls. "Hope we can do this again soon."

"Bye, now," Beatrice adds, sounding bored. She's wearing the watch I found, the band sliding up and down her forearm as she waves to me. "Who knows, maybe next time we'll find a real body for you." She grins, but I can't force myself to return it.

I continue walking, Parrish at my side.

"They can't help it," he says. "Especially Beatrice. Even if you *did* find a dead person, she would be just as heartless, trust me."

I look over at him. "Thanks for walking me to the door," I say. "You don't have to. I'm . . . I'm so embarrassed."

"Don't be," he says. "You did nothing wrong."

I smile. "I almost feel worse because you were the only one who seemed to believe me."

We climb up the porch stairs and he pauses in front of the door, kicking the toe of his sneaker at the wood slats of the floor. "Of course," he says. "I mean, that should have been the first instinct. Not to, like, steal the watch."

"That's a good point," I say, looking back at Beatrice in the car. I turn to Parrish, appreciative of how kind he is to me. Especially after this.

"Although I'm glad you were there tonight," Parrish says, avoiding my eyes. "Maybe next time . . . next time ask them to hang out during the day, when they're less homicidal."

He looks at me, and there's something between us—attraction, sure. He's gorgeous. But it's more, as if he's trying to tell me something without saying it out loud. I feel it reach into me, pulling on my stomach, drawing me to him, and I move closer.

Parrish licks his lips and holds out his hand. Just as I reach to take it, wanting to be closer, the door flies open.

Marco walks out, stopping abruptly when he sees me and Parrish. "What are you doing out here?" he says, flashing an unwelcoming look at Parrish, who draws back. "Dad's been losing his mind. You never texted him."

"Yeah," I say, shaking my head to clear it. "I forgot my phone in the car. But I see you're feeling better?" I motion to him.

"I feel great," Marco replies. "But it's late, Theo." He looks at Parrish again. "You should let Dad know you're home." He starts past me, and I reach to take his arm.

"Hey," I say, holding him by the elbow. "Be careful tonight, okay? It's been kind of a wild night."

"Sure it has," he says with a laugh. He shakes off my hand, flashing me a wide smile. I stare at him, surprised by how much better he seems. Healthier? No . . . he's pale and has circles under his eyes. But he's radiating energy, like a walking Red Bull.

"What?" he asks, trying to read my expression.

"Nothing," I say, shaking my head. "You just look . . ." I pause, unsure how to describe it.

"Good," Marco finishes for me. "I look good. You can admit it." He blows out a low whistle and then, inexplicably, pulls sunglasses out of his front pocket and slides them on. "See you tomorrow," he adds. He takes off down the steps toward the car of girls.

"Tomorrow?" I repeat. But he holds up his hand in a wave and continues his walk to the car. Okay . . . well, that was strange.

"Sorry about that," I say, turning to Parrish. "My brother is more arrogant than usual tonight."

"I should go before they leave me behind," Parrish says, motioning toward the driveway. "Although that wouldn't be the worst thing," he adds with a smile.

I turn toward the car and find Beatrice staring daggers in our direction.

"On a scale of one to ten, how much do they hate me now?" I ask.

"It's fine, trust me," Parrish says. "They'll get over it. But, listen, I wouldn't be offended if you never hung out with us again." He smiles softly. "Even if you are a queen of the Dive."

I laugh. "I promise that I won't let the power go to my head," I say, feeling the warmth between us. Now that I know there's nothing going on with him and Beatrice, I'm more than a little interested. I hope he feels the same.

Parrish watches me a moment longer, his eyes sad but deep and inviting at the same time. "Maybe I can . . . Can I call you tomorrow?" he asks.

"You really should," I reply. Butterflies flutter in my stomach. This is definitely happening.

A horn beeps, making me jump, and I look angrily at the car. They're going to wake up my grandmother. Annemarie pushes Beatrice's shoulder, as if telling her to knock it off, before offering me an apologetic shrug.

Obediently, Parrish heads back to the convertible. Beatrice beckons him to hurry, her long nails flashing red. Minnow is sitting on the top of the backseat again, Marco next to her like he belongs with them. Like he's always belonged with them.

Parrish hops in the back and leans into the seat cushion, away from the group. Minnow studies him and then smiles at me before waving goodbye. I return the wave awkwardly, feeling somewhat left out. I realize I didn't ask them to bring me home. They cut my night short and are now going out with my brother. That stings a little.

Beatrice turns up the music and pulls out onto the road. The tires squeal as they speed down the street, the girls singing as if they don't have a care in the world.

I go inside, pausing as I shut the door to listen for my father and grandmother, but the house is quiet. My head is throbbing, so I go to the kitchen for some water. There's a plate of cookies in the center of the table and I take one. But it tastes . . . blah. Like sawdust. The alcohol from earlier must have affected my taste buds. I throw the cookie in the trash and sit down to think over tonight's events.

Although I've been drinking, I don't feel drunk. I was definitely disoriented earlier, and I did . . . see things when I was by the fire. But when I found the body in the sand, I felt pretty clear. At least, I thought I did.

I try to retrace my steps and my heart starts racing again, the evening more like a movie I'm watching than an actual event I took part in. I see myself walking along the dunes until I notice the silver watch. I climb up to check it out and find it attached to a clearly dead arm. I start screaming and run to tell the others. Call the police. But when the girls go over to check, there is no body. There never was.

I think back to the start and go over it all again. But each time, I'm sure there's an arm. I can see the hair, the bloated skin, the bite marks. When I went back, it was gone. The body couldn't have been moved that quickly. So it was never there. It was just a watch left behind in the sand.

I'm still confused about the entire situation. I put my hand on my forehead, wishing the pounding would stop. This must have been how Marco felt this morning. It's awful—like the worst hangover in the world.

I get up and grab the bottle of aspirin. I fill a cup with water and gulp down the pills, hoping they act quickly.

With my mind working overtime, I come to another conclusion. When I was with Elijah and Felix today, they talked about bodies on the beach. About Felix's friend with scratches and bites on his arms. They told a pretty good story. A scary one. And then . . . I drank a little.

I sigh, thinking this makes much more sense. "Damn it," I say to myself, embarrassed that I called the cops. I should have put this together sooner.

The horror story got inside my head, and in my haze, my imagination got the best of me.

Wait until I tell Willa. She'll never let me live this down. I check my phone to see if she's texted me and find missed messages from my dad and Marco. I'm not sure when my brother started feeling better, but I'm glad his hangover didn't last forever. Hopefully by cutting the night short, I'll be spared the worst of it.

I turn off the kitchen light and go upstairs. I get into my pajamas and plug my phone into the charger on the nightstand, then search "body found on Sunrise Beach" and scroll through the results. But there's no mention of it anywhere—not on social media or the local news websites either. I consider listening to one of my murder podcasts, but my heart just isn't in it.

Instead, I check the *Scare Me Silly* site for the second episode on Nightfall, but it hasn't dropped yet. I'm not sure if I'm disappointed or grateful. I probably don't need more nightmare fuel before bed.

I set my phone aside. My head still hurts and my body is sore—almost like I've just finished a hard practice. It must have been shock; it tightens your muscles.

It doesn't make sense—even now. I let the questions swirl as the night drags on, my eyes getting heavier until they close altogether. And then, I slip away into sleep.

CHAPTER NINETEEN

I wake up with an intense headache, the room blurry around me. I stay in bed for a long time, processing my condition and trying to recall the night. I remember the girls picking me up in the convertible and drinking from the flask. The invitation to walk in the parade. Then we went to the beach and I watched them do cartwheels in the sand. It gets a bit fragmented after that, but I remember the bonfire blazing to life. Parrish talking in my ear. And then of course, there was a watch in the sand, glinting in the moonlight.

"Oh no," I murmur, rolling over to bury my face in the pillow. I called the cops, thinking I'd seen a dead body. A body exactly like the one the podcast boys described. Of course there was nothing there.

I groan and sit up. Wow. Drinking and hallucinating on girls' night. I really am worse than Marco. Ugh—kill me.

With humiliation weighing me down, I roll over and grab my phone, hoping Willa is awake this early so I can get her advice. I pull the phone free from the charger and am surprised to see I have a text, sent at 3:33 this morning. I don't recognize the number and I click open the message.

Hey, it's Parrish. I couldn't wait until tomorrow. Sleep well, Arizona.

I have a rush of excitement paired with an immediate scan of my memory, trying to figure out when we exchanged numbers. But nothing comes to mind. Still, I smile. I must not have made too bad of an impression.

I'm not sure how to respond to Parrish's text. But ultimately, it's only seven a.m. I don't want him to see me respond the second I wake up. I have to play it a little cooler. And I guess he was right—they do stay out late.

I climb out of bed, get dressed, and head downstairs. My father is on the couch, reading Olivia Miles's latest book, which makes me smile. Normally, he'd be reading *Five Rules for Effective Product Marketing* or something equally dry. This is definitely better for his soul. He looks up when I walk in.

"Morning," he says, and then licks his thumb to turn the page in his book, engrossed.

"Hey there," I say. "Get to the good parts yet?"

He chuckles but waves me away as if I'm bothering him.

"Theodora?" my grandmother calls from the kitchen, drawing my attention.

I walk in and find Nonna at the table having her morning soda. She stares me down.

"You went to the beach again," she says by way of hello. "Same with your brother. There's sand all over my entryway. I told you to avoid that place. We talked about this."

"You also said I had a working brain," I point out, and then smile at her.

"I overestimated your willpower," she says.

"Nonna," I say, "isn't it too early for you to be this mean?"

She must be able to tell I'm not feeling well, because she

softens and gets up from the table and comes over to me. I'm surprised when she brushes my hair back, studying me.

"Let me make you breakfast," she says abruptly. She walks past me and puts a pot on the stove.

Confused but also hungry, I sit at the table and rest my face in my palm, watching Nonna as she begins cutting up vegetables and tossing them into the pot before adding some stock. I have no idea what she's making. At one point, she plucks a purple dried flower from her windowsill, much like the ones out front. She brushes off the petals and twists the hardened stem, knotting it as she forms another little doll. She takes a jar from a cabinet and dips the figure in it, coating it with something that looks like metal.

Rather than complain about the smell, this time I just sigh and indulge her.

I turn to stare out the sliding glass doors, noting how heavily overcast the sky is. I also notice the patchiness of Nonna's yard, especially the dead grass under the old tree. With how meticulous the rest of her garden is, I'm surprised she hasn't torn it up yet. Little dots of rain begin to tap at the glass door.

My grandmother finishes making a soup that she says will fix me right up and sets a bowl in front of me. And then, for good measure, she sets the little stick doll on the table next to my spoon.

IT HASN'T STOPPED RAINING all day and the weather is making me lazy, although my headache is now thankfully gone. The house has been quiet since morning. My dad left while I was eating breakfast, saying he and Olivia were getting coffee near the ocean to *bask in the splendor of Nightfall.* Which sounds like something a romance author would say, I guess. Marco has been in the attic, sleeping off whatever he went through last night. Even Nonna went out to meet her friends for a while, though she's back now. It's not lost on me that even my seventy-year-old grandmother has a better social life than I do.

I sit on the couch, the rain pattering against the living room windows. Nonna and Marco are both upstairs and I'm all alone and bored. None of the girls have texted me. They may never want to hang out with me again. I wonder if I'll still be walking in the parade.

I open Parrish's message again. He seems to be fine with my delusions of dead bodies. I wonder if he listens to murder podcasts too. I decide enough time has passed for me to write him back and I tap out a reply.

Another beautiful day in Nightfall, I write, followed by an umbrella emoji. I chew on my lip, waiting to see if he'll reply.

Paradise, he answers, making me laugh. *Hey, what are you doing right now?*

Not too much. You?

I'm about to head downtown for a bite, he writes. *Feeling up to joining me?*

My heart skips and I smile madly. *Sure,* I reply.

I have to run an errand first, he adds. *But I can meet you in front of Scoops in 20 minutes?*

Sounds good, I reply. Although I'm not sure how I'll get down there just yet. I wonder if Marco could drop me off.

See you then, Parrish writes.

I sit a moment, kind of stunned. Okay, so is this a date? Do I want it to be? I mean, I just met Parrish. We had a very

strange night out together—a few, in fact—that I'm still perplexed about. At the same time . . . I'm not that confused about
him. I like him.

I tap on Willa's name, about to text her to get her opinion,
but realize I don't have the time to explain. I'll call her when I
get home. By then, I might have an actual update to give her.

While I change clothes and run to the bathroom to brush
my teeth, I text Marco to ask him to drop me off downtown.
I'm annoyed when he doesn't answer. It's after three—he should
be up by now. I spit out my toothpaste, frustrated that I'll have
to go all the way to the attic to shake him awake. But as I wipe
my mouth, I hear the downstairs door open and my dad call out
that he's home.

Never mind, I text Marco. *You suck.*

My dad agrees to give me a ride, quiet but seeming content
during the drive. The rain is still falling and I don't have an
umbrella. In fact, I didn't even see one in Nonna's house. I'll
just have to deal with it.

"Right here is fine," I tell my dad, and he double-parks across
the street from Scoops.

He watches me a moment, his lips pursed as if he's debating
something. I smile nervously.

"What is it?" I ask.

He waits another beat and then shakes his head. "Nothing,"
he says. "You have fun. And call me if you need a ride home."

I have the sneaking suspicion he wants to talk to me about
Olivia. I wonder how serious they're getting. Seems pretty fast,
even if they did know each other years ago. Still, I have noticed
how much happier he has been here.

I climb out of the car and put up the hood of my sweatshirt, then dash across the street to stand under the striped awning of Scoops and wait for Parrish. I wave to my father as he drives away.

The lights are on inside the ice cream shop, but the Closed sign is turned face out. When I look in the window, no one is there. The chairs are pushed back from the tables, an empty cup of ice cream still sitting where one of the girls must have left it last night. Doesn't seem like they cleaned up after we met. Strange they're not open yet. Is Erika off today?

"Hi," a voice says next to me.

I turn and find Parrish, his black jacket soaked and his wet hair plastered to his forehead until he rakes his fingers through it to give it some height again. Water drips off his face, yet he still looks incredible.

"I think I may have underestimated the forecast," he says, and then his mouth spreads into a devastating smile. "How are you feeling today?"

"Uh . . . I'm good," I say, nodding as my cheeks flush. Under his attention, this close as the rain falls around us, I'm absolutely smitten. "A bit hungry," I add, motioning down the street. "You had a place in mind?"

"I did," he agrees as if he'd forgotten why we're here. "It's for locals only, really. But I think you'll like it."

I fall into step next to him, and about a block down the street, we stop at a diner called Abigail's Nest. It's set back from the street just a little, entrance on the side of the building down an alleyway.

We go inside. The decor is interesting, to say the least. Mismatched picture frames cover the walls, most of them featuring black-and-white or sepia-toned photos of families or men on farms. There are plants everywhere, wood floors, and a beamed ceiling. A fire, cozy and welcoming, burns in a large stone fireplace in the center of the room.

"What do you think?" Parrish asks.

"This is perfect," I reply, smiling.

"Two?" a server asks abruptly, grabbing menus. She casts an annoyed look at Parrish before turning away and starting into the dining room.

Uncomfortable, I glance at Parrish, but he just shakes his head as if telling me not to worry about it. I wonder if this really is a locals-only kind of restaurant. Despite the chilly reception, I follow the girl to a small table in the back pushed up against a faux-brick wall.

"You order from there," she tells me, pointing to the counter, where a few people are seated. "They'll give you a number and I'll drop the food off. What would you like to drink?"

"I'll have a hot chocolate, please," I say.

"Good choice," she replies.

"I'll get a coffee with—" Parrish starts to say when the girl drags her gaze to him.

"No cream," she replies. "Yeah, I know."

The server leaves, and Parrish laughs to himself and passes me a menu.

"Friend of yours?" I ask, nodding in the direction of the server.

"Sure," he says. "It's just that I come in here a lot with the girls. Beatrice makes a scene sometimes. But hey, breakfast all day," he adds, holding up his menu. "Nothing better on a rainy day like this. I mean, other than clam chowder, but I know Mo's is probably packed right now with tourists. Figured you'd like this better."

"I love it," I say, glancing around. "And I already know what I want," I add, closing my menu. "It's a pancake day."

"I'll go put in the order," he says, getting up and taking the menus with him.

Parrish heads to the counter, and while he's gone, I survey the room again. A toddler in a booth near the fireplace catches my eye. She has red pigtails, freckles, and a polka-dot jacket. Super cute. She's staring dead at me while her parents talk to each other distractedly.

I smile at her and wave. She doesn't smile back. Just . . . stares.

Well, good for her, having boundaries with strangers, I guess. I look away just as Parrish returns, setting a metal stand with a card with the number 26 on the table. The server drops off our drinks and ignores Parrish when he thanks her.

Yikes. Even though I've only hung out with Beatrice a few times, I can imagine what kind of energy she's brought into the place. I'm sure the server has a good reason to not want to fraternize with her, and by extension, Parrish.

My phone buzzes and I take it out. *Mom* flashes on the screen and my conscience nags at me, but I click Ignore and flip the phone facedown on the table, though not before I see Parrish eye the screen.

"Not to be nosy," he says, "but the other night your brother mentioned that you haven't spoken to your mom since she moved in with her boyfriend. How long are you going to do that?"

"Until I'm not pissed off anymore?" I say, a little surprised he's bold enough to bring it up.

"I understand," Parrish says, nodding. "But if you've got some things to resolve there, you might want to consider—"

"I'll deal with it," I say sharply.

He holds up his palms in surrender. "I apologize," he says,

and drops his hands to wrap them around his coffee cup. "It's none of my business."

Which makes me feel like a hot pile of garbage. I shouldn't have snapped. I open my mouth to say just that when the server appears with our food.

She sets down a plate stacked with pancakes and another with eggs and a rare steak. She snatches the number off our table and disappears back into the restaurant, leaving us alone with the tension I created.

"Sorry," I whisper.

Parrish nods that he understands.

"And you're right," I add, watching him cut his steak. "I do need to deal with my mother. But right now, I'm going to destroy these pancakes."

"It's all about priorities," he says, devouring a forkful of meat before winking at me.

I laugh and look down at my napkin, only now realizing that I don't have any silverware. "Damn," I say. "She forgot my fork."

Parrish wipes his mouth and moves to stand, but I stop him.

"I got it," I say, and get up and go to the counter.

When I arrive, I realize that Jerry, the guy from the bonfire in the Wombats T-shirt, is working behind the counter. *Nooo* . . . I immediately regret not sending Parrish for the fork, embarrassed all over again about my colossal overreaction last night.

Jerry takes his time chatting with the server before looking in my direction. When he finally notices me, he chuckles to himself and comes over to the counter, leaning on his elbows in front of me.

"Well, well," he says, grinning. "If it isn't our resident detective. How are you doing on this beautiful day? Tracking down leads?"

I smile sheepishly. "Sorry," I say. "I was having a strange night, and—"

He waves me off. "I'm just messing with you," he says. "You're fine. It's not like we're scared of the sheriff." He laughs. "Now what can I do for you?"

"Can I get some silverware, please?" I motion back to my table, where Parrish is waiting.

Jerry's eyes slide over there, pausing a moment before returning to me.

"Sure thing," he says, reaching under the counter to pull out a napkin-wrapped set. He holds it out to me, but then yanks it back just out of my reach. He smiles. "How long are you in town for again?" he asks.

"For the summer," I say. "My dad's actually from here. We're visiting our grandmother."

This seems to pique his interest. "Practically local," he says. "Well then. I'll be seeing you around, new girl."

He holds out the silverware again. Once I take it, he straightens and knocks once on the counter.

"And be careful with that one," he adds, aiming a finger gun toward Parrish. "He's pretty and all, but a real heartbreaker. Leaves poor Beatrice on read all the time."

I have a flash of insecurity at the mention of Parrish's odd dynamic with Beatrice.

Jerry studies me, before leaning back in with a smile. "You know, if you're just looking for someone to pass the time with, I'm free after dark. It could be our little secret."

"No, I'm good," I reply. I think I just lost my appetite.

Jerry grins and walks away. Parrish was right—Jerry is a dickhead.

I turn and find Parrish watching me, patient even as his food gets cold. I hold up the silverware triumphantly and head back to the table.

CHAPTER TWENTY

Parrish and I eat, and when I'm finished, I lean back in my chair and watch him drink his coffee.

"So," I say, breaking the silence. "How was my brother last night? Did he find any bodies or . . . ?" I smile and Parrish laughs.

"He was in a lot better shape than the first time I met him," he says. "I think he's getting the hang of it. But the rest of the night was pretty boring in comparison."

"Well, I think I figured out my temporary insanity," I offer.

"Do tell," Parrish says, leaning in.

"The other night I met these two guys who have a podcast—*Scare Me Silly*?" I study his face for a sign of recognition, but he just shrugs. "Anyway," I continue, "we had lunch the next day and they told me the history of Nightfall, or at least some really fucked-up version of it. I think it got in my head."

"What did they say?" he asks.

"For starters," I say, "the Midnight Dive. Now it's a parade, but they told me that in the beginning, the mayor of Nightfall would force townspeople to drown girls. Like, they would march down to the ocean, drown their daughters, and then chop off their heads." I flinch at my own words. "And they also said bodies washed up on Sunrise Beach, recently. Plus . . . a friend with bite marks . . ." I motion to my own arm, but I trail off as Parrish's brows pull together in disbelief.

"They told you all that?" he asks.

My stomach sinks. "Yeah," I say, my voice weaker. "Why?"

He pauses. "Because that's kind of a fucked-up story to share when you first meet someone," he says. "Were they trying to scare you?"

"Probably," I admit. "It's a horror podcast, so . . . I just, I mention it because I think that's why I saw the body last night. They described something similar to me, and I think with the drinking and the smoke from the fire, I let my imagination get the best of me. They got inside my head, you know?"

He's quiet for a moment, and then he nods. "That makes sense," he agrees. "And yeah, I'm sure some of it's true. People are animals. But I'm also sure those guys probably exaggerated for their show. I promise," he adds, "you have nothing to be afraid of here."

As he holds my gaze, his eyes are soft and dark, deep enough to draw me in. He licks his lips and then looks away.

"We should go," he says. He takes out his wallet and drops some money on the table before I can offer to split the check. "I was thinking . . . since you like history, there's this awesome museum at the top of the hill if you want to check it out."

Surprised, I get up. "That sounds . . . yeah, that sounds great," I say. I remember the place he's talking about from our drive into Nightfall. I'd figured I'd have to drag my father there.

"But do me a favor," Parrish adds with a soft smile. "Try not to ask anyone there about drowned girls and bite marks."

THE LIVA MUSEUM IS IMPRESSIVE. It's an old mansion that has been preserved and added on to, giving it a charming and vintage atmosphere. There are a few tourists, and Parrish and I take our time going from room to room, admiring the tall ceilings, the ornate furniture, and the homey details, all from another time. There are even paintings of the family still up on the walls.

After that, we hit the gift shop. I buy a key chain souvenir to help support the museum and slip it into my pocket.

"I love that you bought a key chain even though you don't drive," Parrish says. "I could teach you, if you want."

"Yeah?" I ask. "You have a death wish or something?"

He laughs. "You have no idea."

I look him over, trying to decide if I'm interested in his offer. I know I'll learn to drive eventually, but it might be kind of cool to go back to Arizona with a story about the cute boy who taught me while I was in Oregon. Plus, it's finally stopped raining—might be a good time to try.

"Are you sure you want to take on the risk?" I ask, eyeing him to accentuate the danger.

"I am absolutely sure," Parrish replies. "So long as you promise that you won't drown me in the ocean if I'm a bad teacher." I push his shoulder, making him laugh.

When we get outside, Parrish already has his keys in his hand. I smile to myself and hold out the key chain I just bought. It's a picture of the museum with the words *You Should Liva Little* beneath it.

"For you," I say, wagging it in his direction. "Payment for the driving lesson."

"A key chain from my own town?" he asks as he takes it from me. "You shouldn't have." He laughs to himself and slips it onto his key ring. I notice how his finger glides over the plastic, gently, and it feels almost as though he's touching me. My heart is beating quickly. The day is turning out much better than I expected.

"I'm parked just down here," Parrish says, motioning to an alley, and I follow him, taking stock of my situation. It's starting to get a little late, and I know that I should probably check in with my dad, but I don't want the distraction. I like being here right now, in this moment.

Parrish points ahead, and I stop. "Wait," I say. "That's your car?"

Just up ahead is a black Charger, the rims black, the interior black leather. And it is *sharp*—like, movie-quality badass.

"You are not going to let me drive this," I say, turning back to him. He's already holding out the keys. "What if I crash it?"

"Then I'll fix it," he replies. "Now get in."

He presses the keys into my hand and then walks around to the passenger door and gets inside. I stand there another moment, looking around to see if someone is going to stop me before I get into this gorgeous car and wreck it.

"While we're still young, Arizona," Parrish calls out the passenger window, making me laugh.

I open the door, the smell of leather and musk drifting out. It's wonderful. I sit down and the seat surrounds me like a glove. I find the lever to slide it up toward the wheel so I can reach the pedals. When I close the door, I look sideways at Parrish, thrilled and absolutely terrified at the same time.

"Seat belt," he says like a driving instructor.

I click mine in, looking over the impeccable interior. It's not too fancy, no dramatic buttons or extras to confuse me. It's also an automatic, which I'm grateful for.

"Let's turn it on and take her for a spin," Parrish says, sitting back in the passenger seat and looking completely relaxed. I, on the other hand, am terribly anxious.

I put the key in the ignition and turn it. The engine roars to life, startling me with its power. Parrish looks over at me with an amused expression.

"It's just a car," he says. "Don't let her intimidate you. Now put your foot on the brake and shift into drive. Don't let off the brake yet, though."

I do as he directs, feeling the car hum with power. It's a bit intoxicating, the vibration of it, the smooth leather handle when I shift gears.

"Check your mirrors," Parrish says, checking his own. "And when it's clear, ease off the brake and gently, *gently,* Theo, press on the gas." He smiles, his voice patient and honestly not nearly scared enough.

I follow his instructions, and then we're easing forward, out of the alley and onto Main Street. At first I have the steering wheel in a death grip, but as we clear the downtown area and move onto empty wooded streets, my tension eases slightly.

The air from his open window blows through my hair softly, tickling my neck. The car is humming, the temperature cool but almost perfect. I can't seem to keep a consistent speed, but otherwise I'm doing pretty good for my first time.

"You're a natural," Parrish says, watching me. "Think how impressed everyone will be when you get home. Maybe your . . . boyfriend?" he asks, laughing a little as if embarrassed.

"I'm not seeing anyone," I tell him, feeling heat in my cheeks.

"That's good to know," he says, resting his head against the seat and watching out the windshield. "I might have been a little jealous if you were."

MY DRIVING LESSON ONLY LASTS about an hour. We cut it short because Parrish has more errands to run, which he is completely nonspecific about. He's mysterious but also kind and self-deprecating in an attractive way.

It's around five when I pull into my grandmother's driveway. Her minivan is there, but my father's car isn't. Maybe he's the one who should be checking in with us.

"So will I see you at the bonfire tonight?" Parrish asks as I turn off the car and hand him the keys.

"I don't think so," I say, shaking my head. "I'm still recovering from last night. But maybe tomorrow."

To be honest, the beach doesn't sound all that inviting anymore. I'd rather stick around home tonight, listen to some podcasts and talk to Willa on the phone. I need time to think over this afternoon with Parrish, do a real analysis of it.

"That's too bad," he says. "But I get it. I'll . . . Is it okay if I text you tomorrow?" He suddenly looks doubtful.

"I'd definitely blame my driving if you didn't," I say with a smile.

He sighs, relieved. "Then I'll text you," he says. "And seriously, you did a decent job today. Could be a professional, easy win at Daytona."

I get out of the car as he climbs out and meets me at the driver's-side door. For a second, we stand there awkwardly, and then I slip past him and walk toward the front porch.

"Have a good night, Arizona," he calls after me. "And thank

you for the wonderful day. It's been a long time since I've had one of those."

I smile and look back him, momentarily troubled by the sadness in his expression. He gets in his car and the engine roars to life, leaving me to sort out my emotions.

I walk inside and I'm greeted by the buzz of the oven timer going off. The house smells fantastic, and the scent is emanating from the kitchen. Before I close the front door, I catch a glimpse of my father pulling into the driveway, arriving home too. Perfect timing.

I wait for him at the door, and he smiles when he sees me.

"Theo," he calls. "How's it going?" He jogs up the porch steps, touching my arm as he passes into the house.

"I'm good," I say. "Had a nice afternoon with a friend. We went to the museum and he gave me a driving lesson."

My father turns to me curiously. "Okay," he says, as if waiting for more details. "This friend—who is he?" he asks. "Because I don't like the liability of you driving around with strangers, Theodora. Legally it's a nightmare."

"A local kid," I say. "His name is Parrish. And we just drove around here. Didn't even try to parallel park, I swear."

He nods, as if thinking that over. "And your brother?" he asks, shrugging out of his coat. "Have you talked to him today?"

"No," I tell him. "I actually haven't seen Marco. In fact, he's probably still in his room."

My father's relaxed expression falters. "All day?" he says. Immediately, he sets his jacket down and we both head toward the stairs to find Nonna making her way towards us.

"Mom," my father says to Nonna. "Have you seen Marco?"

"Marco?" she repeats. "He's not here."

I stare at her. "What do you mean?" I ask.

"I mean what I said," she tells me. "He's not here. I checked the attic."

My father throws up his hands in relief. "Good," he says. "He's up and about. I thought something had happened to him. Well, either way," he says, turning back to me, "you're only allowed to drive with me or your brother from now on, understand?"

"Sure," I say. Although if I took driving lessons with Marco, I have no doubt I'd want to crash the car on purpose after he yelled at me about a turn signal. "Where did he go?" I ask my grandmother.

"What am I, psychic?" Nonna asks, heading to the kitchen, where the buzzer is still sounding. "I'm sure he's out with his new friends," she adds quietly.

My father and I follow her and watch as she puts on oversized oven mitts. She pulls a tray of what look like stuffed peppers out of the oven and my father grabs plates and hands them to me to set the table.

"He could have texted," I say, feeling left out. Although now that I think about it, my last text to Marco was to tell him he sucked.

Through the sliding glass door, I see that the evening sky has grown hazy with clouds, foreboding and miserable. I'm guessing my brother is with Minnow. I consider texting Parrish just to get some insider information, but I don't want to make it weird.

Nonna sets a plate aside for Marco, and then brings the food to the table as we sit for dinner. The meal passes quickly, and after we've eaten the last stuffed pepper, I get up and collect the dishes to wash them. When I'm done, I force my dad and grandmother to watch a few episodes of *The Office,* but Nonna looks confused the whole time and my dad reads his book, missing the best parts of the show.

With all the fun sucked out of the evening, I head upstairs and text my brother.

Hey, I write. *Where are you? Come home and explain comedy to Nonna.*

I wait a moment, but the message doesn't go through. Spotty service. I know it's not Marco's fault, but I'm annoyed. I like to think my brother and I are friends. It's kind of rude how he keeps ditching me.

With nothing much to do, I climb under the sheets with my phone. I go to the *Scare Me Silly* blog, but there's still no new episode on Nightfall. I wonder if Elijah and Felix are out of ideas. They did mention they were having a party this week, but I haven't heard from them since our lunch. I'm going to blame the phone service so I don't feel ignored.

With my phone otherwise useless, I search through the *Scare Me Silly* podcast and find an earlier episode, one that sounds interesting from Alaska, a place I'm not currently living, in case my brain wants to give me more hallucinations.

I settle in to listen, watching the shadows in the room shift in the evening light. When that episode is finished, I'm on to the next.

The show is fascinating, but at some point I drift off to sleep. I'm startled awake sometime later by a high-pitched scraping sound. Elijah's voice is still talking in one of my ears, and I pull out the earbud, the other lost somewhere in my sheets.

There's the noise again, almost like nails on a chalkboard. It sends a shiver down my spine; my jaw tightens. Slowly, I look around, waiting for my eyes to adjust to the dark. The sound stops, but then, I swear, I hear a soft laugh.

I reach for the lamp, fumbling in the dark. When I finally click it on, light floods the room and I shield my eyes, then stop short, my breath caught in my chest. Someone is in my room.

Marco is standing near the foot of my bed.

"Marco," I say, catching my breath. "What the hell are you doing?"

He doesn't say anything at first. He's just breathing heavily, staring at me. But then he relaxes slightly and looks around the room as if he's just realizing where he is and he's unsure why.

"Marco?" I repeat, my heart racing.

"Sorry," he says, and he sounds upset. "I'm sorry, Theo. I must have been sleepwalking."

"You don't sleepwalk," I say, confused. "Wait, did you just get home?" I grab my phone to check the time and see it's nearly five a.m.

"Yes, right," Marco says as if just realizing. "Minnow and the girls dropped me off." His voice sounds far away as he looks out my window. I follow his gaze and I'm startled to find the window slightly open, the curtains billowing softly in the breeze.

I get up, the floor freezing under my bare feet, and push the window closed. But before I draw the curtains, I see Minnow, Beatrice, and Annemarie standing in the driveway, staring up at me. The convertible is parked next to them with the lights off. I hold up my hand in a wave and Minnow smiles back, and then the three of them get into the car.

Unsettled, I turn back to my brother. He looks awful. He's pale—paler than I've ever seen him, and he seems utterly lost. "Did you . . . did you want to stay in here tonight?" I ask, worried about him. He shakes his head no, but his hands are balled into fists.

"Okay," I say. "Well, do you need me to walk you up to the attic?"

"Please don't," Marco says, examining me. Then he swallows hard. "I'll take myself to bed," he adds. "But . . . Theo?"

"What?" I ask, frightened.

"Lock your door behind me."

His words send a shiver down my spine, and my voice is weak when I agree. I'm terrified as I walk with him out into the hall and watch him head up to the attic.

When he's gone, I go back to my room and lock the door, just as he said. And then, for good measure, I lock the window, too.

CHAPTER TWENTY-ONE

When I wake up it's close to nine. I sit up, disoriented at first. I think I had a terrible nightmare. But then my stomach sinks when I see that both the bedroom door and window are locked.

So it wasn't a nightmare. Marco was really in here last night.

Why was my brother standing in my room? And why the hell was my window open? He must have opened it for some reason, which is not only creepy but dangerous—he could have fallen out if he was drunk. Not to mention the girls in the driveway, staring up at me. What were they waiting for?

I head downstairs, to talk to my dad. He must have noticed the changes in Marco's behavior, too. Then again, my father has hardly been around lately. Could that be why my brother is acting out? It's just . . . it's not like him.

Lock the door behind me.

My brother's words chill my skin. He sounded scared. And in return, he's making me scared. Why does he have to be so . . . ?

A flash of movement beyond the window on the front porch startles me, and I pause to peer out. I'm stunned to see Erika, the cashier from the ice cream shop, pacing in front of the door.

What in the world? How does she even know where I live? Tentatively, I open the door and Erika turns, surprised.

"Hi," she says awkwardly. "I'm sorry to just show up, but the phones aren't working right, and I don't even have your number."

"But you have my address?" I ask.

She pauses before laughing to herself. "Yeah, well, everyone knows your grandmother, Theo."

It's a small town, so that's probably true. But she says it like she actually *knows* Nonna—as if they're in the same book club or something.

I'm about to ask more when I realize how disheveled Erika looks, her hair falling out of a low bun and her socks mismatched. Clumps of mascara cling to her bottom lashes.

"Are you okay?" I ask.

"Not really," she answers simply. "I'm leaving before the Dive. I can't do this anymore. I'm not sure where your family stands, but I just couldn't leave without . . ." She scratches her cheek, a nervous movement, as she glances behind me into the house. "I'm sorry," she says, smoothing down her hair as if pulling herself together. "I don't mean to put you in the middle, but I wanted to give you this. I think you're smart enough to figure out the rest."

She reaches into her coat pocket and takes out a brightly colored hacky sack. She passes it to me and I look it over, perplexed.

"What's this for?" I ask.

"Return it to Parrish for me," she says. "Tell him it's his to deal with now. He'll understand."

"Why me?" I ask, holding the hacky sack up. "Why can't you give it to him yourself?"

"Because I really want to make it past the town line," she says, and then laughs softly as if she's only joking. "Because," she adds more seriously, "I think it'll mean something more coming from you. Who knows, might even change things for the better." Her eyes soften for a moment. "Hey, I've got to go," she says. "Take care of yourself, Theo. I mean that."

"Uh . . . you too," I say, although I am utterly confused in every way.

Without another word, Erika bounds off the porch toward a silver car parked on the street. Before she opens the door, she glances back at me, her face twisted with worry. Then she climbs in and drives away.

"What the hell was that about?" I murmur. I look down at the hacky sack, turning it over. Does Parrish . . . kick it or whatever? I have to imagine this is some kind of inside joke between them, or maybe not even a joke. Erika was a mess. She was . . . scared, I think.

I set the hacky sack on the entry table, knowing I'll mention it to Parrish when I see him again. For now, I head to the kitchen, expecting to see my grandmother drinking a soda at the table. Instead, it's just my father pouring a coffee.

"Oh, good. You're awake," he says, with a bright smile. "I've been wanting to talk to you about something."

"Good," I say tentatively. "I need to talk to you too. It's about Marco." He tilts his head with concern, his smile fading. My stomach sinks and I quickly shake my head. "But you go first," I tell him.

My father watches me an extra moment before he walks over and puts his palms on my upper arms, startling me. How serious is this about to get?

"Dad?" I ask, worried.

He breaks out into a wide smile. "I met with a real estate agent yesterday," he says. "And . . . I put an offer in on a house. We're moving to Nightfall permanently."

For a second, I'm too stunned to speak. Moving? Here?

"What are you talking about?" I ask him. "When did you decide this?"

His brow furrows. "I was going to tell you over dinner tonight," he says. "But I couldn't wait. Isn't it wonderful?"

"No," I say immediately, drawing back from him. My shock is wearing off and transforming into anger. "It's not wonderful. Were you just going to move us out here and not even tell us?"

"Theo, relax," my father says. "Of course I was going to discuss it with you, but I wanted it to be a surprise."

"A surprise?" I repeat. "Dad, a surprise is a birthday party at Chuck E. Cheese or maybe even a trip to Disney. It's not moving to a forever home twelve hundred miles away."

We've never talked about moving to Oregon, not even the remote possibility of it. He can't force us to move here.

But then it hits me that I don't have anywhere else to go. Would my mother let me stay with her and Dale in Phoenix? Would I have to share a room with one of his kids?

"I'm sorry," my dad says abruptly. "I didn't see the point in telling you until I found us a place to live. Real estate here is in short supply." He pauses, a crease wrinkling the skin between his eyes. "It's the best choice for us, Theo."

"Why would you think that?" I ask. "And why would you think you could uproot my entire life without at least consulting me first?"

He winces. "You're right," he says. "But you've been having

a good time. You've made friends. And your brother is . . . happy here." He tilts his head. "We can all be happy here. I thought you could see that too."

"Dad," I say, softening slightly, "I . . . I'm glad you've met someone. Honestly. But I don't want to stay in Nightfall. And as for Marco, I don't think you can call him happy. Not sure if you've noticed, but your son is the very definition of weird right now." My father looks away, his jaw clenched in annoyance. "I'm not moving to Oregon, end of story," I add. "I don't care if I have to share a bunk bed with Dale's five-year-old, I'm not staying here."

My father nods, but he's clearly upset. "Tell you what," he says, his voice controlled. "Why don't we sit with the idea for a little bit. Olivia is coming to dinner tonight. Your brother invited Minnow. You're welcome to invite someone too," he adds, and then pauses. "Everyone wants to be happy, Theo. Maybe . . . you could try a little harder."

" 'Try harder'?" I repeat, confused. And then I'm pissed again. "Try harder to what, Dad? Forget my life in Phoenix? Yeah, no thanks."

My father takes a deep breath and blows it out, tilting his head back to look up at the ceiling in exhaustion.

"I'm not sure what else you want me to say, kid," he replies before looking at me again. "So let's stop and take a moment. Return to our prospective corners before we come out swinging again."

I flinch. "Are we in a fight?" I ask.

He stares at me, seeming to debate it. Then he shakes his head. "Of course not," he replies. "Now, I've had a few projects pop up at work and I want to finish them before the day gets away from me. I'll see you at dinner."

Although his words are calm, I feel scolded, nonetheless. His disappointment radiates through the room. He walks past me as I stand there, shell-shocked by the entire conversation.

NOW THAT MY FATHER is avoiding me and Nonna is out doing whatever it is that Nonna does, I am suddenly very alone in this old house on the Oregon coast. Everything about it is unfamiliar—like I'm living someone else's life instead of my own.

I wonder how my grandmother feels about my dad's plan, especially when she didn't want us here in the first place. I wish my father had listened to her. I could be sitting by the pool right now, completely ignorant of Nightfall, Oregon—completely in the dark about the siren and her secrets.

But all this raises the question: What does Marco think? Would he really not mind leaving all of his friends for his senior year? No matter what's going on with him lately, I don't think he'll walk away so easily. I need to talk to him.

I go upstairs and pause at the attic door, debating waking my brother. After last night . . . I'm a bit frightened of him. It's outrageous to admit that—it's *Marco*. I need him right now, need him to back me up with Dad. Still, my heart is beating quickly as I yank on the attic door.

But at first, it doesn't budge. Confused, I try to turn the handle; it doesn't move. It's then that I notice the key is missing and the door is locked.

I quickly look around. The door to my dad's room is closed— I can hear him typing as he works behind it. Did he . . . No. He wouldn't have locked my brother inside. And Marco couldn't have locked himself in.

Hesitantly, I move toward my grandmother's door and put my ear against it, listening. She's not home. At least, I don't think she is—I didn't see her van in the driveway. I don't hear anything, so I slowly turn the handle and push her door open.

I'm immediately struck by the smell of herbs, not surprised to see several stick dolls around her bed. The room itself is small and quaint. There is a queen bed with a flowered quilt and a large crucifix above it, a dresser with some folded tracksuits on top. There is a wooden chest at the end of the bed, the top of it propped open and the contents spilling out onto the floor.

I'm very much violating Nonna's privacy, but I'm too curious to stop, and I go in. There is a photo album on top of the chest, opened, the pages yellowed with age. I notice a newspaper clipping tucked into the fold of the binding. Carefully, I take it out and open it up.

Sylvia Ware, missing.

It takes me a moment to remember that Sylvia Ware is the artist who painted the siren mural. She went . . . missing? I scan the article, discovering that Sylvia disappeared nearly forty years ago. But then my breath catches. "Seriously?" I murmur.

Sylvia was last seen by her friend Josephine Maggione of Primrose Lane. If anyone has information on Sylvia's whereabouts, they're asked to contact Sheriff Wyndell.

My grandmother not only knew the artist behind the Siren of Nightfall but was friends with her? She was the last one to see her? Nonna never mentioned this, although I understand it's not polite dinner conversation. Suddenly her warnings make more sense—why she doesn't want us out late or at the beach. I need to find out more. What if Sylvia was one of the girls who went missing in the '50s?

I flip the pages in the album, hoping for a picture of Sylvia

Ware, but she never appears, not in a single photo. But I do find pictures of my grandmother when she was younger, beautiful. There's a photo of her with a man who looks just like my dad, and I feel a splash of warmth when I realize my grandmother is smiling. She looks . . . happy. I sort through the rest of the album, enjoying the photos of my grandfather, and my dad as a child. I can definitely see where my brother gets some of his features.

There is a creaking noise above me and I look toward the ceiling, reminded that Marco is still locked in the attic. This trip down memory lane was nice, but it doesn't change the fact that my father is trying to ruin my life and my brother is becoming the kind of psycho who wears sunglasses at night.

I put the photo album back on the chest and glance around, my stomach sinking when I spot the key to the attic on the nightstand next to my grandmother's bed. *So she was the one who locked Marco in.* I pick it up and rush back to the hall and jam the key in the lock. I twist until I hear a loud click, then push open the door and head up the stairs toward the attic.

The attic is impossibly dark, with only the soft glow of light coming from the circular window that's covered with a sheet. And Marco isn't in bed.

Alarmed, I swing around, my heart in my throat. After a moment, I see my brother lying on the floor next to the large trunk. He's curled up there with a blanket.

"What are you doing?" I ask, rushing over to him. I touch his shoulder, and he stirs. "Marco," I say. "What are you doing on the floor?"

He blinks at me, his eyes bloodshot and red along the rims. "Theo?" he says. "What time is it?"

"No idea," I say, taking his arm to help him up. "But I have to talk to you."

"Now?" he asks. Marco shakes me off and heads toward the bed. He walks hunched over, like he's in pain. He looks terrible.

"Are you . . . are you okay?" I ask, concerned.

He eases down on the mattress and curls away from me. "I'm tired," he says, annoyed.

"Look," I say, "I have to talk to you. Dad . . . Dad says we're moving to Nightfall—permanently. Did he tell you that?" I brace myself for his reaction. He's going to be so pissed.

"Nightfall is great, isn't it?" Marco replies, turning to look at me, a smile tugging at the corners of his dry lips. "I think it's an awesome idea. Honestly, Dad should have raised us here from the start," he adds. "Instead he let Mom keep us away."

I'm stunned by his comment, by his reaction. "Wait," I say, my voice shaking. "You knew what Dad was planning?"

Marco exhales heavily and rubs his eyes. "Of course," he says.

"Why didn't you tell me?" I demand. "Marco, we can't move here. And why would you want to?"

He snorts a laugh. "Okay, Theo. As if you have something so great going on in Arizona. At least here there's a sense of community. People look out for each other."

"What?" I say, on the verge of shouting. "You sound like a suburban mom. What the hell are you talking about? Marco, do you remember last night? You were standing in my room, hovering at the end of my bed like a damn ghost."

A flash of guilt crosses his expression. "I . . . I'm sorry."

"Not accepted," I say. "Something is up with you. And it's getting worse. And now Dad is acting strange and . . . Are you seriously not seeing this?"

I'm devastated at how far away my brother seems. Marco and I have always been close—especially during our parents' separation. I need him right now.

"What's wrong with you?" I demand, furious. "Is this about a girl?"

"It's about family, Theo," Marco replies, staring me down. "We're meant to be here, together. We always have been."

I'm in disbelief. It's like I don't even know my brother right now.

"I thought we were a team," I say, my voice raw with hurt.

My brother looks me dead in the eyes and shrugs. "Guess we're not on the same side anymore," he says.

I physically recoil from the coldness in his statement. I walk to the attic stairs and then turn back, hoping for an apology. But Marco already has his phone out and is texting someone— probably Minnow. I exit the attic, closing the door behind me and leaving the key in the lock.

CHAPTER TWENTY-TWO

get back into my room, casting a hateful look at the porcelain dolls lining the shelf. It's a problem that the most normal person here is now my grandmother, who creates stick figures to ward off evil spirits.

I grab my phone to call Willa, and see a missed text from my mother.

Please call me, she writes. *I miss you. I hope you're having fun.*

I swallow hard, missing her, too. I'm not even mad anymore. Suddenly, something breaks inside me. I don't want to fight with her. I sit on my bed, tears welling up. I miss my mother. I shouldn't have been ignoring her all this time.

When our parents first sat Marco and me down to tell us they were separating, my mother chose to move out. She was working crazy hours getting her newest restaurant off the ground and needed to be closer to it. Marco and I told her right then, and I still remember the shocked look on her face, that we were staying with our father. The way my mother's dark eyes weakened before she smiled and told us it was okay still haunts me sometimes.

It hurt my mother. She never came out and said it, but I know how she felt. Instead of showing the hurt, though, she hugged us both and told us that she only wanted us to be happy.

I felt betrayed when she moved in with Dale. But if I'm honest . . . I know they're going to get a bigger place. They were already looking when we left. Mom couldn't stay in her condo; the building had been sold. But I didn't care about the details. I wanted to believe that nothing mattered more than me and my brother. That she could magically fix everything.

And now look where I am. My dad is going to uproot my life and my brother is a stranger. I haven't spoken to my mother in over two weeks.

I wipe the tears off my cheeks as they fall. Sometimes a person just needs their mother. I pull up her contact and press call. She answers on the first ring.

"Theo," she says. Her voice is a warm blanket around my shoulders. My heart aches at the sound of it. "I'm so happy to hear from you. I've been worried. How are you, my love?"

I forgot how my mother can swoop in and completely change the mood of a room, filling it up with oxygen so we all breathe a little easier, even if it means we have to keep up with her energy.

"I'm sorry," I say, regret thick in my voice. "I'm so sorry I haven't called you. I—"

"Shhh . . . ," she says. "You have now. Let's talk now."

I nod even though she can't see me.

"How are you?" she asks. "Hopefully it hasn't been raining on you too hard. I know how much you'd hate that."

"The sun came out for about a half hour the other day," I say, sniffling away my tears. I'm relieved at how normal it feels to talk to her again. "Expect me to be very tan in August," I add, and she laughs.

"Luckily you're naturally tan," she replies. "Now, how's Marco doing? I know he was pouting before he left. By the way, I saw one of his ex-girlfriends at the restaurant. She had the nerve to ask when he was having another party. Can you believe that?" She tsks and I hear her take a drink of something, the ice rattling in her glass. She's probably in the back office at the restaurant, dropping everything just to take my call.

But the mention of my brother has put me on edge. "Marco's fine," I say, my voice tight. I really want to tell her about him creeping around, looking like a cadaver on one of the *CSI* shows. But I can't bring myself to say it out loud. It feels like tattling on him, even though I know that's ridiculous.

"What about you, Mom?" I ask to change the subject. "How are you and Dale?"

"Oh, we're good," she says. "But I know you didn't call to ask about him. What's the matter? I can hear it in your voice. Is your grandmother being a pain?"

"It's not Nonna," I say. "Not really."

"Nonna?" she repeats with a laugh. "Oh, I like that for her. Then what is it? I know something's wrong."

Before I get into specifics, there's a question gnawing at me. "Mom," I start, "why didn't you like Nightfall? Dad said you weren't happy here at all."

She grows quiet, the sounds of the restaurant now clear in the background. "Oh, I don't know," she says, sounding far away. "It just wasn't for me."

My mother is lying, or at least leaving something out. "I want to know," I say.

"Theodora . . ."

"Mom, really," I say, sitting up. "Tell me why you didn't like it here."

She waits a long moment, and then her voice is closer, like her mouth is against the receiver. "It was a long time ago," she says. "But I . . . I didn't feel welcome in Nightfall. Someone told your father while I was standing next to him that I wasn't the 'right fit.'" She laughs dully. "As you can imagine, that was awkward. Your father, though, well, he loves it there. We almost broke up because he was so distant during our trip. I just . . . I couldn't stand it. I decided to leave right in the middle of one of their festivals."

"The Midnight Dive?" I ask.

"Yeah," my mom says, amused. "That's what it was. Anyway, your father met me at the town line, telling me he was coming with me, and that I was right—Nightfall had terrible Mexican food."

She laughs, but when I don't return it, she sighs heavily.

"Like I said," she tells me, "it was a long time ago. Your father assured me that you and Marco would be fine in Nightfall— that they'd welcome you because of the family history. Has something happened? Do you need me to call him?" There is a hint of apprehension in her voice. I can tell that she doesn't want to talk to my father.

And to be honest, I don't want to talk to him either. I look toward the window, then at the porcelain dolls lining the shelf. "Mom," I say, misery clear in my voice, "I want to come home."

"Oh, Theo," she says. "We've talked about this. But . . . if you can't stick to the plan, maybe we can figure something out. If Dale's older kids bunk together, um . . . the little one can sleep with us, I guess. Or I could see about renting another place until . . ."

I hear the strain in her voice and I wince. I'm a burden. There's no room for me in her new life. I should have known better. I should have known better than to even ask.

"Never mind," I say, closing my eyes. "It's fine, Mom. Never mind."

"Oh, my love, are you sure?" she asks. I can't tell if it's relief or guilt in her voice.

"Yeah," I say, forcing myself to sound calm. "I'll be back in August." My despair turns to resolve. I'm literally trapped in this place. I can't cry about it anymore. I have to get through it and convince my dad that we can't stay here. I have to be rational.

"Well, I do have some good news . . . ," my mother adds hopefully. "I've been waiting for the right moment to tell you. Dale and I are getting married in the fall, after you and your brother get back. A big event at the Scottsdale Princess. I want you to be my maid of honor."

Her announcement is a shock, even though I'd been expecting it for a while. Numbly, I murmur, "Okay," unable to say anything more.

"Really?" she asks happily. "Oh, Theo. That means so much to me. We're going to have such an amazing time. I've already—"

Off the line, someone at the restaurant is calling, "Rosalinda!" She sighs. "I'm sorry, my love," she tells me. "I have to go. But I should be done around ten. Call me later if you need anything, okay?"

"I will," I say, sick with disappointment.

"Love you!" she sings out, and then hangs up.

I sit a moment with the phone in my hand, looking around the guest room, feeling alone. Forgotten. My mother's getting remarried. I don't know why it hurts so much, but it does, and

I know it'll hurt Marco, too. If anything, it'll be an additional reason for him to stay in Nightfall forever.

For a moment, I wonder if anything at home will ever be the same anyway. My mom is off with her new life. Marco and my dad are obsessing about Oregon. I have no one to talk to, no one who really understands. I look at my phone again.

Hey. You around? I write to Willa, and hit send.

Practice in five, she replies. *Call you after?*

That's right. My friends are practicing without me. Building plays and laughing together.

Sure, I write back.

I think about the conversation I had with my father and remember suddenly that he said Olivia Miles was coming to dinner. Same with Minnow. He said I could invite someone, and I consider it. Really, there's only been one person who seems to understand me in this town.

I scroll through my phone and find Parrish's number. Nervous, I tap out a text to him.

Would you want to come to dinner tonight with my family? I write. It feels a little presumptuous to ask him, and it doesn't help my nerves when the icon that he's writing back flashes but then disappears. Oh no. I shouldn't have asked. How embarrassing.

What time should I be there?

I smile, letting out my breath. Part of me is just happy not to be alone, thrilled by the idea that someone actually wants to hang out with me. But it's more than that—I like him, and I'm pretty sure he likes me. And that's exciting *and normal* and fun.

Dinner is at 7, I tell him. *Thank you. I need the backup.*

Anytime, he writes. *I'll text you when I get there.*

Knowing he's going to be at dinner has settled my nerves slightly, but only slightly. Things are still an absolute mess.

I check the time and consider going downstairs to confront my father again, plead my case to go back to Arizona. But then I get thinking about Olivia Miles. She seemed fine when we met, but she's the reason that my father just completely uprooted our lives. I'm angry at her, even though I barely know the woman.

I grab my laptop and click into the search engine and type "Olivia Miles author."

Her image pops up and I recognize it as the one from the display window in the bookstore. Her hair is airbrushed and the lighting is overly soft. I click to a second photo of her with her dog, Cyrus. The large white animal is truly majestic, even if he trashed my grandmother's flowers. I navigate to Olivia's website and skim her bio, smiling to myself: "Wrangler of strays, both dogs and men. Never mess with a romance writer." Okay, I still like her.

She grew up here in Nightfall, although she went to college in Corvallis. She's never married, no kids. Well, at least that means if things get serious with my dad, she won't pick her kids over Marco and me. I wince, trying to remind myself not to be mad at my mother. I know she loves me. Life is . . . complicated. I just wish I weren't the complication in my own mother's plans.

I take a deep breath and close my laptop. Yes, I need to talk to my father before dinner—otherwise things could get really awkward. And I have to be convincing. If I have any hope of setting my life normal again, I'll need to make him see reason.

I go to my door, and just as I open it, my grandmother appears at the top of the stairs, looking startled to see me. She's wearing a navy blue tracksuit, her gray hair freshly curled, probably for the upcoming parade. She takes a few steps toward me before her gaze falls on the key in the lock of the attic door.

Nonna darts a look toward my father's bedroom, narrowing her eyes at his closed door.

She sighs heavily before turning back to me.

And I swear, she reads it all—understands everything.

"Oh, now," she murmurs sympathetically, and opens her arms.

Without even thinking about it, I rush forward and hug her. Nonna is tiny in my arms, but her hold is a weighted blanket, calming my nerves. She smells of fresh herbs and soap, and her voice is soothing next to my ear.

"Don't go crying," she whispers. "The sun will be out today."

CHAPTER TWENTY-THREE

My grandmother and I don't discuss my father's plans for moving us here. I'm sure she knows, but she doesn't bring it up. And to be honest, I don't want to talk about it anymore. Not now. Her hug sort of brought me back to life.

I also don't ask her why she locked my brother in the attic. Guess we both have our secrets. Maybe she knew he was wandering around late last night, being creepy. In fact, a small part of me hopes she locks him in there again tonight. And yes, that thought does correlate to me being mad at him for not telling me about our father's plans earlier.

But, instead of digging in my heels about the move, I ease up, planning to take a slower approach. I have to be smart, plan it all out. Like a detective—never ask a suspect a question you don't already know the answer to.

It's almost seven o'clock when the doorbell rings. I'm still getting ready for dinner, attempting to wrap a braid around my head in a way that looks summer chic instead of milkmaid. I've already put on makeup, thrilled about seeing Parrish again. Dinner with my family is definitely a date-like move.

The doorbell rings again, and I groan, dropping my hair to let the braid fall over my shoulder. Where is everyone else?

I head downstairs, assuming it's Olivia at the door since Parrish texted earlier to let me know he'd be a few minutes late. Despite the obvious issues with moving to Nightfall, I'm excited about seeing Olivia again. I'm glad my father has found someone. Hopefully his behavior will make more sense when she's around. He could just be a little lovesick—I've definitely seen my brother get caught up in relationships before. Including now.

Which reminds me . . . where the hell *is* Marco?

The doorbell chimes again, and I walk up to it, plastering on a smile to greet the famous author. I yank open the door, a cool breeze blowing in around me—the sun long hidden behind the clouds. My breath catches in surprise.

There's a uniformed officer standing there, and a police car parked beside Nonna's minivan. The man is tall, well over six feet, with broad shoulders, bushy black eyebrows, and thin lips. His cheeks are ruddy. He's an imposing figure in the small doorway.

"Can I help you?" I ask weakly.

"Yes, you can," he replies. "I'm Sheriff Wyndell. We received a call the other night from out at Sunrise Beach. I believe that was you?"

"Um . . . I—"

"Sheriff Wyndell," my father says, coming up behind me. He grips the edge of the open door like he's going to slam it in the sheriff's face at any second. The hostility is off-putting and out of place. "What are you doing here?" my dad asks.

"Your daughter called 911 the other night to report finding a body," the sheriff says with a note of arrogance in his voice.

"Of course, when we arrived at the location, the beach was deserted and there was no body. There was, however, a bunch of alcohol and a recently extinguished fire. I'm thinking maybe things got out of hand."

My stomach sinks. My father breathes heavily out of his nose, and I'm worried he's having flashbacks to the house party my brother threw. Then again, my father already told me that he used to hang out at Sunrise Beach when he lived here. So he doesn't have much room to judge. Still, I quickly try to refocus the conversation.

"I actually made a mistake," I tell the sheriff. "I thought . . . I thought I saw a body, but it was a watch someone left behind. I'm really sorry."

The sheriff smiles. "Ah yes," he says, turning his sharp gaze on me. "Well, here's a tip for the next time you want to file a report. When you see a *real* dead body, you're sure it's real."

He's patronizing and I'm incensed. At the time, I *was* sure.

My father takes a step forward. "There you go," my father says. "You have her statement. Anything else?"

Sheriff Wyndell turns to him, his lips hitching up in a bitter smile. "And when exactly did you get back in town, Joseph?" he asks.

"A couple of days ago." My dad smiles. "But I might stay permanently, Wyatt. Help my mother out."

Just then, as if summoned, Nonna comes out of the kitchen. "Are we going to leave this door open all day?" she asks. "You coming in or out, Wyatt? I'm not running a boardinghouse for mosquitoes."

The sheriff nods at Nonna, averting his eyes as if realizing he's overstepped. "I'll be out," he says, moving back. "And

I'm sorry to bother you, ma'am." She huffs out a sound, arms crossed over her chest. The sheriff holds up a finger to me. "And you stay out of trouble."

"Okay," I say, feeling accosted and slightly guilty.

He starts to walk away, then stops short, nearly tripping down the porch steps. Minnow and Marco are walking up the driveway, holding hands. Minnow grins at the sheriff, her expression wide and open.

"Nice to see you, Sheriff Wyndell," she calls. "You're looking sharp this evening."

The sheriff takes off his hat in greeting. "Minerva," he says, bowing his head.

Minerva? I thought her actual name was Minnow. The nickname is cute, but it's like a sudden new peek into her life. I'm not sure why it catches me off guard so much, but it does.

The sheriff looks back at us standing in the doorway, as if contemplating saying something else.

"Night," my dad calls rudely enough to let him know he's not welcome. Guess they really don't get along.

As Sheriff Wyndell turns and walks swiftly to his squad car, I look sideways at my father.

"What's that about?" I ask.

"Long-standing rivalry," he replies. "Wyatt was an abject criminal when we were kids. Figures he became sheriff."

"Never liked that one," Nonna agrees, watching the car drive away.

"To be fair, Nonna," I tell her, "you really don't seem to like anyone."

She glares at me, a hint of a smile on her lips.

"Yeah, yeah," she says, waving me off. "Just don't forget to shut the damn door." She walks into the kitchen with my father as I wait for my brother and Minnow.

I haven't decided yet if I'm going to tell Marco about our mother getting remarried. But I'm hoping that he's more himself tonight. I need him to be normal so that I can believe things are still normal. At least for now.

As Minnow walks up to the porch, I'm struck again by how stunning she is. She's wearing a black crop top and faded black jeans, the cuffs folded up, and sneakers. Gold bracelets jangle on her wrists and small gold hoops dangle from her earlobes.

"Theo," she sings out. She holds her arms open and I pause a moment before walking over to meet her. She leans in to hug me and I return it, albeit awkwardly.

Other than waving from my driveway just before dawn, I haven't heard from Minnow or her friends since our ill-fated girls' night. In fact, I was sure they were upset with me. But right now, she looks absolutely thrilled and I smile in return.

Marco, hovering just behind her, looks cooler than he's ever looked before. My normally basketball-shorts-loving brother is wearing midthigh shorts, shoes without socks, and a black T-shirt, his curly hair wild and windblown. He's wearing reflective aviator sunglasses and his complexion, although still paler than usual, is clear and dewy.

"I hope you're feeling all right after the other night," Minnow says to me, holding on to my arms. "I was worried about you. Hopefully the sheriff wasn't harassing you," she adds, glancing back toward the street. "Sheriff Wyndell is a hopeless mess."

She takes a step back and looks around the porch. "You know I've always wanted to see what this old place looked like on the inside," she says. "Thanks for inviting me in the other night. I'm happy to take you up on the offer now."

She walks toward the doorway, pausing slightly before stepping over the threshold. Once inside, she tilts her face up to look around the house.

"Beautiful," she says. "I can practically feel the history." She turns back to me and smiles. "Give me a tour?"

"Oh . . . ," I say surprised. I'm not exactly sure what to tell her. I've only lived here for a few days.

Marco slides his hands casually into his pockets. I can't tell if he's looking at me because of the sunglasses.

There is the thump of footsteps behind us and I turn to see Parrish jogging up the porch stairs. He nearly stumbles when he sees Minnow inside the house, and pauses on the top step, darting a quick look from me to her. Minnow offers him a wave and then beckons Marco inside, where he goes to meet her.

Parrish is wearing a charcoal-gray button-down shirt, his hair combed and smooth.

"Hey," he says, a little out of breath and shy in an adorable way. "Sorry I'm late. I didn't know what to bring. I can go grab bread or something?"

"No, you're good," I assure him. "We don't need anything. Well, my brother needs a brain transplant," I say quietly. "Not sure if you can help with that."

"I can scrub in," he offers, and then smiles. "Why, what's going on with Marco?"

I look back inside the house. Minnow is studying the pictures on the walls, but my brother is facing in my direction. His sunglasses hide his eyes, but his head is tilted to the side . . . like he's listening even though he's too far away to hear our conversation.

Either way, it feels invasive.

Quickly, I take Parrish by the sleeve and pull him toward the garden.

"Did something happen with the girls?" I ask him, thinking about Erika stopping by the house. "A problem with them and Erika?"

"Probably just the usual small-town stuff," he says, pausing to clear his throat. "Why? Did you hear there was a problem?" His words are clipped as he stretches his neck, pulling on his collar. He rubs under his nose, his eyes watering as he blinks quickly.

"Well, she . . . Wait, are you okay?" I ask.

His eyes dart around before stopping on the flowers. "Your grandmother grows wolfsbane?" he asks on a cough.

"No idea," I say. "Is that bad?"

"Well, it's poisonous if ingested," he says, and then motions to the newly planted purple blossoms. "And the smell is . . ." Parrish puts his fingers under his nose, blocking the smell. "Let's move upwind," he suggests, pointing to the porch.

To be honest, it just smells like dirt to me, maybe a hint of sweetness. But Parrish could be allergic.

"Figures my grandmother grows poisonous flowers," I say, looking back over my shoulder at the pretty purple flowers. Although the dog ruined most of them, my grandmother brought home a whole new batch and had my father and me plant them. They're all over the yard, practically surrounding the house.

"I hope I'm not too late," a voice calls, and we both turn to see Olivia Miles approaching the house. I'm reminded how tiny she is in person, barely five feet. She's wearing black capri pants, ballet flats, and a burnt-orange cardigan. Her tortoiseshell glasses have slid down her nose, her blue eyes blazing behind them. I assume she knows about my father's big plans, but I look for it in her expression anyway. As if I can tell her true feelings at a glance. She smiles nervously.

"It's nice to see you again, Theo," she offers. "I'm glad we have the chance to get to know each other better."

"Yes, hi," I say, remembering my manners. I walk over and hold out my hand and she grips it firmly.

The three of us walk onto the porch, the front door now closed. Olivia glances sideways at Parrish and furrows her brow.

"I'm guessing you're not Marco?" she asks good-naturedly.

He shakes his head. "I am not," he says.

"Didn't think so," she replies, scrunching her nose.

"He's with me," I say, and then stop abruptly. "I mean, I invited Parrish to dinner as my friend. I . . ." Just stop talking.

Next to me, Parrish is fighting back a smile.

"Okay, then," Olivia says, looking from him to me. "I'm sure you don't want me to ask any follow-up questions there. It's nice to meet you, Parrish," she tells him. He nods at her.

"Please, come on in," I say, opening the door. "I think dinner is almost ready."

Olivia glides into the house, looking around as if drinking it all in.

"Amazing," she says, and turns back to me beaming. "This place hasn't changed since I was a kid. This house is a true relic. Your grandmother—"

"Olivia!" my father says, waltzing out from the living room. He leans in to kiss her cheek, putting his arm over her shoulders before they both turn to me. It looks well-rehearsed, as if they've been together for years. I'm slightly offended by it, although I shouldn't be. It just seems—well, it *is*—way too soon.

"And you must be Parrish," my father says. He stretches his hand toward him and Parrish jumps forward to shake it.

"Nice to meet you, sir," he replies.

Next to my father, Olivia smiles widely as if impressed. I

guess I am too. It's not easy meeting a parent, and Parrish is making a good first impression.

"Let's head into the kitchen," my father announces. "We're just about to sit down." Olivia smiles as my father leads her away.

I wait a moment, unsure of how to proceed with any of this. I haven't even had the chance to tell Parrish about my father wanting to move us to Nightfall. I really want his opinion, but my father was right about one thing—everyone does seem happy. Even me, right now. It's nice to have Parrish here. It's nice that my father has a . . . girlfriend—it's still weird to use that word. I'm even glad my brother has a girl who seems to truly like him. What if I *am* the one being unreasonable?

"My dad . . . ," I start, but the words trail off when I notice Parrish standing there with his jaw clenched, his posture rigid. He's staring at the entryway table. "What's wrong?" I ask.

He looks up, studying my face for a long moment before picking up the hacky sack. That's right. I forgot about that.

"Where did you get this?" he asks stiffly.

"Oh," I say. "That's what I was trying to ask outside. Erika came by this morning and asked me to give it to you. She left town, apparently. No idea why. Is it yours?"

"No," Parrish says, and sets the hacky sack back on the table. "What else did Erika say?"

"Not much," I tell him, a bit confused by his behavior. He's not mad exactly. But he's clearly thrown off. "She said she wanted to make it to the town line and that I was smart enough to figure things out. But I'm sorry to say," I add with a laugh, "I must not be because I have no idea what she's talking about. Please tell me you do?"

"I do," he says, and then shifts his gaze to meet mine. The

look is so intense, it actually knocks the wind out of my lungs. It's a feeling that pulls at my gut, drawing me in. "Did she say anything else, Theo?" he asks. "Anything at all?"

"No," I reply. "Nothing."

Parrish holds my gaze a moment longer and then exhales heavily, forcing a smile. "She loves to be cryptic," he says. "It's fine. I'll figure it out. I'm sure it's just another errand I have to run."

"What kind of errand?" I ask, a bit disoriented.

"Theo?" my father calls from the kitchen. "It's time for dinner."

Parrish starts in that direction, but I pause to look at the hacky sack again. If Erika wanted me to know something important, she probably would have just told me. Right?

When I turn, Parrish is waiting at the entrance to the kitchen and I hurry that way to catch up with him. Inside, my dad is standing with Olivia by the stove, talking with Nonna. For her part, my grandmother holds a wooden spoon poised just above the pot as if she can't be bothered to put it down.

Olivia smiles. "It's wonderful to see you again, Josephine," she says. "You got quite a haul from the farmers market this week—barely left anything for the rest of us."

I forgot that they knew each other from when my dad lived here, both stuck in the same small town.

"Good to see you, too," Nonna replies. She turns back to stir the sauce in the pot. "Food will be ready in a minute."

My dad hands Olivia a glass of red wine from the counter, and then they come over to the table.

Marco breezes into the room, Minnow at his side. He's taken his sunglasses off finally and I see that the dark circles under his eyes are more pronounced. He looks at my dad and Olivia, and then, without waiting for my father to say anything, he holds out his arm as if presenting Minnow onstage.

"Dad," he says, "this is Minnow. The girl I told you about."

Our father smiles widely. "Minnow," he says, reaching over to give her a quick hug. "It's great to finally meet you!"

"It's nice to meet you, too, Mr. Maggione," she says, flashing him a grand smile. "I hear you're really enjoying being back in Nightfall."

"I am." My father nods. "It always feels good to come home. Oh, and this . . . ," he says, turning to Olivia. "This is Olivia Miles. Not sure if you two know each other." He looks from her to Minnow.

"I've seen your display in the bookstore," Minnow replies, looking Olivia up and down. Seemingly judging her. "And I read your latest book," she adds. "It's good. Really good. Can't wait for the next one."

"Oh my goodness, stop," Olivia says, holding up her hands. She seems to be genuinely embarrassed by the attention. "And, Marco," Olivia says, turning to him, "it's great to meet you finally. You look just like your father."

My brother frowns at the comment.

"Now," Olivia says, looking around at our group, "let's eat. I'm starving."

CHAPTER TWENTY-FOUR

The table is packed when we all sit down for dinner.

Nonna is at the counter pouring the pasta into a serving dish. She rejected any offers of help, although we all seem to feel guilty watching her do the work alone. Which is maybe her point.

"Now, how about you, Minnow?" my father says, leaning his elbows on the table. "Did you grow up in Nightfall?"

"No, I'm originally from Chicago," she says.

Her comment catches me off guard, and I quickly look at her. She told me she grew up in a small fishing town near here. I don't say anything, I don't want to be rude. But why would she lie to me about that? Or is she lying to my dad for some reason?

"*Chicago?*" my father says, as if he's been there and loves it. To my knowledge, he's never been to Chicago, other than maybe the airport. "Well, we're glad you're here now," my dad adds. "Marco has really blossomed under your attention."

My brother and I both groan at the use of the word *blossomed*.

"We get it, Dad," Marco says, still cringing. "But feel free to keep any and all thoughts to yourself for the rest of the meal."

"Puberty has been rough, huh?" Minnow asks, casting an amused glance at my brother.

Olivia reaches to pat my father's hand just as he attempts to apologize. "Don't worry, Joey," she tells him encouragingly. "I'm sure your planned icebreaker about menses will be a huge hit."

Parrish chokes on a sip of water. I can't help but laugh at Olivia's joke, and when she flashes me a smile, I return it.

Nonna comes over and sets a large bowl of pasta in the middle of the table, sauce sloshing over the side of the bowl and splattering across the table. She serves everyone before serving herself, then sits at the other end of the table, opposite my father and Olivia.

As we start to eat, Minnow glances sideways to Nonna's end of the table. "You have a beautiful home," she says to my grandmother. "I love the entire property. It's just enchanting."

"Thank you," Nonna replies, keeping her eyes on her food.

"I agree," Olivia says, picking up her wineglass. "That tree in your backyard has to be at least a hundred years old."

At the mention, I lean to my side to look out the sliding glass doors into the yard. The tree is old and withered. As if it's in a perpetual state of dying.

Olivia turns back to us and smiles. "We have all the best greenery here," she says. "Best flowers, gardens, you name it. There's just something about Nightfall."

"Absolutely," my father agrees, lifting his glass. Olivia clinks her glass against his.

I have to force myself not to roll my eyes, my hand clenched in my lap. If it were up to me, I'd already be on my way back to Arizona. Instead, I'm watching my dad and brother transform into Nightfall townies.

"And what about you, sweetheart?" Olivia says to Parrish, her voice warm. "You just graduated, right? I thought I saw you on that stage this year. College plans?"

His lips part and he darts a look at me before answering. "No, college isn't really in the cards for me," he says. "Not anymore." He sips his drink.

He seems so sad, it hurts my heart.

"Why not?" I ask.

Parrish looks across the table at me again and offers a shrug. "It's a long story," he says. "Not really dinner conversation."

"Well, now I'm curious," my father says, leaning in.

"Oh, let him be," Olivia says, tilting her head sympathetically. "Sounds like a personal decision to me." She looks at Parrish. "I can respect that."

He watches her for a moment before thanking her and looking away.

"Well," Olivia adds. "Depending on how the next few days go, we might be inheriting two new Wombats." She smiles at me and Marco. The mention makes me sick and I force myself to take a bite of food so I don't have to answer.

Parrish looks at me suddenly, his expression alarmed. "What's that?" he asks, looking around the table. "What does that mean?"

I swallow hard, not wanting to respond. Luckily, Marco answers first.

"We're moving to Nightfall," he says. "My father's waiting to see if his offer on a house is accepted."

Don't cry, I tell myself. *Hold it together and stay rational.*

"But Theo is throwing a fit," my brother adds. "She's always so dramatic."

"Or maybe you're just an asshole, Marco," I say. I turn to him, shaking with the start of self-righteous anger. How dare he call me out at the table in front of others, especially when I'm the only one making any sense?

"Both of you," my father snaps, clearly embarrassed. "Enough."

"But, Dad," I say, "we—"

"Theo," my grandmother says quietly.

I turn toward her and see her hand out on the table, palm down as if to calm me.

"I'm *so* sorry," Olivia says apologetically. "I didn't realize it was a touchy subject." Her face sags with regret. I feel bad for putting her in this position.

"It's not your fault," I say with a miserable shrug. "And I'm sorry that we reacted that way. Can we just . . . ?" I look around the table. "Can we change the subject?"

Everyone seems to agree, although my father is definitely pissed. He takes a monster gulp of wine and then refills his glass.

"I have a topic," Minnow offers. She smiles at me. "Theo, Annemarie was wondering when she could come over with the costumes for the parade. She's really excited."

"The parade?" Olivia says, and then claps her hands and turns to me. "Were you invited to walk in the parade?"

My dad looks at me, seeming startled by the news. Then, slowly, he lowers his eyes to where his fingers grip the stem of his wineglass.

"Yeah," I say, turning to Olivia. "Minnow and the other girls told me I could join them, so . . ."

"Isn't she perfect?" Minnow asks. "Both she and Marco will be with us this year."

"You're going to have a great time," Olivia says. Her spirits have definitely risen. "Don't you think?" she asks my father. He glances up and smiles.

"Absolutely," he says.

"What about you?" Minnow asks Olivia. "Will you be walking this year? I'm sure you still have a few costumes in your closet."

Olivia laughs. "I'm a little old for it, I think. But we'll see." She looks at Parrish. "And you?" she asks him. "Will you be there?"

"Wouldn't miss it," he says dryly.

"He's usually so shy," Minnow says, grinning at him. "It's nice to see Parrish putting himself out there and making friends. We're all so proud." She puts her hand theatrically over her heart to tease him.

Parrish pauses and looks dead at her. "I'm glad you approve, Minnow," he says.

Minnow smiles and stirs the food on her plate, bringing an empty fork to her lips to lick the sauce. "Yum," she says, and smiles at Nonna. She turns back to Olivia. "So, Ms. Miles," Minnow starts, "what's it like being a famous author?"

Olivia laughs, shaking her head. "Oh gosh. I don't know how famous I am. But I love writing. Always have. Of course, it's not entirely glamourous. Sometimes I have to lock myself away for weeks to finish a book. But I'm trying to get a social life again. It's all about balance."

"Inspired," Minnow says, gazing at her.

It's becoming clear that Minnow doesn't like Olivia. I have

no idea why, because to Olivia's credit, she's being completely kind to Minnow. Like Parrish said earlier, probably just the usual small-town stuff.

"Well, we all have coping mechanisms," Olivia replies, and then holds up her glass as proof before taking a sip. "Some more socially acceptable than others."

Despite the mention of the parade, I'm still angry at Marco for calling me dramatic. In fact, I've lost my appetite. I turn to my grandmother.

"Nonna," I say quietly, "I'm finished. Can I be excused?"

"Already?" my father asks, overhearing. "We haven't even had dessert. Your grandmother made an apple pie."

"I'm full," I reply, glaring at him.

He stares back at me, as if ready to hash out our argument right now. But my grandmother waves her hand between us.

"Oh, let her go," she says. "She's eaten enough."

Everyone else at the table seems shocked at my dessert-free exit, including Parrish. But I'm grateful when he stands up along with me.

As we clear our plates into the garbage, I notice that he hasn't eaten a thing either. Seems none of us were very hungry tonight. I quickly rinse the dishes and set them aside.

Minnow looks at my father. "I'll stay for dessert, Mr. Maggione," she says. "Apple is my favorite."

"Great," he says to the group. "I'll get the pie."

The happy little family sitting at the table—a family that doesn't seem to include me anymore. I feel absolutely abandoned, even though I'm the one who left. Nonna glances in my direction, her dark eyes unreadable.

As my father gets up to walk to the fridge, Olivia Miles smiles gently at me from the table.

"It was great to chat with you again, Theo," she says. "I'm sorry tonight was . . ." She pauses. "I hope you know that your father adores you," she adds.

I swallow hard, a stab of guilt in my gut. Although she's nice, I don't need anyone else speaking for my father. He's free to use his adoration to send me back to Arizona.

"Thank you," I say quickly to her, and then duck my head as I hurry out of the room.

When Parrish meets me in the foyer, he looks equally concerned.

"Your dad is moving you to Nightfall?" he asks in a hushed voice. "How did that happen?"

"He just told me today," I say. "But Marco already knew and is being insufferable about it. They both are."

"I'm sorry, Theo," Parrish says, sounding truly regretful. The sadness in his voice pings off my heart.

"It's not your fault," I tell him. "But thanks."

He takes out his phone, and as he reads a message, his jaw tightens. "I should go," he says as he slides it away.

"Oh . . ." I thought Parrish would want to stick around after dinner, but he seems to have other plans. "Everything okay?" I ask.

"Yeah," he says. "Sorry—just . . . I have to get things ready for the parade. Should have been there an hour ago." He smiles. "But I really wanted to come over tonight. I wanted to see you."

Heat crawls over my chest, up my neck. "I'm glad," I tell him. After a second of silence, I nod toward the door. "Let me walk you out."

We walk onto the porch and down the driveway. The night has gotten chillier since he arrived. I really wish he could stay longer. I feel like there's still so much I want to ask him.

Parrish pauses at the driver's-side door of his car, and I wrap my arms around myself in the cold. He looks down at me with a soft smile.

"I forgot to bring my jacket for you," he says. He places his hands on my upper arms, rubbing them to warm me. His touch is soft, cool, and gentle. Flutters begin in my stomach and I find myself moving closer to him.

We gaze at each other for a long moment. In the fading light, I can see the softness in his eyes, see him lick his lips.

"You can, uh . . ."

I was going to tell him he could kiss me, but Parrish seems to read my mind and he leans down to softly press his lips to mine.

My eyes slide closed and I rise up on my tiptoes. His hand rests on the side of my neck, his body against mine as if he's kissing me with his whole self. I don't want to stop, but Parrish pulls back and laughs quietly.

"Are you sure you have to leave?" I ask through my smile.

Disappointment sweeps over his face when he looks at me. "Unfortunately, I do. But we'll be at the beach tonight if you want to join us."

Right. The beach. "Uh, maybe," I say. He nods, seeming to understand my hesitance.

"I'll text you later," he tells me, reluctantly backing away to open the car door. "And thank you for dinner."

"I didn't cook it and you didn't eat it, but you're welcome," I say, making him laugh. I shiver again in the cold.

"Now get inside, Arizona," he tells me, pointing at the house. "You're still too thin-blooded for this weather."

"Absolutely true," I say.

I wave goodbye, and then I cut across the front lawn to the porch. Once there, I pause to watch Parrish drive away. I touch my lips, still kind of shocked that we kissed. I'll admit that right now, Nightfall doesn't seem so bad.

But I'm still not moving here.

CHAPTER TWENTY-FIVE

The entirety of Nightfall seems to have Midnight Dive fever as the weekend arrives. The local news has been covering the constant activity and crowds, the day packed with preparations for tomorrow's celebration. But here at Nonna's house, things are quiet.

Thursday night's dinner was a mess. And now neither my father nor my brother are speaking to me. We've been avoiding each other, my grandmother sighing every time she walks in a room, as if frustrated by the stubbornness of the entire Maggione family.

Parrish and I have been texting nonstop. He's been busy, but he's managed to stop by a couple of times, a few stolen minutes here and there between errands. A few kisses. I'll admit that I've fallen pretty hard. I haven't told Willa about this development yet. I haven't told anybody. What's the point? No matter how adorable Parrish is, I'm leaving Nightfall the first chance I get.

The house is quiet as I get out of the shower and get dressed for the day. I plug in my phone, and when I do, a reminder alerts me that the next episode of *Scare Me Silly* will be out tomorrow. I pause a moment, the story of Nightfall clicking back into place, feeling closer now that I have my own story of a missing body—sort of. I think . . . I think I need to talk to Elijah and Felix again.

I haven't heard from them since our lunch, but it occurs to me that they might be able to help with my current situation. I need a reason for my family to leave Nightfall—proof we shouldn't stay. Clearly *something* weird is going on. So even if Elijah and Felix can't provide hard evidence, they might have some insight into why my brother and father are acting like Stepford Wives. Who better to help me figure it all out than the boys who study spooky towns for a living?

I gather my courage and text Elijah.

Hey, it's Theo, I write. *Want to grab a coffee?*

I have a burst of anticipation as I wait for his answer, but it's mixed with anxiety. What if they don't want to talk to me again after our lunch? After all, I did question the facts of their podcast.

It's about time you reached out, Elijah replies, making me exhale with relief. *Yes to coffee. We have a lot to talk about. See you in 15?*

Perfect. Um . . . any chance you can pick me up? I ask, wincing even though he can't see me. When he agrees, I send him my address.

With that settled, I grab a sweatshirt and head downstairs to wait. Maybe now I can finally get some answers.

Elijah arrives ten minutes late, and I dash outside. His car is an older-model Range Rover but still pretty nice. When he sees me, Elijah tentatively holds up his hand in hello. I can't tell his mood, but he's watching me, inspecting me, it feels like.

I get in the warm car, immediately holding my cold hands in front of the heater.

"Where's Felix?" I ask, glancing in the empty backseat.

"He's prepping the house," Elijah replies. "We're having a party tonight, remember? I'm hoping you'll be there."

"Right," I say, although I kind of forgot. "Yeah, sounds fun."

Elijah adjusts his glasses and peers out the window toward the lawn. "I see your grandmother's growing wolfsbane," he says, motioning to the purple flowers in the garden. "That's industrious."

I peer out the window at the bed of purple flowers. "Okay," I say, confused, "you're the second person to mention them. Are they rare or something?"

Elijah takes in a long breath. "You definitely don't see a lot of wolfsbane in Nightfall. Now," he adds, turning back to me, "start from the beginning."

I have topic whiplash. "The beginning of what?" I ask.

"The beginning of whatever made you ask me to coffee." He puts the SUV in reverse, checking the mirror as we back out of the driveway. "I know you didn't believe us at lunch when we told you about the town history. But I think you're starting to." He glances sideways at me. "There are some rumors about you calling the sheriff from the beach the other night."

I'm mortified that I've become town gossip. "Great," I say, leaning my head back against the seat. "Well," I continue, "to be completely transparent, I still don't believe some of your details about the town history. *But* strange things have been happening. Including my father suddenly deciding to pick up our lives and move us here permanently. And my brother, well, he was already strange, but it's worse now. Like . . . a lot worse."

I shudder when I think about Marco standing in my room, the open window, and the girls looking up from the driveway. Even now, I want to explain it all away. I want an easy answer, an easy fix. I turn to Elijah.

But I don't tell him any of that. "Can you help me convince my father to take us home to Arizona?" I ask a little quieter.

He seems to think it over. "It honestly depends, Theo," he says. "I don't know how deeply involved they are. It might be difficult to pull—"

"Involved in what?" I ask, confused.

He tilts his head as if unsure. "Something definitely bad," he replies.

I can't gauge how serious *definitely bad* is. "Wait, so you think there's something bad going on in town, and yet you're having a party?" I point out.

"I'm a researcher," Elijah says. "And monsters, ghosts, devils— they love the spotlight. They'd never hurt us."

"Monsters?" I repeat, staring at him. I almost laugh. Cults? Sure—I can buy those. You know, maybe even ghosts to some extent. But monsters? No.

"If it makes you feel better," Elijah says. "I think you're safe. At least, I don't think your body is going to wash up on Sunrise Beach, if that's what you're afraid of. Your family is from here. It gives you some level of clout."

"What a relief," I say sarcastically. I wait for him to laugh, but when he doesn't, a knot tightens in the pit of my stomach.

Elijah stops at a red light and turns to me. "Now, start from the beginning," he says again, undeterred by my skepticism. "I want to know what happened at the beach."

So I indulge him. I tell Elijah about going with the girls to Sunrise Beach, how the night took an unusual turn. And when I tell him about thinking I found a body in the sand, he tightens his grip on the steering wheel. He finds a parking spot in front of the library, and we idle at the curb.

"Then the body disappeared," he says, turning to me. "Just like the other ones."

"Yeah, but . . . ," I start, thinking it over. "It wasn't like in your stories. The body didn't *go* missing. It was literally never there. Is it possible that something is causing hallucinations? Or that we're being drugged?"

He considers it, or at least pretends to, before answering. "I wish it was that easy, Theo. And I don't have the answer—not yet. But I'll know more after tonight's party."

I glance over at Scoops and think of Erika.

"Hey," I say to Elijah as he turns off the car, "did you talk to a girl named Erika by chance? She worked in the ice cream shop, but the other day she came by my house to tell me she was leaving town before the Dive. She left in a hurry. I don't think she even told anyone."

"I never met her," Elijah says, looking at the ice cream shop. "But that's too bad. Sounds like she could have been a good lead."

A ray of sunlight peeks through the clouds and falls on the dashboard.

"That's our cue," Elijah says, nodding toward it. "Let's go get those coffees."

Although the sun is out, I don't have time to enjoy it today.

Downtown is even busier than I anticipated—we have to dodge laughing children racing up the block; a couple taking selfies in front of the mermaid mural. When I look at it now, the mural seems more sinister than I originally gave it credit for. I think . . . I think the mermaid is smiling.

As we pass Scoops, I look over and find it still untouched from the last time I was there—lights on, chairs out. Only now, I notice the door to the back room is slightly ajar. Pretty sure it wasn't like that last time.

I think again about the hacky sack Erika left for Parrish. He hasn't mentioned it again, although I did notice it was gone from the table in the entry. I don't remember him grabbing it on his way out.

Elijah heads to a coffee shop called Short and Stout. I quickly follow and when we get inside, I see it's super charming with pale green walls, a shit ton of plants, and painted wood floors. There are no other customers as we make our way up to the counter. I wonder if this is another shop for locals. When the barista comes out from the back to take our order, my breath catches.

It's the blue-haired girl from the bonfire—Sparrow. She snaps her gum and smiles when she sees me. I have a flash of an image, of her smiling and standing behind Jerry near the sand dunes when I was panicked about the body. Her smile was . . . mocking.

"Hi there," she says in a fake-friendly voice. "How can I help you? It's Theo, right?"

"Yeah," I say, nervous. "It's nice to see you again."

Sparrow turns to Elijah and any pleasantries drop away. She runs her eyes coldly over him. "I don't know you, though," she says with no hint of interest. "Now, what can I get you?"

243

"I'll have an iced macchiato," Elijah says. He turns to me. "You?"

"Oh," I say, glancing up at the menu board. "Just a . . . vanilla frappe."

"Coming right up," Sparrow says, spinning around and walking to the coffee station.

Elijah fidgets, occasionally looking at me as the machine whirs to life, blending my drink. He widens his eyes as if to tell me that Sparrow is unpleasant, which is true.

When she returns, Sparrow puts our drinks on the counter and Elijah pays for them. I thank him profusely and then we head to a table that faces downtown.

We sit down and I taste my drink, enjoying the creamy whipped cream on top. Elijah stares out the window, his face screwed up as if he's making calculations.

"Can I ask you something?" I start. He turns to me and nods. "How did you get into all this? The whole horror podcast part."

"Well," he says, taking a tentative sip of his drink, "Felix and I started the podcast once our blog and social media started taking off, got sponsors. But as far as the topic? I've always been interested in the occult, the unusual, the scary stuff. Even when I was a kid—nothing scared me. Instead, it fascinated me. I considered becoming one of those ghost hunters, or even pull a real-life conjuring, like that couple." He smiles. "But ultimately, the podcast pays better and there's less chance of us getting possessed."

"So you believe it all?" I ask. "The things that you've seen—you believe they're supernatural?"

"Sometimes, yeah." He nods.

He seems to believe what he's telling me. Which raises a major question. "Then what do you think is going on here?" I ask. My heart is thudding, my anticipation at his answer tinged with fear.

"How open are you to believing me?" Elijah asks.

"Depends," I say, quietly. "How much do you know for certain?"

"At this point," he admits, "it is all speculation. My and Felix's working theory. Are you ready for it?"

Am I? There is an incredible chance this might give me nightmares. But here we go.

"Yes," I say, nodding. "Tell me everything."

Elijah leans into the table, dropping his voice low. "The girls," he whispers. "We believe the beautiful girls in this town are luring tourists here to kill them."

I sit very still, making sure that what I heard is what he actually said. My fear calms slightly, but I have no moment of laughter bubbling up either.

"I assume there's more," I reply, curious.

Elijah smiles. "Of course," he says. "Now, I don't know how, or really even why. But I think your friends . . . I think they're something else. I think they're monsters."

Okay, now there is a bit of laughter brewing. "The *monster* word again?" I say, fighting back my smile. "Let me guess," I tell him. "They're sirens?"

He stares at me, completely humorless. "Sirens aren't real," he states.

Now I laugh, and then quickly cover my mouth so I don't draw Sparrow's attention. She looks over anyway and I duck down to talk to Elijah.

"Then what kind of monsters are we talking about?" I ask him quietly. "And why would they just kill tourists?"

"We're not sure of all the details yet," he says. "That's why we need more research. But I think we'll know by the end of the night." He swallows hard, leaning in. "The thing is, Theo, I wanted to talk to you because I think some of the locals know, too. Whatever is going on—it's an open secret. Which means—"

"My family knows," I say, worry making me straighten. "At the very least, my grandmother. And you think my father knows, too?"

"I do," he says with a nod. "Which is why I'm glad you texted. You are an important part of this research for us."

Research? It stings a little, the idea that he might be using me to get information on my family for his podcast.

"Sure," I say curtly. "I'll ask my dad if his hometown is full of monster girls who murder tourists. But here's the problem with your theory," I add. "I've listened to hundreds of true crime podcasts, and the killer is rarely a teenage girl. It's more likely to be a well-mannered male neighbor, a local fisherman, or the husband. Not the queens of the Midnight Dive."

He sits back in his chair, clearly disappointed by my reaction.

"Look," I tell him, "I appreciate what you do, honestly— I'm a fan. But I'm actually worried about my brother—*for real* worried about him. And my dad. It might be cult shit or drugs or something, but it's not sirens, it's—"

"There's no such thing as sirens," Elijah reiterates.

"It's not monsters either," I whisper harshly. "So yes, something is going on in Nightfall. Something real. When you have an idea of what it really could be, not the podcast version, I'm ready to listen."

Elijah gnaws on the corner of his lip, thinking. Then he

nods. "I understand," he says. "Trust me, I've never gotten any-where being impatient. I'll help you. I promise."

"And I won't just be research to you?" I ask.

"No," he says. "Can we . . . I want us to be friends."

My hurt is alleviated slightly. "You'll help me find real an-swers?" I ask. "No embellishing?"

"None," he promises. "I'll figure this out, I just need a little more time. For now let's talk to people. Socialize to get a bet-ter sense of the town. Come to the party tonight," he offers. "Everyone will be there. And bring your brother."

To be honest, I'm not sure my brother will hang out with me, but I'll ask him. Some normalcy, a night with me, could snap him out of whatever is going on. And maybe that's the answer, time together—actually talking to each other.

"Okay," I tell Elijah. "I'll ask Marco, but no guarantees there. And I'll help gather info, but you have to tell me everything you find out too. I need a reason to get out of here."

"Swear," Elijah says, crossing his heart. He smiles hopefully at me. "Don't worry, Theo," he adds. "It's going to be all right. We'll get you back to Arizona in one piece."

That is a morbid way to put it considering our earlier con-versation.

"Let's get out of here," Elijah says, finishing his drink. "That girl Erika you mentioned, any idea where she was headed?"

"None," I say. "But now I wish that I'd asked more ques-tions."

"That's all right. Felix's a pro at tracking people down. Hopefully this Erika can shed some light on what's going on here."

We both stand up, and although I didn't learn any key de-tails, our conversation has helped me realize that I need to talk directly to my brother. The first step is always communication, that's what the divorce-court-appointed therapist always told me.

"You two have a nice day," Sparrow calls out as we leave. "And be careful out there. I heard it's going to rain."

Both Elijah and I groan at the idea of losing the sun, and then we're out the door.

CHAPTER TWENTY-SIX

'm apprehensive when we arrive back at my grandmother's house. Knowing I need to confront Marco about acting creepy is different from actually confronting him. I'm worried he'll shout at me, or worse, never talk to me again. A week ago the idea of never speaking to Marco again would have seemed impossible. So much has changed.

"Thanks," I tell Elijah as he parks in the driveway. I unbuckle my seat belt, moving to get out. "I'll see you tonight."

"Be careful, Theo," he says, sounding truly worried.

I climb out of the car and head for the house, but as I climb the first stair to the porch, I'm startled by a shifting shadow. I take a tentative step closer, and I realize it's Marco. He looks thin and pale, but he's smiling widely.

And yet, he doesn't look friendly.

"Hey," I say to him, and my nerves ratchet up.

My brother nods a hello, flipping his gaze from me to Elijah's SUV as it drives down Primrose Lane. "That the podcast celebrity?" he asks, stepping out of the shadows. "What the fuck did he want?"

I flinch at how harsh he sounds.

"We went out for coffee," I say, inching forward. "But hey. Can we talk?"

Slowly, Marco sits on the top stair of the porch, shrugging as if agreeing. He blinks against the overcast morning light, his demeanor softening slightly. I sit next to him, but he leans away from me. I have to fight back a wave of anger and sadness.

"Listen, I know we're not . . . great right now," I admit. "But there is a lot of strange stuff going on in this place. Including you."

He laughs. "This coming from the girl who called the sheriff about a scary watch she found at the beach?" he replies, resting back on his hands and stretching his legs out.

"This isn't about the watch, Marco," I say, flushing with embarrassment. "You and Dad are practically unrecognizable. You were in my room in the middle of the night, and Minnow and her friends were standing in our driveway. I'm getting scared. Do you seriously not see that something is off here?"

There's a sudden break in the clouds, and several rays of sunlight beam down. One of them hits the porch, and Marco draws his sneaker back from it, his posture rigid.

"What I see," he says in a measured tone, "is that you're self-sabotaging again. You pushed away Mom, and now you're pushing away me and Dad too."

There is a sick twist in my stomach. "Don't do that," I say, tears stinging my eyes. "Don't you dare."

"You know I'm right," he tells me. "And now there are girls here who want to be your friend, and what do you do? You call the cops to break up their party. You hang out with Parrish and then go out for coffee with this other guy. To what? Talk shit about everyone who lives here? Just stop, Theo."

"You are so wrong about all of this," I say, my voice shaking. "And you're being a real dick right now."

"Yeah, well," he says as if he doesn't care. "Tough shit. Now stop talking to me. The smell out here is giving me a headache."

The smell? I don't smell anything other than the earthy flowers in the garden. The purple ones are blooming brightly. I have a sudden and wild thought. Parrish said they were poisonous. Is it possible . . . ? Could they be making everyone sick?

I get up and head inside to look for my grandmother. What if that's the answer? I need to talk to Nonna, but she's not in the living room or the kitchen. I jog upstairs to her bedroom, but she's not there either.

I find my father at his desk in his room.

"Hey," I say, drawing his attention from his laptop. He looks me over with a bored expression before tapping on the keyboard again. I'm aware that it's the first time I've addressed him since our family dinner.

"Theo," he says in greeting.

His coldness is an attack, but now I might have a way to fix him.

"Do you know where Nonna is?" I ask. I try to keep my voice soft, but my feelings are hurt. My father has never been this indifferent. I'd rather he scold me for twelve solid hours on a car ride than give me the silent treatment.

"Your grandmother is out for the day," he replies. "Is there something I can help you with?"

Can he help me? I debate asking, so I tread carefully. "Do you know if the flowers in the garden are poisonous?" I ask. "The wolfsbane?"

He pauses, and a slow realization comes over his face. "You know," he says, "that's a great catch, Theo. I should tear them out."

"Oh . . . ," I say, surprised at how easy that was. "You sure they—"

My father gets up from the desk and heads right past me into the hall and down the stairs. I follow him to the top of the staircase, only to see him reappear a moment later holding a trowel like a sword. He yanks open the front door, holding up his arm momentarily to block some of the filtered light. And then he slams the door and sets out to tear up my grandmother's garden.

Well, there's one possibility down. We'll see if it helps.

I take out my phone and text my grandmother. I have no idea if she even uses her phone, but I have her number saved and decide to use it.

I need to talk to you, I write. *It's an emergency.*

I hit send. To my frustration, the text says *undelivered.*

"Of course," I murmur.

I start for my room when my phone buzzes. I look down to see a text pop up, but it's from Parrish. Okay . . . who is his service provider?

Heard there's a party at the definitely haunted Victorian house tonight, he writes. *Want to be my date?*

I smile, despite the ridiculous day I'm having. Seems pretty doubtful that Marco will go with me at this point. Then I wonder . . . what does he know about the girls? Could there be any truth to Elijah and Felix's theory of murderous definitely-not-sirens? Because Parrish has been pretty clear that he doesn't like having to be with the girls all the time. He might have a huge clue to what's going on. I just have to figure out how to bring it up without sounding insane.

I'd love to go with you, I tell him. *Meet you there?*

He sends back a thumbs-up emoji.

With that settled, I text Elijah to confirm I'll see him soon. But again, the text doesn't go through.

Yeah, definitely need to switch phone plans. My texts to Parrish went through just fine.

MY GRANDMOTHER DOESN'T COME home before I have to leave for the party and my father is out with Olivia. Marco never came in the house after our porch conversation, so I assume Minnow picked him up.

I'm just going to hope that destroying those flowers has helped somehow. They are completely gone from the yard, upturned dirt left in their place. Nonna is probably going to be pretty pissed, but I'm sure once I explain . . . It's not like she can hold *my* superstitions against me.

After getting dressed, I head out for the party at the purple Victorian alone. It's not quite dark yet, and the streets are quiet. I spend the walk examining the houses. Behind one of the windows, I see a family gathered at the dinner table, smiling and chatting. Enjoying their time together. I can't even remember what that's like at this point. I'm having serious abandonment issues.

There is rustling from a bush on my right, and I quickly look that way. When I do, the sound stops, the leaves still swaying. I swallow hard, really hoping I don't get attacked by a wild animal. The feeling of being watched clings to me as I hurry onward.

Even under the glow of the streetlamps, I can't shake the sensation of something just over my shoulder. When I finally see Elijah and Felix's house lit up with a party, I breathe out my relief. All of the lights blaze in the windows, and a dozen or so cars line the street. I hurry up the pathway to the house, and as soon as I reach the stairs, I spin around to check behind me.

I yelp my surprise when I see Annemarie walking up the drive, an oversized purse on her arm. I swear she wasn't there a moment ago. She immediately waves, delighted.

"Theo!" she calls. "I didn't recognize you. You look amazing."

"Thanks," I say, my hand over my heart as I wait for it to calm. "Did you . . . walk here?"

What I really want to ask is if she was hiding in the bushes, following me. But that would be ridiculous.

"I just got dropped off," she says, meeting me on the porch. "Oh, and your brother and the girls will be here shortly. Look!" She holds open her bag. Inside is a mess of sequins and brightly colored fabrics. "I have the costumes," she tells me. "We can try them on."

"Great," I say, still a bit off-balance from her surprise appearance.

I look past Annemarie toward the street and find Parrish there with his phone to his ear. When did he arrive? He notices me and smiles, but then his attention is drawn back to his call. He holds up his finger to let me know he'll be over in a minute.

There's suddenly a lot going on and it's left me uncentered, trying to catch up. I was alone just seconds ago.

"I've never seen him so happy," Annemarie coos next to me, staring at Parrish. "Well, to be clear, I've never seen him happy at all," she adds. "So you're really doing the devil's work, Theo." She grins at me and then takes my arm and turns me toward the front door. "Shall we?"

She pulls me inside before I can answer.

The music is loud, but the lighting is fantastic. I see Elijah right away. He's on the staircase talking to Jerry, who is in another Wombats T-shirt. I keep forgetting to check online for one, but I'm not so sure I want it anymore. They're laughing as if they're old friends. Elijah notices me and waves.

"Theo, you made it!" he announces brightly. Jerry grins at me.

"I'm here," I say, slightly awkward but happy to be inside. I force myself to breathe deeply, my anxiety dissipating a little. It's a party. Of course other people would be arriving at the same time.

"Thanks for inviting me to your home," Annemarie says to Elijah as she steps inside. When she does, she licks her teeth and smiles brilliantly. "My goodness . . . ," she says. "This is a beautiful house. You're so lucky."

"Well, we're just renting," Elijah says with a laugh. "But someday."

"Yay!" Annemarie says suddenly, noticing Sparrow standing a little way ahead of us, sipping a drink. She darts an apologetic look at me. "I'll catch up with you later, Theo," she says, and then peels off toward her friend.

I'm glad to have some space from her. Our vibe feels off, and I'm not sure if it's because I called the sheriff the other night or because Elijah's story of murderous girls has rooted itself inside my head. Rationally, I'm sure the adorable, five-foot-tall hitch-hiker hasn't killed anyone.

Just then, Parrish appears next to me and touches my arm. I jump, gasping in a breath.

"Sorry," he says, slipping his phone away. "Didn't mean to scare you. And sorry I'm late," he adds. "Had to deal with a life-and-death situation, apparently. You look lovely." His lips spread into a slow smile, a dazzling one that I can feel all the way in my stomach.

Elijah watches us from the stairs, his brow furrowed. He says something to Jerry, and then comes down to meet us.

"It's nice to see you again," he tells Parrish politely. "There are drinks in the kitchen, help yourself."

"I think I will," Parrish says. He turns to me. "You want anything, Arizona?" The way he says it feels suddenly intimate, and my cheeks flush.

"Maybe in a bit," I tell him. "I'm good for right now."

He pauses a beat before nodding. "Cool," he says, smiling at me. He turns, scanning the room for a moment before walking off toward the kitchen.

"Did you come with him?" Elijah asks me, sounding confused.

"I met him here, yeah," I say, a bit evasive. Again, not a secret, so I'm not sure why I feel so protective about it. "We're sort of . . . we're just hanging out," I add. "Why?"

Elijah looks in the direction of the kitchen, and when I follow his gaze, I see Parrish with a drink in his hand already. He's talking to Annemarie, although he doesn't appear to be listening to her. He looks over then and catches us watching him. Parrish lifts up his drink to me in cheers.

"Does *he* know you're just hanging out?" Elijah asks quietly through his smile.

"I like him," I say, matching Elijah's tone. "And he's been consistently normal, which is high praise, considering."

Elijah turns to me. "Fair enough," he says. He takes my arm and pulls me off to the side, to an area that's a little more private. "So, what's the latest update?" he asks. "How did it go with your brother? I didn't hear from you."

"About that," I say. "I'm having terrible cell reception, but I tried to text you earlier. I think I figured something out." My voice pitches upward with my excitement at my discovery. "I had my father tear up all the wolfsbane in the garden in case it was poisoning my family," I tell him, anticipating an aha moment.

Instead, Elijah's eyes widen in surprise before he puffs up his cheeks and blows out a breath. "Well, that's not great," he says, and takes a sip of his drink. "You should have left it there, but it doesn't matter. It's only a mild deterrent anyway."

"What?" I reply, disappointed. I kind of thought I had solved it. "A deterrent of what?"

He sniffs a laugh. "Pests," he says. "Now, what about your brother?"

"But . . ." I want to argue my point about the wolfsbane, though his complete lack of interest makes me rethink it. I guess . . . I mean, my grandmother would know her own flowers. And I don't think she would intentionally poison us. Damn—I thought I had figured something out.

"Theo," Elijah says, snapping his fingers. "About Marco?"

"Oh," I say, shaking my head. "Yeah, my brother didn't really want to talk to me. But Annemarie told me that he and Minnow are on their way." I furrow my brow. "Did you invite them?"

"I invited everyone," Elijah says seriously. "Had to see what we were dealing with."

"Still not sirens?" I ask teasingly, earning a sharp look from him.

"Nope," he responds, taking another sip of his drink. "But Felix was able to track down that Erika girl on social media. She was evasive, pretty unhappy to hear from us. But eventually, she hopped on a phone call. And you were right—she's scared. She's local, but she's not like the other girls here. She ended up . . . well, she filled in some details about Nightfall. Now Felix and I have a new theory." He glances sideways at me. "And you're really not going to like this one."

Before I can tell him to spill it, the front door swings open. Elijah and I both turn to see Beatrice standing at the threshold. Her blond hair is in ringlets and she's wearing a pale green '50s-style party dress with fluttering fabric. Next to her is a boy I haven't seen before in red Converse and a T-shirt staring adoringly at her.

Beatrice grins, taking in the room. "Hello, boys," she announces. "The cavalry has arrived."

She walks into the foyer, winking at Annemarie when she sees her across the room. The two meet at the foot of the stairs, both laughing at a joke that no one else is in on. Together, they take up all the air in the place. Everyone stops to stare at them.

Beatrice turns to me with a playful grin and comes over to take my arm like we're best friends. I play along, not sure how to react, and shiver at the sight of the silver watch from the beach on her wrist.

"And where have you been hiding?" she asks me. "Digging up more dead bodies?"

She and Annemarie laugh, and when I glance at Elijah, he casts a nervous look back in my direction. Wait, why is he worried? It's making *me* feel worried.

Beatrice drops my arm and points to the other room.

"Oh goody," she says to Annemarie. "You've tracked down Parrish. Let's go chat with him, find out if he's ready to stop avoiding us."

They walk off, and I turn back to Elijah, a bit startled by the entire exchange.

"That was the watch you found, wasn't it?" he asks. "How cryptic of her. The guy who owns it probably died on that beach."

I examine him, trying to decide if he's joking, but he's entirely calm. Serious.

"Do you really think he's dead?" I ask as dread pools in my stomach.

"Oh, definitely," Elijah replies without pause.

I wait a moment, considering his statement. Truth is . . . I still think I found something that night. Deep down, I feel the truth of it.

"You believe I found a body on the beach?" I whisper. When Elijah nods, my skin starts to prickle. "Then what . . . what happened to it after? How was it gone when I went back to check?"

"Because they moved it," Elijah says, keeping his voice low and nodding at partygoers as they pass us. He inhales deeply and turns to me. "They're vampires, Theo."

I blink quickly. His words are nonsensical—yet the simple way he says them makes it sound like he's reciting a fact. "Excuse me?" I ask.

He takes a sip of his drink, keeping the edge of the glass to his lips as he speaks. "Nightfall is the epicenter of a vampire nest. And we're standing in the midst of its hatchlings." He looks sideways at me. "They're beautiful, right?" he asks, studying my expression. "That's the glamour. It makes you see things, relaxes you, and sometimes—it makes you forget. It's a great trick, honestly. Vampires are just dead people with magic tricks."

I know he said monsters earlier, but *vampires*? Even for him that feels like a stretch. I have seen some strange things, I don't deny that. But can't they just be homicidal maniacs?

"And you're not scared?" I ask, forcing myself to stay calm. "If this is true, you're not scared—you just want to use it for the podcast?"

"Nightfall isn't the only place with monsters," Elijah says, sounding offended. "Ultimately, Felix and I are just trying to document it all while not getting killed. So far we've been successful," he adds.

"What about this party?" I ask, confusion warring with rising anger inside me. "If you know it's dangerous, why set yourself up like this? Why invite other people—including me—here?"

"I told you that you're safe," he says. "They've invited you into their world. And as far as the podcast, sure, this has all the makings of a great story. But that's not the point. It's never been the point for us. People deserve to know. We're just following the truth."

I look around the party, newly paranoid. They can't be vampires—it's not possible. But at the same time . . . the authority in Elijah's voice is making it *sound* possible.

Annemarie reappears at my side, a wide smile on her lips, holding out an unopened can of beer to me.

"I got this for you," she says. "You looked nervous."

"Oh, thanks," I say, trying to keep my voice steady. I take the beer, avoiding her eyes.

"Hello again, Annemarie," Elijah says warmly. It's amazing how easily he can change his tone, like an actor in a play.

Annemarie reaches over and touches his arm. "Where's

Felix?" she asks with a pout. "You know I *adore* him, but I haven't been able to find him anywhere."

There is a flash of panic in Elijah's eyes before he recovers. He pushes up his glasses.

"You know, that's a good point," he says, nodding. "He's probably running around doing a hundred things while I socialize. I'll go find him."

He turns back to me and I can see that he's frightened. The fear in his eyes reminds me that he believes his theory, and in turn that I might . . . I might believe it too. "I'll catch up with you later, Theo," he says, nodding as if telling me to be careful.

I don't want him to leave, but I can't say so in front of Annemarie. So I smile, trying to get a grip on the situation I find myself in.

Elijah slips into the crowd and disappears, and I look apprehensively at Annemarie. She smiles at me, her teeth very white between her pink lips. I paint on a grin in return, hoping I'm as convincing as Elijah.

"Come on," Annemarie says, looping her arm through mine. "Let's try on the outfits."

I consider making an excuse, but I can't think of anything to say. Besides that, Annemarie has never given me a reason to be scared of her. She's always been sweet. Forcing myself to relax, I let her lead me up the stairs toward the bathroom, the oversized bag still on her shoulder.

I leave my drink on the counter as she closes the bathroom door and locks it. My heart jumps with a spike of fear. Was this a bad idea?

"So let me show you what I'm thinking," Annemarie says. She reaches into the bag to pull out a gown, the material a shimmering shade of champagne pink that reminds me of the sunset.

"Oh wow," I say, reaching for it. The delicate fabric slides through my fingers. It's honestly the prettiest dress I've ever seen. Annemarie smiles, seeming proud as she puts it away.

"That one is yours," she says. "The other girls and I have similar looks, but yours is definitely the best one. We really wanted to show you off."

Annemarie comes over to take me by the shoulders and turn me toward the mirror. When she's reflected behind me, my tension eases slightly. See? Not a vampire.

She smiles at me in the mirror and then begins to gather my hair, piling it on top of my head to make a chic bun with tendrils hanging down. There is a cool breeze on my neck.

As I stare at my reflection, the world feels softer. I look beautiful. I look like one of them.

"You know," Annemarie says, taking some bobby pins out of her bag, "Parrish has been talking about you a lot. Ever since you met on the beach."

My cheeks grow red, even as I try to play it cool. "Really?" I ask. "All good things, I hope."

"Of course," she says, studying my reflection as she makes an adjustment to my hair. "And he's very handsome. I still remember when he came down from Seattle, Beatrice practically had to beg him to hang out with us. He eventually accepted, and look at him now, he's part of our group."

Is he, though? I wonder if Parrish is really part of their group at all. Even Beatrice said he was avoiding them. And Parrish has always had this bit of sadness clinging to him, loneliness—especially when he talks about the girls.

"To be honest," Annemarie adds, "Beatrice kind of has a thing for him, but we all agreed you might be better suited, if you're interested. We'd allow it. You seem to have a connection."

I look at her in the mirror. They'll *allow it*? What the hell does that mean?

And for a moment, Annemarie's reflection seems to waver. A ripple like water. I lean forward to look closer when there is a swift knock on the door, startling us both.

Annemarie groans, annoyed, and moves to answer the door. And in that split second, I swear her reflection disappears altogether.

I gasp, falling back a step and knocking her bag into the sink with a loud clatter as a few products spill out. Annemarie pauses at the door, her hand on the knob. She looks back at me and I force a smile, my heart racing.

"That knock scared me," I say weakly. She waits a beat and then turns to answer the door.

The moment her back is to me, I grab the edge of the sink to steady myself. *What the hell just happened?*

On the other side of the door, Sparrow is standing with a drink.

"There you are," she sings out to Annemarie, passing her the cup. "Oh!" she says, noticing me. "Theo, your hair looks amazing like that."

"Wait until you see her dress," Annemarie says, coming back to collect her bag. "Complete stunner," she whispers, smiling at me.

It's then that I realize I'm terrified of her. Elijah's story about magic and glamour—it's impossible, but it's true.

"You'll let me know if you need help getting ready before the parade?" she asks. "I'll drop the dress off, but I can do your hair again."

"I think I got it," I say, a small tremor in my voice. "It looks amazing," I add quickly, touching my hair. "I love it. Thank you."

She smiles, watching me a moment longer. Then she sighs as if her work is done for the night and grabs her friend's hand before heading back downstairs.

CHAPTER TWENTY-SEVEN

Once Annemarie is gone, I lean my palms on the top of the sink and let my head hang, trying to catch my breath. It must have been . . . a trick of the light. I look at my reflection again and see the fear in my eyes. No—it was real.

I think back on what Annemarie just said about Parrish. His reactions make more sense now—his sense of melancholy. He knows what is really going on. I need to ask him, just outright ask him.

Quickly, I head downstairs. The minute I get there, most of the locals seem to notice me, gazing at me as I pass, smiling. Watching. I realize my hair is still done up, but it's more than that—as if . . . as if they were waiting for me.

I want to escape their hungry gazes, and I hurriedly make my way through the party, searching for Parrish. But everything is a blur of smiling faces. It's overwhelming, like a sudden weight is pressing in around me. Across the room, I see Annemarie and Sparrow smiling at me.

With my heart racing, I escape into the kitchen, grateful when I find Parrish standing at the counter. He smiles, oblivious to my fear as his gaze sweeps over me. Warmth reaches out to pull me toward him. My energy shifting from frantic to a sense of relief.

"There you are," Parrish says softly. "I thought maybe I hallucinated the whole me-asking-you-on-a-date part."

I laugh, though the lighthearted sound feels wrong. How out of place it is in the madness. I glance back and everyone is suddenly normal again, laughing and chatting. I want to convince myself that I was overreacting, but I know what I saw. I need to stop gaslighting myself.

I lean against the counter next to Parrish, annoyed that there is another couple in the room, making drinks. I can't be as direct with him as I want.

"I need to talk to you," I say quietly. "Alone."

Regret sweeps over his face, and he lowers his eyes. He knows what I want to ask him about—I'm sure of it.

"You can still go home," he says, almost to himself. "Back to Arizona. And you should. I wish I could go home, too."

His voice is absolute misery. "Why can't you go home?" I whisper, touching his arm.

There is giggling as the couple in the kitchen takes their drinks and returns to the party. Parrish and I are finally alone.

He swallows hard and then takes a long sip from his cup. "I have nowhere to go," he says. "My parents died while we were in Nightfall two summers ago. Car accident along the coast. I was with them, but I . . . I survived."

The story is devastating, and every bit of that pain is reflected in his expression. Any thought of vampires leaves my mind for a moment, and I squeeze his arm in support.

Parrish slides his hand over mine and turns to me. Tingles race over my skin, heat on my cheeks and chest. "I survived," he whispers. "But there wasn't a scratch on me, Theo. Not a single fucking scratch. You . . . you can't stay here, even though I want you to."

As I watch him, I'm sure his eyes are growing darker and I feel myself leaning closer, listening to his every word, hanging on them. He is incredibly beautiful, complex. I want to study him. Know him. He smiles softly, and I wet my lips, waiting for him to kiss me again.

But then he looks away to take another sip of his drink.

When he does, I'm left feeling kind of dreamy, unsteady. My gaze drifts over his shoulder and out the window. There's a ping of reality, a soft click.

There's something out there.

Parrish starts talking again, and I try to clear my head and decipher what I'm looking at in the yard. I move away from him, my hand falling from his as I wander toward the window.

I glimpse what looks like a pair of legs poking out from the side of the house, as if someone is lying in the grass. The legs are moving, the heels of the red Converse digging into the grass, piling up mud on either side of them. I tilt my head, trying to understand what I'm seeing.

Yes, it's a person in the grass. But above them, seemingly floating in air, is this light green hue. No, it's fabric just . . . floating above the legs. Where is it coming from?

Behind me, Parrish stops talking.

I lean forward, staring out the window. The legs stop moving, and the fabric disappears. And then, so fast and violently that I actually jump back, the legs are pulled behind the house and out of view, leaving furrows in the grass.

I'm terrified, my breathing coming fast and the hair on my arms standing on end. There is another flash of movement, and then Beatrice comes walking out from behind the house, the color of her dress matching exactly the fabric I'd seen floating in the air. Beatrice . . . she was . . . she was floating.

Beatrice, her mouth smeared in red, is walking toward the house. She draws her hand over her mouth and then licks each finger clean. And when she does, I see the flash of her big, pointy teeth.

I scream as my hand flies to cover my mouth. Elijah was right about them. Beatrice isn't a regular girl—she's a vampire. And she just killed someone. She just . . .

I'm frantic, ready to run from the room and scream for help. Parrish grabs me by the shoulders and spins me around to face him. I'm shaking. It's real. It's all real.

But as I watch, Parrish's eyes grow deeper, darker. He starts talking, but I can't focus. I'm absolutely overcome by the horror of it all. I have to run.

"You didn't see anything," Parrish adds quickly. "Listen to me, Arizona. You didn't see anything out there. Do you understand?"

And I can feel him reaching inside my head. The invasiveness of it. The intoxication of it. The lines of my memory start to blur.

"No," I say suddenly. "Get away from me!" Terrified, I push him off me. He tries to grab me again, but I dodge away from him, toward the door, back to the party.

Where's my brother? I have to tell him what's happening. I'll make him believe me. I take out my phone and text Marco. *I NEED YOU. SOMETHING HAPPENED,* I write. I hit send, but the message immediately returns as undelivered.

Panicked, I get out into the foyer. Elijah is next to the stairs with Felix, laughing with a person I don't recognize. I have to tell them what happened. I have to warn them. I rush over, trying my best to look calm. When Elijah sees me coming toward him, his expression falters. He murmurs something to the others, nodding meaningfully at Felix, and meets me halfway.

"Theo, what's wrong?" he whispers, his voice tight with fear. "What happened?"

I get close to him, paranoid but afraid to look behind me. "There was someone on the grass outside," I say, my voice unsteady. "And Beatrice was with him . . . she . . . she was licking blood off her fingers. She was . . . she wasn't right."

Elijah pulls back to stare at my face, his chest rising and falling quickly. "You think she just killed someone?" he whispers. "Here?" I nod and he puts his hand over his heart. "Okay, shit," he mutters. "I need to think for a minute."

I look around the room, and I'm surprised to see that my brother has made it to the party after all. He's standing across the room with Minnow. But he looks unwell. He's all sharp angles and bruised flesh. He's watching the action around him, not really a part of it.

His red-rimmed eyes shift to the staircase as Felix heads upstairs alone. Marco licks his lips, revealing a flash of sharp white teeth.

I gasp, my entire body bursting with horror.

He's one of them.

Marco slinks off the wall and walks slowly toward the staircase. He reminds me of a cat stalking a mouse it's about to torment to death.

What is he going to do?

I start toward Marco, who's already halfway up the stairs. I follow him and just as I get to the second-floor landing, I hear a noise, a loud thump coming from the bathroom. I run to it and throw myself against the door. It only opens halfway. There's something blocking it.

When I peer inside, I'm horrified to see that Marco has Felix on the floor, one hand over Felix's mouth and his neck exposed. Felix's eyes are wide with terror.

"Stop!" I shout, and throw my entire weight against the door.

It gives, knocking Marco off Felix. My brother rolls to his feet, crouched like an animal ready to attack. When he looks up at me, his eyes are murderous. Terrifying. A low growl escapes him as Felix tries to get up off the floor.

Without thinking, I leap forward and punch Marco hard in the face, to drive him back from Felix. My knuckles explode with pain, and I cry out, gripping my fist to my chest. Marco ignores me, moving to slash at Felix, his fingernails incredibly long and sharp.

I dart over and grab my brother's arm. But he thrashes and slams me into the tiled wall, knocking the wind out of me, my head banging painfully against the tiles.

I gasp and slide to the floor, the world spinning, my breath caught somewhere in my throat. My eyelids flutter.

There is a moment of stillness as my brother freezes, staring down at me. Then he inches toward me.

Frightened, I put up my hands to protect myself. "Don't hurt me," I tell him. "Don't—"

But instead of attacking me, Marco gathers me in his arms.

"Are you okay?" he asks, his voice rumbly.

Dazed, I pull back to look at him. His eyes are normal, although his face is still angular and pale. But . . . it's my brother.

Felix scrambles to his feet and races from the bathroom, but

Marco doesn't even notice. Instead, he's focused on me, touching the spot on my head that hit the tiles and making me wince.

"You hit your head," he says, concerned. "What happened?"

"What . . . happened?" I repeat. "Marco, you just . . . you just attacked us. You just tried to bite Felix."

My brother gives a startled laugh, and then looks around the small bathroom, clearly confused. His expression falters.

"How did I get in here?" he asks, and when he meets my eyes again, his face is drawn and scared. "Theo," he whispers. "What's happening to me?"

The way my brother is looking at me now, the misery and vulnerability, the fear—he needs my help. He needs me to protect him.

"We have to go," I say with renewed clarity. "We have to get out of this house."

He takes my arm so I can get to my feet; I'm dazed, a pulse in my head where I hit it on the wall. Marco helps me out onto the landing, or maybe I'm helping him, I'm not sure anymore.

There's a loud stomping and I see Parrish racing up the stairs toward us, taking the steps two at a time. "Are you okay?" he asks me, and when I jerk back from his touch, there's a flash of sorrow in his eyes.

"I don't know, dude," Marco tells him, shaking. "I'm fucked up."

But Parrish is watching me, waiting to see what I'm going to say. I have no idea if he'd hurt me. But I can't wait to find out. I wrap my arm around my brother and walk past Parrish without a word.

I look downstairs and find a crowd has gathered. Minnow's

standing by the front door, faking concern. Because the worry doesn't reach her eyes, which are narrowed in amusement.

Elijah is standing at the entry to the living room, holding a visibly upset Felix, who is turned away from us. Elijah's expression is pure anger, and I have no idea what I can say. He knows what just happened, but more than that, he knows what it means—what Marco is.

Thankfully, Marco regains some of his composure by the time we get to the bottom of the stairs. There is a soft laugh, and I look over to see Beatrice biting down on one of her long red nails.

"You sure you want to leave so early?" she asks us. "Things were just getting fun."

Next to her, Annemarie is fighting back a smile but makes an attempt at normalcy. "Oh no," she says. "You wrecked your hair." She touches her own and I realize my curls have fallen down around my face, some still twisted in bobby pins.

I don't respond, staring back at her, speechless. In the matter of one night, my entire reality has shifted; the world is completely insane. Parrish comes down the stairs slowly. They're closing in around us.

I have to get my brother away from here.

I tug on Marco's arm and then we're out the door. Just as we step off the porch, Elijah comes running out after us.

"Theo!" he yells, and I turn back to him. "I need to talk to you."

"I have the minivan," my brother says to me. He shakes his head once as if to clear it. As Elijah approaches, Marco swallows hard. "I'll pull up to the curb," he adds quietly before heading away.

I'm relieved. Despite the insanity of this situation, I've

missed this mostly normal version of him. At the same time, a wave of fear and confusion sweeps over me. What the hell do we do now?

Elijah appears in front of me and gets right up in my face, making me stumble back a step, startled. His voice is low, his eyes intense.

"You saw him, didn't you?" he demands. "You saw your brother turn into one. Just like you saw the girl in the yard."

I wish I could deny it. "Yes," I murmur, horrified. I can't believe this is happening. Marco almost killed someone.

"Fuck!" Elijah says, folding his hands on his head. When he looks at me again, his expression is a mixture of anger and sympathy. "They turned him," he says. "Your brother is a new vampire. Shit, Theo. He almost killed Felix."

I close my eyes, wishing I would just wake up, wake up from this walking nightmare. When I open them I see Parrish in the doorway, watching us. I'm reminded that I'm not safe, none of us are.

Which side is Parrish even on? Because at this point, I'm certain it's not mine. He was trying to make me forget what I saw in the backyard. And he must have known about Marco. Maybe he was part of it. Betrayal is thick in my throat, leveling up to the fear already there.

Beatrice walks up next to Parrish and takes his arm possessively. She lifts her chin—defiant—as she watches me.

And it's clear to me, more than ever. I have to get my family away from this town. Far from the vampires of Nightfall.

Marco pulls up in the powder-blue minivan, the wheels hissing as he stops at the end of the driveway. I meet Elijah's eyes, a reminder that he's vulnerable too.

"Come with us," I say, reaching for his arm. But he laughs.

"Trade in these vampires for a baby one?" he replies, hiking his thumb toward the house. "No thanks. I'll take my chances with the established vamps. They tend to be more stable. Your brother is way more likely to kill us."

I gulp, turning to look at Marco behind the wheel. I have no idea if his murderous intent extends to me, but I'm going to have to take my chances.

"Good luck," Elijah says when I turn back to him.

Without a goodbye, I spin and run to the minivan. Behind me, I hear Elijah announce to his house of guests, "Show's over, everyone! Time to move your party to the beach."

As soon as I'm inside the minivan, Marco hits the gas and we take off down the street. He's still a bit out of it, and at several points I reach over to straighten his shoulder when he starts to drift to the right of the road. I watch the side of his face, the horrific realization just too much to bear.

"You're a vampire," I whisper.

Marco turns to me sharply. His eyes begin to well up before he turns back to the road. "That can't be true," he replies, even as a tear rolls down his cheek. "There's no way, Theo."

Over the next few minutes, I tell him about Beatrice in the yard with blood on her face. Her pointy teeth. And I tell him he was stalking Felix and how I followed him. I describe finding him in the bathroom attacking Felix. And then I tell him about his changing eyes and fingernails.

Marco shakes his head from side to side, his expression fearful. "That's . . . that's not possible." My heart aches, and I have to turn away. "That can't be true," he adds, sounding small. "What am I going to tell Mom?" he murmurs to himself.

I feel helpless, unable to stop whatever's happening. Unable to make it instantly better. But then I look back at my brother.

"Do you have any bite marks?" I ask him with one last gasp of hope. "Are you sure you were really bitten?"

Marco swallows hard. He pulls the collar of his shirt to the side, exposing two small puncture wounds that have scabbed over.

CHAPTER TWENTY-EIGHT

When we arrive at Nonna's, Marco kills the headlights and turns into the driveway. The house is dark, thankfully. I'm pretty sure I'm in shock—assuming shock feels like a combination of disbelief, numbness, and utter terror.

Marco is silent as he follows me into the house and up to the attic, where he sits on the edge of the bed and drops his head in his hands. I'm unsteady as I ease down onto the trunk. What the hell are we going to do?

My brother lifts his head, the circles underneath his sunken eyes are blue. "I don't feel too well, Theo," he says quietly. "My stomach hurts with hunger."

"Not a comforting thought," I tell him. He holds my gaze before looking away, ashamed. Of course, I'm now reminded of the threat he poses to me. To our family.

I'm not certain Elijah will answer my call anymore, but I need to talk to him. He has to know how to help. Service is spotty; I hope I'll have better luck with the landline downstairs.

"Wait here," I tell my brother. "I'm going to make a call."

"You're leaving me?" he asks, frightened. "But, Theo—"

"You'll be all right," I reply, trying to reassure him. "Just don't . . . don't do any monster shit, okay?"

"Okay," he responds automatically.

In the upstairs hallway, I glance at my grandmother's closed bedroom door. I consider waking her for help, but at the same time . . . I'm scared. What does Nonna know about this town and how long has she known it? Also, considering that she planted wolfsbane in her garden, I have to worry about how she'll react to her grandson being a vampire. She might hurt him, lock him in the attic forever.

With that thought, I lock the attic door myself and take the skeleton key with me. I head straight for the phone, find Elijah's number on my cell, and dial it. I bring the receiver to my ear, grateful when I hear the phone ring.

"Who is this?" Elijah answers.

"It's Theo," I tell him. "We're back at my grandmother's house. I'm calling from the landline. I'm glad it worked," I add, relieved.

"I'm not so sure I am," he returns. "Maybe you don't get it, but your brother nearly killed my boyfriend. I'm *pissed*."

I wince. "I'm so sorry," I say. "And Marco is sorry too. That wasn't him—at least, he would never have done anything like that before. He's never even been in a fight."

"So you say," Elijah responds, but his tone has softened a bit. "And where is Marco now? Snacking on rabbits in the garden?"

"He's locked in the attic," I tell him, looking up at the ceiling.

"That's a start."

"And he . . . he, um," I continue, "yeah, he's a vampire. He even has a bite on his neck. And he's not feeling well, Elijah. You have to help us. How do I change him back?"

He's quiet for a long moment. Then, "Your big brother is

a bloodsucking vampire. You can't help him. You have to kill him."

My stomach tightens, little pinpricks of fear racing across my skin. Just the words have set fire to my heart. "Don't ever fucking say that," I hiss into the phone.

"I'm being serious, Theo," Elijah says, sounding practical. Cold. "You have a vampire in your house. You have to destroy his heart with a wooden stake or chop off his head."

"Neither of those things are going to happen," I shoot back. "What's your next best option?"

"Okay, if not him, you have to kill the queen. The vampire queen."

"Who the hell is the vampire queen?" I ask.

"I don't know," he answers. "But since there's a nest, there's a queen. Find her and kill her."

"Can you please just give me an option that doesn't involve murder?" I ask, frustrated. "I can't believe I'm even having this conversation. I'm not a fucking vampire slayer. I haven't even graduated from high school yet!"

"I'm sorry," Elijah replies, sounding like he might actually mean it. "But those are the only two options. Unless you want your brother to become a killer who slaughters tourists."

"Marco wouldn't do that," I say.

"Uh . . ."

"Right," I reply. "Okay, what about a cure? Some kind of spell or relic. My grandmother has these little stick dolls. Does anything like that help?"

"Are we going to do this for the next hour?" Elijah asks. "There's no answer I'm going to give that you'll like. It's too late. Your brother started dying the moment he was bitten. And after the Midnight Dive, the transformation will be complete."

"Wait," I say with a spring of hope, "the Dive? What does the Midnight Dive have to do with any of this? Are you saying my brother isn't actually a vampire yet?"

"He is," Elijah says with a sigh of exasperation. "Your brother has been . . . infected, let's call it. He thirsts for blood, can glamour when he's strong enough, et cetera. But he needs to complete the transformation. Remember when I told you that we talked to Erika about Nightfall?"

"Yeah . . ."

"She filled in some of the details," he continues. "But Felix and I put together the rest after the party. Bits and pieces of overheard vamp conversation, town history, and some internet searches on reanimation curses. Basically," he says, "during the Midnight Dive, the girls lead the parade as part of a ritual for the people they've chosen to stay in Nightfall. They lead them to the water and drown them."

"Drown them?" I repeat, confused. "Like Alfonse Cardelli drowned the girls back in the day?"

"Yeah, except they're not going to chop off Marco's head," Elijah clarifies. "Cardelli destroyed the vampires, at least that's what I think happened based on some vague mentions in personal journals they had in the library. But now the Midnight Dive is used to turn those who have been bitten—those chosen by the girls—into full-fledged bloodsuckers. They drown the human bodies, and from there, the curse takes over. The dead are reanimated into vampires."

"And no one notices?" I ask, incredulous. "They just . . . You're telling me the townspeople just let that happen?"

"Some of them, I suppose," Elijah says. "Especially the ones who date back several decades. But others are glamoured. Either way, it's part of the ritual, like I said."

I'm trying to think over everything, every part seeming more impossible than the one before. But I saw what my brother has become. I won't let him stay like that permanently. There has to be . . . Wait.

"Elijah," I say suddenly, "what if Marco doesn't go to the Midnight Dive? What if they don't drown him?"

"Then he will wither and die in the light of the new morning," Elijah says. "It's how the girls pick and choose. They might bite several tourists throughout their time here, but only some shall stay. The ones they bring back on the night of the Dive. The rest die."

"What about Felix's friend?" I ask. "Brecken. He had bites and he went home."

"About that . . . ," Elijah says. "Brecken died shortly after arriving in Loma Vista—the morning *after* the Dive. At the time, we didn't know what killed him. They found him in the back of the bus, curled up and just . . . dead. Even though he ran before he could be drowned, the curse still got him—the infection—even all the way in another state."

"Why didn't you tell me that?" I ask, frustrated. That's a pretty important part of the story.

"We were still investigating," Elijah says. "In fact, all the pieces didn't fit until after the party," he adds. "But . . . if I'm being honest, it was pretty obvious at the beach that your brother was going through something similar to Brecken. The best we could do was monitor the situation to learn more."

"I don't think that was the best you could do," I reply.

But it doesn't matter what Elijah tells me now. I won't let him convince me that Marco has to die. There has to be a better way.

"So if Marco doesn't go to the Midnight Dive and get

murdered, he dies?" I ask, my heart pounding. "And if he does get murdered there, he comes back as a vampire—a stronger one?"

"Yes," Elijah says. "Which is why you have to destroy him first," he adds, a hint of sympathy creeping into his voice. "Before he bites someone else and spreads the infection."

"I'm not cutting off his head," I reiterate fiercely. "And he's not getting drowned either."

"Then he'll be dead the day after the Dive anyway," Elijah says.

"Okay . . . so say he changes," I tell him, desperate, "I'll just take him back to Arizona, make sure he stays out of the sun. We'll figure something out. Feed him rare steaks and shit."

"Theo," Elijah says, "vampires are very possessive. Whoever bit your brother will come for him. They're not going to let him leave—dead or alive. Especially not a town descendant. Nightfall has claimed your brother. He belongs to them now."

"Fuck that," I say. "No one claims Marco but himself." I run my hand through my hair, my fingers snagging on the bobby pins. I yank them out and toss them aside. "At least give me some pointers," I tell Elijah. "What else can these vampires do besides bite people? What am I dealing with?"

"Like I said earlier," Elijah says, "your brother isn't there yet—he's more like a rabid dog. But the other vampires in town can change their appearance or make people forget things with a glamour. They can make you calm, make you yearn, or make you miserable. They're talented hypnotists. At the same time, vampires are very social creatures. They want to be adored—no amount of love is ever enough."

"So you threw them a party," I say, thinking back on tonight, how thrilled Beatrice was when she walked inside. She really is a psychopath.

"We played along," Elijah says, "pretending they were just locals, too beautiful and cool to contemplate. But we miscalculated—Felix and I underestimated them. I'm sorry, Theo, but we're wrapping up our production and leaving as soon as we grab a few things."

"How nice for you," I say bitterly. Elijah and Felix stirred things up and now they're leaving us behind. "Marco and I don't have the luxury of leaving, it seems. So how do we protect ourselves? How do I kill them?"

"Beheading or stake through the heart," he replies. I recoil at the idea. "From all the research I've done, those are the only two ways to kill vampires other than direct sunlight. But you don't get much of that around here. Wolfsbane helps with the hypnosis part—cuts through a glamour, plus it's deadly if ingested in large quantities. Garlic is a skin irritant, causing wicked burns.

"And of course," he continues, "they need to be invited in. Don't count on that, though. Vampires always find a way to get inside. Like I said, social creatures."

There is a thump from the top of the stairs. Marco may have just realized I locked him in the attic. I don't want to frighten him . . . or anger him.

"I have to go," I tell Elijah.

"Be careful," he says. "And . . . I'm sorry, Theo. Truly."

The defeat in his voice steals my hope. I can't even say goodbye. Instead, I hang up and walk upstairs to the attic door. I pause there, slowly taking out the key. I listen for a moment, but don't hear anything else. Quietly I unlock the door and make my way up into the room.

My heart sinks when I open the top door and find Marco sitting on the bed, his arms wrapped around himself, shivering.

He looks weak and pathetic and I've never wanted to protect him more in my entire life.

"You didn't have to lock me in," he says miserably.

I feel a little guilty, but he *did* try to get out. What if he hurts our dad or grandmother? What if he hurts me? Despite that thought, I walk over to the bed and sit next to him. I'm admittedly anxious, but then Marco leans forward to rest his head in his palms.

"I don't want to be a vampire," he murmurs. "There has to be a way to stop this."

"There is," I tell him definitively.

"What if we leave?" he asks, looking at me. "Do you think it would stop if we went back home?"

Hearing him say *home* sends a splash of grief through my chest. That's I want right now and yet it isn't possible anymore.

"I guess it doesn't work that way," I tell him. "I'm sorry, Marco. But I won't give up. I'll find—"

There's a knock at the door, and we both jump. The door opens slowly and our father pokes his head inside the room. Marco tenses and I grab his arm.

From the doorway, our father takes a moment to look us over. I almost open my mouth and tell him everything, including the fact that Marco nearly killed a guy tonight. But then I remember what Elijah said, that some of the townspeople are in on the secret. I don't think our dad is one those people—he wouldn't have brought us here otherwise. But I don't want to take the chance. I don't want to put him in danger either.

"Hi, Dad," I say, plastering on a smile. "What are you doing up? Midnight snack?"

Our dad smiles and steps inside, closing the door behind him. He wanders around the room for a bit before leaning against the closet door. "So," he says, "what's going on with you two?" He motions to me and Marco.

Does he already know? My entire body tenses, but I do my best to seem normal. "We're fine, Dad," I say. For his part, Marco is smiling awkwardly.

Our father steeples his hands. "That's good," he says. "Because I wanted to talk to you both for a second."

"Okay . . . ," I reply, glancing at Marco. He is terribly pale and his lips are twitching.

"I know the past few years have been hard on you both," our father says. "And part of that is my fault. But you know how much I love you. This family . . . it's everything to me."

I smile for real, heartened at the idea of our family.

"And I'm sorry, Theo," he adds. "About surprising you with a move. Being insufferable. It was unfair not to discuss it with you first. But I know you're going to love it here."

My stomach drops, but I hold very still, not wanting to give away how terrifying the thought is. For a moment, I wonder if he's infected too. But there are no obvious marks under the loose collar of his nightshirt. No, I think he's lovesick—completely ready to uproot our lives for Olivia Miles.

Our father walks over to us. Marco leans into me as our dad bends down to kiss the top of his head and then mine.

"Let's all go to the Midnight Dive together tomorrow," our father says. "I hear it'll be overcast and rainy, which is just perfect in my opinion. We'll go as a family."

"That sounds fun," I tell him weakly. My brother nods.

"I really do love you both," our father adds, his eyes glistening with tears. I'm struck by the sentiment; I feel the same. Our dad goes to the door and leaves, closing it behind him with a soft click.

CHAPTER TWENTY-NINE

wake up with the worst headache, probably from the endless nightmares I had throughout the night. And for the first time, I remember them—every terrible second.

I didn't trust that Marco wouldn't kill us all in the night, so I locked him in the attic again. This time he agreed it was the best idea for now.

It's a long morning and an even longer afternoon as I wait for my father to leave the house to meet up with Olivia. The plan is for the four of us to rendezvous at the parade downtown this evening, although there is no way in hell I'm bringing Marco anywhere near that place.

My grandmother is nowhere in sight. I have no idea where that woman even goes. I only saw her for a brief moment this morning. She looked at me funny and I considered asking her if she knew about the vampires in Nightfall. But what would it matter? She's a little old lady. It's not like she could help us fight them off. Better to keep her out of it.

In the early evening, I head upstairs to let my brother out of captivity.

Marco is disheveled, his hair a mess and sticking out in

various directions. His cheeks are sunken, the circles under his eyes darker. His shoulder blades are sharp under his T-shirt. He's fading quickly—starving, I realize. Along with that comes the uncomfortable thought of what he's hungry for.

"Where is everyone?" Marco asks, scratching at the collar of his shirt, just above where the bite marks are.

"Dad's out with Olivia," I say, watching him closely, "and Nonna has been gone all day. The parade starts in a few hours."

I'm dreading what happens next. Even if we don't go to the Midnight Dive, will others die? Will my brother die? And does my father want us there, for family bonding? Or something more . . . sinister?

"Marco?" I ask. "Do you think Dad knows? About the vampires? About . . . about them wanting to kill you to keep you here?"

It might just be the question I'm most afraid to ask. Our father brought us here, against the advice of his mother. And he's kept us here. Are we . . . are we sacrifices to the town of Nightfall?

"I'm not sure what Dad knows," Marco says in a quiet voice. "I'm honestly not, Theo." His posture sags from the thought. "But I really hope not, okay?"

"Okay," I murmur, although when we look at each other, our eyes are welling up. Have we ever been more alone than now? It occurs to me that it's me and Marco against the world. Again. All we have is each other.

And with that in mind, I tilt my head, looking him over.

"You don't look so good," I tell him.

"That's because I'm ravenous, Theodora," he snaps, making me jump. He turns away and winces. "I'm sorry, that just came out. I'm losing my mind."

"No, you're not," I say, trying to calm him. "Here, sit down. I'll . . . I'll make you a steak."

Although it's disgusting, I serve Marco a bloody, rare slab of meat. I watch as he gobbles it down using his hands, keeping my distance by the stove—my hand on the skillet in case I need to use it as a weapon. Marco is an animal, tearing through flesh, blood dripping from his lips. My stomach turns with every bite. Pretty sure I won't be eating meat again anytime soon.

When he's done, Marco looks over at me, his eyes dark and wild, the skin around his mouth stained red. I hold up one finger to him.

"Shut it down, blood breath. I'm not about to become dessert."

My brother stares at me, his chest heaving, remnants of steak clinging to the corners of his mouth. But slowly, too slowly for my liking, he begins to come back to himself. And then he blinks and shakes his head as if to clear it.

"I'm sorry," he says, his voice rough and grating. A few more moments pass and then he leans back in the chair, sighing loudly. "That was hard," he says, sounding like himself again. "I wasn't sure I'd be able to hold back."

I'm terrified that this is really happening. That my brother wants to kill me. That I'm some monster keeper, the only thing standing between my brother and a baby vampire rampage. But I'm not giving up hope.

"What did you . . . what did you feel just now?" I ask tentatively.

"That I wanted to tear you apart." He looks over at me apologetically, and I tighten my grip on the skillet. "But it passed," he adds. "I just had to keep reminding myself who you were."

"Which is?" I ask.

"My pain-in-the-ass sister."

"Fair enough," I say. Just then, there's a soft knock at the front door.

Marco and I exchange a worried look.

"Stay here," I say. "I'll check it out."

My heart is pounding as I approach the door. I turn the lock and slowly ease the door open, my breath catching when I see it's Minnow. I'm struck silent with fear. I'm not sure if she's here to hurt us, but I remember Elijah's strategy for dealing with vampires: act like they're just insanely attractive locals. Regular people.

"Minnow?" I say, opening the door a bit wider. "What are you doing here?"

Her beautiful face is lined with worry, but her outfit is once again on point—red tube top with a plaid flared skirt, chain belt, and sneakers. She's holding a duffel bag and passes it to me.

"Annemarie wanted me to drop this off," she says. "It's for the parade. Should we meet you there around nine?"

"Oh . . . uh . . ." I take the bag from her, looking down at the shimmering pink fabric of the dress inside. "Sure," I say with absolutely no intention of meeting them anywhere. "Thanks."

Minnow smiles brightly. "I also wanted to check on Marco," she adds. "He hasn't answered any of my texts since he ran out of the party last night." She looks past my shoulder into the house. "Is he around?"

I bring the door toward me a bit more, blocking her view. She backs up, and then flicks her eyes to mine.

"He's not feeling so great," I tell her. "But I'll let him know you stopped by."

"You sure you don't want to just let me in?" she asks, her voice low-pitched. "I've already been invited, remember?"

My stomach sinks. She knows that I know, and yet we're playing a game. I have to fight to keep the fear out of my voice.

"I remember," I say, and try to smile. "It was the night Marco nearly puked on you at the beach."

"That was the one," she says, matching my smile. But the air between us is filled with a menacing sort of tension. Minnow runs her tongue over her teeth, and then shrugs. "Okay, then," she says.

She turns and walks off the porch before turning to look up at the attic window. Then she steadies her gaze on me. "You know I could come in if I wanted, right?" she asks, simply, as if it isn't a threat.

Terrified, I nod—not trusting my voice.

"See you tonight," she says, and smiles.

Minnow walks down the driveway, but I wait at the threshold until she turns the corner and disappears, and I breathe a sigh of relief.

Then I close the door and lock it.

CHAPTER THIRTY

f we're going to beat this vampire curse, I need more information. Right now my only source is a pair of podcasters who
want my brother dead. There's Nonna, but the more I think
about it, the more I'm convinced she might just drive a stake
through Marco's heart herself. She doesn't strike me as the kind
of person who would indulge vampire nonsense. I'm going to
have to be my own detective.

With that thought in mind, I leave the bag with the parade
dress by the entryway and go find my brother in the kitchen.

"Who was it?" he asks, but I shake my head.

"Doesn't matter," I tell him. "But I have things to do, so I
need you to get in the attic."

"Again?" he asks, sounding like a kid. "But why?"

"Because I only have a few hours to figure out how to keep
you alive and I can't spend them worrying that you'll bite me."

"I wouldn't—" he starts to argue, but stops himself. "Fine,"
he adds, disappointed.

Despite his reluctance, I get Marco into the attic and lock
the door. Maybe there's a way I can stop the Midnight Dive

ritual or even reverse it. But it's getting close to dusk—I won't have much time.

I pull my ASU hoodie on and stuff my feet into my sneakers and head out.

Walking, it takes me close to twenty minutes to get downtown. Before I turn onto Main Street, I hear music and the buzz of the crowd, the smell of popcorn and hot dogs. There are kids at the face-painting tent, and laughing tourists taking pictures with the mermaid statue. It's a literal party, people everywhere and the road closed off to traffic.

As I work my way toward the library, I keep my head down, unsure of who I can trust and doing my best to hurry but trying not to outright run and get noticed. Just up ahead, I see the awning for the ice cream shop. The lights are still on, the Closed sign facing out.

Erika made it out, left Nightfall behind. She came to me with a gift for Parrish, although I have no idea what it meant. Still, it might have been a clue. She didn't seem to be a vampire, but she knew what was going on in town. Perhaps . . . perhaps she left something in the ice cream shop. Something that could help us now.

I stop in front of the building and peer through the window—everything is still undisturbed. I try the door and it's locked. Rain drizzles onto the awning above me, and I glance around, not seeing any of the people I recognize as vampires. Then it occurs to me—they're getting ready for the parade. On the horizon, the sun is close to setting.

I go around the building to the back door. There's a big green dumpster and a few empty parking spaces. I find the delivery door for Scoops, the one we used when I came here with the girls.

I have a flash of hope and try the handle—locked. I knock even though I'm sure no one will answer. When I'm met with nothing more than the dull roar of the band on the street, I take one last look around to make sure no one is watching. Then I pick up a big rock from the ground next to the dumpster. I take the rock back to the door and slam it down on the handle with a loud clank.

The handle doesn't break off right away like I'd hoped. It's just dented. I drive the rock down again, and then once more before the handle finally gives way and falls to the ground. I drop the heavy rock next to it.

With a new jolt of adrenaline, I pull open the unsecured door and slip inside.

I'm immediately met by the sickly-sweet smell of vanilla, but over that is the foul smell of garbage. Something rank and rotting. I pull my shirt over my nose and move further inside the building.

The hallway is dark, the light from the lobby barely making its way back here. I want to flip on another light switch, but I'm scared that someone outside will notice. I'm a criminal at this point. I can't believe I'm breaking and entering, and then I can't believe I'm worried about breaking the law when I'm trapped in a town full of vampires.

"Focus," I whisper to myself.

I don't want to stay in the shop any longer than I have to—the smell is absolutely horrific, unbearable. As I head toward the front, prickling heat begins to race up my arms as the realization settles over me. The smell . . . it might be a body. In fact, I'll admit that it's pretty likely—I've heard it described enough times on my true-crime podcasts.

My eyes well up, with both fear and disgust. I should call

the police, but I'm not sure how complicit they are. And who else can I call? My only hope is that Erika left behind something I can use to figure out how to get Marco out of town.

Staying low, I swing behind the counter and look around. Ice cream has melted in a container on the counter, a metal scoop left abandoned next to it. I make my way toward the kitchen.

When I push open the door, I gasp. There is a pair of legs sticking out from the walk-in freezer. All I want to do is run, but I cover the lower half of my face and move closer to see who it is. The light grows dimmer the further into the kitchen I go.

A man is lying there on his stomach, his head turned in my direction. His open eyes have a milky film over them. It's Asa, the hitchhiker I saw on my first day in Nightfall. Annemarie told me he went home, to Joshua Tree. He looks like he's been dead awhile—probably since that first night at the beach.

My breath catches when I turn and see a hacky sack on the counter. The same one that Erika left for Parrish. So he's . . . he's been here. He's seen this. I stumble back a step, trying to keep my wits about me.

The freezer door is open and I walk toward it, stepping over Asa's body to look inside. When I do, my stomach turns. There are more bodies stored there. One of them I recognize immediately—Greg from Texas. The guy whose watch I found in the sand. His bloated face is coated with sand, proving he was exactly where I thought. On his neck, there is a gaping wound, a chunk of flesh missing. But there is no blood. He's so pale he's almost blue, and there isn't a drop of blood on the floor, even though the area around the collar of his shirt is soaked with it.

Hanging from a hook, his back to me, is a man in uniform. I swallow hard, backing up until I bump into the wall with a jolt. That's . . . the sheriff. Sheriff Wyndell. They killed him, too.

I spin away from the carnage, horrified. But when I look up, a face is staring back at me, and I let out a scream. It takes a second for my brain to compute that I'm looking at a missing persons poster.

In fact, there are a lot of them. The bulletin board is littered with flyers, some of them dating back to the '80s, but most from the past few years. There are so many that they've been stapled on top of each other before spilling onto the wall.

This mixture of bitter death and ice cream sweetness is stomach churning and I wrap my arms around myself. I'm in the middle of an absolute nightmare. I'm barely holding on at this point, and that's when I see it.

Missing: Alexander Parrish—Seattle, Washington.

At first, the picture doesn't totally look like him. The guy staring back is smiling, with full cheeks and reddish-brown hair. He's cute, but . . . average. He's the boy next door. But those eyes—dark and deep. Those are unmistakable.

I put my palm over my mouth, holding back a fearful cry as I stare at his image. How close I was to the danger without realizing. How naive I have been.

I look at the bodies again, desperate for escape. I quickly run through the shop and out the back door. I spin around to look at the door as I back away, making sure none of the corpses have gotten up to chase me.

My heart is beating so fast that it's hard for me to think. I might pass out. The sounds and smells around me are overwhelming. I need to go. I'll report the dead bodies once I get out of town. For now, I need to figure out how to get us out of Nightfall.

I slip between the buildings and head out to the sidewalk, sliding into the crowds on Main Street, doing my best to seamlessly blend in. The rain has stopped, but I pull up my hood to be more inconspicuous.

I'm about to cross the street when there is a blip of a police siren, and I jump.

I step back from the curb as a police cruiser edges toward me. I'm immediately panicked. Someone must have seen me break into the ice cream shop. Maybe there was a camera. I don't know what to do. Should I run for it? Should I tell them about the bodies? I'm absolutely terrified as the cruiser eases to a stop in front of me.

The window rolls down. The officer is younger than the sheriff and has a black mustache and dark skin. He nods at me.

Please don't arrest me, I pray. *Please don't turn me over to the vampires.*

"Theodora Maggione, right?" the officer asks, studying me. "I'm Deputy Brooks." He motions to my sweatshirt hood as if telling me to pull it down.

With a shaking hand, I push the hood off my head, my hair damp and my ears cold. I try to read his expression, but I'm getting nothing.

"Yes," I say, confirming my name. "Is something wrong?" I hope the answer is no. Just say no.

"Yes, actually," he says. My stomach sinks, my chest growing tight with anxiety.

The deputy shifts the cruiser into park and gets out. I watch, terrified as he comes to stand in front of me, looking me over from head to toe before studying my eyes.

I do my best to look concerned, not guilty. But I'm not sure if I'm pulling it off.

"The other night," the deputy says, "Sheriff Wyndell came by your house."

"Yes," I say, swallowing hard. "The sheriff talked to me and my family."

"What time would you say he left?" he asks.

I'm struck with guilt. Do I tell him what I found? What happens if I do? It's not like he'd just let me go home. At the very least, I'd be at the police station, giving a statement while the girls in town drown my brother in the ocean.

"What was that?" I ask, trying to focus.

"What time did the sheriff leave your house?" the deputy asks, annoyed.

"Around seven, just before dinner," I tell him. "Wh-what is this about?"

The deputy narrows his eyes. "The sheriff didn't come home Thursday night," he says. "His wife called me. Did you see him after he left your house?"

"No," I tell him. "I didn't see the sheriff after he left."

Sheriff Wyndell never made it home from his visit to me. I think back to him on the porch and realize that he was scared of Minnow. The same Minnow who is about to unalive and then re-alive my brother.

The deputy studies me, and I try to breathe normally. But behind me there are dead bodies piled up in the ice cream shop. Any longer and I'm going to break.

Finally, the deputy nods and takes a step back and it's like a weight has been lifted off my chest.

"If you see anything," he says, "call the station immediately, understand?"

"Of course," I say, breathing out, relieved.

The deputy opens the car door but stops before getting in and looks at me. "I heard your father was buying a place over on Carnation Drive," he says. "I'm glad you'll all be staying. Nightfall is a nice town. So long as you don't cause any trouble."

I force a smile. "Thank you," I say.

"Now, you let your grandma know I said hi," he adds, and gets in the car. He runs his siren once, making me jump again, and then pulls out into the street and slowly drives through the crowd.

I hate this town. I hate it.

We need to go, take our chances on the road. I dash across the street and start for home, but as I approach the library, my plans disintegrate. My heart leaps into my throat and I stop, my shoulders bumped by moving tourists.

There is a figure sitting on the library's large stone steps, hands folded between his knees. Parrish shrugs miserably when our eyes meet. He was waiting for me.

I'm struck with fear as I take a tentative step toward him. "What do you want, Alexander?" I ask, my voice barely carrying over the sound of the band.

He flinches at his first name. "Haven't been called that in a while," he says, and motions to the spot next to him on the step. "I'm just here to talk."

I could refuse, of course. I could walk past him or run all the way home. But . . . he could also kill me. Any of them could. In the end, I'm looking for information on monsters. Who better to better to ask than a monster closely tied to the vampire girl gang terrorizing my family? Reluctantly, I nod.

Blood pumping quickly, I climb the stairs and sit next to him, careful not to get too close.

"So now you know," Parrish says, exhaling heavily. "I saw you go into the ice cream shop. I assume you found Asa, Greg, and the sheriff. I told the girls to clean up their own mess. Erika inspired me."

"That's normally your job?" I ask. "Is that what Erika was saying with her gift, for you to stop helping them?"

He lowers his eyes. "She's been telling me that for a long time," he says. "She isn't a vampire, but she got stuck helping them. She's a good person. In fact, she tried to save me once. But it was too late. She's safe, by the way," he adds, looking at me. "For now at least."

I try to discern if Parrish plans to hurt her. But I don't think so. He looks absolutely beaten down and dejected.

"I'm sure none of this has been easy for you," he adds. "And for that, I'm sorry. I didn't want any of this, if it helps."

"It doesn't help," I say. To be honest, I'm sick of his nice-guy routine. He's a vampire. He's not my friend. He's not my moody love interest. He's a killer. "Now, how do I save my brother?"

Parrish blows out a breath and stretches out his legs as if settling in for a long story. "Nightfall is a vampire town," he says. "We run this place. Or should I say, the girls run this place. Even if they believe you, none of the locals are going to stop them, so there's no point in asking for help."

He confirms my greatest fear with ease, and I look around at the quaint little buildings of downtown with a new kind of resentment.

"How many vampires are here?" I ask.

"A dozen or so," he responds. "For now. The girls are looking at expanding. A way to bring in more food." He pauses. "More tourists."

I cringe at the thought of being considered a meal.

"You know, not everyone we bite becomes a vampire,"

Parrish says. "That's just in the movies. Some can't tolerate it—like poor Asa in there. But the rest, like your brother, have been chosen to join us. He's not leaving here, Theo. I'm sorry about that."

"And me?" I ask. "What's my part in this?"

"I don't know yet," he says. "Annemarie wanted to keep you, but I stopped her. And then it was on me. They chose you for me. I'm supposed to bite you tonight. Before the Dive."

"If I refuse?" I ask.

He winces. "You can't," he says, looking over at me guiltily. "Not if I really wanted to bite you."

I should be scared of him, but there is vulnerability just under the surface. The human side of him, I guess. A piece that's still there.

"And then what?" I ask. "I'll become a vampire or die?"

"That's the rule."

"How did this happen to you?" I ask. "Who changed you?"

"Beatrice bit me at the beach two years ago," he says, looking away. "Just like your brother. And then she brought me to the Dive, and with my parents not ten feet away, she drowned me in the ocean. Glamoured my parents so they couldn't see me, couldn't even hear me calling out for help."

Parrish's voice catches, and he blinks away tears before they can fall. I swallow hard at the horror of his story.

"When I woke up, I knew it was too late. And yet," he says, almost wistfully, "I tried to escape. I got in the car with my parents, told them to drive fast even as I ached with hunger. But we didn't make it far. On the way out of town, Beatrice and the others ambushed our car. Drove us off the road, killing my parents. Imagine my horror when I survived. That I have to fucking live like this."

He motions to himself, his face a portrait of misery.

"Why can't you run again?" I ask. "Take off when they're all at the Dive."

"Because I wouldn't get far," he says. "Even if I avoided the light, fed discreetly, they would come for me. That's the thing, I can't hide from them—we're connected, as much I would love to sever that bond. Annemarie just got back from killing a guy out in New Mexico who ran. No one gets away, even the locals. In fact, I'm supposed to find Erika after the Dive. I either bring her home or kill her."

I swallow hard, scared of what I'm about to suggest. "Then why not just kill the girls first?" I ask.

He laughs. "Like Beatrice?" he says. "Trust me, I've tried. But she is stronger, faster, smarter. She's broken my neck more times than I can count."

"And Minnow?" I ask.

He laughs. "Not a chance. She's the strongest."

"The queen?" I ask, a quick jolt to my heart.

"Yeah, I guess you could say that," he replies. "But they're all strong—all three of them."

So it's Minnow—I should have figured. Of course Marco had to fall for the vampire queen. And if Parrish won't even try to kill her, what hope do I have of defeating her?

Parrish looks at me with pain in his eyes, so close to human that I almost forget he's not.

"But you," he whispers, "you can still leave. I won't chase you. But you can't take your brother with you. They've chosen him. There's no stopping that now."

"But why?" I ask. "What does that mean?"

Parrish tilts his head, and his expression changes. "The town has to go on," he says. "But they're careful about which outsiders stay. They don't trust them. Bloodlines run deep here. Your family is an especially prized possession. They—"

"Well, well," a voice sings out. "Isn't this a sight for sore eyes?"

I turn to see Minnow on the sidewalk, watching us. My heart leaps into my throat. I'm completely exposed, all pretenses gone.

"I knew you two had something special," she adds, climbing the stairs slowly. "Chemistry is off the charts."

"Minnow, we—" Parrish starts, but Minnow snaps her head in his direction and silences him with a look.

"Run along now," she tells him. "Theo and I have some business to discuss."

To my alarm, Parrish stands up, about to leave me behind with the head of a vampire coven.

"Wait," I say, reaching for his arm.

He turns back to me. "I can't," he says. "I'm sorry, but I can't." Then he hurries down the stairs and I watch as he falls into step with a group of tourists, then disappears around a corner, leaving me completely vulnerable.

"Stop looking so worried," Minnow says, sitting down next to me. "I'm not going to hurt you. I thought we were friends."

"We're not," I say, trying to keep my voice steady. She has the nerve to look offended by my comment.

"So," she says, "what did Parrish tell you? He's always been a sucker for a pretty girl." She laughs at her own joke.

"That he doesn't want to be a vampire," I say, "and you assholes won't let him go."

"Whoa," Minnow says, holding up her hands. "Let's not start name-calling. I was trying to give you a compliment. And don't go singing the praises of the guy who has been planning to take your life since he first saw you by the water. He's not innocent. None of us are."

The revelation shouldn't be a shock and yet my heart feels plucked and raw. I don't want to know the number of times I nearly died at their hands.

"Minnow," I say, trying my best to sound forceful, "leave my brother alone. Just tell me how to change him back."

"Your brother's with me now," Minnow says. "We're bonded. We belong together."

"That was before he knew you were a vampire."

"Is it?" she asks. "You act as if he wasn't a willing participant. Your brother was hungry for attention, and I fed him. He needed to be loved. There's no going back anymore. And he doesn't want to, not when you give him the choice between this life and the one he used to have."

"I think I know my brother better than you," I say.

"You don't even know yourself," she says. "This town is in your blood too—you drank it at the bonfire, remember? Drank it greedily from my flask."

"What?" I say, recoiling. "No, that was sambuca."

"Was it?" Minnow asks with a smile. "Or did I just tell you it was? Parrish may have slowed things down, but you'll see soon enough. Nightfall is your home whether you like it or not. It's a part of you."

"Like hell it is," I say. "I'm not staying here. Neither is Marco."

"Your brother will wither away painfully if he doesn't change tonight," she says. "Now, would you make him suffer? For what? Some broken home back in Arizona?"

"Fuck. You," I say clearly. "I'm going to find a way to save him."

I'm feeling emboldened, stronger. But, of course, that's only because Minnow is letting me feel that way. She reaches out and grabs my chin hard, her nails biting into my skin. I wince, unable to pull away.

"I'm done playing these games," she says, her eyes bright with fury. "Marco belongs with us," she asserts. "He will be at the parade tonight. And if you still want to be part of his life, your family's life, you'll be there, too. There's still time for you. But either way, this is our town. Our rules."

She shakes her hand, releasing my face, and there is stinging pain. Minnow starts down the stairs as I touch my chin. When I draw my hand back, my fingers are covered in streaks of blood.

I jump to my feet and realize that Minnow is already gone, vanished into downtown Nightfall among all the other people.

The sun is nearly set, the sky growing dark. I have to get back to my grandmother's house. Marco and I are out of time. The parade will start soon. Several families are already setting up spots along the curb to watch. Do they know? Are they the townspeople watching along the beach in the mural?

There's no time to consider the answer. I start running, bumping into several tourists and ignoring their cries of protest. I'm terrified that I won't be able to protect my brother. That I won't get to him in time.

Minnow is coming tonight—they're all coming. I need to save my brother and get us out of Nightfall.

CHAPTER THIRTY-ONE

take out my phone as I rush toward Nonna's house. I call Marco, but he doesn't pick up. The phone rings and then beeps as it drops the call. I try again.

"Come on," I breathe out, frustrated. When I can't get through a second time, I click to call my father instead. Although my dad has been part of the problem, I have to tell him what's going on. At this point, there's no other choice.

The line clicks and my heart leaps.

"Dad," I say quickly, "Marco is in danger. He—"

Before I can finish my sentence, the call disconnects. I immediately try my father's number again, but there is only a series of beeps before the call drops.

I stop running, fear creeping up my throat.

When I look at my phone, the bars are gone, replaced with a small *x*. No service. Please not now.

I open my messages and find my brother's number. I quickly type, *We have to run!* and hit Send.

The message turns red—undelivered.

"No," I say, wanting to cry. I call Elijah, but the line drops again. "No!" I scream, and then try my mother.

Beep, beep, beep.

Nothing is working, no calls or texts are going through. I look around. The neighborhood is quiet and calm. Most people are already downtown.

I have to get home. I have to get to Marco before they stop me.

My body already tired, I break into a run again.

Rain starts falling quickly, creating a mist and hitting my face with painful little taps, but I don't slow down, even though I'm out of breath, my throat burning. I have to get home.

Finally, I can see Nonna's house. I'm winded as I jog up the driveway. Both her minivan and my father's car are gone. I run up the steps and pull out my keys, unlock the front door and get inside the house. As I'm locking the door behind me, though, I see the house phone on the floor. The cord has been slashed.

My fear explodes and I dash up the stairs, to the attic. I have to make sure Marco is okay. I fish the key out of my pocket, but just as I clear the top step, I freeze.

The handle has been broken off the attic door, and splintered wood is cast across the floor.

"No," I gasp. Slowly, I make my way up to the attic, terrified at what will be waiting for me. The room has been tossed, sheets and clothing on the floor, the trunk half-destroyed. The mirror smashed. And my brother is gone.

Marco is gone.

I drop down on the bed, tears running down my cheeks. The girls have gotten to him and taken him away. I'm too late. I've failed him.

Overwhelmed, I curl up on my side and cry. I have no idea how to fix this. I don't know how to save my brother.

There is the slow screech of the front door opening. I shoot up with a new surge of hope. I quickly clear the tears from my face and dash toward the sound.

I practically trample down the stairs. "Marco?" I yell, hoping to hear him call back. Instead, when I get into the entryway, the door is closed. I turn to see my grandmother sitting calmly in the living room recliner as if she's been waiting for me.

"Nonna!" I say, immediately breaking down as I run to her. She needs to know everything that's happened. That Marco is in danger. She has to help us.

But if my grandmother can tell I'm distressed, she has no noticeable reaction.

"Nonna," I say stopping in front of her. "It's Marco. We have to—"

"Sit down," she tells me calmly, nodding toward the sofa.

"No, we have to find Marco," I say, waving her up. She clearly doesn't understand the urgency. "Come on, we have to go."

"There's nowhere to go, Theo. Now sit down."

I have a spike of fear as I stare into her dark eyes. A sudden realization slips over me, and I stumble back a step, falling into a sitting position on the couch. I can't believe I didn't see it before.

"Nonna," I say, panic climbing up my throat, "are you one of them? Are you . . . a vampire?"

She stares at me for a long moment, and then slowly leans in. I hold my breath, terrified of the truth.

"That has to be the stupidest thing you've ever said," she says slowly. "I thought your brain worked."

I'm caught off guard by her response and let out a startled laugh. Okay, first good thing to happen today. My grandmother isn't a vampire. "Wait," I ask with a new flash of terror. "Is my father a vampire?"

She purses her lips like it's another bad question.

Now I'm just confused by her calmness when everything is so out of control. "Then what is going on?" I ask. "You need to tell me everything. Marco has been . . ." I look out the front window into the dark night. "Marco's been bitten."

"Obviously," she says.

I swing back to her, studying her face. The beginnings of anger building in my chest. "So you *do* know about the vampires?" I ask.

"I live here," she replies dully.

My anger intensifies. "And you didn't think to warn us?" I demand. "Protect us?"

Her expression weakens slightly, and I'm reminded that she didn't want us here in the first place. Which means she didn't want us here with the vampires. In her way, she did try to protect us. My anger fades back into dread.

"What do we do?" I ask, desperate.

"Not much you can do," she says in low voice. "Not now."

Her words send a wave of hopelessness through me, but I can see that she's distressed. No, I'm not giving up. It won't end with me sitting here, doing nothing.

"You need to explain," I say. "Because I won't accept this. I'll burn this entire town to the ground if I have to."

"Killing more innocent people isn't going to help," my grandmother says as if I'm the one who has gone too far. She eases back in the chair and then pushes herself up. She walks toward the kitchen.

Wait, where is she going?

I scramble to my feet to follow her and pause in the kitchen doorway. Nonna is stirring a steaming pot. Next to it on the counter is a line of tiny stick dolls.

"What do those dolls do anyway?" I ask, motioning to them. "What was the point?"

"They're made of dried wolfsbane stems. It helps with the glamour," she says. "It's easier to see through it if you know what to look for. Vampires also hate the smell."

"You could have mentioned that a few days ago," I say.

"There wasn't a vampire sleeping under my roof a few days ago."

She kind of has a point, but so do I. A little more notice would have gone a long way. I'm going to need more information than this. It's time to loop in my father.

"Where's my dad?" I ask her. "And how much does he know?"

"He's already downtown with Olivia," Nonna says, pausing before speaking again. "Theo, your father knows all about Nightfall," she adds, looking back at me. "Of course he does; he grew up here."

Prickles of heat race over my skin, and tears sting my eyes. "Why would he . . . why would he bring us here, then?" I demand.

"Sometimes Nightfall calls you home," she says solemnly. "The lure of comfort, peace—especially when you feel lost. This place *is* special. Sometimes I think the whole damn town is a glamour."

Nonna clicks off the burner on the stove and sets the pot aside. She turns back to me, her lips pressed together sympathetically.

"You have every right to be angry with him," she adds. "Your father took a chance coming back to this place after getting out all those years ago. But he should have been safe here," she emphasizes. "The vampires would never hurt a local—it's our pact, our bond even. That meant you should have been safe too—bloodlines mean something. But . . . someone stepped out of line and bit your brother."

"And now Marco's stuck here as a monster?" I ask, feeling betrayed by my father. "And my dad just, what? Sacrificed him to the town?"

"When you're from Nightfall," Nonna replies quietly, "you learn to accept the situation, and sometimes you even grow fond of it. Glamour can be a hell of a drug for some. For others, it can be the only thing that softens their pain."

She pauses, and I have a flash of my father back home, sitting alone in the yard after the divorce. Lonely. Quiet.

"But I promise you," Nonna continues, "no matter how foolish he's acting, your father was *never* going to abandon Marco here. In fact, he bought a house to stay with him once he realized he'd been bitten. He accepted what he couldn't change."

I run one palm over my face, overwhelmed and sickened. Still confused. Our own father knowingly brought Marco and me to a *vampire town*? The house he bought was to stay with my brother?

"And what about me?" I ask, looking at my grandmother again. "What was supposed to happen to me?"

Nonna swallows hard, and looks away. "He wanted you to stay, Theo," she says. "Your father loves you both so much. He wanted to stay together. And he thought he could protect you, thought you'd come to accept the town as he did. But he didn't understand the dynamics in Nightfall were changing. New vampires can get out of control sometimes. Normally, there's people keeping them on course, like me and the sheriff."

"Well, the sheriff's dead," I tell her, more harshly than I intend. I immediately regret the tone when my grandmother's back straightens, her lips set in a straight line.

"Now, that's too bad," she murmurs. She grinds her teeth a moment, as if lost in a thought. Then she grabs a kettle and fills it with water and puts it on the stove. "Although to be honest," she adds, "I never did like him. Now sit down. I'm making tea."

"We don't have time for tea," I say, incredulous. "We have to get Marco out of here."

"You have time," she says. "They won't bring Marco out until the parade starts. We have more to talk about."

When the tea is ready, Nonna brings it over and sets a mug in front of me. She sits on the other side of the table.

"I've done my best to look after this town," she says, staring down at her tea. "But I've gone and gotten old. I've gotten tired."

She looks up at me and there is a zap to my heart at the vulnerability in her expression.

"You're not *that* old," I offer to make her smile. When she does, the skin around her eyes is wrinkled with age.

"I will protect this family until my last breath," she tells me. "But it's not always easy—especially if they don't listen. Still . . . you love them anyway." She reaches over to grip my hand, her fingers hot from the cup. "You protect each other no matter what," she says.

"I understand," I tell her. "And we will, Nonna. That's why I need your help."

She lets out a breath, and then releases my hand. She takes a sip of her tea, setting it down gently. For a moment, she's lost somewhere inside her head.

"Why would you stay in a town infested with vampires?" I ask.

She looks up, surprised by the question. "I'm not going to be driven from my home," she says. "I'm not going to leave my neighbors. Besides, those girls maybe have gotten out of control the last few years, but . . ."

"Yeah, out of control like killing unsuspecting tourists?" I ask.

Nonna stands and walks over to the sliding glass door to stare into the backyard. She clicks on the light. When she does, I look past her to the old, withered tree and the patch of dead grass beneath it.

"My first husband, Xavier, was the one who cursed this town," Nonna says quietly.

For a moment, I'm not sure I heard her correctly. First, who the hell is Xavier and why didn't anyone tell me that Nonna was married before she married my grandfather? And secondly, *what?*

"What do you mean?" I ask, apprehension spreading over my skin. "Who is he? How did he curse the town?"

"He was the mayor once," she says. "Survived a shipwreck and was hailed as a hero. But he was a cruel man."

"Wait," I say, thinking suddenly of the podcast. "Are you talking about Alfonse Cardelli? Nonna, that was in the 1800s. I know you said you were old, but—"

"That's him," she says. "Alfonse has lived many lives. He originally came over as a stowaway." Nonna continues to stare out at the yard, sounding more like she's talking to herself than to me. "But when he began to devour the crew, they discovered what he was. The port of Nightfall was just ahead, and the men feared he would slaughter the town. So they sacrificed themselves by driving the ship into the rocks, hoping to kill Alfonse in the process.

"He didn't die though," Nonna continues. "No, unfortunately he did not die. He came ashore and took over the town, using his glamour to fool people. He picked off the girls in town and blamed it on outsiders. A few girls survived his attacks, becoming vampires themselves. When they weren't content to do his bidding, he had them killed. It was a cycle of terror; the people lived in fear. It was like a witch hunt, townspeople dragging their daughters into the ocean at his behest, killing them for him. Not all of those girls had even been bitten—innocent lives lost."

I stare at her back, my breath coming faster and my pulse quickening. I know part of this story already, but I didn't know my family was tied into it.

"Just as the sailors feared, Alfonse tore quickly through the town," she says. "But soon, people became suspicious of him, of how he never aged. Of the destruction that started with his arrival. They ran him off, and rather than kill them all, he decided to bide his time. He went south for a generation, hunting and feeding along the coast. Once he was gone, the town began to rebuild.

"When I was eighteen, I met a young man who had just arrived in town—a tourist. He called himself Xavier. We were married and he bought this house"—she motions around—"an old house that belonged to a long-ago mayor who no one ever talked about. At first, Xavier was kind to me. A beautiful house, a doting husband, and my best friend, Sylvia, living close by. She would stay here all the time—she even had her own room in the attic. Some afternoons, she would paint in the yard, just under that tree. She was so talented."

"Your friend Sylvia who painted the mural?" I ask, remembering the newspaper article in the scrapbook.

"Yes," Nonna replies, and I can hear a soft smile on her lips, even though her voice is tinged with sadness. "But then . . . things started to change in Nightfall. Young girls started disappearing again. There were murmurs about restarting the drownings . . . and all of us girls feared what that would mean. Would we be targeted?"

My grandmother takes a moment, looking down at her hands.

"What happened, Nonna?" I ask. "What happened to your husband?"

"One day," she says, "I came home from the market and found Xavier feeding on Sylvia. My husband looked up and his face . . . his face wasn't his own. His glamour had slipped away. "He was a vampire," she says, her voice bitter. "He was Alfonse, the mayor of Nightfall. Blood poured from Sylvia's wounds as my husband backed away, hissing that this was his town. That he could do what he wanted. But I had to stop him. I had to protect Sylvia and all the girls in Nightfall."

Nonna pauses, swallowing hard. "I grabbed the poker from the fireplace and drove it straight through his chest, piercing his heart," she says. "But he didn't die right away. So I kept stabbing him"—her voice catches—"but he just. Wouldn't. Die. Sylvia crawled over, blood pouring from her wounds, her eyes wild with hatred and hunger."

She stops and I can hear her breathing heavily.

"Before I understood what she was doing, she began to feed

on him," my grandmother says. "Tearing open his throat, biting off whole chunks as she furiously drank his blood. And I . . . I pushed her away, unable to watch another second. Then I grabbed the metal shovel from the fireplace. I stood over my husband and I chopped off his head. When I did, Sylvia screamed, clutching her stomach as if in pain, skidding back from me, hissing. I burned Alfonse's head in the fireplace. And while Sylvia continued to die, moaning in pain, I dragged my husband's headless body into the yard and buried him."

"What?" I ask, startled, as I push back from the table. I look immediately at the spot in the yard, knowing exactly where Alfonse is buried.

"His rot still kills my grass," Nonna continues. "A stain on everything he touches."

She turns and comes back to the table to sit in front of her tea as if she hadn't just recounted her husband's brutal murder. As if she isn't a badass vampire slayer.

"If you killed him," I say, leaning toward her, "then how did the town get like this? How did this lead to Minnow and her friends? How did the girls of Nightfall become the ones to be afraid of?"

Nonna closes her eyes. "It's my fault," she says quietly. "Sylvia didn't die that day, or rather she didn't stay dead. Killing Alfonse would have ended the curse, but she fed on him as he died—his blood still flows in her veins. I didn't realize . . . I promise you, I didn't know that I needed to kill her too," she continues. "All I saw was my best friend in pain, her gaping wounds, blood everywhere. I knew she was dying, so I brought her to the water to let her slip away at the beach that she loved."

"What happened to her?" I ask, trying to picture my grandmother doing all these things. She was obviously young once, but I envision my tiny tracksuit-wearing grandmother as the one dragging a body through downtown Nightfall.

"I laid Sylvia in the water," Nonna continues. "I said goodbye as she slipped away. But then . . . she emerged from the water reborn. Not as a monster like Alfonse—Sylvia was powerful, and yes . . . she needed blood to feed." My grandmother winces. "But she understood what that vampire had done to the girls of Nightfall, and she vowed that it would never happen again. I took that vow with her.

"Sylvia painted the mural downtown as a celebration and a warning: we killed the beast of Nightfall, finished the job of the sailors. We wouldn't hesitate to do it again. Sylvia even started the Midnight Dive to honor the town's past. She promised me that she would always remember when to draw the line—she knew I didn't want more vampires in Nightfall."

Nonna takes a slow breath. "But you don't forget being murdered like that," she says. "That trauma stuck to her. She couldn't stand her own name anymore, so she faked her death three, four times—whenever the memories began haunting her again. But after a decade with that curse running through her veins, Sylvia broke her promise to me. She began to turn other girls in town into vampires, using the Midnight Dive to drown their mortal bodies and transform them. Soon after, tourists began disappearing, and the local townspeople grew fewer, more isolated. But no one stopped her, not even me. We kept her secret, because despite everything she still protected us. Until now, not a single townsperson has been murdered in Nightfall since Alfonse died in 1954. Not a single one. So when it came to Sylvia, it was always best to just leave her be."

"And my dad?" I ask, trying to keep up with the logic. "He knew about *all* of this?"

"No," my grandmother says, shaking her head. "I never told him that story—I'd lost track of her by then. I haven't talked about Sylvia Ware in a long time."

Although I don't mean to be sentimental, I feel a splash of warmth at my grandmother's confiding in me.

"When your father was your age," she continues, "he was close friends with a few of those girls. Eventually, he went away to college, and when he returned with your mother, their relationship created a problem. You see, although he was local, your father been chosen by one of the girls. But before he could be bitten, before they could drown him at the Midnight Dive, your mother left town. Joey chased after her and it saved his life."

"My mother didn't know, right?" I ask, worried that she had also kept these secrets from me. My grandmother quickly shakes her head.

"No," she says. "Rosie was bright, though. She felt something was off. As for your father, after being away all those years, away from the glamour and the beach, his memory of this place had faded a bit. I'd hoped by coming back, he could find a little piece of himself again.

"But now I see that the vampires are out of control," she continues. "They've killed Wyatt, which is out of bounds, even for them. They will have to be dealt with. But . . . like I said"—she breathes out heavily—"I'm too old now."

It occurs to me that Minnow isn't the leader of the vampires. She may be strong, but killing her wouldn't solve anything. "Sylvia . . . ," I start. "Is she the vampire queen?"

My grandmother considers the question. "I suppose she is," she replies after a moment. "But whatever you're thinking, it's no use. Like I said, it's best to just leave Sylvia Ware alone. She would be too strong by now."

"Then what am I supposed to do?" I demand.

"You need to leave town, Theo," Nonna tells me, although it seems to pain her. "They'll let you go. But your brother must stay. Your father will watch over him. We both will."

I'm disappointed and sickened. I'm not going to give up, and I can't believe my grandmother is. It's betrayal; it's heartbreak.

"I'm not leaving Marco," I tell her angrily. "And I think you're a coward for even suggesting it."

My grandmother lowers her eyes and I walk back into the living room, pausing at the phone on the floor. I wish I could call Elijah and ask him for help, but I'm on my own now.

In the entryway, I scoop up the bag with the dress that Minnow left for me. Fuck the queens of the Dive. I'm going to the parade to save my brother.

CHAPTER THIRTY-TWO

'm anxious, terrified, and determined. Wearing the dress Minnow left for me and a pair of sneakers that I can run in, I go downstairs. My grandmother looks over from her recliner but doesn't say anything as she watches me leave. She's already told me her story—she won't help me beyond that.

I start the long walk to downtown, hyperaware of every swaying bush, every rustling tree.

A car pulls up next to me. Reluctantly, I look over with my heart in my throat, sure it's one of the vampires. I'm relieved to see it's the Range Rover. Felix rolls down his window.

"I'd say you look nice," he starts, "but I feel like you're on your way to do something really stupid." He smiles. "Now get in."

I cast one more look around and then climb into the backseat. Elijah looks back at me from the driver's seat, taking in my outfit. He nods his approval.

"You're still in town," I say, relief thick in my voice. "I thought you were leaving?"

"Yeah, I guess it turns out we're a couple of heroes or

something," Elijah says, shrugging. "Either way, we had to stick around to make sure you got out of here okay."

I smile, my heart swelling. "I really need the backup," I say.

As Elijah pulls into the street, heading toward downtown, Felix turns to me.

"I wanted to thank you for saving my life," he tells me. "If you hadn't come into the bathroom when you did . . . I don't know. Anyway, in all of the madness, I didn't get the chance to say it. So, Theo, thank you for punching your brother in the face."

"I've always wanted to," I say. But in truth, I feel guilty for Marco's behavior, even if it's not my fault.

"Are you doing okay?" Felix asks. "With the whole . . . vampire stuff?"

"I really think the answer there is no," I say, holding back tears. Felix reaches back for a hug and I lean forward, resting my cheek against his shoulder.

"We tried to call you," Elijah says. "We went by your place and your grandmother told us you were heading downtown. I assume to the parade?" He motions to the dress.

"I have to get there before the Midnight Dive," I tell him.

"Is there a plan?" he asks, hopefully.

"Sort of," I reply. "I planned to walk in the parade, get close enough to Marco to talk to him, and convince him to make a run for it. Think it will work?"

"No," Elijah says simply. "But I'm not sure we have anything better."

"I finally got some answers today," I say. Felix turns back to me as Elijah watches me in the rearview mirror.

I go on to tell them everything, starting with finding the

bodies in the ice cream shop and then Parrish talking to me on the steps of the library. Then I pass along Nonna's absolutely bonkers story about the history of Nightfall and her friend Sylvia Ware.

"I need your help," I say. "If something happens to me before I can get to Marco, I want you to help my brother."

Felix frowns and glances at Elijah.

"Just try to get him away from here before they drown him," I add, trying to overcome their reluctance. "Bring him home to our grandmother if you can. Don't . . . chop off his head or anything. Okay?"

"We'll try," Elijah says, averting his eyes from mine in the mirror.

They have no loyalty to my brother—after all, he tried to kill one of them—but I'm hoping they'll respect my wishes anyway.

Elijah finds a parking spot behind one of the shops. The night is loud, people cheering, music playing. It sounds like the parade has already started, and I have a panicked moment that we've missed it. But when I check the time on my phone, it's only 11:45. They shouldn't have gotten to the water yet.

I jog ahead, the podcast boys close behind. I'm moving too quickly to be afraid, my mind focused on finding Marco. Once we're on Main Street, there is an explosion of people. The parade is passing us. There are people with balloons and wearing comically big hats. Some are in wigs and feather boas. Mermaids everywhere. Everyone's moving slowly toward the promenade. It's sensory overload.

"Where do I start?" I call back to Elijah and Felix, my voice barely audible above the noise. Elijah holds up his hands, as if saying he has no idea.

I gaze down the street toward the promenade where the parade will end. It's lit up and crowded with people waiting for the parade to come through. The girls are going to lead everyone into the water, and then they'll drown the ones they've chosen—all while the crowd cheers, most of them not even knowing what's truly happening.

It's then that I catch sight of my father standing on the curb opposite us with Olivia Miles on his arm. They're sharing cotton candy, laughing as they point out their favorite costumes. Olivia looks up and notices me. She smiles brightly and waves, tugging on my dad's arm to let him know that I'm here.

My father spots me and his face lights up. I can't help it. I feel tears welling up, knowing how much danger surrounds us. Knowing that my brother will likely die tonight and that's the best-case scenario. As a tear slides down my cheek, my father's smiles fades. Something like guilt crosses his face. And then I turn away. I push through the crowd and into the parade and begin to march with the locals.

It's a swirl of fabric and noise, laughter and cheers. The older man next to me is grinning from ear to ear, a woman with red hair throwing candy to families along the curb. It smells of sweat and salt and . . . blood.

And then I feel him behind me. I have a sense of calm even when I know I should be afraid. Peace amid chaos. I turn slowly just as Parrish falls into step next to me. He looks at me, his gaze sweeping over my dress.

"I hope you don't mind me telling you that you look absolutely beautiful tonight," he says, leaning toward me.

"I do mind," I reply. I'm reminded of how devastatingly

handsome he is and resent him for it. Glamour. Pretty good glamour at that.

"I'd hoped you left town," he says. "You're putting me in a tough spot."

He looks at me again, a flash of anger in his eyes. He glances at my neck. "I could turn you, you know?" he says, frustrated. "Then you'd have to stay here."

I nod, playing my hand. "But you won't," I say, and his eyes weaken. "You won't because you would never want that for me."

He holds my gaze, and once again, glamour or not, I like him. Despite what he is, the human Alexander Parrish was a good person. I wish it had ended differently for him. And just like that, Parrish nods.

"You're right," he says miserably. He reaches over, his cool fingertips brushing my arm, and then turns and walks off into the crowd, disappearing.

I face forward, missing him in a way. But then I focus on my mission and begin to push forward. I've lost Elijah and Felix. Hopefully they're looking for my brother, too.

Minnow is the first one I see. She is a vision, clapping her hands above her head, all eyes on her. She's calling out and singing, dancing and laughing. Next to her, Beatrice turns as if she senses me. She grins.

"There she is!" she yells, waving. Annemarie appears and begins to jump up and down when she notices me. She fights the crowd, making her way back in my direction.

She's gorgeous, they all are. And as Annemarie gets closer, I feel the pull of it—the life, or rather the vampire life with them. It's like when I was standing as we raced down the highway, the sense of weightlessness. Freedom.

"It's almost time!" someone shouts, grabbing my attention. I look over and see a couple clinging together, their phones out. They being to count down from twenty.

The Midnight Dive. Annemarie has almost reached me, and I frantically search for my brother. He has to be here.

"Twelve!" the people around me cry out. "Eleven!"

"Marco!" I scream. I can barely be heard over the count down, the whole parade revving up to run the rest of the way to the water. "Marco!" I call again.

And it's then that I see him. Marco is at the front of the crowd. He's impossibly thin and wearing sunglasses and a Hawaiian lei around his neck. He's swaying on his feet as if he doesn't even know where he is.

"Marco!" I scream, and push my way forward. Out of the corner of my eye, I see Annemarie making her way toward me. But I don't care. I need to reach my brother.

"Three!"

"Two!"

"One!"

The entire parade surges forward, rushing toward the ocean.

When the water hits my ankles, it's a jolt of cold that yanks the breath out of my chest. I gasp, wading forward as I try to reach my brother, the water rising up my legs.

He's not far, I'm almost there. I see Minnow embrace him, smile before she kisses him. And then she grabs him by the neck and submerges him in the water.

"No!" I scream, and splash ahead, the cold water covering my thighs and then my waist. The dress is heavy now, each step growing more difficult. There are people in my way and I try to move past them, screaming for Marco, who is still under water as Minnow grins, holding him down. Bubbles floating up around her.

And the people around me—they're smiling and laughing. They can't see through the glamour. They don't even realize that Minnow is killing my brother.

Suddenly, two arms wrap around me from behind, lifting my feet off the sandy seafloor and swinging me around with a splash. I feel a face next to mine, a mouth at my neck. My arms are pinned at my sides, useless. I scream.

When I open my eyes, I see Annemarie paused a few feet away, staring at whoever is holding me. She flashes her pointy teeth. And then she nods and turns away.

I'm confused until I hear Parrish's voice, his lips still close to my skin.

"I'm not going to bite you," he whispers. "But it's too late for your brother."

And still I struggle to get free. "Please, Alexander," I say, beginning to cry. "Please, I'm begging you. Save my brother."

"I'm sorry," he murmurs into my skin. "It's too late."

And I know he's right. Marco has been underwater for too long. I stare at the area, Minnow no longer holding him down. Instead, she's laughing with Beatrice as several bodies float facedown around them. Including my brother.

I'm choking on my tears, my body shivering so hard that I stop fighting. Slowly, Parrish lets me go, but I don't move right away. I let the ocean waves push me back and forth, knocking me into other people.

A lone girl, me, crying in the middle of a celebration. Lost and alone.

With a long look at me, Parrish begins making his way back to shore. He stopped me from saving my brother—but he spared my life. I wonder if they'll kill him for that, just like they killed the sheriff for trying to interfere in their affairs.

I watch my brother's body floating in the water and then I scream, my arms wrapped around myself as I double over. Sobs tear from my throat at this incredible sense of loneliness that I never thought possible. I'm going numb in the frigid water, but all I can think is that Marco must be cold too. I don't want him to be cold.

I start to move toward my brother again, just as the townspeople and tourists head back toward shore. The fun is over for them. No one notices the bodies, at least six floating in the water. One man pushes the body of a young girl aside as if she were seaweed.

My dress is heavy, the water cold. I'm almost to my brother, knowing I need to bring him home to our mother. All we can do now is run, run forever if we have to.

I'm nearly to him when there is a sudden shift of movement and one of the bodies floating in the water suddenly stands up, screaming. Roaring.

I fall back, losing my balance, and temporarily go under. I sputter out salt water as I stand again, brushing my wet hair from my face. The rest of the bodies are also standing, growling and seemingly disoriented.

The town vampires are laughing, hugging each other.

And then Marco pops out of the water, his hair matted, his eyes squeezed closed as he screams. But it's not really his face anymore. It is cold and dead, stretched out and vicious. It's not my brother.

Minnow catches my eye and smiles, pure and inviting. She thinks I've been changed into a vampire, I realize. But her smile fades quickly as she processes my condition, her expression twisting into something like loathing. The other girls see me too, see me as perfectly human. The crowd around them is too thick for them to reach me quickly. Annemarie's eyes darken with a flash of rage. I was supposed to die tonight.

Well, too fucking bad.

And with that, I turn and begin to wade toward the shore.

CHAPTER THIRTY-THREE

t's nearly impossible to run in water, but as I make my way to shore, I rush past the lingering townspeople. They're cheering and joyful as I'm shivering and crying.

Just as I reach the sand beach, I see Elijah and Felix. They're running toward me. Elijah pulls off his jacket and wraps it around my shoulders and rushes me toward the sidewalk.

"They turned him," I tell them, my teeth chattering. "Marco's a vampire now."

"Don't stop," Felix says, casting a look around as he grabs my arm. We jog toward their car, my feet sloshing in my wet sneakers. "I saw Parrish a minute ago," Felix adds. "I overheard some hairy guy tell him that the girls will be coming for us tonight. They plan to kill us, Theo."

"Then we have to get out of town before they can catch us," I say, starting to get my wits back. I hold tightly to Elijah's jacket, letting the warmth of it bring me back to life. "Once we get past the town line, we can—"

"Not going to happen," Elijah says. "The deputy's helping them and has a checkpoint set up—heard it on the scanner. He says it's for drunk drivers, but I think it's to stop certain people from leaving. And that includes us. By morning, those who didn't change will be dead. Bodies will go missing, things will be sorted out. We can slip out then. But that means we have to survive Nightfall until dawn."

"How do we do that?" I ask just as we reach the Range Rover. Elijah clicks the locks and we all jump in.

"We need to get prepared," he says.

Elijah spares no time racing back to the old Victorian, taking the turns hard enough to squeal the tires. He bumps over the curb as he pulls into the driveway. We quickly get out of the car and run for the porch.

"Get inside," Elijah says, waving us forward. "Come on," he says more urgently. "Get inside!"

The three of us rush up the stairs, and when we get on the porch, I spin around, nearly stumbling. No one is there. And yet . . . there is an odd, deafening silence, as if the entire world has gone still with fear.

Elijah pulls me inside the house with Felix right behind me. Then he shuts the door and turns the lock.

"Is this a good idea?" I ask, frantic. "Is there nowhere else we can go?"

"It won't matter," Elijah says. "I don't know anywhere in this town they haven't been given permission to enter. I'm sorry we invited them here," he adds. "We really didn't think that one through."

He casts an apologetic look at Felix, who gives him a hug in return.

"We have to be smart," Elijah says, and turns to me. "Are you prepared to defend yourself?"

"Yes," I answer immediately. "But I have one condition: not

my brother." Elijah groans, and I grab his arm to explain. "I'm ready to take your advice," I say. "Let's just . . . let's just kill the rest of them." I honestly can't believe this is what it's come to. Suggesting murder as the better option.

"You'd be surprised how difficult it is to kill a vampire," Elijah says seriously. "I've had to put down a few monsters before, and—"

Suddenly, the power goes out.

I yelp as we're submerged in a darkness. After a moment, my eyes adjust. Moonlight filters through the stained glass window above the door, setting everything in a hazy blue-gray glow.

The three of us immediately take out our phones and click on the flashlights. Seeing only bits and pieces of the room makes it all seem more dangerous. There are shadows everywhere.

"Fuse box?" I ask quietly.

"I think I saw it in the laundry room, through the kitchen," Felix replies. "Come on." He waves us toward the other end of the house.

Felix and Elijah pause at the end of a dark hallway, shining their phones in that direction.

"Laundry room is through there," Felix says. "Wait here." He starts down the hall, feeling his way along one wall until he disappears into the blackness.

I hear an audible gulp from Elijah, and then he's next to me and we're holding on to each other. There are quiet taps on the floor as my dress drips ocean water.

"So, recap," Elijah starts. "Death blows are a wooden stake through the heart or beheading. In a pinch, garlic will burn their skin, but that would be nothing more than a distraction. Wolfsbane beats glamour, but we don't have any. And, of course, sunlight really pisses them off, but that doesn't help us right now."

"Good to know," I say, trying to keep my breathing steady. I'm freaking scared, and impatient. What is taking Felix so long?

"We can't outrun them either," Elijah continues. "Best we can do is injure them enough to have a shot at killing them. Any chance you found out who the main vampire is? There's still a possibility we could end the curse if we kill it."

"My grandmother killed the head vampire years ago," I say. "Next one in line was the mural painter, but my grandmother said she started a new life. I don't know who's in charge now—but I assume it's Minnow."

Elijah groans. "That's probably not going to work. Fine. Then we have to kill them all."

The casual way we're discussing this should be horrifying, but instead it's our only hope.

A flash of light makes me jump, then it turns into a beam waving in our direction from the end of the hall, and then Felix appears.

He shakes his head. "Seems the power was shut off from the outside," he says. "I'm thinking it's not a great idea to head out back to find the utility box."

There's a giggle and then a shadow passes by the kitchen window. Felix curses and moves to yank open a drawer, the sound of metal clattering together. He grabs a meat cleaver and holds it in front of him.

My lack of protection has left me feeling vulnerable. "What other kind of weapons do you have around here?" I ask.

"Uh . . . there's some garlic next to the fridge," Felix says. He darts over and smashes some bulbs with his fist, pieces flying everywhere. He adds the garlic to a pitcher of water on the counter and then motions to it as if we should be impressed.

"Thanks," I say. "But I'm looking for something a little

sharper." I scan the room and my gaze lands on the table. "What about a chair leg?" I ask, shining my light on one of the chairs and its spindly legs.

"Theoretically it would work," Elijah says. "But do you have any idea how difficult it is to drive a blunt object through someone's chest?"

"I haven't really had the opportunity to consider it before now," I say.

There is a loud crash and I shine my light over in time to see that Felix has kicked apart a chair. He rips a leg off the bottom of the seat. "We'll give it a try anyway," he says, tossing it to me.

Armed with three dull chair legs, a cleaver, and a pitcher of garlic water, we look at each other, our faces in shadows. There is a terrifying voice and we turn toward the front of the house.

"Little pigs, little pigs . . . ," a girl sings—Beatrice—I think, followed by a high-pitched laugh. "Let. Me. Come. In."

Next to me, Elijah adjusts his grip on his makeshift stake.

There is a series of creaks from the porch, and as we run to check from the window, the front door flies open and smashes into the wall. Minnow walks right in, Beatrice and Annemarie coming to stand at her side.

I waver with fear, my heart in my throat as Minnow looks around until she sees us crowded in the living room, just outside the small kitchen. She laughs.

"Thanks for inviting me to your superfun party," she tells Elijah. "This place was always impossible to get into. You've made this all *so much* easier."

Beatrice laughs again, and on the other side of Minnow, Annemarie loudly chews gum, but as she tries to blow a bubble it pops on her sharpened molars.

The girls are still dressed up for the night, although they've changed from their parade dresses.

Beatrice is wearing another vintage prom dress, this one red with gobs of crinoline underneath. Her hair is in a deep side part, her lipstick matching the color of the fabric. Annemarie is in a gold-sequined dress with tall high-heeled boots. But it's Minnow who would take my breath away if I were ready to pay her a compliment. She's wearing a white strapless dress, fitted and gorgeous against her skin.

I can't believe they stopped to change. What absolute assholes. "Just leave us alone!" I shout.

"Can't do that," Minnow says, sucking on her teeth. "Although I'm sure you wanted to leave, you wouldn't have gotten far. You see, Theo, this town has needed fresh leadership for a while. Now they're loyal to *me*. We would have tracked you to the ends of the earth if needed."

Quickly, I exchange a look with Elijah. So it is Minnow in charge. We need to kill Minnow.

"Look," Felix says, pointing a shaky finger out the window toward the front yard.

Outside are people from the town: Sparrow and Jerry along with several others I vaguely recognize. The guy with the guitar is already playing as if this is some kind of party. They're all vampires. Beside them are the others from the ocean, baby vampires newly turned. But my brother's not among them. *Where's Marco?*

I swallow hard and turn back to Minnow.

"You don't have to do this," I tell her, my voice verging on hysterics, my body shaking. "Let me take my brother home."

"He is home," Minnow says with a smile. "Deal with it."

And then Minnow's smile widens—her mouth enlarging,

her sharp teeth glistening in the moonlight. Her eyes glow with an amber sheen and her fingernails break through her skin as they extend, small dots of blood hitting the wood floor. Her face is completely transformed.

I back into Elijah, who holds my arms to steady me.

Beatrice and Annemarie laugh at my reaction and then their faces change, too. They are no longer beautiful—they are hideous beasts.

There is a flash of light beside me and we all look at Felix, who has his phone raised in the girls' direction, taking a picture. He winces and turns to Elijah and me. "Sorry," he whispers. "I didn't realize the flash was on."

"Give me that," Minnow growls, taking a step toward us, clawed hand outstretched. The three of us take a step back. Minnow stares at us a moment and then laughs, her friends joining in. "I'm just going to kill you and destroy your phone anyway," she says.

Felix immediately ducks behind Elijah. Next to me, Elijah's fingers tighten on the dull piece of wood in his hand.

There is the creak of footsteps on the front porch and I turn toward the door, hoping for some kind of rescue. But it's Parrish who appears, pausing a moment before taking a very deliberate step inside and exhaling.

"I see you didn't take my advice," he says, looking pointedly at Beatrice.

"No," she replies. "We don't give a shit what you think."

"Nice," he says, shaking his head. He looks over at me and winces apologetically. "For the record," he tells me, "my vote was subtlety."

"I'm with Beatrice," I reply. "I don't give a shit what you think either."

He has the nerve to appear hurt. "They're not going to hurt *you*, Theo," he tells me. "And I would never hurt you. Unfortunately"—his entire face changes into that of a beast, his tongue licking his sharpened teeth—"I have to tear your friends apart."

"Fuck," Elijah murmurs under his breath.

"You're not going to kill any of us because I won't let you," I tell Parrish, sounding much braver than I feel.

Beatrice laughs. "And what are you going to do, sweetie?" she asks. "Bore us to death?" Annemarie giggles next to her.

Serious assholes.

"You know," Annemarie adds, "I should have bitten your father at the Midnight Dive all those years ago. It would have kept you from being born and wrecking this year's parade."

First, that's a messed-up thing to say. And second, I'm weirdly grossed out that she knew my father when he was a teenager.

"Door to the yard," Elijah whispers to me, drawing my attention again.

I start to move with him when suddenly, Felix jumps forward with his pitcher of garlic water, looking ridiculous as he holds it in front of him as a weapon.

Parrish grins. "What you got there, buddy? Offering us some lemonade?"

Felix's eyes flash with terror. Then he yells, "Burn, bitches!" and tosses the contents of the pitcher at the group of vampires, splashing them all with the liquid.

"Ew!" Beatrice says at first, shaking out her hands. But then she begins yelping, trying to wipe the liquid off her skin, the rest of them crying out in a mixture of disgust and pain. Minnow coughs and wipes her eyes, while Annemarie gags and runs toward the dining room, where she dries her face with a curtain.

We stare a moment, a little disappointed they didn't start melting or something equally dramatic, but then Elijah tugs me back, and the three of us run into the kitchen. Just as we get to the back door, Annemarie pops up in the window on the other side of the porch, her face steaming from the garlic as she hisses at us through the glass.

"Upstairs, upstairs!" Elijah shouts, and then we're running through the foyer again. Beatrice and Minnow are still flailing, temporarily blinded by the garlic as we rush past them toward the stairs.

Our feet pound up the steps, and at the upstairs landing, I stop and turn at the sound of Marco saying my name from downstairs.

My heart leaps. *He's* here. I turn to find him, but Parrish is rushing toward us, taking the stairs two at a time. Elijah directs us to the master bedroom across the hall and we slam and lock the door just as Parrish throws himself against it, rattling it on its hinges.

Elijah keeps his shoulder against the door. "Dresser," he calls breathlessly, pointing at it.

Felix and I get on either side of the dresser and push it over to the door. It's heavy, but we manage to slide it across the room, taking healthy chunks of the wood floor along with it. We secure it against the door while Parrish beats on the other side.

The three of us look at each other, and Felix finally drops the empty pitcher on the floor.

"We're screwed," Felix says, gasping to catch his breath.

I turn to Elijah. "Got any ideas?" I ask.

"No," he says. "I honestly thought the garlic would do more."

"So you're just winging it?" I ask, disappointed. "I thought you said you'd killed monsters before."

"I never said I killed *vampires*!" Elijah responds.

"Yep," Felix says over the banging on the other side of the door. "Totally screwed."

"Are your phones working?" I ask, raising my voice over the noise.

"Nope," Elijah says. "Service has been out all day. Preparation for the Dive, I guess."

"Besides, there's no one to call," Felix adds. "They won't help us."

"They're probably scared," I say.

I think about what Nonna told me. The town was being terrorized by a vampire mayor. Despite what the townspeople had done in service to him, they found a hero in Sylvia—a siren of Nightfall watching over them. But now the same heroes tasked with defending them are not just picking off tourists but also killing their own.

"Yes, they're probably scared," Elijah says, nodding.

The banging on the door suddenly ceases. The silence might be more terrifying.

"This door isn't going to hold through the night," I tell Elijah and Felix quietly. "We need another way out."

Just behind us, there is a high-pitched scratching noise. When we turn, we find Annemarie floating outside the second-story window, running her nails along the glass and grinning at us, her gold dress glittering in the moonlight.

Felix lets out a scream, and without hesitation, he grabs a lamp off the nightstand and throws it at Annemarie, smashing through the window. We all duck as shards of glass fly and Annemarie laughs. Felix just gave her easy access into the room.

Bracing her hands against the window frame, Annemarie murmurs, "Idiot," but the word comes out as a gurgle. Her eyes widen in surprise as a stream of blood bubbles from her mouth. Glinting in the moonlight, a large piece of glass is lodged in her throat.

Annemarie fumbles for it, her feet perched on the window frame. She yanks out the shard of glass and an arc of blood sprays across the room, landing just in front of my white sneakers. I shuffle back from it.

Annemarie is gasping, and before she can heal, Felix rushes forward with his arms outstretched and pushes her out the window. We all scream as she falls back, and then there's a loud thump, a crack.

Felix stands completely still, arms still extended in front of him. Slowly, Elijah and I walk over and peer down at the driveway.

Annemarie is splayed across the pavement, her head cocked to the side with a gaping wound in her neck, one of her boots lying in the grass. Blood pours from her body and runs down to the street.

I swallow hard. "Do . . . you think she's dead?" I ask, glancing at Elijah.

Before he can answer, a piece of the windowpane breaks off and soars down. It lands on Annemarie's throat, chopping her head clean off and sending it spinning toward the road. My eyes widen in horror.

"Uh, yeah," Elijah says with a nod. "I think so."

There is a roar from inside the house, and we all cringe, feeling it in our bones. The other vampires have sensed Annemarie's death, and the pounding starts again on the bedroom door, furious and insistent. It's terrifying.

I look down at the bloody driveway again, considering the

distance, but the leap would be too steep to survive it. Besides, there are vampires waiting for us out front. Would they kill us right away if we tried to escape or would they hold us for Minnow? I'm going to guess we're screwed either way, as Felix put it. We're essentially trapped in this room. The banging stops abruptly.

"Theo?" a small voice says.

I turn toward the door, my stomach sinking.

"Theo, it's me," Marco says. "It's okay. We're both okay. Come on out."

I press my palm to my mouth, horrified.

"Theo," Marco whispers again. "Before they come back. I'd never let anything happen to you. It's me and you, remember? We're a team. I want to go home, Theo. I want to see Mom again."

A tear drips down my cheek when I blink. I lower my hand from my mouth and move toward the door. Elijah catches me around the waist and swings me to the other side of the room.

"You can't do that, Theo," he says, shaking his head. "I can't let you do that. He's lying."

"Theodora Maggione, open this door," Marco calls out, banging on it once. "You're not allowed to abandon me. You promised."

"We can't kill him," I tell Elijah with a whimper. "Please. We can't kill my brother."

"I'm sorry," he whispers miserably. "There's no other choice."

There is a soft thump on the other side of the door, and then I hear crying. I push Elijah aside and run to the door, putting my palm against it.

"Marco?" I say.

"I'm dying," he murmurs. "Let me in, Theo. I'm dying."

I close my eyes, pain ripping through my chest. "You're dangerous," I whisper.

"Please open the door," Marco says. "I promise no one will hurt you. Just come out." He pauses. "Come out or we have to kill all of you."

I step back. Terror runs through my body, and then Elijah and Felix are next to me. Felix puts his hand on my arm as I lean into him.

"You still have a chance, Theo," Marco says, his voice growing stronger as if he senses the others next to me. "Hand them over and prove your loyalty. Then we'll run this town. Nothing before matters. Nothing can hurt us now."

"I am not abandoning my friends, Marco," I say, wiping the tears off my cheeks. "And I'm going to kick your ass when this is over for putting me through this."

Marco laughs, and the sound is nails along metal, high-pitched and earsplitting. "Have it your way, then," he says, his voice getting farther away. "Stay human and die with your friends."

Suddenly, there is a sharp crack, rattling the door and making us all scream in surprise. There's another bang, and this time the top of the door splits and a glint of light shines through from the other side.

CHAPTER THIRTY-FOUR

We watch in horror as another crack splits the wood wide open and a girl's hand snakes through, gripping the edges to quickly pull the door apart. There's a flurry of movement, and then Beatrice is visible, her face that of a demon. She smiles at us.

"I'm going to enjoy devouring you," she says, licking her teeth.

Elijah throws himself against the dresser to hold the door closed, but it's useless. Beatrice is strong, and with the top of the door torn away, she grabs the dresser and pushes it to the side, taking Elijah with it. He falls to his knees, only to quickly scramble up as Felix runs over to me, holding the meat cleaver out in front of him.

Beatrice opens the door, a monster in a red prom dress, and smiles. "Who's first?" she asks.

Elijah balls up his fist and punches her in the jaw, but her head barely moves. He curses and Beatrice backhands him across the cheek, knocking him onto the bed.

"Stay behind me," Felix says bravely, holding his arm out

in front of me while he waves the meat cleaver with the other. "Don't come any closer!" he yells at Beatrice, making her laugh.

"You're all so pathetic," she says. "Honestly, we should have drained you the first night. I thought you'd be more of a challenge. I listen to your podcast."

Felix pauses, seeming flattered. "Really?"

Elijah rushes Beatrice from behind, but she knocks him aside again, this time sending him headlong into the bedpost before he falls to the floor, clutching his forehead. When he lifts his head, blood runs down from the cut that opened there. When Beatrice sees it, her eyes flash and she growls at him, drool slipping from her mouth.

"Leave him alone!" I scream, terrified, as she moves to attack him.

Felix rushes forward, cleaver in the air. While Beatrice is distracted, he brings it down on her shoulder, the wet *thwack* audible as it slices into her muscle. She howls in pain and spins on Felix, the cleaver still in her shoulder, and wraps both her hands around his neck.

Elijah runs over and begins punching Beatrice and then I join in, trying to pry her fingers from around Felix's neck. We're all moving, shuffling, as we drag her out the bedroom door and onto the landing. In the process, I break off one of her nails. Beatrice turns to me, pissed.

Elijah takes that moment to kick her hard in the thigh, sending her to her knees. She lets Felix go and he scrambles away. But before we can claim any victory, Beatrice catches Elijah by the arm as he tries to hit her again. The world freezes for a moment as they stare at each other, and then she stands and flings him over the railing, sending him falling to the first floor.

There is a loud crash. Felix screams and grabs his table-leg stake from the floor. But as he lunges for Beatrice, there is a flash of movement on the stairs and Felix goes flying backward into the bedroom, skidding across the floor until he hits the wall, knocking a few more pieces of glass out of the window-pane.

I'm breathless as Parrish stands there, teeth bared. He glances at me, and for a moment, there is a hint of regret in his inhuman eyes before he goes for Felix.

"Stop!" I scream. Beatrice grabs me, but I yank away, her nails slicing into my skin when I do. I haul back my elbow and jab her in the face as hard as I can and I run past her to help Felix, afraid that when I get into the bedroom, he'll already be dead. I find him getting to his feet and looking around for a weapon. The stake is across the room.

In front of me, Parrish grins at Felix, cracking his knuckles. "I just started listening to your show," he tells him. "I'll be honest, it could have better production value."

Felix's eyes flash with anger. "Take it back!" he yells.

Parrish laughs and steps up, kicking Felix square in the chest, knocking him back against the wall again, where he crumples to the floor. Felix looks up at him, eyes wide and terrified. Parrish punches him in the face and blood sprays from his lips.

He's going to kill him.

Before I think twice, I rush forward and scoop the stake off the floor. Parrish opens his mouth to tear Felix apart and I run at him. My body connects with his in a jolt of pain as I knock him off Felix and into the closet door.

Parrish looks at me just as the wood pierces his chest and strikes his heart.

He cries out, and I stumble back, shocked at what I've done.

Parrish takes in a shaky breath, hands on the stake sticking out of his body. Then he rests his head back against the door and he closes his eyes, smiling.

"Good for you, Arizona," he breathes out. "Good for you." And then his legs give way and he collapses to the floor.

I kneel down next to him. "I'm so sorry," I say, putting my hands around the stake as blood pours out. Although I didn't want Parrish to hurt Felix, I didn't want to kill him either. I really didn't.

Parrish reaches to run his fingers along my cheek, his dark eyes locked on mine. Then his hand falls to his side, his eyes drifting toward the open window.

And then, Alexander Parrish dies.

I pull back in disbelief and stand up. A sharp pain of regret, grief. But I had no other choice. I know that.

When I turn back to Felix, his left eye is swollen and his teeth are bloody.

"Are you okay?" I ask, and Felix's good eye widens.

Pain explodes in the back of my head as I'm hit and thrown to the floor. I roll over, sure I'm about to throw up, and Beatrice steps over me. The meat cleaver is no longer in her shoulder, but the gash in her muscles leaks blood, leaving a trail along the floor as she walks toward Felix.

She licks her teeth. "Boy, do you smell good," she tells him.

Felix's face twists in disgust and I drag myself to my knees, my head pounding. I touch the back of my head and my fingers come back covered in blood.

Beatrice and Felix dance around the room, and I look toward the door, wondering where my brother and Minnow are, worried they'll attack us from behind. But it's quiet beyond this room.

Felix swings at Beatrice and she ducks away, then slashes his back with her nails, shredding his shirt and opening bright wounds on his skin. He arches his back and, in that moment, Beatrice grabs him by the neck.

She opens her mouth, teeth glistening with drool, and leans in to bite him.

"No!" I scream, running at her. I grab a fistful of her hair and pull her with me to the floor. Felix breaks free and runs for the stake, but Beatrice throws out her arm and clotheslines him. He holds his throat, gasping for breath.

When I open my hand, I'm holding a fistful of blond hair. I throw it aside, inching away from it.

Beatrice trains her murderous eyes on me, hand to her head where a chunk of hair is missing. "Chosen or not," she says, "you're dead. I've been sick of you from the start."

"I'm glad the feeling was mutual," I say, climbing to my feet.

I take a step back and my sneaker hits Parrish's body. My heart sinks seeing him there, but I lean down and rip the stake from his body with a loud sucking sound.

"When I'm finished with you," Beatrice says, "I'm going to tear apart that little nonna of yours."

A shot of adrenaline hits my bloodstream and my muscles tighten. I bare my teeth at her, and for a moment, *she* recoils.

"Don't you ever threaten my grandmother!" I scream, and lunge for her. I'm surprised at how strong I am when I knock Beatrice to the floor, scrambling on top of her like a wild animal, scratching and hitting. She knocks the stake out of my hand, sending it flying out of my reach.

We're a flurry of motion, and it's not long before she gets the upper hand and knocks me into the hallway. I quickly slide back along the floor, and when I look up, she's unhinged her jaw to make her mouth even wider. She runs at me, letting out a primal scream.

My foot touches the discarded meat cleaver, and before I can think twice, I grab it from the floor and swing it out wildly. It's all in slow motion. As Beatrice bears down on me, I draw the edge of the cleaver across her throat, slicing it open and sending a wave of blood splashing over me.

The world is cast in pink as warm liquid washes across my face. Beatrice is frozen in pain and surprise, and then she falls toward me.

I spin out of the way and she lands cheek-first on the floor. I crawl to my knees and hold the cleaver above my head to finish the job. But I can't do it; it just seems too cruel.

"I'm . . . going to . . . kill you," Beatrice gurgles.

"Seriously?" I say.

In that moment, Felix takes the cleaver from my hand and chops off Beatrice's head. I don't look away. I watch Beatrice's face as she turns back into the girl she was—no filter of glamour, no impossible beauty. Instead, she's just a normal, dead girl on the floor.

Felix pulls me to my feet and we stand facing each other—both of us covered in blood.

I give him an affirmative nod, and then we both turn and look over the railing. Elijah's in the entryway, sitting up. Felix gasps in relief and rushes down the stairs to kneel beside him, taking stock of his condition.

"You okay?" I call down, and they both tip their heads to look up at me.

"My leg is broken," Elijah calls back. His dark skin has taken on a grayish tint. "Broken in at least two places. And I have no idea where your brother and Minnow are . . . so if you have an idea on how to get us out of here, I'm all ears."

As if on cue, the overhead lights click on. There is the sound of shuffling feet, and when I look toward the front door, I see Nonna standing there. I'm absolutely speechless.

My grandmother is wearing a gray tracksuit with her thick black shoes, her hair set and curled. A large purse dangles from her left hand, and in her right she's holding a very sharp wooden stake. She looks around the house, her gaze stopping on Felix and Elijah, then looks up and fixes on me at the top of the stairs, bathed in bright red blood.

"What a mess," she says, sounding disappointed.

CHAPTER THIRTY-FIVE

rush forward down the stairs, pausing at the bottom as my grandmother puts her hands on her hips, surveying the damage.

"Nonna!" I say, worried. "What are you doing here? How did you even get in here—you're going to get hurt." She might have slayed a vampire in the past, but she's in her seventies now.

"You mean those foolish people outside?" she asks sharply. "I sent them home. Picked up that poor girl's head to show them and told them the night was over. They're gone now."

She . . . picked up Annemarie's head? Damn. I can see why everyone in town seems to know her. My grandmother does not fuck around.

Nonna walks to where Elijah and Felix are on the floor, looking them over before tilting Felix's head to examine his neck.

"You'll be okay," she tells him, and pats his head affectionately. "But get this one to the hospital." She motions to Elijah before walking to the staircase.

She passes me, making her way up slowly.

"And where is your brother?" she asks me impatiently, as if Marco has just missed curfew and isn't a blood-lusting vampire.

"I don't know where Marco is," I say. "But, Nonna, he's—"

"Yeah, yeah," she responds as she gets to the top of the stairs. She waves off the rest of my comment and disappears into the bedroom, then reappears and stops next to Beatrice. She tsks, shaking her head.

"Oh, Sylvia," Nonna mutters under her breath. "What have you done?"

"So what happens now?" I ask my grandmother. Ready for someone with an actual plan.

"Go get in the car, Theodora," she tells me. "The van is out front."

"And what about Marco?" I ask, afraid she's going to kill him.

"Theodora," she repeats, but I shake my head.

"I'm not leaving until this is over," I say.

Nonna's expression softens for a moment, and then she opens her purse and pulls out another stake. "Then take this," she says. "But be careful with it—it's sharp."

"Thank you," I say. As I take it from her, she holds on to it an extra second before letting go.

Nonna heads toward the kitchen while I make my way to the other side of the house, where the dining room is. It's painfully quiet, the world so still I swear I can hear my heart beating.

"Maybe they just—" I start to say.

Suddenly, something grabs my arms, swinging me around as I flail painfully into the dining room table, my body folding over it before I roll off and hit the floor. For a moment, I see stars.

I blink and turn my head slowly. My brother is standing there, heaving in breaths, his mouth wide and monstrous.

"Marco?" I say, fumbling in my surprise and dropping my sharpened stake to the floor.

He takes a step toward me, teeth glistening. His eyes are vicious.

"What are you doing?" I ask, putting up my arms to protect myself. "Marco, snap out of it!"

He doesn't seem to hear me, instead focused on the blood seeping from my various cuts and wounds. I slide backward, knowing I'm running out of room. I have to distract him to buy some time.

"Mom's getting married at the end of the summer," I blurt out, and he stops in his tracks.

It takes a moment, but then his eyes soften and tears well up. I keep talking as I pull myself to my feet.

"I talked to her the other day," I continue, "and she wants us to be in the wedding, a big event at the Scottsdale Princess. She said it would mean the world to her. We have to go *home,* Marco. We have to go back home to Arizona. Please," I tell him. "We can still go home and—"

"Not a chance, Theo," Minnow announces, strolling into the room, her face as beautiful as ever. "He's not going anywhere with you. We belong right here, together."

My brother goes to stand next to her and I can't describe the feeling of betrayal at the way he ceases to recognize me. He becomes a creature again.

Minnow shakes her head slowly. "You killed my friends," she says, angry. "I was going to let you live, let you join us, but now . . . Well, now you'll have to pay for what you've done. You've ruined everything, Theo."

"And what about you?" I shoot back. "You kill people too.

You bit my brother! How did you become like this? How did you end up a monster?"

"You think I wanted to be like this?" Minnow demands, offended. "I had plans, dreams. I was going to be a singer and travel the world. But in one night it was all stolen away."

"Sylvia bit you?" I ask, trying to keep her talking until I figure out how to escape.

"I showed up in this godforsaken town to play the Midnight Dive four years ago," Minnow continues. "The night before the parade, Sylvia found me and bit me. Then, while my bandmates watched, she drowned me in the ocean during the Midnight Dive. No one saved me. When I woke again, Sylvia told me that together we'd protect the town from outsiders who would harm us. That we were free to build our own community—pick and choose who stays. But it wasn't until after I fed that I realized what I'd truly become. And I hated her, and this place."

She looks out the window at the town with pure contempt.

"And I wasn't the only one," she adds. "Turns out Annemarie and Beatrice were like-minded girls. They'd been stuck with Sylvia for decades, but they were done with her rules too—respecting the town limits, not feeding on locals, blah, blah, blah. So we decided we weren't going to listen to some old-ass vampire anymore. We wouldn't stay trapped in Nightfall. But first we need more vampires. So we lure in as many tourists as we can, keeping the ones who can help us, who can survive the change, and feeding on the rest."

"Where is Sylvia?" I ask. "My grandmother said she moved on. Are you saying she's here?"

"*Your grandmother said,*" Minnow repeats, mimicking my voice before laughing bitterly. "That woman is loyal to the end."

What did that mean? Did Nonna lie to me? After all this, she still had to lie?

I focus on Minnow again. "It wasn't fair what happened to you," I tell her, slowly getting to my feet. "But please, let me take my brother home."

"I need him," Minnow says with a flash of vulnerability. "Thanks to you, he's all I have left. Now enough talk. It's time to feed."

She growls and then widens her mouth until her entire face transforms. I fall back a step, nearly tripping over the stake I dropped earlier.

Marco's teeth flash in response to Minnow's, but then his expression falters slightly, his eyes horrified—human eyes, as he sees me backing away and terrified.

"No!" he yells as Minnow charges in my direction.

I drop to the floor and grab the sharpened stake. And just as Minnow descends on me, I hold the stake up, driving it straight into the center of her chest. Bright pain blossoms along my neck as her nails slash my skin and I scream at the same time she does.

Minnow collapses on the floor, writhing in agony. Marco roars and backs away, putting his hands over his ears, and cowers in the corner.

I touch the wound on my neck, scared of how deep it is. Blood is pulsing down my skin and pooling at the neckline of my dress, but it doesn't feel like she got an artery. As I steady myself on my feet, I realize my mistake.

Minnow isn't dead. She's in agony; her screams are visceral, haunting. I don't understand her condition, but I kneel down beside her, regret pulling at my soul. In this moment, she's someone dying—painfully and all alone. I can't help it—I take

Minnow's hand in mine, wanting to comfort her even now. She didn't choose this life. She didn't choose this curse.

There is the sound of footsteps, and I look up to see Nonna marching in from the foyer, her mouth set in a determined scowl.

"Move aside," she say, nearly knocking me over as she comes to stand over Minnow's body.

Nonna reaches for the stake and pulls it out of Minnow's chest with a loud sucking sound. Startled, I fall back as Minnow gasps, her body jolting before she lies still, bleeding everywhere.

Nonna leans in to examine the wound, dipping her index finger in to check its depth. She nods, satisfied, and then opens her purse. She drops in the bloody stake.

"It's not deep enough to kill you," she tells Minnow. "Just a nick of the heart."

I stare at my grandmother, shocked at how easily she's managing this macabre insanity.

Nonna takes a small vial of blood from her pocketbook and presses it into Minnow's hand.

"Drink this and heal," she tells her. "It's good quality. It'll work fast."

Minnow is still gasping, still clearly in pain, but she stares up at Nonna, seemingly stunned.

"Go on now," Nonna says, motioning toward the bottle. "Before it gets worse." When Minnow continues to hesitate, Nonna tilts her head impatiently. "I know what I should have done all those year ago," she says. "I know it every damn day. But I can't change the past and neither can you. Now go ahead and heal yourself. And then you leave my family alone. Do you understand?"

Minnow slowly nods. She's too weak to sit up, tears leaking

from the corners of her eyes, but with effort, she takes the top off the vial and hungrily drinks the blood. Judging by the strange look on Nonna's face, I think it may be her blood.

"She . . . she . . ." Minnow is gasping, trying to talk. "She won't let you live."

"You let me worry about that," my grandmother says. "If it's my time, then so be it." Nonna stands straighter and snaps her pocketbook closed.

I turn to find Elijah and Felix watching the entire scene, a combination of horror and fear on their faces.

Minnow slowly sits up, still taking labored breaths. When she gathers enough strength to get to her feet, Nonna puts out her arm to help steady her. Minnow towers over my grandmother, but she looks weak. I wonder how long it'll take her to fully heal.

Minnow and Nonna exchange a long look, something unsaid passes between them as Minnow nods. And then the beautiful girl who started a vampire war and took over an entire town walks into the foyer. She walks right out the front door, never once looking back at my brother.

I turn to Marco, finding him huddled against the wall, staring at the empty vial of blood that Minnow left behind. As he starts to move toward it, Nonna reaches out to smack him across the side of the head.

"Don't you even think about it," she says. "I've had enough of your nonsense. Self-control is not one of your strengths, Marco."

He stares at her, his face still that of a monster, but Nonna is watching him as if he's a little boy. Her expression softens.

"I love you," she tells him. "I'm going to fix this. You trust me?"

I look at her, unsure what she means by that. How is my grandmother going to fix this? She told me there wasn't a way to do that. But as I wait for an explanation, Marco's face slowly turns human again and tears begin to stream from his eyes. And then my brother nearly collapses as he runs to hug my grandmother. She pats his back and lets him sob.

"There you go," she says kindly. "There you go."

"Shit," I murmur, starting to cry myself.

Nonna looks over at me and sighs, then waves me over to join in the hug. I rush over and the three of us cling together. It's exactly what I need, I realize. This love. This care.

"Enough slobbering on me now," Nonna says, pulling away from us and spoiling the moment. I laugh a little, clearing the tears off my face. "Now you get yourself to the hospital to get those scratches looked at," she tells me. "I'll have your father meet you there. And you," she says, taking Marco's arm, "are coming home with me so I can keep an eye on you."

Nonna pulls him toward the foyer. I follow, and when I look over at Elijah, he laughs.

"Wow," he says, looking us over. "Gory. Felix, get a picture."

Felix takes out his phone and snaps a pic, but Nonna blocks her face with her purse. Felix takes Elijah's arm to help him to his good leg, the broken one hanging limply behind him. Felix has deep bruising on his neck, one eye swollen shut.

"Mind if we get a ride to the hospital with you?" Felix asks me in a raspy voice. "I'm seeing double. Triple even."

"Oh," I say, looking at my grandmother and then back at Felix. "I can't drive."

"You'll be fine," Nonna tells me. She reaches into her purse and pulls out a set of keys, holding them out to me. "I'm sure he wouldn't mind," she adds quietly.

I feel a flash of hurt when I see the *Liva Little* key chain. Nonna must have grabbed Parrish's car keys when she checked on him earlier. When I make no move to take the keys, my grandmother jangles them.

"Theodora," she says impatiently, "take the damn keys. I have to get your brother home."

Reluctantly, I take them from her hand. I guess that driving lesson will come in handy after all. That one perfect afternoon with Parrish. A final goodbye.

Elijah and Felix meet me at the door. Nonna leads the way outside, and when we get onto the porch, the other vampires and local conspirators are indeed gone. I'm impressed with Nonna's sway in town, even now. To top it off, she takes a business card out of her pocketbook and hands it to Elijah.

"You go ahead and call Bill Heeler," she says. "He can help you clean this house up. Just tell him Nonna sent you and he'll know what you need."

She walks ahead and gets into her minivan, and Marco quietly goes around to the passenger seat, his head hanging low.

The rest of us go over to the black Charger, the outside slick and shiny. A real beauty. Felix whistles as he helps Elijah into the back. "Nice wheels," he says.

"Sure are," I say.

I climb in and get behind the wheel. When I turn the keys, the car roars to life, vibrating with power. I think of Parrish sitting beside me in the passenger seat with all the patience in the world. I touch the steering wheel and slide my hand around it.

Good for you, Arizona.

A salty tear falls on my lips and I glance at Elijah and Felix in the backseat. "You both realize I don't have my license or my learner's permit?"

Elijah smiles. "Not even the fourth most dangerous thing today, Theo," he says. "Just take it slow."

We idle for a moment in the driveway as I adjust the seat and mirrors. In front of us, the lights are blazing in the trashed Victorian. All of us are covered in blood, Elijah's bones broken, Felix's eye swelling. The stench of death is all around us.

And then—because what else are we going to do?—we all bust up laughing.

CHAPTER THIRTY-SIX

didn't need stitches. But I have fourteen butterfly sutures closing my wounds. The doctors warned that I'll probably have faint scars, but the nurse told me to put some ointment on them and that should minimize them. I know I'm lucky to be alive.

Turns out I'm a natural behind the wheel of a car and only curbed it twice. I'm definitely going to get my permit when I get back to Arizona.

I left Elijah and Felix at the hospital. Elijah has indeed broken his leg in two different places and the doctors are debating surgery here or back in California when he gets home. Felix has a concussion, but no permanent damage was done to his neck and his scratches were superficial.

I pull into Nonna's driveway and park behind her minivan. My father never showed up at the hospital, and with the phone lines still down, there was no way to call him. Honestly, I'm not sure what I would have said to him anyway. I have no idea where we go from here, but . . . fact is, Marco is a vampire now. At least my dad has a plan to deal with that.

We didn't kill Minnow, but we made a pretty good-sized

dent in bloodsuckers tonight. Nightfall might be a bit more peaceful for a while.

I go inside the house and make sure the door is locked before setting the keys on the entryway table and kicking off my bloody sneakers. My dress is still damp from the ocean and the blood, and I can't wait to take a shower.

"Nonna?" I call, heading into the living room to check on her and my brother.

"In here, Theo," Marco calls from the kitchen, sounding pathetic.

I'm scared to see him—scared that he's still a monster. But I walk over, hesitantly peek into the kitchen.

My brother is at the table, sweating and pale, his hands trembling in his lap. A blue towel is wrapped around his shoulders, his hair matted to his forehead. My grandmother is ladling some broth into a bowl over by the stove. On the counter, I see some crushed purple flowers.

They're blocking the glamour, because Marco looks like literal death right now.

"I'm so sorry about everything," my brother says to me. Immediately, he breaks down crying. My heart sinks and I walk over to hug him, his body cold in my arms. "It wasn't me," he says. "I would never . . . it wasn't me, Theo. I'm sorry."

"I know," I tell him.

"Bloodlust will cloud the mind," Nonna says from the stove, startling me. I cringe at her casual use of the word *bloodlust*.

She walks over with a bowl of soup and sets it front of Marco. "Finish it all," she tells him, handing him a spoon. She stands over him, watching.

The spoon scrapes against the bowl as Marco scoops up broth and slurps it. He forces it down, seeming to hate every second of it. And soon, Marco's eyes start to get heavy, each blink longer and longer.

"I don't feel right," he says, dropping the spoon in the bowl with a clatter. He reaches up to touch his head. I glance up at my grandmother, and she waves for me to help her.

"Let's get him to the recliner," she says. Without argument, I get up and do as she asks.

My brother is barely conscious as we lead him to the living room. With Nonna on one side and me on the other, we drop Marco into the recliner. His head falls to one side and his eyes slide closed.

"So what did you give him?" I ask, stepping back to look over my brother. "Some old-fashioned vampire elixir?"

"No," she replies. "I crushed up Valium and put it in his soup. Couldn't take the chance he gets up in the night for a snack." She looks pointedly at me.

"We'll lock him in the attic later," I say, and she nods.

Nonna and I go back into the kitchen, and I watch as she cleans up.

"Well?" I ask. "Are we going to talk about tonight?"

"Your father will be home soon," she says, "and I'm sure we'll discuss it then."

I have so many questions, some of them about my father, but I have to prioritize.

"Why didn't you kill Minnow?" I ask. "How do you know she's not going to keep coming after us?"

"Minerva was someone's child once," Nonna says. "I don't get to pass judgment on when she dies. It's not up to me. Besides," she adds, turning to look at me, "she wants the same thing you want."

"And what's that?" I ask.

"To be free of this town," she says. "By creating more vampires loyal to her, there would be no one to stop Minerva from leaving, no one to drag her back here. She was misguided, yes. But she might get her wish still."

"What does that mean?" I ask. "What are you planning to do, Nonna?"

Just as she starts to answer, the front door opens.

"Oh, I'm sure she has a plan," a woman's voice calls out.

I glance at Nonna, then we walk into the living room and toward the foyer. Olivia Miles comes gliding in the house as if she owns the place. "Josephine always knows what to do," she adds with a smile.

Olivia stands there in a brown-and-white polka-dot raincoat. Her blond hair is fluffy from the humidity, her white shoes spotless. My grandmother lowers her eyes and disappears back into the kitchen.

In hindsight, I should have realized the truth sooner. But that doesn't mean I'm any less shocked as my heart sinks to the floor.

"So you're Sylvia," I say.

She breathes out a huge sigh before unzipping her coat. She shrugs it off and sets it aside. As she comes into the living room, she transforms with each step. Her blond hair becomes a dark bob, her laugh lines fading away. She removes her glasses and drops them on the floor.

By the time she's in front of the fireplace, she's twenty-two again. The year she was bitten by Alfonse Cardelli. Sylvia Ware, the artist, perfectly unaged.

"It feels good to be young again," she says with a smile. "It's never fun to glamour older, but it keeps them guessing. And how are you, sweetheart?" she adds, looking me over. "You look like you've had a rough night."

I'm standing in a blood-soaked dress, covered in bandages. "A rough night?" I repeat. "Are you fucking kidding me?"

I can't believe she called me *sweetheart*. Can't believe she has the nerve to say anything to me at all. She's a vampire. She's literally queen of the vampires!

"What do you want with my family?" I demand. "Where's my father?"

"Enough with the tantrum," she says, walking right past me toward the kitchen. She glances briefly at Marco's sleeping body in the recliner and smiles to herself. "By the way, your father is fine," she tells me, continuing our conversation. "He's at the new house picking out some paint colors now that Marco will be staying indefinitely. And hopefully you too. Your father is going to marry me, Theo. We're practically family."

"The hell we are," I say, following her.

"You really have to clean up that language," she says. "Now, where did Josie run off to? Tell her to put on the tea and grab—"

There is a whoosh and an iron skillet swings out, striking Olivia hard on the side of the head with a loud thud. I scream in surprise as Olivia falls against the wall, catching herself.

When I look, my grandmother is breathing heavily, the skillet hanging from her hand.

"Oh, Josie," Olivia says, resetting her jaw as she straightens. "You're not going to make me kill you after all this time. I'd never forgive myself."

The two women stare at each other, and I'm reminded that they're the same age. Or at least, they were once.

"I told you to leave my family alone," my grandmother says.

"I've watched you take and lose our town. You don't care about any of us. I've abided by a lot of things, Sylvia. But no more."

"So honorable," Olivia says, pulling out a chair and sitting down. "I'm sure you remember me warning you about Xavier, telling you that something was off. But none of that was enough for you, was it? I had to confront him myself. And now, well, look at us. You're old and I'm forever young. I guess it pays to be the good guy. The good girl," she corrects herself.

"You stopped being good a long time ago," my grandmother says. "I should have killed you that night."

"Life is a series of choices, Josie," Olivia says. "But at least you've lived long enough to regret yours."

"So what do you want with us?" I ask. "Aren't you a little"— I curl my lip—"old for my father?"

Olivia laughs. "Don't be ageist," she says. "Besides, I'm as old as I want to be. But to be fair and answer your rude question, I've known your father for years. Back when I first became Olivia Miles, studying creative writing. Your father was just out of high school. A good local boy—friends with Annemarie and a few others. It didn't bother him that they were vampires because he had the right vision," she adds, nodding. "He truly loved Nightfall. So I decided that he should be my partner. Only some shall stay, Theo." She references her own mural. "And only some should rule."

She picks at her nails, which are growing longer as she talks. They tear through her skin, but she doesn't seem to register the pain as blood drips down her arms.

"But before I could reveal myself to him, *choose* him, your father left to chase after that girl," she says with a dismayed sigh. "He left me brokenhearted. But I found plenty to do, not the least of which was build a book empire. No small feat, by the way. And then, imagine my surprise when Joey Maggione was out in front of this very house, finding his way back to me after all this time."

She's insane. My dad's . . . girlfriend is a vampire and she's insane.

"He and I clicked again right away," she adds. "Of course, Joey will be a little upset when he learns who I am, but he'll understand—especially with what's happened to your brother. Unfortunately, Minnow took things upon herself *yet again* and bit Marco." She rolls her eyes. "I swear, that girl . . . thorn in my side."

She glances at me as if looking for sympathy. Yeah, I'm sure it's tough leading a nest of murderous teen vampires. Poor her.

"Here's the thing, Theo," she continues. "While I was playing the part of Olivia Miles, my girls got a little out of control—overzealous. Thank you for handling that for me."

"I didn't do it for you," I say. "In fact, I wish I knew it was you from the beginning because I would have cut off your head immediately."

Her smile fades. "Fair enough," she replies. "Well, it's time for a grand reset. I've done my best to understand you humans over the years. But the loyalty never lasts. Your grandmother just hit me with a skillet," she says, motioning to Nonna. "And she's my oldest friend. My own girls turned against me. It's chaos out there."

"What do you want?" I demand. I'm sick of listening to her talk.

Olivia leans into the table. "I'm taking back the reins of this town. Chosen ones only, fewer tourists, less attention. I need to be surrounded by people I trust. By my new family." She smiles at me. "I may be cursed, but I am not prey," she adds.

"He's dead, Sylvia," my grandmother says, her voice echoing in the room. "I killed him. Alfonse will never hurt you again."

"Until the next one," Olivia says sharply. "What's to stop more of them from coming? Or even another man, a human one? You think they're not capable of that destruction? Do you even watch the news? No," she says, shaking her head. "I choose who stays here."

"It's not that simple anymore," Nonna says. "You see that, don't you? You've kept the town safe for many years. But it's time to let them go—it's time to free them all."

Olivia watches her, and then glances to where my brother is passed out in the recliner before smiling sweetly at me. She turns back to my grandmother. "You can't stop me," she tells Nonna. "Once Joey has changed, these will be my kids too. My family."

My stomach turns at the thought. This creature, this vampire, as my stepmother? Fuck.

"No," Nonna tells her. "I'm sorry, old friend. But my grandkids are going back to Arizona."

CHAPTER THIRTY-SEVEN

About fifty years ago, my grandmother murdered her husband and spared her best friend's life. In return, Sylvia protected the town, even painted a mural to honor that agreement. But decades later, things have changed. Nothing ever really stays the same. And Sylvia's motivation, maybe pure at first, became skewed. It became murderous.

Standing here now, I realize what my grandmother is saying. I hear the pain in her voice, a combination of guilt and resignation. She's about to kill her best friend.

I look at my grandmother and she catches my eyes for just a moment before she holds up the skillet again. Olivia is out of her chair, fast as lightning. She crosses the room and slams my grandmother into the wall, hand on her neck as she chokes her.

Quickly, I grab a stick doll off the counter and press it to Olivia's cheek. For a moment, she's a corpse, rotten and dead— her glamour gone. There is a singeing sound and she howls in pain as the silver on the stick figure burns her skin. Then she swats me away and I go spinning along the counter, my hip bones banging painfully against the granite.

I notice my grandmother's purse looped around the top of a kitchen chair. I don't have time to think, don't have time to check on Nonna. I grab one of the stakes out of it and rush forward at Olivia.

Just before I reach her, she senses me. She drops her hand from my grandmother's neck and slams her palms into my chest, sending me flying into the cupboards. As I crash against them, the breath is knocked out of my lungs and I fall heavily to the floor. My grandmother lowers herself next to me, gasping for breath but seemingly okay.

Olivia grabs me by my hair, hauling me to my feet. Her face has transformed into a monster's, the skin cracking at the edges of her mouth, drool glistening on her teeth. She's more hideous than any of the others, and I punch her square in the face. She doesn't seem to feel it.

She growls, her mouth expanding, and in that instant, my life flashes before my eyes.

I think of my dad. I think of him always beaming with pride at my volleyball games, at Marco's swimming events. The way he cried after my mom left. And my mom . . . her flourish of life, always swirling around us. Her smile. And my brother, helpless but purehearted most times. I remember him standing on the roof of our house, begging me to watch as he jumped into the pool.

And then there's Willa and my friends. There's Arizona—there's home. I close my eyes, tears streaming down my cheeks.

The memories slip past as Olivia leans in to bite me, dragging me toward perpetual night with her very sharp teeth.

But before she can, I'm suddenly rocked forward and my eyes fly open as I'm pushed aside. I land painfully on the floor and quickly look up. When I do, I gasp.

Olivia's monster face is frozen in pain, and protruding from her chest is a bloody wooden stake. My grandmother is still on the floor, watching the horror unfold. But standing behind Olivia and holding the stake that's impaling her is my father.

He looks just as surprised to be the one holding it.

Olivia's eyes slowly slide closed. Her face begins to transform, her glamour falling away. She ages rapidly, skin puckering, neck sagging. Her dead flesh turning into dust. My father takes a step back, letting Olivia fall to the floor in a heap of bones. I quickly move away from her.

My father stands in the middle of the kitchen, completely aghast. Beside himself. He turns to me and my grandmother, his hands covered in blood.

"I'm sorry I'm late," he says, looking around wide-eyed. He stares back down at Olivia's remains, then he focuses on me, still heaving in breaths. "We're leaving as soon as the sun comes up," he says.

I'm still in shock, but I laugh at the comment. "Finally," I reply, making him smile as he wipes a splatter of blood off his cheek.

My father spends the next hour apologizing for everything, for bringing us to Nightfall in the first place; for not warning us about vampires, including Annemarie, who he recognized when he saw her hitchhiking the day we arrived. Of course, he had no idea he was dating Sylvia Ware, literal vampire queen of Nightfall.

"I swear I would have killed her sooner if I knew," he says as we're sitting together at the kitchen table. "The minute I learned that Marco had been bitten, I would have stopped Olivia. But I didn't know what she was, and even if I did, I thought the curse was irreversible. All these years, I'd accepted that vampires were just a part of Nightfall. I . . . I'm sorry I didn't figure it out sooner."

Nonna looks down at her hands, guilty for keeping that secret, no matter the reason.

"I was trying to do my best, Theo," my father adds, regret thick in his voice. "Can you ever forgive me for failing miserably at it?"

"Well," I say, looking around at the carnage in the kitchen, Olivia's remains a few feet away. "You came through when it counted, right? And to be fair, Marco really sucked at figuring this all out too. So you're not alone."

My father laughs, sniffling back his tears. But I think we're both hurting more than we're willing to admit in this moment. Maybe for a while.

"We're starting therapy again as soon as we get home," he offers.

"Oh, definitely," I reply.

IT'S EASILY THE BEST night of sleep I've had since arriving in Nightfall. Whether it's because the monsters are dead or because my grandmother secretly drugged me too, I can't say for sure. But when I open my eyes, soft light is filtering through my bedroom window. I never closed the curtains and the overhead light is still on. Those damn porcelain dolls watch from the shelf. Although now, I've lowered their terror rating. Real monsters are way scarier.

I lie there, motionless for a moment as it all floods back. Every bloody second. I wish I could have amnesia instead. I pretty much ache all over and I have a massive headache. I have cuts and scratches, but otherwise, I'm okay. At least I'm not a vampire. And neither is my brother. With Olivia dead, the curse has ended.

My phone is on the nightstand, and when I check it, I realize that I have service again. There are several three a.m. messages from Felix.

Elijah doesn't need surgery, he writes. *We're leaving as soon as we're discharged.*

And then, an hour later, *By the way, your grandmother knows some pretty scary dudes, but they promised the house would be spotless. Thank her for me.*

I smile. *I'm glad Elijah doesn't need surgery,* I write back. *Please keep in touch.*

Felix sends back a heart-and-bloody-knife emoji and I smile again.

I open one more message and send a text to Willa.

On our way home.

It's early, but I'm sure when she sees it, she'll call me. I can't wait to see her again.

There's no delaying the start of the day at this point. I grab a change of clothes and head to the bathroom to shower. As I strip down, I know that I'll be throwing away this dress. I never want to wear formalwear to a vampire slaying again.

I shower for what feels like hours, scrubbing myself raw. When I'm done, I pull on a comfy T-shirt and leggings, stuff the dress into a trash bag I found under the sink, and head back to my room. I take a moment to change the sheets, stuffing the old ones into the bloody bag.

My phone buzzes with a text. I check and see it's from my father.

Bring down your stuff, he writes. *I want to get going.*

I stare at his words for a moment, waiting to see how I feel about everything. I wanted to go home from the start, even before I knew there were vampires. Surprisingly, I have a twinge of sadness. Not about leaving Nightfall—I still hate this place. But I'm going to miss my grandmother.

The house is bustling as my dad helps Nonna with a few things. Marco sits on the front porch with a blanket wrapped around his shoulders like he just survived the sinking of the *Titanic*. I go out and sit next to him.

"How are you feeling?" I ask.

"The same way I look," he says miserably.

"Then we'd better call the coroner," I reply. He doesn't laugh and I lean over to bump his shoulder.

We watch as our father plants another row of wolfsbane for our grandmother. In one corner of the yard a large white dog on a leash waits for his chance. Turns out Cyrus is pretty sweet, so Nonna is taking him in. He keeps tearing up her flowers, though.

"When I woke up this morning," Marco says, "Nonna was burying a body in the backyard. She told me what happened with Olivia. Or Sylvia, I guess her name is."

"She was burying her?" I ask.

"Under the tree," he says, nodding. "And then she made me stand in the sunshine to prove the curse was really broken. No sunburn." He holds out his arm.

"That makes me feel better," I say. "After what you put me through, I'm glad Nonna's torturing you a little."

Marco laughs, and then winces and touches his throat. "Still sore from the ocean water," he tells me. "They fucking drowned me, Theo. I was . . . dead." He shakes his head. "But I guess when the curse ended, it sort of returned things. Heart started beating again, all that."

"Just in case," I say, "you should avoid human blood for a while."

"Noted," he says.

We're quiet for a moment, then he sniffles once. "What you said about Mom," he says. "Was that true?"

"About her getting married?" I ask. "Yep. And I'm going to be her maid of honor."

Marco tries to read my expression. I smile, letting him know we're fine—actually fine.

"She's happy," I tell him. "We'll be happy for her, too."

He watches me another second and then nods. "Mom's getting married," he repeats, and then laughs to himself. "To fucking Dale."

"Yep," I say. "I'm pretty sure he's not a vampire."

"Dad apologized to me earlier," Marco says. "Let's make a pact to never let him forget how badly this went if he ever tries to plan a vacation again."

"Deal."

"Okay," our father calls, slapping his hands together to clear off the dirt. "You both ready? We need to get out of here before your grandmother makes me clean the gutters, too."

"You hush," she tells him, slapping his arm.

My dad turns around to hug his mother, stooping low so his chin rests on her shoulder. Marco and I stand up, our bags waiting on the edge of the porch. I'm already feeling tightness building in my chest at the impending goodbye.

"Bye, Mom," my father says, kissing his mother on the cheek before backing away, holding in tears. "We'll miss you."

She waves him off, although her own eyes are misty. "You take care," she tells him. "I'll be down there to see you all at Christmas," Nonna adds.

As my dad brings the bags to the car, I walk over to Nonna and smile at her. I'm getting a little emotional saying goodbye. To think, I didn't even know her a week ago, and now . . . she's the most interesting person in my life.

"Thank you for everything, Nonna," I say quietly. "You're a badass."

She nods. "And you're a good girl, Theo."

I pull her into a hug, startling her with my affection. Nonna is stiff in my arms for a moment, and then she pats me on the back and tells me to have a safe trip home.

When I draw back, there are a few tears on my cheeks. I'm so glad our relationship has evolved. We're a team, me and my vampire-slaying grandma. I gaze at her. "I love you, Nonna," I say warmly.

She stares back at me for a long moment and then sighs. "You're always so dramatic, Theodora," she announces impatiently. "Goodbye."

She goes back inside, closing the door behind her.

"And that's why I didn't try," my brother says from the stairs. "Just kidding," he adds. "I was crying on her all morning."

The three of us get into the car to begin the drive back to Arizona. The sun is shining brightly; it figures it would show up now that we're leaving. I consider turning on one of my podcasts, but honestly, I've had enough murder for a while.

My father takes the turn onto Main Street, the pavement littered with the remains of yesterday's party. As we drive through downtown, we see a police car and fire truck outside Scoops, yellow tape blocking off the entrance. They must have found the bodies. I'm glad they will be put to rest. And hopefully Erika is free, starting her life fresh.

The breakfast place is open and busy, locals waiting to get

in. I think of Alexander Parrish, wondering if he'd be glad this is all over—even if he didn't make it out alive. He really hated being a vampire. But no one can hurt him anymore. And for that, at least, I'm happy.

As we pass the former church, where we first saw Minnow and her friends, I notice a girl sitting on the low wall, all alone.

It's Minnow. She looks up as we pass, watching after us. There's no glamour anymore, but she's still pretty. She just looks younger. Smaller in some way.

Marco turns in her direction and as their eyes lock, she holds up her hand in a sad wave. My brother doesn't return it, but I can feel his grief. I think he really did like her—it wasn't all glamour. . . .

I bring my face close to the window as we pass, watching as Minnow lowers her hand, a soft smile on her lips. And then she disappears from view as we crest the hill.

Finally, we pass the mural—the Siren of Nightfall. I'm surprised to see that someone has gotten to it. The mermaid is gone, painted over with bright yellow paint—transformed into a giant sunrise shining over the town.

"Only some shall stay," I murmur to myself as we pass. The dark history of Nightfall is finally behind it. The nightmare over. The tourists and townspeople safe.

And I'm glad that we're finally going home.

ACKNOWLEDGMENTS

Writing a book can be lonely sometimes. Spending hours at the computer . . . Did I say hours? I meant full days. Full weeks. Months? But I've been lucky to feel supported professionally by a great team.

Thank you to my agent, Lane Heymont at Tobias Literary. We both love some bloody good fun in our books, and I'm happy with how you've embraced my horror. Thank you to my editor, Krista Marino, who immediately got every '80s and '90s reference I made. It took ten years, but I finally convinced you to publish one of my books. Thank you for making that dream come true.

Huge thanks to my writing pals Amanda Morgan and Trish Doller. Don't know what I would have done without you answering my "Wait, does this suck?" emails.

Of course, none of my books would happen without my family. This includes the constant interruptions by my children, which remind me how precious writing time is. And my fantastic husband, who orders takeout when he knows I've lost track of time at my computer. Of course, I'm also grateful to my dogs, who bark at every single person who walks by the office window so that I have to keep the blinds shut and work in the dark. It's really helped me get in the zone.

But mostly, I thank my readers. Every message, every tagged review, every video saying that I broke your heart with my words, thank you. It reminds me why I do this.

ABOUT THE AUTHOR

SUZANNE YOUNG is the *New York Times* bestselling author of the series The Program. Originally from Utica, New York, Suzanne moved to Arizona to pursue her dream of not freezing to death. She is an author and an English teacher, but not always in that order. Suzanne has published more than twenty books for teens, including *Girls with Sharp Sticks*, *All in Pieces*, and *Hotel for the Lost*. Follow her and her three photogenic dogs on Instagram at @authorsuzanneyoung.

authorsuzanneyoung.com